**Praise for *New York Times* bestselling author
Katy Evans
Author of The REAL series**

"Evans [takes] writing to a whole new level. She makes you FEEL every single word you read."

—Reality Bites

"Saturated with palpable tension and incendiary sex, this tale packs an emotional wallop."

—Library Journal on *REAL*

"Smoking hot and completely mind-blowing."

—RT Book Reviews on *ROGUE*

"What a rare gift for an author to be able to actually wrap her arms around her readers and hold them. Katy Evans does just that."

—SubClub Books

"Whoa. Why was I not told I'd need one of those walk-in freezers while reading this book? Apart from being one of my most scorching reads of the year, the 'realness' of the love story took me totally off guard, and held me captive until the very last word."

—Natasha Is a Book Junkie on *ROGUE*

"Seductive, wild, and visceral."

—Christina Lauren on *REAL*

"Wow—Katy Evans is one to watch."

Little Pixie

D0451596

manwhore

KATY EVANS

G

Gallery Books

New York London Toronto Sydney New Delhi

G

Gallery Books
An Imprint of Simon & Schuster, Inc.
1230 Avenue of the Americas
New York, NY 10020

First Gallery Books trade paperback edition March 2015

GALLERY BOOKS and colophon are registered trademarks of Simon & Schuster, Inc.

For information about special discounts for bulk purchases, please contact Simon & Schuster Special Sales at 1-866-506-1949 or business@simonandschuster.com.

The Simon & Schuster Speakers Bureau can bring authors to your live event. For more information or to book an event, contact the Simon & Schuster Speakers Bureau at 1-866-248-3049 or visit our website at www.simonspeakers.com.

Design by Davina Mock-Maniscalco

Manufactured in the United States of America

10 9 8 7 6 5 4 3

Library of Congress Cataloging-in-Publication Data is available.

ISBN 978-1-5011-0153-3
ISBN 978-1-5011-0156-4 (ebook)

To the slow burn;
we never see it coming until we catch fire.

PLAYLIST

ADDICTED by Saving Abel

UNDISCLOSED DESIRES by Muse

SUPERHEROES by The Script

CLIMAX by Usher

STAY WITH ME by Sam Smith

PEACE by O.A.R.

I BELIEVE IN YOU by Kylie Minogue

KISS YOU SLOW by Andy Grammer

TALKING BODY by Tove Lo

MY HEART IS OPEN by Maroon 5

BROKEN by Lifehouse

NEED YOU NOW by Lady Antebellum

1

DREAM JOB

I walked into Helen's office this morning certain she was going to fire me. It isn't really my boss's job to fire me. It's HR's. But the HR department has been cut. *Edge,* the magazine I have written for and loved since I graduated from college, is hanging by a thread.

Three steps inside the cluttered room stacked with old magazines, ours and our competitors', and my breakfast—coffee with two sugars, and strawberry jam on whole-wheat toast—turns into a stone inside my stomach.

Without even looking up from the folder in her hand, Helen signals to the chair across hers.

"Rachel, sit down."

I sit silently, a thousand things leaping to my tongue: I can do better; I can do more; let me do more, two articles a week rather than one. Even: I will work for free until we can find our feet.

I can't afford to work for free. I have rent, I'm still paying off my college loan, and I have a mother I love with a health condition and no insurance. But I also love my job. I don't want to be let go. I have never wanted to be anything else other than what I am now, at this moment, as my fate rests in her hands.

So it's with dread and an impending sense of loss that I sit here and wait for Helen to finally lower that folder and look at me. And I wonder, as our eyes meet, if the next story I have to tell in my life is the one of her firing me.

I am in love with stories. How they shape our lives. How they mark people who don't even know us. How they can impact us even when an event didn't exactly occur in our own lives.

The first things I ever fell in love with were the words my mother and grandmother told me about my dad. In those words I got what I didn't have in real life—a dad. I would collect them into groups, memorize the stories they formed. Where he'd taken my mother on their first date (a Japanese restaurant), if his laugh was funny (it was), what his favorite beverage was (Dr Pepper). I grew up in love with stories and with *all* the facts and details that enabled me to shape, in my mind, memories of my father that have been with me for life.

My aunts said I was dreaming when I said I wanted words to be a career, but my mother kept quoting Picasso's mother. "Picasso's mother told him if he got into the army, he'd be a general. If he became a monk, he'd be the pope. Instead he was a painter and became Picasso. That's exactly how I feel about you. So *do*, Rachel, what you love."

"I would do it more happily if *you* were doing what you love too," I always replied, miserable for her.

"What I love is taking care of you," she always came back with. She's a lovely painter but nobody else thinks so but me and one tiny gallery that went bankrupt months after its inception. So my mother has a normal job, and the Picasso in her has quieted.

But she's sacrificed so much to give me an education and more. Since I'm actually a little shy with strangers, I didn't have encouragement from a lot of my teachers. None of them believed I had the stomach for hard-core reporting, so I ran with the only thing I could: the sole motivation of my mother and her belief in me.

Now I've worked at *Edge* for almost two years, the job cuts started over three months ago, and my colleagues and I have all been afraid we'll be the next. Everyone, including me, is giving 110 percent of what we've got. But to a flailing business, it's not enough. There doesn't seem to be any way of salvaging *Edge* except with a huge investment that doesn't seem forthcoming, or with stories much bigger than what we've been running.

The moment Helen opens her mouth to speak, I dread hearing the words *We've got to let you go.* I'm already thinking of a story, an idea, I can pitch for my next column, something edgy that could put our name out there and somehow allow me to hang on to my job a little longer.

"You've been on my mind, Rachel," she says. "Are you currently seeing anyone?"

"Um. Seeing anyone? No."

"Well, that's just what I wanted to hear!" She shuffles her paperwork to the side and pulls out one of the magazines from the shelf, dropping it on the desk between us. "See, I've got a proposition for you. It might require you to bend your morals a little bit. In the end, I think it will ultimately be rewarding for you." She shows me an old magazine, a rueful smile on her lips. "This was our first issue. Fifteen years ago."

"I love it!" I say.

"I know you do—you've always taken an interest in how we started. Which is why I like you, Rachel," she says without any warmth at all. Just a fact, it seems. "You know, *Edge* used to stand for something. All those years ago, we weren't afraid of breaking rules, venturing where other magazines wouldn't. You're the only one who seems to have preserved that. The Sharpest Edge is always our column with the most comments. You focus on the trends and give your raw, unfiltered opinion. Even when people don't agree with your opinion, they respect you for the fact that you share it so honestly.

"This is why I suppose you're in my office now, instead of Victoria." She jerks her chin in the direction of outside where my greatest competitor, Victoria, must be busy in her cubicle.

Vicky. She's the only other overachiever at *Edge* and somehow always lucks out at overachieving more than me. I don't want enmity with Victoria. But it still feels like there's a popularity contest here I didn't sign up for. She always seems so damn happy when Helen isn't pleased with what I wrote, and sometimes I can't write a word simply because I'm worrying about what Victoria will come up with.

"See, I'm thinking of ruffling some feathers. If we want to stay in business, it's becoming clearer and clearer we need something more drastic. Something that will make people take notice of *Edge.* Are you with me?"

"I agree. If there's anything to breathe new life into *Edge*—"

"We're doing so poorly, we've all grown so scared; we're all reporting from safe, scared places, afraid to push the button in case we explode. We're already withering here. We need to write about the topics that scare us, fascinate us . . . and nobody fascinates this city more than our billionaire bachelors. Do you know who I'm talking about?"

"The playboys?"

Her lips twist. "The worst of them all." She pulls out another magazine. I stare at the cover, which says *Saint or Sinner?*

"Malcolm Saint," I whisper.

"Who else?"

The man staring back at me has a perfectly structured face, beautiful lips, and eyes greener than the bottom of a beer bottle. His smile is all mischief. It says he likes to cause trouble and, most of all, that he likes getting away with it. But there's something very closed off and somehow icy in his eyes. Oh yeah, those green eyes are made of green ice.

"I've heard of him," I admit, starting to get nervous. "I wouldn't really be alive in Chicago if I hadn't."

Ruthless, they say.

A complete manwhore, they say.

And so ambitious he'd put Midas to shame. Oh yeah. They say Saint won't rest until he owns the world.

"Victoria thinks that you're too young and inexperienced to take on such a risqué project, Rachel. But you're single, and she's not."

"Helen, you know how much I enjoy writing about trends, but you also know that I really want to write bigger stories, stories about people's homes, security. I want to earn that chance, and if this is how I can do that, then I won't let you down. What kind of story do you see for him?"

"An exposé." She grins. "One where we get to hear juicy little tidbits about him. I'm thinking about four things, specifically. How he manages to stay so calm and in control all the time. What's the deal with his father? What role do all these women play in his life? And why, oh why does he have this obvious affinity for doing things in *fours*? Now"—she slaps her hand on the desk for emphasis—"in order to get to the meat . . . Let's be honest, Rachel: you must try to get close. Lie, little white lies. Ease into his world. Saint isn't an easy man to access, which is why nobody's been able to figure out even one of these things, much less all four."

I've been listening. My curiosity is fully engaged. But I've started to squirm. *Lie. Little white lies.* True, I've lied sometimes. I'm human. I've done right things and wrong things, but I'd rather stick to the right side. I enjoy my sleep, thank you. But *this* is the opportunity I've wanted since I started college.

"And if Saint wants to make a play for you," Helen continues, "then be prepared. You might need to play a little bit back. *Can* you do that?"

"I believe so," I say, but I sound much more confident than I feel. And I just . . . I'm not sure how many opportunities like this I'll get. I'll never be able to move into reporting things that are important to me if I don't make a stronger effort to be heard. Tackling a topic that fascinates the public so much will give me a voice, and I really, really want that voice.

"Do you think you can do this? Or . . ." She glances outside.

No. I can't bear for Victoria to get the story. It's not a pill I want to swallow. In fact, it's downright bitter, and I don't want to swallow it.

"I'll do it. I'm hungry. I want a good story," I assure Helen.

"We can always wait and find you another good story, Rachel," she says, playing devil's advocate now.

"I'll do it. *He's* my story now."

"He's Chicago's story. And Chicago's darling. He has to be handled with care."

"He's the story I want to tell," I assure her.

"That's what I like to hear." She laughs. "Rachel, you are absolutely beautiful. You are a doll. You're funny and you work hard, you give it your all, but for all that you've lived, you're still an innocent. You've been here two years, and even before you graduated you were working it. But you're still a young girl playing in a world for grown-ups. You're too young to know there are protocols with the rich in the city."

"I know we usually cater to the rich."

"Just remember, Saint could crush the magazine. He can't see it coming. By the time he does, he'll see his face on the newsstand."

"He won't catch me," I mumble.

"Okay, Rachel, but I want intimate revelations. I want every detail. I want to feel like I stepped into his shoes and walked his everyday walk. What is it like to be him? *You're* going to tell the whole city." She smiles happily and wakes up her computer with a wiggle of her mouse. "I look forward to hearing all about it. So off you go now, Rachel. Find the story in the story and write it."

Holy crap, Livingston. You've got your story!

I'm so dazed and exhilarated, I'm euphoric as I head to the door, fairly trembling with the need to start working.

"Rachel," she calls as I open the glass door, my stomach in a whole new tangle. She nods her head. "I believe in you, Rachel."

I stand there, completely awed that I finally, finally have her trust. I didn't expect it would come with a huge fear of failure on my shoulders. "Thanks for the chance, Helen," I whisper.

"Oh, and one last thing. Saint isn't normally accessible to the press. But there have been exceptions, and I can think of a way you could get lucky. Check out his new social media site, Interface. Use it as an approach. He might not like the press, but he's a businessman and will use us to his advantage."

I nod with some self-confidence and a ton more self-doubt, and as soon as I'm outside, I exhale nervously.

Okay, Livingston. Focus and let's do this.

I've got so much information on Saint that I email myself dozens and dozens of links to continue researching tonight at my apartment. I place a call to his office and talk to a representative, asking for an interview. She assures me they'll let me know. I cross my fingers and say, "Thank you, I'm available anytime. My boss is very excited to run a piece on Mr. Saint's latest venture."

Done for the day, I head home. My place is close to Blommer Chocolate Company, in the Fulton River District. I wake up to the smell of chocolate in the air. My building is five stories high, on the edge of downtown.

Sometimes it's hard to believe I'm living my dream, or at least half of it; I wanted the briefcase, the mobile phone, the heels and matching jacket and skirt. I wanted to be self-sufficient enough to buy my mother the car of her dreams, and a home of her own where she wouldn't get evicted because she couldn't pay the rent. I still want those things.

Unfortunately my market is tough. A freelancer before I even graduated college, I had no steady income. You live by your muse, and she's not always ready with ideas for you. Then I answered an advertisement in the *Chicago Tribune*. *Edge* was looking for weekly columnists for topics such as fashion, sex and dating, innovations, decorating tips, and even fancy pet discoveries. The office covered two floors in an old building downtown, and it hardly represented the corporate environment I'd envisioned.

The top floor is littered with reporters at their desks. The floors are wood, the editorial offices peppered with bright colors and satin cushions, always full of the buzz of phones and people chattering. Instead of the business suits I imagined wearing to work, I write in an oversize, trendy T-shirt-with-an-attitude and a pair of socks that have the words *I Believe* on the toes. It's a crazy magazine, as crazy as some of the stories and columns we put out—and I love it.

But bloggers are putting us out of work, our circulation growing tinier by the second. *Edge* needs something cutting-edge, and I'm desperate to prove to my boss that I can bring it to her.

"Gina!" I call to my roommate when I stroll into our two-bedroom flat.

"We're over here!" I hear Gina call.

She's in her bedroom, with Wynn. They're my best friends. Wynn's a redhead, freckled, pink and sweet, very unlike the dark, sultry Gina.

We're like Neapolitan ice cream. In height, Gina and I are the tallest, while Wynn is an elf. Gina and I try to use logic; Wynn is "Team Feelings" all the way. I'm the career girl, Wynn is the nurturer, and Gina is the sexpot who hasn't yet realized she could use men as her personal dildos (if she wanted to). She doesn't want to. Really.

Dropping my bag at the door, I spot their huge Chinese food picnic and join them on the floor.

They're streaming an old episode of *Sex and the City.*

We eat in silence and watch a little bit, but I'm not even paying attention to the screen. I'm too wound up, and finally blurt, "I've got my story."

"What?" They both stop eating.

I nod. "I've got my first full story. It might be three pages, four—hell, five. Depending on how much information I end up with."

"Rachel!" they yell in unison and come toward me.

"No tackle hugs! Shit! You spilled the rice!"

They squeal and then ease back, and Wynn goes to get the Dustbuster. "So what's it about?" she asks.

"Malcolm Saint."

"Malcolm *Saint?*"

"What about him?" Wynn asks.

"It's . . . almost undercover." They're practically popping out of their skin with anticipation. "I get to meet him."

"How?!"

"I'm trying to get an interview to ask about Interface."

"Aha."

"But I'll also be researching him in secret. I'll be . . . unlayering him," I tease.

"RACHEL!" Gina bangs my arm, knowing I'm usually straitlaced.

Wynn shakes her head. "That man is hot!"

"What do you two know about him?" Gina asks.

I pull out my laptop. "I was just online liking all his social pages, and the guy has over four million Instagram likes."

We hop onto other sites and check out his Twitter feed.

I'm not impressed by what I read.

"His rep wouldn't give me an appointment—she wrote me down on a list. I wonder if I'll have better luck reaching out on social media."

"Let's look for a smexy profile pic in case Saint himself sees it."

"Not happening," I say.

"Come on, Rachel, you have to make yourself as appealing as possible. This one." She points at a picture in one of my old social media albums where I'm wearing a secretarial skirt and blouse, but the three buttons between my breasts are about to burst.

"I hate that shirt."

"Because it shows off what you've got. Come on, let's do it."

I change my profile picture, then send him a message.

Mr. Saint, this is Rachel Livingston with Edge. I'd love it if
you granted me the opportunity for a personal interview in
regard to your rising new star, Interface. I've put in the request
through your office as well. I'm available anytime. . . .

I include all my details and shoot it off.

"Okay, fingers crossed," I murmur with butterflies in my stomach.

"And toes."

Later, after Wynn goes home and Gina goes to sleep, I head to my bed. I settle on my pillow, my laptop on my lap, sucking on a Fruit Roll-Up. "Interesting reading," I say to an online picture of the man. I stay up until midnight, reading more and more. I've already dug up quite the dirt on him.

Malcolm Kyle Preston Logan Saint. Twenty-seven years old. His family is such old money in Chicago, he got a headline the day he was born. At age five, he was in the hospital with meningitis, and the world was on pins and needles to see if he'd make it.

At age six, he'd already earned a black belt in karate, and on the weekends he flew with his socialite mother from one state to the next on one of his father's jets. At thirteen, he'd already kissed most girls in school. At fifteen, he'd been the world's biggest player and smoothest liar. At eighteen, he was the perfect bastard, and rich to boot. At twenty, he'd lost his mother but was too busy skiing at a Swiss alpine village to reach the funeral on time.

By twenty-one, he and his two best friends, Callan Carmichael and Tahoe Roth, had become the most notorious trust-fund babies of our generation.

He's the owner of four Bugattis: license plates BUG 1, BUG 2, BUG 3, and BUG 4. He has houses all over the world. Luxury cars. Dozens of gold watches, including a rose gold perpetual calendar he bought at auction for $2.3 million. He's a collector, you could say. Of companies, toys, and, apparently, women.

Malcolm is an only child, and after inheriting his mother's millions and displaying an uncanny flair for business during the following years, he became not only a billionaire but an absolute symbol of power as well. Not political power, but the good, old-fashioned power that comes with having money. Saint isn't linked to the shady dealings of the Chicago political machine, but he can press that machine's buttons if he wants to. Every politician knows this—which is why being on the playboy's good side is in their best interest.

Saint doesn't back just anyone. The public, somehow, trusts that Saint doesn't give a shit about what they think—he won't back anyone he doesn't plan to own, so, indirectly, anyone backed by Saint can't be owned by anyone else. He's the champion of the underdog. Using his substantial inheritance, Saint became a venture capitalist at a very young age, funding the tech projects of many of his Ivy League school buddies, many of which soared to success, making Saint a few hundred million wealthier than his own father. He still manages venture capital investments from within the offices of M4. Named for his initial and his favorite number, M4 is a company he created in those early years when several of his investments ended up listing on Nasdaq—one for a few billion, to boot.

Latest cover of the *Enquirer*—
Malcolm Saint: Our Favorite Bad Boy, Revealed
How many women has he slept with?
Why isn't he interested in marriage?

How he became America's hottest manwhore bachelor
And more!

Twitter:
@MalcolmSaint I wish I'd never laid eyes on you!
#eatshitanddie
YOU'RE FUCKING DEAD! @MalcolmSaint you fucked my
girlfriend you're so fucking DEAD
Free drinks anyone? @MalcolmSaint paying at Blue Bar
downtown!

Facebook wall:
Hey Mal, remember me? I gave you my number last week. Call
or message me!
Saint—drinks next weekend, I'm in town with the wife. (Not
that I'd bring her. She's fawned over you enough.) PM me to
set a place.
Looking good in the yacht pics, Saint. Have room for a few
more? My friends and I would love to party with you again! :)
XOXO

Wow. "You're a real gem, aren't you?" I whisper, slamming my
laptop shut around midnight. I bet half the things on the internet are completely overblown and untrue, which is why, of
course, I need more reliable research—firsthand research. I grin
and check the time, realizing it's too late to tell my mother that
I've finally got my story.

2
NEW RESEARCH

Twitter:
@MalcolmSaint please follow me on Twitter!
@MalcolmSaint to throw the first ball at Cubs game

My personal inbox:
EMPTY.

I've already got a two-inch-thick file on Malcolm Saint, but no call from his PR contact.

Today's plans with my mother are a no-go too.

I was supposed to meet her to show our support for our community's End the Violence campaign, but she calls to say that she's not going to make it. Her boss asked her to cover for someone. "I'm sorry, darling. Why don't you ask one of the girls to go with you?"

"Don't worry, Mother, I will. Take your insulin, okay?"

I know she takes it, but I can't help mentioning it every time we call. I obsess about her like that.

In fact, I worry about my mom so much, Gina and Wynn worry I'm going to make myself sick over it. I want to get a big cushion of savings so I know I can take care of her insurance and be sure she has a good home and good healthy food, and good care, too. I want to give my mom everything she's given me so she can retire and finally do what she loves. Everybody deserves to do what they love. Her love for me and her desire to provide for me as much as she could have held her back. I want to do well enough that now *she* gets to follow her dreams.

This exposé could lead to so many more opportunities, that one door opening to a plethora of new ones.

I'm clicking Malcolm Saint links like crazy when Gina finally pads out of her bedroom in her comfiest outfit.

"I told you it needs to be something you won't mind getting paint on," I remind her. "Aren't those your favorite jeans?"

"Oh fuck, I heard that! Why did I forget when I went into my closet and saw these?" She thumps back into her room.

An hour before noon, at a corner of the park near the basketball courts, Gina and I—along with what looks to be several dozen people—finally gather in anticipation of slapping our paint-covered hands onto a mural-size canvas.

"We've *all* lost someone to this fight. Our loved ones, our grocer, a friend . . ." one of the organizers is saying.

I was two months old when I lost my dad.

All I know is from my mother's account: that he was an ambitious man, hardworking, and full of big dreams. He swore to her that I would never have to work . . . he was obsessed with giving us the ideal life. We didn't ask for it, but it didn't matter to my dad.

All it took was one gun, and none of it happened.

I didn't get to have a memory of his eyes, gray, supposedly like mine. Never heard his voice. Never knew if, in the mornings, he'd be grumpy like Gina's dad or sweet like Wynn's. I remember the neighbors bringing pie for years as I grew up. Their daughters coming over to play with me. I remember playing with other people's kids too, my mother taking me over to play with other children who had lost someone to violence.

Now, twenty-three years after my father died, every time something bad happens I wish we could make it stop, and I never want to forget how it feels, this wanting to make it stop.

We've been criticized over our methods of pleading for a safer city—some say we're too passive, others that it's pointless—but I think that even the quietest of voices deserve to be heard.

Per one of the organizers' instructions, I pour a half an inch of red paint into my oversize plastic tray, and then I plant my hand on the surface. Thick red paint spreads to my fingertips.

"We're putting our hands on this huge mural as a symbol to stop the violence in the streets, in our communities, in our city, in our neighborhoods," the organizer continues.

My phone buzzes in my left butt-cheek pocket.

"All right, now," the woman hollers.

On the count of three—one, two, three!—I press my hand to the wall, while Gina does the same, her hand red like mine and a little bit bigger.

Once we've all left our prints, we hurry to the water fountains to clean up. Gina leans over my shoulder and I yelp and try to ease away.

"Dude, you're getting paint all over me!" I cry, laughing as I dry my hands and step aside to let her wash. While she scrubs off her paint, I pluck my phone out.

And my stomach takes a dive because I've got a reply.

3

MESSAGE

Malcolm Saint—

Ms. Livingston, this is Dean, Mr. Saint's press coordinator. We
have a ten-minute opening today at 12 p.m.

So I get that notification right now, Saturday, at like 11:18 a.m.

"Shit, I got it!" I tell Gina as I show her the message. But
instead of high-fiving me because I freaking landed this and I
rock, she glances pointedly at my coveralls.

"Oh no," I groan. "I can't see him like this!"

"Okay, take my belt."

"OMG, really? I look ridiculous!"

She ties it around my waist and cinches it. "Rachel, focus.
There's no store around, you don't have time to go change."

We share panicked looks, then we both survey my clothes.
I'm now wearing a jean coverall with a tank top beneath and a
red belt, with paint splats here and there. "I look like an absolute slut on a washing day!"

"You have paint on your cheek," says Gina, wincing on my
behalf.

I groan and whisper to the universe: Next time you make
one of my dreams come true, can I please be dressed for the
occasion?

As if reading my mind, Gina tries to pep me up. "Come on, clothes don't make the girl. Hey, at least you're not naked."

I've tried to twist my hair this way and that, and no, my appearance hardly improves. I'm passionately hating on this entire situation while riding in the back of the cab, sitting sideways because I suspect that, when Gina washed her hands after me, she got some paint on my back. Just seconds ago I felt it sticking to the cab vinyl, and now I'm hating on this situation so bad, my stomach hurts. I ask the driver to drop the passenger mirror, and I stare at my face.

"Ohmigod," I say.

And there I am. My long blonde hair twisted into messy pigtails, a slash of paint on the side of my neck, stark like blood against my pale skin. "Ohmigod," I moan.

This is the woman the renowned Malcolm Saint is going to see?

And, if I thought in the back of the cab that I really loathed this situation, I had no idea how much more I would hate it when I got to the M4 corporate building.

The building itself looms with its fancy mirrored windows piled up almost as high as the Sears—supposedly-called-*Willis*-now-but-screw-that-name—Tower. Inside the lobby, from one end to the other, marble and granite floors spread out beneath my feet. Steel structures hold glass staircases leading to a second lobby floor, while see-through elevators zoom up and down.

M4 is about as edgy as a nightclub but as quiet as a museum. I feel like a balloon delivery girl who forgot the balloons as I walk past the revolving doors and deeper toward reception.

Oh fuck me, this is so not optimal right now. *Everybody* in the lobby is looking at me.

I can't do this, I can't do this, I can't do this.

Livingston! Focus. YES. You can.

I thrust my chin out and proudly walk up to the receptionist. "Rachel Livingston for Malcolm Saint."

She eyes me quietly. Inspects my ID card. Frowns a little.

At five foot seven, I'm not short by any means. But I feel smaller and smaller. I am shrinking, right here, as I wait. Humiliated quietly.

"Top floor," she says, eyeing me down to my Converse sneakers.

Fuck. Me.

I head to the elevator with as much pride as I can muster.

The elevator zips up to the top floor, dropping my companions—all of them in sharp black-and-white exec suits—along the way until it's just me. And a knot of nerves tightening more and more. I bet Victoria wouldn't be caught dead wearing this. Not even if she were paid to do it.

But Victoria isn't here, Rachel. You are.

The elevator tings, and I step out.

There are four desks, two to the right, two to the left, and huge frosted-glass doors leading to . . . his lair. I know it's his because of how the frosted doors give the impression of a glass fortress that is both bold and strangely understated. It signals accessibility while being completely out of reach from the world.

A woman comes around a desk and gestures for me to take a seat in a section to the left.

Thanking her under my breath, I perch on the edge of a chair for a few minutes, watching all four of his assistants—all of them sharp and attractive in different ways—take continual calls. They work in absolute perfect synchronicity.

An elevator opens and a glimpse of a tall, striking man hits me with a jolt of pure feminine awareness as he steps out with a trail of businessmen behind him. Shoulders a mile wide, jet-black hair, crisp designer suit, snowy white shirt, and a stride to eat up the universe. He's taking the folder that one of the other men extends and, after issuing some sort of command that sends his followers dispersing out with bullet speed, he charges forward. He passes me with the simmering force of a hurricane and disappears into the glass cave, leaving me dizzy and frantically absorbing my last sight of the dark hair, broad back, and the hottest male ass I've ever seen walking Chicago.

For a second I feel like the world moved faster, that somehow ten seconds were all crammed into the space of one—the one where this man went past me. Like a lightning bolt.

One of the assistants leaps to her feet and goes into the glass office where he vanished, while the other three stare at the door as if they wish the lightning bolt had hit a little bit closer to home.

Then it hits *me*.

That the storm was Malcolm Saint.

Yes, the hurricane was *Saint*.

I feel a prick of dread.

I glance at my sneakers. And yep. They're still sneakers. Urgh.

I notice the assistant left the door slightly ajar, and I can't help but lean forward, straining to hear her whispers.

"Your twelve o'clock is here. You have ten minutes."

I can't hear the reply through the nervous pounding of my heart.

"Oh, and Mr. Saint, this . . . reporter . . . she's dressed a little bit unconventionally."

God, I still can't hear.

"From *Edge,* a low-circulation magazine. Dean thought it important we use whatever outlets we could to push the new Facebook."

My skin pebbles when I hear a low, excruciatingly deep male voice murmur something unintelligible.

"Rachel Livingston," the assistant answers.

I feel shivers when the indiscernible but deep sound of his voice reaches me again. The shivers race from the top of my spine down to my tailbone.

I've never shivered like this before, not even when I've been freezing my ass outside. Is this from nerves?

"Yes, Mr. Saint . . ." the assistant finally says.

She comes out and can't quite manage to conceal the fact that she's flustered. Shit, and *I'm* the one going in next. Looking like I was just tossed into a blender with a can of paint and I'm the result of that fun little expedition.

She calls me over to the door. "Mr. Saint is truly pressed for time today. Enjoy your ten minutes," she says as she pushes it open.

I try to reply, but I'm so nervous only a little croak of a "thank you" comes out as I step inside. Stock tickers scroll on one wall on dozens of different screens. There are no live plants, nothing but technology and natural stone floors, and a lot of space, as if this man needs it.

The windows have an open view of the city of Chicago, but I can't absorb it for long because I see him—quiet, storm-like intensity in Armani—walk toward me in that hurricane force that is almost otherworldly.

Wow. Wow on every part of him. His face, his presence, his shoulders, his eyes. His eyes are glowing, alive—green and deep, like moving rivers, but there's no missing the little shards of ice glinting inside, almost screaming for me to warm them.

"Miss Livingston."

He extends his hand, and it's when I slide my fingers into his warm grip that I notice that I can't breathe.

Nodding and swallowing and pasting a stupid smile on my face as I pry my hand free, I watch him with mounting awe.

Once in his chair and leaning back comfortably, he sits there, the pose deceptively casual, but I can feel the energy humming from his being.

"Mr. Saint," I mumble at last, never more aware of my attire and how out of place I must seem amid such polished luxury.

He's staring too, in a slightly puzzled, quiet way. I bet I'm the only woman he's ever seen in coveralls. In sneakers. I bet everyone wears their best when they're going to see him.

Shit.

He glances at his watch, startling me when he speaks. "Clock is ticking, Miss Livingston, so you might as well shoot." He signals to a chair across from his desk, and . . . can I just say that his voice is really quite an experience?

His *presence* is quite the experience. No wonder people talk about it online—hell, to whoever will listen.

His jaw all lean bone, his eyebrows two dark slashes above thick-lashed, deep-set eyes. His lips are sensual, slightly tilted at the corners. The kind of lips Gina calls "edible."

"Thank you for seeing me, Mr. Saint," I say.

"Saint is fine." He leans back in his chair.

Adrenaline courses through me as I finally have no other choice but to attempt to sit on the chair he indicated, every effort I make focused on my movements. I'm trying not to recline to avoid getting paint on the fabric—a bit stiffly, I pull out the questions I wrote on my phone on my way here.

"So my main interest is, of course, your new social media platform, the first to ever really compete against Facebook . . ."

I can't help but notice he's distracted by my clothes as I sit across from him. I can feel his eyes on me, checking me out. Is he disgusted by my outfit? I can feel his hot eyes on me, and I'm just about squirming.

He shifts in his chair, a hand covering his face. Is he hiding a smile? Ohmigod, is his chest moving a little? He's laughing because of my clothes! Because I'm rigid as a mannequin here, nervous and frantically wondering if I have paint on me or not.

"As you know," I force myself to continue, but god, I'm *mortified,* "investors have not only been wondering whether it will remain privately held . . ."

I trail off when he stands and walks to the far end of his office. He walks in a way only confident men walk. It's unsettling when he walks back to me, extending what looks to be a clean men's dress shirt.

"Here, put this on."

Holy crap. Is this *his* shirt? "Oh no."

His eyes are extraordinary up close, peering down at me with a curiosity I hadn't seen there before.

"I insist," he says, with a hint of a smile.

My heart speeds up. "Truly," I protest, shaking my head.

"You'll be more comfortable." He gestures down at me, and I feel myself go hot. He just smiles, a twinkle in his eye.

Standing to take the shirt, I pluck each button open with shaky fingers, then slip my arms into the sleeves. I start buttoning it up as he heads back to his desk, his strides slow this time, almost predatory . . . because he won't take his eyes off me as he walks around.

The faster I try to make my fingers move, the more inept they feel. The shirt falls to the middle of my thighs—a shirt that has touched him, his chest, his skin, and suddenly I can't stop being aware of what he's doing; slowly lowering Chicago's most coveted male body back into his chair.

"Okay," I announce.

But it's not okay. It's so not okay right now.

I'm blushing to the tips of my ears, and his eyes are twinkling mercilessly, as though he knows it. "You wear it better than I do," he assures me.

"You're teasing me, Mr. Saint," I say under my breath, lowering myself to the chair again. His shirt smells of soap, the collar starchy, loose around my neck. God. My knees feel *weak*. I couldn't feel more vulnerable if I'd bared myself naked in front of him.

"All right, so now that you've managed to dress me properly," I tell him laughingly, then scorn myself for my familiarity. Pull out your questions, Rachel. And while you're at it, pull out your objectivity, too.

His cell phone rings. He ignores it, and I realize he's smiling over my comment. Lips curled seductively at the corners, teeth perfectly even and white against his tan.

His. Smile.

Oh.

My stomach dips unexpectedly. "Would you like to answer?"

"No," he says bluntly. "Go ahead. This is your time."

It rings again. He glances at the screen, narrowing his eyes.

"Please go ahead," I encourage.

I really *need* for him to look at something else for a hot second.

What is going on in my life?

I'm wearing his shirt!

He finally murmurs, "Excuse me," and takes the call and turns his chair a bit as he listens into the receiver.

Exhaling as I pull my questions up from my phone again, I lift my lashes and watch his profile as he listens attentively. Just sitting there doing nothing but taking a call, he sucks up all the oxygen in the room. He screams class, money, sophistication, and purely powerful things.

They say he once leaped from the top of his office building.

He's been called bold and daring both in business and out of it.

I hadn't believed everything I read last night.

I'm not sure it's all a lie now.

There's quite an energy under those business clothes.

He wears those clothes like second skin—hell, as if he sometimes sleeps in them. Under his white shirt, I can see the impressive muscle tone of his arms and chest. No picture I saw online truly captured the effect of that tanned, well-structured face in person. Absolutely none. His face is walk-straight-into-a-wall stunning, and I won't even dwell on his body, but now I understand why his bed is the most coveted spot in town.

He hangs up and settles back down, and we stare again for a moment. "Do you want to go ahead now, Miss Livingston?" he prods, gesturing to my phone.

"I amuse you," I blurt.

Hiking up one eyebrow, he seems to turn the question in his head a bit, steepling his fingers before him. "Intrigue me, yes. Do you paint?"

"I was at a neighborhood park this morning. Members of my community get together sometimes; we're trying to stay active against street violence, gang fights, drug selling in general."

"Are you now?" he says, without inflection.

I'm not sure if he's really intrigued or has simply decided he doesn't want to allow me to interview him after all. Thinking back to my questions, and how much I need to draw out the most information that I can, I open my mouth to try to get on his good side—maybe a little flattery?—but one of his assistants interrupts.

"Mr. Saint, China calling," she says as she peers through the doors. "And the car's ready."

He eases out of his chair, and his muscles ripple under his shirt as he maneuvers his arms back into his crisp black jacket. He grabs the Chicago Cubs cap sitting on the side of his desk, and as he looks at it, a muscle jumps in the back of his jaw as if he's suddenly irritated about something.

I don't want to overstay my welcome so I force myself to stand.

He lifts his head to briefly spare me one last glance. "It was interesting. Rachel," he adds.

A horrible sense of loss weighs down on me, growing heavily with each sound of his sure, steady footsteps heading toward the door. *Oh god, that's it?*

"Mr. Saint, could you see me again . . . ? " I begin.

He's already at the threshold of the open doors. His assistant hands over a couple of yellow Post-its, and he bends his dark head as he quickly skims them. He has an extremely toned back, an inverted triangle from his broad shoulders down to his waist—covered perfectly by that black designer jacket. As another one of his assistants goes to summon one of the elevators, one of his employees catches up to him with a ball.

A baseball. Of course. Either he's getting it signed by the players today or throwing that ball out at Wrigley Field.

I glance around at his assistants. Two are typing. One is

waiting by the elevator. And the one who's always hovering by his side is . . . hovering by his side. All their eyes are on him as he boards. It seems like nobody is breathing until he leaves, not even me.

When the elevator takes him away, his assistants return to their desks. Other than me, I've never met people more eager to get back to work.

I smile as I approach the one who let me into his office. Her name plaque reads CATHERINE H. ULYSSES. "He's got an effect, hasn't he?" I fished. *Does he sleep with any of you girls?* is what I really want to know.

She scowls a little. Protective? "Can I help you?"

"Yes, I'd like to see about the possibility of booking another appointment with Mr. Saint. We couldn't cover the subject I'm interested in. I'd love at least an hour with him, even two, if it's not too much to ask."

She says she'll keep me posted, and the four of them stare at the shirt I'm wearing and none of them looks happy. Sigh.

His assistants hate me, and he's probably banning me from M4 for life.

I'm so disappointed when I ride the cab back to my apartment that I replay the scene over and over, trying to find something I can use. It takes an effort to push away my embarrassment first, digging underneath to the gist of the meeting.

I jot down—

Punctual

Respected by his staff = good boss?

Even when he sat there, there always
seemed to be something happening in his
head (what was he thinking? Mergers?)

His stare is ... the deepest I've ever seen (indicates a man who can read people?)

He gave me his shirt

I look down at his shirt and study the buttons, the lapel. It's an unexpected gesture, that he gave me his shirt. *Unexpected.* Yes, that's him. Cool and composed, with a tight leash on his exhilarating hurricane energy, hiding something deep and interesting inside him.

I roll the sleeves to my elbows and jot that down. Sometimes my stories start with a list of words. I end up with this list of five things. So this is what I got out of the meeting? Five things with very little concrete evidence to back them up, and a strange knot in my tummy. And his incredibly nice-smelling shirt.

"What's a man's shirt doing here? This is sacred feminine space," Gina protests when she gets in from work.

"He was embarrassed for me and gave me his shirt."

I'm sitting in front of a blank computer screen, and I'm not that thrilled. Usually I love blank computer screens—they're like my playground. But a playground with one lone subject and no information to play with leaves me grumpy. I've got a bag of yogurt pretzels from Whole Foods sitting right beside me, and even that won't lift my mood.

"He *covered you up* rather than told you to remove your coverall? What kind of manwhore is he?"

"Gina! We were in his office. He has a good work ethic. He clearly doesn't mix business with pleasure."

Gina comes over to dive into my yogurt pretzels. "Saint

lives for pleasure; he's the tsar of pleasure. . . . What's with the frown?"

I groan and set my laptop aside and plop down on the bed. "I need to give that shirt back, and the stain on the inside from *your damn handprint* won't come off."

"Why would you need to give it back?"

"Because! I've never . . . you know. Gotten gifts from a guy. It makes me feel uncomfortable."

"You missed out on a dad giving you stuff. Or a brother. Or even a boyfriend. Still, you need to take stuff when you can get it because, trust someone who knows this shit, it doesn't come that often."

"I'm not keeping his shirt. What does that even say about me?" I shake my head and *tsk*.

She chows another pretzel and kicks off her shoes. "He's a billionaire, he's probably got a dozen more still with the tags on. Were you just planning on dropping by to hand it over? Are you like a permanent badge-holder of M4 corporate, or what?"

"No," I admit, and I reach to my bureau for my phone and open my internet so she can see for herself the message I got.

Malcolm Saint
Miss Livingston, Dean again. Mr. Saint can see you Monday. If you don't mind that we're squeezing the interview in between some of his other obligations, he's open to seeing you at 3 p.m.

"Rachel!" she says, jabbing my arm. "You go, girl!"

I grin quietly and stare at his shirt hanging on the back of my bedroom door again.

They say when you want something, you should visualize getting it and it will materialize. Well, this is the first time in my life I've wanted something bad enough, to prove myself so much, that it's finally taking shape.

He gave me another interview. He's got other obligations, but he will see me again. Even after that first mess of a meeting. It's so beyond perfect I can't stop a fresh wave of story-giddiness creeping up on me until finally 3 p.m. Monday rolls around.

4

MONDAY

A shiny black Rolls-Royce is parked at the very center of the M4 driveway, the sun gleaming on its rooftop. The moment I hop out of a cab, a uniformed driver approaches. "Miss Livingston?"

Mutely, I nod. Formally, he tips his hat to me and briskly opens the rear door. I spot Saint inside, issuing a string of impatient commands to someone through his phone. Oops. I don't think he's in a good mood today. He's not yelling, but he doesn't seem like the kind of man who needs to yell to be heard. His voice is exactly as I remembered, but the words today are sharper, laced with absolute authority and finished in steel. I inhale sharply when I realize I'm supposed to get in this car with him. *Oh boy.*

Ignoring the sudden weakness in my knees, I slip inside. The instant the driver shuts the door behind me, the car seems to shrink a whole size. Saint seems to occupy all the space with his not-too-subtle body sprawled on the bench across from mine. He's wearing a white button-down shirt, partly open to reveal a smooth expanse of chest. His jacket is tossed to the side along with a few folders and an iPad. "Don't make excuses and don't talk about it. *Do* it," he growls impatiently. He hangs up, then seems to quickly pick up another call. "Santori, talk to me."

Stroking his jaw, he regards me thoughtfully as he listens to the other man. I settle back for the ride while the car pulls into traffic. Trying not to make noise or distract him, I take out my phone and email myself some notes as he speaks. *Businesses? Buying or selling? Names—are they first names or last?*

All this time, I watch him through my lashes, trying not to get caught staring. Strangely, though, sometimes when he grows silent and listens to whatever the person on the other end of the line is saying, his eyes slide down the length of my seat and they . . . stick like glue to me.

I quickly look down at my phone, going hot all of a sudden. He's so intense, this man. And there's that maddening hint of arrogance, clinging to him with everything he does.

There have been legions of women who've been with him in bed—he's a challenge and a prize, I've seen. But in all of last night's research, I found nothing on any office affairs involving him and anyone at M4. *Saint does not mix business and pleasure?* I wrote down last night.

Sitting in the back of a black Rolls-Royce now, I realize this man doesn't seem to mix *anything* with business. He sits across from me and gives me a perfect view of his face as he engages in multiple transactions. He really is quite beautiful, even when frowning—and he seems to be wearing a thoughtful frown right now as he . . .

Uh, stares at me.

"In business, *no* is not an answer," he says, low and deep, into his phone. *"No* is simply an invitation to bargain."

Smiling at the frustration in his voice, I glance out the window as he mumbles something to his employee.

He hasn't stopped for a moment so I can get a single question in, but I'm not complaining. I'm getting a prime-time, front-row view of the labyrinth of his mind, and the complete impact of his personality.

I thought *I* was a workaholic, but there's really no way to describe the kinds of deals Saint is handling while doing something even as passive as riding in the back of a car. *Passive*—I don't think that's a word in this man's dictionary. The guy is getting things done, and I'm going to take a page from his book and use this same push to get my exposé.

I get caught up in the drama of a bidding war. Adrenaline pumps in my veins as he keeps saying numbers, shooting them off. Is he buying a company? Something from Sotheby's? I write down the name of the person he's talking to—Christine. And the numbers he's reciting. He's upping his bid by 100k increments and ends at a little over two million. He murmurs, "Good," and judging by the dazzling, toe-curling smile that appears on his face, I assume he got what he wanted.

I almost miss the rush when—at last—there's silence and the sound of his phone hitting the leather seat.

Pulling my eyes away from the Chicago streets, I spot his phone now lying next to his jacket and then, with the strange knot in my stomach he sent me home with last time, I notice that his full, undivided attention is on me.

A strange heat spreads up my neck because he's finally going to speak to *me*. "Is the moon yours yet?" I ask.

He grabs a water bottle from the wet bar to one side, cracks it open, and takes a swig. "Not yet." He smiles at that, then he frowns and reaches for another water bottle, extending his arm to hand it to me. "Here."

When I take it, he lounges back for a moment, twists his neck to the side . . . taps his fingers on the back of the armrest . . . and I'm unnerved by it. Is something wrong?

I'm not in coveralls anymore. I'm wearing . . . I instantly rehash because his stare makes me nervous. Black slacks, white button-down shirt, a cute white jacket, my hair held back with a black band. I look professional and clean, ready for business. Don't I?

"Is it all right if I ask you some questions now?"

"Shoot," he says, aloof.

As I pull out my note cards, he sips his water, his eyes coming to rest on me. His face is such an absolute distraction, I try to alternate between studying my note cards and looking at him in a professional manner. "When did the idea for Interface originate?"

"When Facebook fucked up its system."

"Their weakness became your gain?"

For the briefest moment, an appraising light shines in his eyes, surrounded by an odd yet exhilarating darkness. "Everyone's weakness is another's gain. Their system could be much improved upon. Better games, better access, faster downloads, and I've got the most capable team on the continent to do that."

"How many workers are currently on board?"

"Four thousand."

"Isn't that a high overhead for a start-up?"

"Considering we've already accomplished our initial user-sign-up goal, no, it's not."

I smile and flip through my note cards just to avoid the intensity of his gaze for a little bit. When I lift my eyes, he's drinking from his water bottle, still watching me.

"You have to know that you're the city's most wanted man. Does that surprise you?"

"Most wanted." He repeats that as if almost entertained by

the concept, a slight smile on his lips. "By whom?" He stretches out his legs wider and sits back comfortably, his hand spreading over his knee as he drops his water bottle into the cup holder to the side and regards me with openly curious eyes.

He's got a huge hand. The kind you see on basketball players or pianists.

"The media. The fans. Even investors," I specify.

He seems to mull it over in silence and never actually answers.

"You grew up under public scrutiny. I can't imagine anyone would enjoy it. Do you ever get tired of it?"

His hand spreads over his knee, wider. He taps his thumb against his leg in a restless way, but still his eyes do not leave me. Not for a second. Not even as he reaches for his water again. "It's always been like that for me."

That stare of his is really messing up my concentration. "All your acts of rebellion," I begin, trying to be professional and keep my eyes on his as well. "You were trying to make a point that you wouldn't be controlled? Did you expect this would endear you more to the public?"

A moment. Two.

That small smile on his lips again.

Those eyes still on mine.

"I'm not endearing to people, Miss Livingston. I'd say people respond to me on four levels and four levels only: they want to pray to me, be me, do me, or kill me."

Surprised by his bluntness, I let out a small laugh; then I blush because of the way his eyes darken when he hears me laugh. "Forgive me the personal questions. I'm interested in Interface and in the mind behind it—though the piece will focus on Interface."

The car is slowing down as it approaches a driveway.

Quickly peering out, I see we're pulling into the drop-off lane of a very high-end business center, and it strikes me we might have reached our destination. *Noooo. So soon?* I turn back to him, but he doesn't seem to share my anxiety. He's the embodiment of relaxation right now, leaning back in his seat, still continuing to watch me.

"I think we're here, and I wanted to ask you so many more impertinent things," I tease.

He smiles at me, a genuine smile that makes him look younger, more approachable. "I'll tell you what." He shifts forward in his seat, a mischievous expression on his face. "Tell me something about you, and I'll tell you one more thing about me."

I jump at the offer, not even hesitating. "I'm an only daughter."

"I'm an only son."

We stare at each other again, the same way we did at his office.

Suddenly I want a thousand and one answers like that one. Personal. Precise. "Can I offer another one of mine in exchange for one of yours?" I ask.

"Ah. I've got a bargainer on my hands." He leans back in his seat, his chuckle rich and savoring.

"Is that a yes?" I laugh too.

"See, the thing about bargains is, you have to have something the other wants."

I stare at him, unsure whether he's teasing me or not.

His eyes are dark, but his lips are smiling.

His eyes—I can never seem to stare enough. The pulsing energy of his being seems to roil in their depths. He's a dark individual. Dark as his hair. Dark as sin. Dark as whatever whirls around him. Something magnetic. Unstoppable. Irresistible. He sits there evaluating me, and I don't even know what to do, how to respond, what it is he's trying to get from me. He's a powerful businessman who gets what he wants and is used to things being done his way. He's also a player who always gets *who* he wants. He wanted to know something about me, and I stupidly jumped in and offered more. But he wanted to know one thing about me, not two.

"I'll think about it, Rachel," he says when I don't reply, as if to soften the blow, his eyes dark and unexpectedly liquid as he looks at me.

God! I could just *hit* myself.

"I always seem to mess up my interviews with you." I don't even know why I'm whispering, but he's such an attentive man, it seems like speaking any louder would deafen someone as sharp as he is.

I duck my head to hide the blush on my face. When I risk another glance, he's surveying me in silence.

Trying not to stare at that distracting face of his more than necessary, I glance out the window and exhale, rubbing my palms over my slacks as the car finally parks before the building entrance.

There's a new tension in the air after my *idiotic fuckup*. As his driver gets out and seems to summon Saint's PR team, Saint taps his hand on his knee, surfs his phone, and dials one number, speaking low into the receiver. "Hey, call the troops for Friday night. Let's chill out at the Ice Box. Send out e-invites to the usual list." He glances out the window for his driver's signal, and though I want to ask more about Interface, I can tell that I've already lost him.

I'm absolutely dismayed when he gets out of the car and lets me know his driver will be happy to drop me off wherever I need him to.

"Thank you for your time, Mr. Saint," is all I manage. I

think he says something back to me that sounds like "Take care," but his team fetches him and he's gone so fast, if it weren't for the empty water bottle by the place where he sat, you'd hardly believe he was just here.

On my ride home, I finally notice other things about my surroundings—now that he's gone. The quiet, beautiful car interior reminds me this isn't my life, or me. My eyes keep drifting to the now-empty water bottle where he sat. Why I'm so obsessed with an empty water bottle all of a sudden, I don't know. I force my eyes away and try to write some impressions on my phone, opening an email to myself.

Insatiable and demanding in business/extremely ambitious

Really . . . blunt (this guy does not sugarcoat anything)

*dropped the F-bomb (I like that his answers were not rehearsed and he just winged it); reason Chicago is so obsessed with him? He is NOT a fake, that's for sure

I try to think of something else, but I can't even land the thoughts and questions in my head. *Patience,* I remind myself. No story was told in one day. No secret revealed in one hour. Nothing lasting built on a single moment.

That night, I look for my Northwestern T-shirt as I get ready for bed, and I spot his shirt in my closet. I stare at it for so long I lose track of time. I reach out and run my finger over it. I feel how strong the collar is, run the back of my knuckles down the sleeve. It's huge and classy and clearly a very expensive shirt, and it somehow seems to take up much more space than it

actually does. I stare at every button, the perfectly folded cuffs—
touching it makes me smile and it makes me frown and it makes
the knot come back full force to my stomach.

And then, suddenly, I know how I'll get him to see me
again.

5

SHIRT

Mr. Saint, this is Rachel Livingston with Edge. I'd love to return your shirt, if possible. And if you'll find it in your heart to give me one more shot to discuss Interface, I couldn't be more appreciative. Looking forward to hearing from you.

Ms. Livingston, Dean again. Mr. Saint has a charity appearance this afternoon. If you can make it to the building lobby by 5 p.m. he'll see you then.

P.S. He says keep the shirt.

"He's seeing me again. Oh god. He's seeing me again, and I can't afford for it to go wrong this time! I need to ask clear questions. Get on his good side so he can see me again, maybe. Gina, it's *imperative* I wear the right clothes. Help me choose."

"What are we going for?"

"We're going for . . ."

I stare at a white skirt and white top—feminine and pure.

"I say go for something stronger that says, 'Here I am, and I'm serious about doing this thing.' " Gina gestures to a gray skirt, a tight, short gray jacket, and red pumps.

"But I wanted to look pure and vulnerable," I groan.

"Come on—this will get the job done."

"Okay," I agree. "This, and some pretty underwear for confidence."

I tell Helen I've got an interview so that I can leave work early on Thursday.

"Are you wearing that?" She points at the outfit Gina and I chose.

I nod.

She scowls. "It's a bit too . . . secretarial. Can we go for something a little more sexual? We want his sexual interest piqued!"

"I'll pop open a few buttons and get some cleavage in," I appease.

"I heard there's a big party this weekend at the Ice Box. Did you get info on that?"

No, but I heard him mention it in the car. "I'll try to get in," I assure her.

I arrive early at M4 and ask if I can see him before we leave. "Five minutes so I can give this back?" I ask, lifting the hanger with the plastic-covered, dry-cleaned shirt.

One of his assistants picks up the phone, whispers something into the receiver, then nods and asks me to sit.

I sit and, after a minute, lightly raise my free hand to my blouse, popping open a top button.

Then I pop open a second, a bit of air caressing the skin between my breasts.

Exhaling, I consider buttoning back up at least a dozen times by the time I'm allowed into his office. And then I forget about it when I see him standing behind his desk, pulling his jacket off the back of his chair.

Six feet three inches of polished businessman, black tie, and smoothly shaven jaw. I never got to watch my father dress for work, or a brother. That has to be why I find the sight of Malcolm Saint reaching for his jacket in that crisp white shirt so completely haunting and beguiling.

I'm helpless to stop myself from staring. I catch his expression the moment he gets a glimpse of me, and he quietly returns my stare. God. He's so disturbing to me in every way. I'm not blind to his attraction. I feel it like a fist in the gut, every look punching me deeper.

His eyebrows rise in curiosity, in question. "What's this about?"

Clearly noticing what I carry, he hooks his jacket behind him and assumes a wide stance—only looking at me—for the longest moment. My legs feel liquid.

I don't think he's even spared a glance "there," but a little bit of cleavage has never made me feel so exposed.

"Mr. Saint." I clear my throat, and a silence stretches between us as he eases his arms into his jacket.

"Rachel," he says, his smile so mysterious, I wish I knew what he was thinking.

I step forward and lift the shirt across the top of his neatly organized desk. "I believe this is yours. I'm sorry it took me a while. I had to dry-clean it twice, one at an eco-friendly place, the other normal, just to try to get a little smudge of paint off."

He looks at his shirt as if amused that he's seeing it again, and all I can wonder is why, if he's not even looking at my cleavage, do I still feel so naked right now? "I told Dean you could keep it," he tells me.

"It seemed inappropriate of me to."

He leans over to his computer and types in several digits, locking it. "Why?"

He finally takes the metal hanger; his fingers curl over mine—warm, long, his grip strong as he takes the shirt back. He crosses the huge expanse of his office to hang it with the rest, and I quickly button up the two buttons I'd undone, finally able to take a breath.

"Have you never gotten a gift from a man before, Rachel?" he asks.

He's too perceptive, too observant. "Well, actually, I . . . no. Not really . . ."

"Not even flowers?"

With a tap on the wall, he opens the hidden closet and keeps eyeing me from across the room. I can't imagine why it matters or why he'd even care, but I manage to answer.

"No," I say.

He shoves the shirt back inside with dozens of others, but by the glint in his eye, he looks fascinated by this news, and I can't begin to fathom why. I groan. "You're going to tease me about it, aren't you?"

A brow raises in question. "Me? Tease you?"

"I think you like teasing me. Your eyes are laughing at me right now," I accuse, pointing at his face as he comes back with that long, sure stride of his and the most beautiful smile he's ever worn in front of me.

"Maybe because I like the way you blush."

I'm blushing pretty hard now.

His stare isn't as icy as I remember. I feel as warm as his eyes look.

"What about your father?" He motions toward the doors and we exit his office.

I want to find something fun and light to say in answer, but

I can never find anything fun and light to say about my dad that actually happened to me. We wait for the elevator. "He was gone before it was time for gift giving," I finally murmur.

The elevator arrives, and he signals for me to board. As I pass, he lowers his face until I feel his breath on my ear. "I didn't mean to make you uncomfortable, Rachel."

When we board, all his assistants and everyone on the floor seem to be on standby, alert to what Saint does. I stand there quietly at his side, just as alert. "You didn't," I whisper so only he can hear. But oh. He really doesn't need to do much to make me uncomfortable. Why does my personal life matter? Will he think me too green, not experienced enough, to be able to interview him the way a man in his position deserves?

One of the assistants calls, "Oh, Mr. Saint," and jumps into the elevator before we can leave.

"Yeah, Cathy?"

She opens a folder and points at something written down on there.

"That's right," he answers out loud.

"Okay," she says. "And this?"

He doesn't wear too much cologne. He smells of aftershave and soap. His lips distract me a little bit as he keeps answering whatever questions the assistant seems to be tapping. They suddenly face me and tip upward slightly, those lips, and when I look up a few inches higher, I realize he just caught me staring.

I'm red as we hit the lobby. "Thanks, Cathy," he tells her.

"You're welcome, Mr. Saint."

Cathy. She's at least one or two decades older and clearly in love with him. How long has she been here? I wonder, and shoot myself a little reminder email.

"You doing okay?" He hands me a bottle of water

once we're in the car. Seated facing me, the guy fills the bone-colored leather seat with broad shoulders that look about a mile wide. He looks relaxed, his hair black and silky—shorter on the sides, a little more generous and playful at the top, slicked back today to reveal his smooth forehead and chiseled features. The green of his eyes is never the same each day. Maybe that's why I can never seem to pull my own eyes away?

"Yes, thanks for seeing me," I finally tell him.

I pull out my note cards, because I'm *not* messing it up this time. He silently sips his water as I start charging forward with my questions. I learn that:

Interface will also offer Tumblr vids, gifs, and YouTube videos.

The site will have high file-sharing capacity.

Its user subscriptions are exceeding their initial estimates by 160 percent daily.

"So Interface is the thirty-fifth company you've begun from scratch?"

"Thirty-fifth, thirty-sixth . . . The number is irrelevant. Each feels like the first."

When we arrive, the event is happening in a huge garden in the back of a mansion. There are several dozen tables with white linens, a podium, and floral arrangements to spare. A huge canopy shields the tables from both the sun and rain, the effect elegant and beautiful.

SAVE AN ANIMAL, the tall banner over the podium declares in navy-blue letters. When Saint stops by a table to get a paddle for the auction, I'm confused.

"I thought you were speaking publicly today?" I ask as I follow him through the tables.

"I'm letting my wallet do the speaking."

"Saint," a guy calls, coming over with a camera. "I thought you didn't do reporters."

I don't remember the guy's name, but I suddenly remember that he worked for only a few days at *Edge*. He's tall, blond, young, and looking at me with all kinds of professional envy.

Saint takes me by the elbow, ignores the guy, and walks us right past him as he states, "Mind your own business, Gregg," in low warning.

"You're my business, Saint!" Gregg yells.

Quiet and curious as to his reaction, I peer up to read Saint's unreadable profile. I'm quickly impressed with how easily he dismisses the guy from his thoughts. He must be completely used to such scrutiny, to the point that we could all be flies, vying for his attention, waiting for him to make a move we can call newsworthy. Sometimes he obliges us, the media—he's been reckless before. How hard must his limits have been pushed for him to lose it?

I notice he ignores most everyone or just greets them amicably—but the attitude he radiates is "I don't give a shit." People, on the other hand, can't resist his magnetism. They seem to gravitate in his direction the moment they spot him. I can't explain the kind of venomous looks I'm getting from the same women who then turn adoring gazes back to Saint.

He sits me down at a table at the very front.

With each place setting there's a small picture catalogue of the loveliest wild animals you've ever seen. "What do you say?" he asks me in a cool, businesslike tone as I flip through one.

"You're saving one of these animals?" I ask, bemused when he nods. "I can't possibly pick one."

"They were in the circus. They'll be euthanized if they don't find a home, and to do that, they need a sponsor who'll help set them up in the care of a local zoo."

"I'm so sad right now." I look at the list of animals and stop on one. "Elephant. I think it's one of the noblest animals. How they are with each other, so nurturing, so strong and so gentle."

"That's your pitch?" he asks, as if not amused.

"No, I'm just getting started," I say, pride pricked. "Elephants are lucky. I bet if you save this elephant today, its luck will save *you* one day."

"I'm absolutely unsavable, Miss Livingston—but let's get the elephant." He hands me the numbered paddle so I can do the bidding, then sits there on his phone, answering emails while I keep on lifting the stick.

I start freaking out as the price rises. "Saint—"

"Keep going until she's yours."

"She's *yours*," I amend.

He shrugs. "If it makes you feel better."

We save the elephant named Rosie, and now she'll have a home for life. He also retrieved the stick from me and bid on each of the other animals, enough to get their prices up and make the others pay out their asses. He didn't say he'd do this—I observed by the fourth animal he was bidding on them all, pushing everyone to their limits until he was satisfied.

It's as if the world is his playground. I'm awed, and also a little frightened.

Saint could crush the magazine. . . .

I just saw a calmly ruthless side of him I hope to never see opposing me.

On our way back, he's on the phone speaking in another language, and I'm trying not to notice how the sound of his voice caressing the foreign tones makes me shift in my seat. I write down notes on my phone to email to myself, especially the one that's most on my mind.

He takes no prisoners. He pushed the prices up as far as
they'd go. Why? He challenges his peers and his peers don't
like it——> How many enemies does he have?

I start blushing when I think of the way he seems to enjoy
teasing me, and I exhale and look at him as he talks to someone
I'm pretty sure is Tahoe Roth. He's different with his friends.
More at ease, less intense. I think of his business calls, of his actions today.

He's driven and relentless—absolutely unquenchable.

When we drop him off at M4, where the shiny BUG 3 waits
for him with someone standing by with the keys, he says good
night. I thank him for today and then sit there tortured, wondering if that was my last interview.

When I get home I wonder how I'm going to get him to
see me again. I feel restless even thinking this is over. I wonder if I will look too desperate if I ask for another interview.
Maybe I'll just keep in touch and then reach out later in the
week.

Opening my Interface inbox and starting a new message, I
search for the auction and find a beautiful elephant picture. I
add a caption saying, *You really know how to treat a gal; my hero,*
and then I write a message:

Mr. Saint, I not only enjoyed learning about Interface but I am
sleeping so much better knowing that Rosie is, too.

I stare at the words and wonder if I'm going a little too
far. I'm teasing him a little because he teased me today. I want
to appeal to his human side so he can share a little more with

me, but I don't want him to feel I'm being unprofessional. I ask Gina what she thinks of me sending an elephant picture.

"What's an elephant got to do with anything?"

I decide it's something only *he* will get, so I gather my courage and send it. Then I groan. Really? I'm not even sure he'll laugh, what kind of moods he has. I end up checking compulsively for messages, and as I wait for a reply, I divert my energies into reading his interviews. I read and read, interested not really in the questions but in the answers, and more than that, in each tiny white space in between the words of his answers, as if any word he didn't say will help me get to know him better.

Still no reply to my message hours later.

There's usually peace in my bedroom, but I seem to have sent it off with the elephant picture. I toss and turn all night.

6

CLUB

I'm staring up at the ceiling of our apartment, terribly confused.

Did I make a mistake sending the elephant picture?

I let my excitement get the best of me and maybe crossed a professional line. I've heard nothing from him today, or from Dean or anyone. Now I don't know what to do, but I know that tonight he's got a posh gathering at the Ice Box. I need to get in somehow. His life seems perfectly compartmentalized; business on the one hand, and what about the other? If the man works hard, he's got a reputation for partying just as hard, or—impossible, but yes—even *harder*.

The media loves to emphasize his whoring around, but can you blame him? He looks amazing, and walking next to him when we got to the auction, there wasn't a single female eye that didn't look at me and then crawl its way longingly up to his beautiful face. Can you blame him for partaking of what women offer when he's such a young, healthy man?

Saint might think he's giving us a puff piece, but he's done more for *Edge* than anyone has lately—cooperating past what I'd have *ever* expected. He's given me more time than anyone even half as important as he is has been willing to give to a struggling magazine like us.

I can tell he's a hard boss, but my gut says he's not an unfair one. Interface and the entire M4 conglomerate are examples of vision and ambition but not greed. From his phone calls alone I can tell he's a remarkable businessman—as remarkable a businessman as they say he is a lover.

During the first interview in the car, when he thought about the Ice Box, who did he call? One of his boys? Roth or Carmichael?

Grabbing our apartment phone from next to the living room couch, I call Valentine, one of my coworkers, the one who's in the social section—who knows everyone, and if not, knows about them well enough to lie about it. "Can you get me into Malcolm Saint's Ice Box party tonight?"

"I can get you anything, woman. The real question is, what do I get in return?"

"Name the price . . . *man.*"

"Ah, I love my snarky Rache! Let me call you back."

Minutes later, he calls me back and says, "You're on the list."

"With Gina, right?"

"Dude, I'm a rainmaker, not a miracle worker. You're welcome. You owe me one."

"And I'll pay," I happily promise—but Gina's not that happy with the news.

"What do you mean I can't go with you?" Gina complains when I tell her. "Wynn is going out, and I have to stay in on a Friday?"

"I'm sorry, Gina." I wince as I frantically fish out some clothing options. "What if Valentine comes over?"

"Oh no." She groans. "I don't trust that man. He's like the gossiping bald guy in *Game of Thrones*, playing everyone." Then she starts texting. "Okay, I texted Valentine *because* he's like the gossiping bald guy from *Game of Thrones*. We might get drinks once I send you off."

I'm still in my terry robe, fresh out of a shower, with Gina and Wynn trying to help me find the perfect outfit, when there's a knock. Wynn leaps to her feet as if lightning just struck. She rushes to the bathroom to fluff her curls, and then walks across the living room to answer the door.

Wynn flings the door open to reveal: Emmett, chef at an up-and-coming restaurant. Her latest man. Her scarf flaps in the breeze generated by the opening door, and Emmett grabs its edges and pulls her to him.

Tall and blond, he kisses her on the mouth, a kiss so perfect and movie-like, any minute now I expect the background music to blare.

I've never been pulled to a man like that. I've never been tossed in the air like an airplane, like Wynn was growing up, or kissed on the forehead by my dad every night, like Gina was.

Wynn has always been the softest of us three. She wants to marry, and is expert at using her femininity to get what she wants. What she always wants? A man. I haven't wanted a man my whole life. I grew up wanting my dad to be alive, and all my wanting has been used up; that well has long since gone dry.

Gina watches them too, and the moment Wynn shuts the door behind her, we both stare at each other with a look that says, *Are we missing out on something great because we grew too jaded?*

Gina is the cynic among us. She dated a guy named Paul a

couple of years ago in college. Paul is such a nice, unassuming name. You'd never think someone named Paul would be lying through his teeth when he said he loved you. You'd never imagine he'd have two other girlfriends with whom he discussed you. You'd never think that the first guy you fell in love with would make being single for the rest of your life something to look forward to.

Gina and I are both married to our jobs, and we both mean for it to stay like that. Gina works at a department store and she lives for her employee discount. I live for my column.

"You look nervous," Gina says as I add some blush to my cheeks. "Relax, Rachel. He's just a man, no matter how godly."

"Don't say that, I'm nervous enough as it is. Clubs were not even my scene when we were begging to be let in."

"Nobody will know it's not your scene. Just make sure to look the part."

We both look at the three options I've set out.

Considering he's seen me in my coveralls and then dressed in a suit, I want to give a completely different message with whatever I wear tonight. His parties are known to be decadent—and I don't want to wear clothes that say I'm a working girl. I want to look like someone who parties with his crowd. I want to look seductive, modern, edgy so the last thing he'll remember if he sees me tonight is that I'm the same woman interviewing him for an Interface article.

"What do you think?" I ask her. "Option 1: a cute white skirt with a flimsy white top; option 2: red, knee-length, very tight dress; option 3: black bandage dress."

"Men love women in white," Gina says. "It's that devil in them that can't resist. Saint's devil is the wildest of them all. They love red too."

"But black is foolproof," I say. "I don't want to scream out,

'I haven't had sex in a while.' I don't want to say, 'Come hither.'
I just want to be there and say, 'Here I am.' "

She nods approvingly, so I go into the bathroom, slide on
my black lace undergarments and the dress, and come out barefoot to slip on my heels.

Gina drops the magazine she was reading as we take in my
appearance in the full-length mirror on the inside of my closet
door.

I'm tall and trim, my breasts small but firm and perky. My
skin is milky apricot and my hair platinum blonde, from my
mom's Scandinavian heritage. For some reason people compli-
ment the curves of my shoulders and neck, so the low-cut dress
shows them off. It emphasizes my slenderness, my slim hips and
small waist, the black material heightening the translucence of
my face and neck. My hair gleams like silvery gold. My eyes are
gray with flecks of blue. The dress hugs me in all the right places.

"Like off a catwalk," Gina assures from the bed, nodding.

"*Definitely* better than I looked when I met him in my
sneakers," I counter.

I run a brush over my hair, then blow-dry it for a few minutes. When I'm done, I expel a breath as I meet my stare in the
mirror. "Ready or not, Rachel."

"Of course you're ready!" Gina woots.

I laugh and turn to look at her, wishing she could come.
My absolute best friend. She's my adopted sister in my heart.
I held her hand when Paul broke her. I passed the Kleenex. I
swore I'd never let anyone break her heart again. I swore I'd be
with her to the end, and I wouldn't let anyone break mine. I
promised we'd be happy and single, because who needed a guy?
And we both ate ice cream and repeated that mantra all the
time. And already I feel that I'm going to the club tonight, an
angel without my wing.

"Go get it," she tells me with that singular excitement of hers.

I swallow and grab my bag and try to tell myself that I can do this. That I want to do this. That when—not if, *when*—I write this exposé, I will finally silence every doubt in my head of whether I can bring it to the table when it's most needed.

I look very different from the girl Saint met in his office. But I don't feel any different. My nerves are frayed to the edges as I give my name to a bouncer at the entrance and I'm allowed into the club, every part of me snug and tight in my dress as my black heels hit the floor.

Whereas M4 was all museum-like, the Ice Box is pure dark decadence. Ice sculptures sit on pedestals around the room. Cages with body-painted dancers hang from the ceiling. A bar with white and blue lights stretches from one wall to another.

Strobe lights flash across the space as I get jostled by the crowd. The bass thumps as the Mr. Probz song "Waves" plays for the dancing crowd. Drinks are flowing on shiny silver trays, and the drinks are so adorned—by fruits, olives, salt glitter, or colorful liquid swirls—they're like artworks. This isn't a normal swanky club. It's the rich boys' club, and everywhere you look are beautiful people wearing beautiful things.

"I met him! God! When he said hi I thought I'd faint . . . !"

My nerves eat at me as I hear that, because I know for sure they're talking about him. Trying to breathe, I wind deeper into the club, wishing for Gina so bad I ache. The room is packed with women, some clearly on the hunt, others already paired with someone, a few hanging out with their friends. I breathe slowly, in and out, telling myself I can do this. It's just a club.

I can have some fun. It's been a while since I've gone out to a club, and never to a club like this, but it doesn't matter. I can interview people, and if I'm lucky, I can do more than that.

After scanning the area and trying to find the best spy spots, I go to the top level, and that's when I get the best look at what's happening downstairs in the most crowded corner.

And speak of the devil. My heart stops a beat when I see that dark head of his, and that loathed, burning knot in my stomach squeezes with a vengeance. I swear, *no one in my life has ever made me this nervous.*

He sits with his arms stretched out behind him, a wine-glass and two women vying for his attention as he chats with his friends. His masculine face is illuminated in certain angles when the lights flash—his beauty unprecedented.

Okay. *Breathing.* Do I want him to know I'm here or not?

A watery sensation seems to spread down my limbs as I force myself to go downstairs. I wend my way to the ladies' room and worm through the throng of bodies toward a wide mirror above a set of modernist floating sinks. A group of women primp and preen themselves while I look at all of our reflections. To my right, a woman pouts her red lips, and to my left, her friend pouts her pink ones. Me? I'm still me, but I look extravagant, like I was born here. I look very different than the young girl in coveralls he met. Will he even recognize me like this?

"You going to the after-party?" Red Lips asks Pink Lips as they retouch their lipsticks.

"No key yet."

"Lookie lookie." Red Lips waves a key card in the air.

There's squealing in the room, and she tucks the key into her bra. "Mine!"

"So there's an after-party?" I ask them.

"At Saint's penthouse," one says, nodding.

"How do you get invited to this party?"

"A hundred keys are distributed during the evening."

A sudden thought of stealing the very key she's just tucked into her bra flickers through my mind. I mean, it's just a key. It couldn't possibly be a felony.

"Babe," she tells me, "stop giving my key the eye! I've been waiting three years to get a key like this. Go and work your ass out there if you want one. Only the finest asses make it."

"Thanks," I say, turning to look at my ass in the mirror questioningly. Gina says I've got a great ass. It's perky and the perfect handful, some would say. But would Saint say that?

I sigh and lean against the wall, then I spot all the little writings on an open stall door. I narrow my eyes, forcing my focus.

Malcolm for my baby-daddy

I sucked Saint's cock

Tahoe rammed me right here

Callan licks cunt like a caveman

I head back into the noise and try to find a good spot for spying when I see him again. The two women won't leave his side, and now my stomach for some reason feels jumpy, annoying me. One of the blondes takes a shot from the waiter, licks the rim, and then adds salt.

Saint edges back and watches her with an expression of casual boredom, but his lips are curled, as if he's having some fun.

I'm so engrossed in watching—a little too fascinated and a little bit disgusted—I don't realize a guard has walked up to me until he's right in my face. He signals to the back of the room—

to where Saint's best friends are now watching me. Saint isn't even looking my way. Oh no, he's too busy being entertained, still wearing that almost-bored smile. Maybe they need to take their tops off to get him excited.

All three men fit in perfectly with the lavish surroundings, but I can't look at the other two. Only at Malcolm. Malcolm's dark good looks blend with the shadows, like Hades in his own little corner of hell.

Suddenly he laughs at something one of the blondes does and he turns a little, his eyes landing straight on me—and stopping there.

I feel his stare like a hit of adrenaline. I want to look away, but I can't, I feel trapped. I don't know if I made this up, but I could've sworn his chest jerked as if he sucked in a breath.

Does he recognize me?

Do I want him to?

Suddenly the atmosphere is so heavy I can't breathe. My lungs feel like rocks and I really can't *breathe*. As he rakes me in one fast, complete sweep of his eyes that makes my stomach quiver nervously, he takes me in, from my pumps up to my long blonde hair, and I become aware of my dress hugging the tops of my thighs, my hips, my abdomen, my breasts, and even my ass. Oh god. I force myself to follow the guard in his direction, every step accelerating my heartbeat. In that black suit and without a tie, the top button of his shirt open and his hair a bit rumpled, Saint is the embodiment of luxurious decadence and sin. He is Sin Itself, and I feel like an absolute . . . virgin.

He stretches his long legs out before him, his stare fixed on mine without any seeming inclination to move away.

"Mr. Saint." The guard clears his throat. "The gentlemen had me summon her."

Although his smile doesn't waver, the look on his face is completely remote and unreadable.

"Here she is, gentlemen," the guard then tells the other two—the blond and the copper-haired man looking at me like I'm lunch.

"Tahoe," the blond says.

"Callan," the copper-haired man says.

Saint merely pats the blondes on the butt and sends them on their way, then he reaches out to take my elbow in a somehow instinctive gesture that brings me a strange sense of comfort. I don't know anybody else here, so when he tugs me to his side, I sit next to him on the edge of the long booth.

And that's when he leans his dark head over to me and murmurs, "Malcolm." His voice is so deep and rumbling I shiver.

"Rachel," I lamely offer.

He raises his eyebrow and stares at me. *What are you doing here, Rachel?* he seems to ask.

I'm wondering what to say, when Tahoe lifts his drink and drains it. "You're up past your bedtime." The Texan oil baby. Oozing charm, drawling out the words.

I don't know why, but I'm acutely aware of the position of Saint's body in relation to mine. He just straightened fully in the booth and somehow shifted so that his arm is very noticeably stretched out behind me.

"Like they say, no rest for the wicked," I answer Tahoe with an extra-wide smile, my heart pounding over Saint's nearness.

Suddenly I can smell him. Just him. Among all the mingled scents in the room, it's Saint somehow in my lungs, in every *breath*. He radiates a vitality that draws me like a magnet. It unnerves me but something in his presence, so close to me, soothes me too.

"Apparently there's a dress code—Saint had to drop his tail

and horns at the door," Callan jokes as a waiter sets a drink before me.

"Oh yes." I tug the hem of my skirt self-consciously. "I had to drop half my dress."

"Did you now?" Tahoe asks.

"T."

One word, one letter, from Malcolm.

"Yeah, Saint?" Tahoe returns, lifting his eyebrows.

"Dibs."

I almost spit out the drink. I cough and slam my hand to my chest, and Saint calmly reaches out to take my drink from my hand and sets it aside. "Okay?" he asks, ducking his head and peering into my face.

I give one last cough and squeeze my eyes shut and nod, and when I open my eyes, Saint is the only thing I see. I find him staring at me in such a penetrating way I can feel the stare in my bones.

"Did you just get in to the party, Rachel?" he asks.

As he waits for my reply, he reaches for my cocktail and extends the glass out to me. His wrist is thick and looks so strong, so golden, his skin smooth, his arm dusted with a little bit of hair as I cautiously take it from him, our fingers brushing.

Tahoe reaches into his coat pocket and waves whatever he extracts in the air. "Saint! May I?"

Excitement leaps in my chest when I realize it's *a key!*

"Not happening, that's not her scene," Malcolm murmurs beside me.

"Aw! Come on, let me give her a key. She's a dime, man," Tahoe drawls.

I'm so disbelieving that I'm not even breathing as Malcolm slowly stands. I follow him up, staring into his face in confusion.

"What do you mean it's not my scene?" I demand. I feel like there's no gravity when he stands so close to me. I'm dizzy. Confused. And unexpectedly hurt.

For the first time since we met, he looks at me like he's actually losing his temper . . . with *me*. He leans closer and puts his lips against my ear. "Trust me when I tell you, it's not your scene. Go home," he whispers. He sends me a look laden with warning and walks away, blending into the crowd.

Tahoe and Callan stare at me, speechless. "That's a first," Tahoe mumbles and heads away.

I feel myself burn in humiliation and confusion. Worse is that, when I go outside, the same man who drove us around the day before walks over to me.

"Miss Livingston, a pleasure to drive you," he says, hanging up his phone as if Saint just called him. He is a huge man with a bald head and no expression. A second later, he's opening the door of the Rolls for me.

Seriously?

Did Saint call him just now and ask him to escort me home?

Aware of people staring and seeing me being led to Saint's car, I climb into the back of the Rolls and murmur my thanks simply because it's not this man's fault.

The car smells new and expensive and like *him*. A bottle of wine and water bottles ride with me. There's music in the background and the temperature is just right. The perfect luxury of it all tempts me to run my hands over my dress and look down at myself in confusion. What is wrong with me?

I feel as if he pulled the rug from under me and reminded me what I'm up against. The top of the species. Somebody ruthless.

I can't take the heat in the back of my ears and on my

cheeks. I sag on the backseat and set my forehead on the window. Focus, Livingston! Exhaling, I grab my phone and try to write down all the details about what I saw, but I can't right now. I just can't do anything but ride here, in his car, wondering why I feel so vulnerable.

At about 11:55 p.m. I tiptoe into the apartment, wincing when the door shuts a little louder than I'd planned. I go to the kitchen to get myself some water and Gina pads out, her hair a tangle. "Hey," I say apologetically. She frowns and squints in the lamplight. "Sorry, G, I didn't mean to wake you. Get back to bed."

"How was the party?"

"Okay," I can only say. "I'll fill you in tomorrow morning."

She rubs her eyelids. "Urgh, it's too late or early. Yeah. We watched *Game of Thrones.*"

She pads back to her room and I go into mine, take off my makeup, then strip out of my dress. As I look for my Northwestern T-shirt, I spy the vacant spot where his shirt used to be in my closet and I stare at it. I should be glad it's not here, but instead its absence makes me ache worse, because I can't even remember if I made up the times he was nice to me. Slamming my closet door shut, I slide into bed in my boy briefs, bringing my notepad with me, forcing myself to write. One word, at least. Just one, because blocking out this evening will not further my goals in any way. I write:

Territorial

And then I Google, simply because I still can't believe he said . . .

Dibs: A claim / rights

Yes. It means exactly what I thought it did.

Frowning, I settle back in bed and stare at the ceiling. Livingston, so what? He didn't like seeing you at his club party—you're a reporter. Did you expect he would? Do you know what this means? All this means is that you need to dig *deeper*!

7

DREAM

*D*eeper. His body's on top of mine—hard in all places. He thrusts, and I like it so much I cry out and arch my body. "Please," I whisper. "Deeper, oh please, *deeper.*"

His lips cover mine in an uncontrolled kiss. Hands squeeze my breasts, palms stroke my nipples. The back of my head is swallowed by the pillow as the weight of his body buries me deeper into the mattress.

I agonize. I agonize because I haven't had sex in so long and it has *never* felt like this, and he kisses me again, with raw hunger. He curls his fingers around one breast and suckles the tip. I curve and stretch my body up wantonly, my thighs parting beneath his hips so he can get inside me, as deep as he can. . . . Please pleasepleasep*please* . . . I never beg, but I can't stop saying *please*.

I nibble hungrily on his full lips and let my fingers trail up the grooves of his back. He feels the way he looks: hard, unyielding. But his body is oh so warm—there's not an ounce of cold in *this* body. If I open my eyes, will his eyes be green ice or green fire? Please be fire, please want me. Please, deeper, I think, tossing my head as his next powerful thrust brings him so deep, every inch of his hard flesh buried inside me, every inch of me taken. He starts to move: out, in, out, in—

I wake up sweating and rolling my hips and just a hair away from orgasm, breathing in fast pants. I groan and roll to the side. 1:08 a.m. He must be at his after-party. Having a three-some. A foursome. God.

Seriously, Livingston! I chide. I'm trembling and it won't stop. I'm already at the edge, just waiting to fall.

Groaning in misery, I slide my hand between my legs, where I'm aching. Don't do it, Livingston, I warn, but I feel fe-verish. I squeeze my eyes shut and slide my finger between my thighs and then, because I just can't stop it, I try to picture a hot actor instead of him. But as the pleasure comes back, icy green eyes look back at me. I bite my lip and want to bite his lips. Fe-verish, I feel his hand between my legs and it's still not enough; I want more of his fingers, I want his weight crushing me. I savor what he's doing to my body and tell myself that I just won't say his name when I come. I won't say it. Because he's not the one doing slow, sweet, sexy things to me right now. Kissing me. Squeezing me. Moving inside me as I—

"*Saint.*"

After an earth-shattering orgasm, I lie in bed, dazed. Then shocked.

"God, I'm such a slut." I turn on my lamp and go wash my hands, then wash my face and scowl at myself in the mirror.

Sighing as I pad back into my room, I open my laptop and find myself pulling up more links about him, putting my-self to work. It occurs to me that right now he's probably with one or two or three or four girls, having the kind of toe-curling, sheet-clawing sex he's known for. I spy his personal social media and tell myself the exposé is the only reason I want to know.

His Instagram page is full of adrenalized pictures:

Saint black-diamond skiing, a black-clad form against a huge white mountain, a clear zigzag dent behind him.

Saint skydiving, flinging himself backward off the plane, hot as ever, the world a tiny blur beneath him.

But there's nothing, absolutely nothing, from the after-party he didn't want me to attend.

8

SUMMONED

"Saint is never up to any good," Gina declares Sunday afternoon from her spot on the living room window seat. "You can count on trouble following this little after-party of his. Did you hear me?"

"Umm . . ." I'm surfing the internet, trying to glean any info on the after-party.

"Rachel Livingston. Hello? Rachel Dibs? Can I call you Rachel Dibs now?" She snaps her fingers to pull my attention away from my laptop, and boy, has she been ribbing me about the "dibs" part. "Whoa. There's a car outside. A big-ass car. Outside our humble little apartment. Do you copy? Earth to—"

"What do you mean, 'a big-ass car'?" I leap up from the couch and hurry to where Gina sits. I pull open the other gauzy living room curtain, and there is the big-ass Rolls-Royce that carried me home this past weekend.

What in the world?

I grab my phone and my heart stops when I see his name on my email.

I'd like to meet with you today. I'll have a car waiting at your place.
M

Ohmigod.
Malcolm himself messaged me?

"Hey, girl, where you going?" Gina hollers as she watches me run to my room.

I'm so nervous I've clammed up and can't talk to her about it. I change into my white jeans that curve around my ass, a tiny top, and silver high-heeled sandals. I spritz myself with a cloud of perfume and shout back to her, "I'll tell you later. Don't wait up!"

I tuck a clutch bag under my arm and take the elevator downstairs. When I step out to the sidewalk, I notice people are actually taking pictures of the car.

The driver spots me and quickly opens the door. I slide inside before they can snap a picture of me too, the memory of the last time I was in here making me feel a little bit uncomfortable. But I'm not wearing anything way outside my comfort zone today. My clothes say modern and sexy, but not seduction. More determined than ever, I'm out for information, and *no* green eyes will distract me.

"Where are we going?" I ask the driver.

"DuSable Harbor," he tells me.

He drives for a while, and the whole time I can't possibly imagine what Saint wants from me. I'm still uncomfortable about what happened the last time we saw each other, but I can't let my personal feelings hurt my story, either.

The car swerves into the parking lot and parks near the most luxurious yacht in the harbor. It's compact enough to fit in the dock, but big enough to stand apart from the others. It glistens, pristine white under the sun. THE TOY is scrawled in navy-blue letters near the bow.

The car door swings open before I can even close my mouth. As I get out, I see the dark-haired man on deck, and my heart leaps. Slowly, I force my legs to move, a part of me wondering if this is actually me heading to this yacht—to the man waiting above. My world tilts a little and I feel as if someone misplaced me and put me on the wrong shelf as I board.

"Mr. Saint."

He walks forward in baggy swim trunks and an open dress shirt, and his abs are smooth and so ripped I could trace the indentations with a finger. His legs are absolutely muscled and the wind teases his hair in a playful way.

He wears his suits as if perfection made them for him, but right now, his surprisingly casual, very sexy, very toe-curling, and still imposing good looks only remind me of my dream and make me wish I hadn't dreamt it. In the sunlight, he's so much more stunning than I remembered. His tan neck is thick and strong, his Adam's apple sexy as he speaks in that deep voice: "Rachel."

I blush beet red.

"I'm expecting friends over. I thought you'd like to join me."

"Why would you think that?"

He steps forward, almost into my personal bubble. I want to cringe, he's so powerful. But I don't. "I have a feeling you were pissed off about the way things ended last time." He watches me with a guarded gaze that misses absolutely no detail.

I don't want to feel the hurt I did and the confusion over what he did, but it surfaces without effort. "Pissed off that you called dibs like you were twelve? And then had the nerve to dismiss me?"

His expression still doesn't change.

And neither does my anger.

"Did you want me here just so you could remind me of my place? Or did you think I was going to bow down at your feet and beg forgiveness for annoying you?"

"No, I wanted to ask you a question." His normally intense green stare accomplishes the impossible and intensifies even more. "What were you doing there Friday?"

"A friend invited me."

He comes closer.

"The truth," he warns.

A hot blush creeps up my neck, and he notices. His voice drops. "Tell me you were looking for me, and then let me make it up to you."

"Oh really? How does Malcolm Saint make something up to someone? Something tells me a simple coffee isn't your style."

"Do you like coffee?"

"Two sugars, actually."

"Noted." He studies me as his lips shape a coaxing smile. "Stay and meet my friends tonight."

His smile is small but so coaxing, my stomach feels hot, as if I swallowed a spoonful of warm honey. I don't know how those eyes of his can be so disturbing and so comforting at the same time.

"Saint! My man!" A yell carries from nearby.

Callan and Tahoe and a handful of girls hop onto the yacht, and I exhale shakily and edge a few steps away from Malcolm as they greet him.

"Rachel," he says, calling me back, and he introduces me to his friends.

9

YACHT

Here's why I'm sucking at my job today: Saint.

Saint lounging in a chaise.

Saint wakeboarding.

Watching Saint strut around his yacht.

Saint calling out to some other guys on another passing yacht.

"Saint! You heard the Cubs got smashed?"

"That's so wrong, dude. That's so fucking wrong."

Then, Saint chatting with his friends.

We've been eyeing each other in quiet puzzlement for a while, Saint and I. There's a closet full of trunks and bikinis, and I ended up slipping into a tiny white one and watching the other women dip into the lake.

This afternoon I've smeared on a lot of sunscreen, enough to let me get a good tan but hopefully keep me from burning. My skin prickles under the warmth of the sun. I can feel the Lake Michigan air, the wind playing with my hair, the soft rocking motions of the yacht as it glides through the water. The engines hum softly, lulling me to a near sleep. But I'm too aware to sleep—I don't want to miss anything. The work calls he makes. How he relaxes but still is somehow alert to his business.

Saint's been dipping into the water all day. I know it's cold, because I went in once too. He's been swimming a little and diving in every half hour, regardless of whether his friends are swimming or wakeboarding. I've been staying on my chaise, warm and cozy under the setting sun, but he's always doing something. It's like he doesn't relax. He exudes a force; no wonder he's always active. Skiing black diamonds, skydiving, flying . . . He takes the risks of someone who has nothing to lose. He takes more risks than anyone I've ever known.

I'm in my tiny white bikini and hungrily circling an oasis of food when his friends, Tahoe and Callan, join me.

I linger by their sides and altogether try to avoid Saint merely because we seem to have come to a truce, but I'm a bit out of my element. In his space, with his friends.

The interest in his eyes, every time I look around to find him watching me, makes me more nervous than I've ever been in my life.

When he brushes my arm with his, I find myself instinctively edging to the side. When he comes to stand beside me, I shrink from the warmth of his touch. I'm unsettled and I don't know why. He ends up heading to the opposite end of the party. He disappears into one of the cabins—on business, the friends say—until a pair of women go and coax him out to "sit" with them. He drops onto a couch, his arms spreading over the backrest. I can feel his stare on me as if it were a touch.

I try to get into the stories his friends are sharing with the group. But out of the corner of my eye, I can't stop watching the girls sitting on either side of Saint nearly blabber their mouths off as they try to get his attention.

We stay on the deck sitting area with the group while Malcolm slowly drains a glass of wine. And then another.

We end up telling drinking stories, friend stories, stalking stories about girls who stalk Malcolm.

"His old man never knew what he was going to bring home since Kalina," Callan explains.

"You brought home a naked girl?" one of his floozies asks him, pouting jealously.

The beginning of a smile tips the corners of his mouth. "She was an artist, and her clothes were painted on. Quite nice, actually."

I feel my mouth quirk up too. His gaze locks on me and his smile fades, his look growing thoughtful.

"So we missed you at the after-party," Tahoe says to me.

"I bet." I steal a glimpse in the direction of where Saint lounges back, aloof, and I notice one of the girls is holding grapes in her hand and is trying to push a grape past his lips. He's looking at me, watching me. I watch him as he absently opens his mouth to munch on the grape but never, for a second, takes his eyes off me.

"One more," the girl whispers at his jaw, pushing another grape past his beautiful lips.

His jaw muscles flex as he crushes it with his molars, and I wonder what he tastes like right now. Fresh. Juicy. His eyes gleam as he watches my reaction, and my entire body begins to vibrate with feelings I can't even process. My cheeks flare with the same heat that spreads across my skin like wildfire. The night only makes him look darker.

Dangerously, primitively darker.

I can't stand the knot in my stomach, completely merciless when he's near. I shift to the side and ask his friends, "What did you all do? You're so famous for your parties, I can't imagine what happens at the after-parties."

"I skinny-dipped." Tahoe grins. "Callan got a bit too far into his cups to remember."

And SAINT?

"Saint and I had a good time," one of the women fawning over Malcolm says.

I feel my cheeks burn. Don't look at him. Don't look at him.

"We gave him quite a show," the other says with a little purr that makes my bile sort of rise.

This is golden information. Really. This is the kind of material that the spiciest exposés are made of. But I can't seem to manage to force myself to stay and hear the rest. The walls of my stomach seem to be caving in, and without being able to stop myself, I quietly get to my feet and ask if I can go into a cabin to rest a little.

I don't even wait for anyone to assent; I just head around to the sitting area, avoiding anyone's gaze—avoiding *his* gaze. Since I'm suddenly craving air, I instead end up heading to the top deck. At the bow, I just lean on the railing and stare out at the lake. At the horizon. At a little piece of moon.

I get my phone out and try to write something. Writing always makes me feel better. Complete.

But I can't concentrate.

I set it aside and stare out at the lake.

Minutes later, fireworks explode in the sky while the group watches and hoots from below. The sight is mesmerizing. I exhale and watch the lights shoot up from Navy Pier and burst up high. It's so still right here, on the lake at night. I've always wanted to find a nice, warm spot where nothing is moving, where everything is as it should be, and I want to stay here, still and quiet, in that spot. Funny to find that spot when your world is spinning out of control.

I type one word into my phone to feel better. The first one that comes to mind when I see the lake and sky touch at the horizon.

Endless

The wind ruffles my hair, and I tie it into a bun at my nape as I turn to the top-deck sitting area. That's when I see him. He's sitting with his torso lightly stretching his shirt, the glow of his phone illuminating his profile. I didn't hear him approach. Why isn't he below? Why won't this stupid knot inside me ease?

"Taking over the world is a full-time job for you, I see," I whisper.

He slowly stands, the button-down shirt he wears casually falling open to reveal his swim trunks and his smooth, hard abs and chest and neck. He seems taller and larger when he steps closer. The air shifts quickly in temperature, or maybe it's me, warming and blushing because he was here the whole time. And he is so beautiful. He's the first beautiful thing I've ever seen that actually hurts to look at.

"I'm sorry, I didn't mean to break your concentration. I'll leave you to it," I whisper.

"Stay."

The abrupt command stops me from leaving. My blush seems to spread to the marrow of my bones because of the way he's staring at me now. His breath moves the hair at the top of my head as he whispers:

"I want to make you blush, from here"—he touches my

forehead and briefly glances at the ground—"to the tips of your feet."

He's smiling down at me, his chest so close I can feel it warm me against the breeze. I feel like he's a hurricane and I'm the lake, calm on the outside, holding a thousand and one secrets within.

"Why couldn't you look at me down there?" he murmurs, his voice breaking with huskiness as he lifts his large hand and runs the backs of his fingers down my cheek.

A hot ache grows inside me. "Saint. Don't."

He lifts his phone and shows me a picture on the screen. "I like this picture of you. You look soft and thoughtful. I can see your chin, one of your elfin ears sticking out of your hair."

"You took a picture of me!"

"I did." His thumb caresses the picture on the screen and my spine tightens, because I can almost feel the touch.

"Erase it," I say, shocked.

"Ah. Bargaining again."

"Saint. Don't. Delete that picture. I'm not interested in you like that. In being on your phone."

He eases back, searching my face. "Come here, sit with me."

He heads to the couch and settles his large body right at the center. Wow. So he expects me to follow?

With a deep breath, I force myself to go there, to that couch he now so thoroughly occupies. I'm sitting at the edge while he continues taking up the center. We stare at each other, me scowling, him in amusement, and then our heads turn and we're staring at the last fireworks in the distance.

"You're mad at me because I had my driver take you home?" he says, his eyes gleaming ruthlessly.

"You said that, not me," I return.

He chuckles softly, the sound low and male, distracting. As

is his big body, somehow sucking up the space around him like a vortex.

"I might have let you come to the after-party if you'd accepted my gift." He drags his thumb thoughtfully along the raspy square of his jaw. "A man has his pride, Rachel. How do you think I feel when I see my shirt back in my office?"

"Aw, does he feel neglected by one girl out of his million girlfriends?"

His voice lowers, his handsome face etched in puzzlement. "Why?"

"What?"

"Why did you bring it back to me? I said keep it. Nobody gives my gifts back. Am I repulsive to you?"

My gaze fixes on the thick tendons of his throat because I don't want him to see that he's *not* repulsive—he's too attractive to let me think most of the time. "I'd rather not accept gifts from men or strangers." I lift my chin a fraction, narrowing my eyes and warning under my breath, "And if you keep teasing me, I'm going home."

He leans forward. "You know, Rosie didn't toss my gift back in my face. She called me a hero . . . and I liked it very much."

He's provoking me. I used to like banter so much better when he wasn't scrambling my head.

"A: Thank-yous from elephants are pretty rare, so I hope you appreciate her gesture. And B: I suppose *you've* been given things your whole life," I say.

His smile turns rueful, and he leans forward. "Everything."

"Everything?"

He nods.

"I don't believe it."

"What could I have wanted that I don't have?" He laughs softly. "I have it all, Rachel. At least I used to." He reaches out and runs the back of one finger along my cheek, awakening every nerve ending in my body.

My throat feels tight all of a sudden. His stare turns dark and hungry, and no man who has everything could hunger like that.

As we grow quiet, the breeze shuffles past us, the air between us different. What game is he playing with me? The picture he took was taken while I was so vulnerable, my profile showing my confusion. I can't bear that he saw me like that.

He's looking at my picture now, serious.

"I realize the company I keep is special. I appreciate being given a chance to make it up to you," Saint tells me soberly, staring at the dark sky where the fireworks used to be. When he turns his head to face me, I have to fight not to look away from that probing green gaze.

"Thanks for inviting me . . . I've had a good time," I say, my voice as husky as I've ever heard it.

Suddenly I feel hungry too.

For him to tease me again, and make me smile, and get that twinkle in his eye that both infuriates me and makes me feel little bubbles in my veins. I feel hungry to know why he called dibs on me, why he wants me to have his shirt.

He smiles amicably and signals at me.

"I'll bargain with you now, Rachel. If you'd like to ask me something, I'll give you an answer—and I'll ask you a question," he says, watching me.

"Really?" I perk up, and when he nods indulgently, I gesture to him. "You go first."

"All right." He leans forward, his muscles straining under the open shirt he wears. "Why couldn't you look at me down there, Rachel?"

"What do you mean?"

"Down there. Why couldn't you look at me? Even now, why aren't you looking up here?" I follow his fingers to where he taps them over one of his eyelids.

I think of my answer.

Before I can even reply, he murmurs, almost warningly, "The truth."

I blush. God, he's always wanting the truth. Does he trust nobody, then?

"You were right about me, this isn't my scene," I say with a shrug. "You're good at reading people, I can tell."

"I can tell you are too."

He waits. I guess it's my turn. I want to ask him things that are personal, like why I couldn't come to his after-party, but I need to focus on the interview. So I focus on him. "The question that's on everyone's mind: Do you think she's out there? One women to embody all your desires?"

I make a quick appraisal of his features, but he reveals no glimpse into his thoughts at all. "Is that really what everyone would like to know?"

"You're answering with a question."

"And you're not asking the right questions."

I scowl and grab from the fruit tray his yacht personnel put upstairs too.

"That's not how it's done," he says. I remember the way he was fed grapes below.

"Excuse me? I'm not part of your harem." I laugh. "Here's your grape."

I toss him a grape. It bounces off his chest. I feel a jolt when his thigh brushes mine as he shifts and grabs a grape too. "I was taught not to play with my food but to eat it."

The mere touch of his hand circling the back of my neck sends an odd little warmth running through my veins.

"What are you—"

"Shh."

My body short-circuits as he leans over. The scent of soap reaches my nostrils as he brings the grape up to me, his pupils so blown up they're all I see.

"Open your mouth," he coaxes.

The gentle brush of the grape across my lips sends a current through my body.

He stares down at me with a wicked smile, and then I feel him brush the grape over my lips again. Instinctively, sensually, I open my mouth and let him feed it to me, breathing hard. By the time I swallow, his smile is gone.

Our eyes hold for the longest of seconds. Then, gently, I feel the brush of his thumbs on my cheeks.

A tremor runs through me as he ducks his head. And then, oh god. He places one single kiss on the corner of my lips. I tremble to the tips of my feet.

The tremor intensifies as Malcolm takes my chin and turns me so that his green, green eyes look into mine. They're cautious and still so hungry. I'm telling myself *this can't* be real! He couldn't possibly want you like this!

I'm afraid to be kissed. Afraid to want it. He smells even better than in my dream, feels even better, and I want him so much more, more than more.

He's breathing fast, clearly fighting for control. And I want him to lose.

No. No, the only one with everything to lose is me.

"Mm. Wow," I say, clutching at the ache in my stomach as I straighten. "Wow, it does taste different when you're being fed. I can taste your germs on it."

He sits there, a small smile lighting his lips like the sun.

"Saint!" the boys call. He doesn't respond to them.

"You two up for skinny-dipping?" That's the first thing Tahoe says when he appears on deck.

"Rachel and I are talking up here, but go on ahead," he dismisses, not even turning. He settles back to occupy most of the couch. I lean back uneasily, and he takes a piece of my hair to play with.

"You're up to mischief, aren't you?" I laugh.

"If you'll join me, yes." He flashes the picture of me on his cell phone screen, his voice dropping. "If I delete this . . . you let me drive you home tonight."

"You've been driving me home for days."

"My driver has been driving you home—not me." His voice is low but firm, final. "There's a big difference, I guarantee it, Rachel."

My smile fades at the predatory air surrounding him. I'm as seduced by it as I am scared.

"I need to get home early. I'm sure you'd rather be with your friends."

"If I would, I wouldn't be asking you." His thumb hovers above the "delete" icon, his expectant gaze on me. "Rachel?" he insists.

"If you delete it, I'll think about it," I offer.

His hard jaw seems to tighten reflexively in challenge, and in one slow second, he lowers his thumb and presses "delete."

"There," he says, his eyes twinkling happily in the dark. "Now I drive you home."

There mere thought of it unnerves me. My apartment is my safe haven. I imagine his presence near all my frilly, girly things. What does he want there? If his shirt invaded my thoughts and my space, I can't imagine what Saint himself will do. I nod, merely because I want, need, to leave an option open, but specify, "Yes, but not tonight."

And then I just need some distance, from his eyes, from the way my body feels overworked—my heart leaping, every part of me overreacting to his smile, his glance, his smell.

So I head down to the lower deck without even telling him where I'm going, and I leap into the cold water in the tiny bikini—*crash!* Cold! And then I swim up, wooting when I do.

Tahoe swims nearby, and he blinks at me, his grin turning naughty. "Well, well, well . . ."

"Cut it, T."

At the voice, I look up. Saint leans over the rail with that small smile, watching me.

I sit that night taking notes feverishly.

Okay, focus on just the facts, Livingston. I exhale and try to push one tiny green grape out of my head. Green eyes asking—demanding—I let him bring me home. And I can't believe I almost said *yes.*

> He's a loner—he seemed detached from the group. Always one step ahead, somewhere else.
>
> He is used to women flocking to him. (Are they an afterthought? Background noise? He didn't seem especially attentive to anyone, but they pole-dance and make out to amuse him!)

I go brush my teeth and head to bed. I settle under my covers. Try to go to sleep. But other things keep coming back to me.

The fact that when he fed me the grape I could feel his hard chest against my breasts and his breath on my face.

The fact that I could always seem to smell him when the air hit me a certain way, and hear him above everyone else.

I try to push these thoughts away, but the more I try, the more they surface. God, I don't want to dwell on this. I don't. But if I want this exposé to be good, I can't block out parts. I can't pick and choose what's convenient for me to deal with and what's not. I grab my pad again and start with one word.

Electric

He electrifies the air.
Then I write down a few more.

Consuming

If he's around, you hardly notice anything else.

Stubborn

He's impossible to bargain with.

HE STILL LOVES TO TEASE ME!!!!!

He poked and prodded me about the picture, the grapes, the shirt, even being Rosie's hero. . . .

I set the pad aside and turn off my lamp, but even in the dark, I still see him watching me in the water from above. And I still feel his fingers on my shoulders as I hopped onboard the yacht again only to feel him wrap a warm towel around me.

10

CAMPOUT

For the last twenty-four hours, I've been surfing the Net and clicking through all his newly tagged pictures. There are also some older pictures of girls in bikinis playing mini golf at his place. And pictures of him getting out of a chopper with girl pilots wearing nothing but tiny shorts.

"It really bothers me, seeing all these pictures, because a lot of these girls go to *him,* he doesn't ask them to come cling to him," I tell Gina.

"Dude, Saint is big on whoring around. Must be all the attention he never got as a kid."

"More like he's a healthy male and women just throw themselves at him. I've seen YouTube videos dedicated to him, of women stripping or washing their cars, offering to come wash his. In fact, look at this. . . ."

We watch a video of a woman with no bra wetting her T-shirt and smiling. "Saint, I'll wash your cars any day, and clean your pipes, too."

We burst out laughing.

"He's got a huge car collection, apparently. There's a picture, see? There are like thirty cars here. Very rare ones. He's got a thousand and one toys. Doesn't that say something?"

"What?" Gina asks.

"When you have everything and nothing is ever enough?"

"How should we know? We barely made rent this month."

"Come on, be serious. When nothing is ever enough, on some hidden level of his psyche there's something about this man's life that's absolutely empty. I see him work, Gina; it's like he . . . is obsessed with it. Like it helps him block out something else."

"What?"

"Forget it."

She laughs. "You're so deep, Rachel. Such a philosopher. Send him the bill and save him the therapist."

I continue with my links and end up viewing a video of him next to his father taken when his father refused his mother's last wish to give Saint a seat on the board of his father's company.

"The only good thing he has going for him is his name," his father says to a reporter who asked why Malcolm had not been allowed into the family business. Malcolm doesn't flinch. He smiles ironically, says nothing, just keeps himself in check. This video only made everyone cheer on Malcolm rather than his dad. Still, did it damage his psyche in some way?

"What an asshole," Gina says late that afternoon when I watch the video one more time, this time watching only Saint's expression, revealing nothing—like he expected the blow and was braced for it.

"No wonder Saint's an asshole—he was bred like that."

"He's not an asshole."

"Excuse me?"

"He's not an asshole," I say casually.

"Who's touchy?!"

"I'm not touchy. I'm just stating a fact."

"Okay. You don't like what we have in the fridge, when it was *your* turn to stock us for the week; you're obsessed with that computer; you have circles under your eyes; you're wearing an *E* for *exposé* on your forehead and an *X* on your ass screaming at Saint to fuck you right there. You're crushing on him, aren't you?"

"No."

"Well good, 'cause you've wanted this your whole life. Look up all the pictures of women all over him. Hell, with their tits almost in his face. *That* is the guy you like?"

I stare at the YouTube video. "I like this one," I mumble as she leaves, then I scowl at myself. No, you don't like him, Rachel. You want to be fair—you want to be truthful.

I go grab my sleeping bag for the End the Violence campout.

My friends think that a campout won't achieve much on its own, really, but I feel good every time I do it, so I do it often, and when my life is unsteady, I do it even more because I feel safer doing it. Focusing on someone else is the only way I know of to forget about your own little pains—but I didn't have a lot of those pains. I had a great life. Have.

My upbringing was different than his. I wasn't told, "You're reckless; the only good thing you've got going for you is your name." My mother gave me so much love that here I am, taking on projects that might be a little too big for me, just because I'm crazy enough to think that I can handle them.

I'm so worried about doing justice to the piece, I need to touch base with her right now. "Hey, Momma."

"Oh, hey, sweetheart. What are you up to? Are you on your way to the campout?"

"Yes, I just wanted to see what *you* were up to. Do you need anything?"

I can always tell when my mother is feeling all right or when she's faking it. I'm relieved that she sounds genuinely happy today.

"I'm quite all right, Rachel. Last I checked, I was still the mother in this relationship," she even teases me. "But how is my girl?"

"I'm good." I can hear her favorite Cat Stevens CD playing in the background. "I'll text you from work tomorrow. Take your insulin, okay?" I wait for her to say okay, and then I whisper softly, "I love you, Mom."

"Rachel! Wait. Is something wrong?"

I hesitate. "What do you mean?" Oh wow, so now my voice is affected? I always tell her that I love her, so that can't have caused her concern.

"Nothing is wrong, I'm fabulous. I'm writing a new piece, I'll tell you all about it soon."

A silence. "Are you sure?"

Shit, she suspects something.

It's futile to tell her, not to worry about me, because then she'll tell me not to worry about her, and I love her too much to do that. But I loathe having her worry over nothing.

"*Yes,*" I laughingly assure her. "I love you. I'll see you soon." Then I hang up and exhale.

Despite my mother having gotten so inquisitive in the end, I really needed that call. I needed to remind myself that she's the thing I most love and that my dream is to get her a nice house, a nice car, good hospital care, *safety.* I can't give her back my dad, but I'd like to give her what I can. I'd like to give her the things he wanted to. In my heart, it means I will honor him—wherever he is—by managing to get for us the same things he wanted to provide. My mom's a diabetic. It's been under control for years, but her continued good health is still a concern for me, even if she refuses to admit it's a concern for her.

The park is not very crowded tonight. A lot of people skip these events and opt for the walks or other sorts of End the Violence events, but I like coming out here with my books, my iPod shuffle, my snacks, and I'm set.

Recognizing some faces, I walk around until I find a nice spot under a tree.

I spread out my sleeping bag, say hi to the young couple nearby whose names I don't know but who I've seen before, and stare up at a bunch of tree limbs and leaves poking into the sky. I rarely manage to get an hour of sleep whenever I camp out here, but I still do it just because I never want to get so comfortable with things to the point I don't want to change them for the better.

After eating some berries and listening to music, I pluck off my earphones, plump my campout pillow, and drift off to sleep, dreaming that I'm lost at night inside a green forest, running in a man's shirt, and when Gina, Helen, and my mom shout for me to come out, I can never find my way out of the deep.

I wake up with a start, sweaty and breathless and staring around in confusion. I'm at the campout. Shivering, I pull out my phone and then blink when I see I've got a message.

If I can't drive you home yet, then at least let me pick you up and take you someplace.

I stare at the text from an unknown number with a wildly pounding heart and a tangle inside my stomach. I know it's him, it has to be him. I think of him and his shirts and his stares and his grapes. I think of his yacht and his secrets and the ice in his eyes and the way he stares at me like he wants me to melt all of those mysterious icicles in him. I think of how restless I feel and how I can't focus on anything else . . . and then I think of the exposé and struggle to center myself with that one goal, that one wish. Exhaling, I text back:

I wouldn't object to a tour of the Interface headquarters

Done

I bite my lip, things that feel like butterflies now seizing me. These have to be story butterflies but I've never gotten them like this. Before I can stop myself I text:

Don't you sleep?

Not when I don't want to

I blush. God, is he womanizing right now? He could be such a great guy for one special girl, it's depressing he lets everyone have a piece of him somehow.

You? Why are you awake now, Rachel?

Your text woke me, I write.

Sweet dreams then, Rachel

I close my eyes and think of his face in the YouTube video, his face at the club after he saw me, his face always so closed off and mysterious, as if he refuses to let anyone see and know who he really is or what he really wants from them.

Same to you—if you want to dream, that is

Oh, I sound so dumb. Urgh. Setting my phone down as if it's suddenly a snapping alligator I just encountered in my scary green dream forest, I don't sleep one wink.

11

OFFICE

At least my writing has benefited from my growing obsession with this tormenting fascination that has nowhere to go. This thirst for information is leaking into my writing, into anything I turn my attention to. I'm like a glutton craving something in particular but stuffing herself on whatever she can get her hands on in the meantime. Even if it's information on something else.

"This piece is phenomenal!" Helen says. "Such fire. I can't wait to see what you do with the Saint piece. What's the dibs on that?"

I gasp. "What?"

She smiles and taps the notebook on my desk with one word, underlined until the page tore.

DIBS.

She props her hip on my desk, and I feel Victoria nearly fall out of her chair in her eagerness to hear what I have to say.

"None," I say, taking the tablet and putting it aside. Really, so I'm doodling "dibs" now?

"Oh, what do you mean, none?" She turns. "Victoria, Victoria." She crooks a finger and Victoria gets up and walks over, casual as can be.

"Helen?" she says. "Hi, Rachel." She beams.

"Help me get Rachel in with that stylist who always has you looking so spectacular? With this face"—she tips my chin up—"there's no way Saint should be able to keep himself from hunting her down. Thank you, Vicky," she says, sliding into her office.

With Victoria near, I suddenly wish I'd said I'd made moderate progress. I wish I'd said anything to keep me from having to see her enormous, gloating smile. I can almost hear her thinking that I can't even write a piece without her help. That I can't get a man without her help.

"It's not necessary, really," I tell her.

"Oh nonsense, I know just what you need. I'm going to borrow this for a second," she says, gesturing to my landline. So she calls her stylist and hums while she waits, and I need to save and close my file because nothing can mess with my mojo as much as someone sneeking a peek at my screen.

I sit there, feeling like a loser and peering into my phone when I see Dean's message.

> Mr. Saint would like to give you a tour of the Interface
> corporate headquarters. Let me know if this is of interest; he's
> looking forward to seeing you.

My toes curl a little and my cheeks are red. Fuck. I text back:

> I'm looking forward to seeing him.

Oh god. Seeing him? I'm *meeting* with him, not seeing him. Professional. That's all. What will I do when I see him again?

I pull out a picture of him I downloaded on my phone and peek at it. His profile is so perfect. He's the only guy I've ever had a picture of in my phone—it came from one of the girls who tagged him, and since it got downloaded it's somehow stayed in my phone. I haven't been able to erase it.

Considering Saint erased my picture, I should do the same, but a part of me enjoys being able to look at him while he's not watching me. And this picture . . . I'm pretty sure this picture was taken that day on the yacht, and what he's staring at in the distance is me. Something about his unreadable expression demands that I figure him out.

Victoria slams down my office phone. "Done. I've got an in for you next week on Friday. Be ready to make Saint weep!" she declares, patting the top of my head and leaving me staring down at my phone to Dean's new message.

Great. We'll have a car at your place on Thursday at 4 p.m.

12

THURSDAY

Thursday.

At 4:01 p.m., I'm exiting my building.

"Oh, I'll get the door for you, Miss Sheppard."

Our neighbor from the third floor (who makes killer coffee cakes every holiday) seems to have been out walking her dog, her cat nestled in her arm. "Rachel, you look lovely with your hair down." The cat purrs as she strokes the back of its ear. "I can't even think of an actress as blonde and fair-skinned as you. Who did your makeup? It's so natural."

"My roommate, Gina." I hold the door open for her. "She works in a department store, in cosmetics, and we're trying out different looks on me."

"Ah, yes. The day I have a ball and a pretty dress, I'll go visit her."

Her dog yaps at my ankle and I wince a little but stand my ground, then turn back to the street once she's inside. I freeze.

Instead of the Rolls, Saint's black and shiny BUG 1 is parked just outside.

He leans against it, watching me. And he's smiling. At me. He steps forward and says, "Hey." To me. And I forget about everything. Even my name. Even that I'm supposed to be working today. My stomach contracts, and so does my throat.

"Hey," I say, taking in his black suit as he opens the passenger door for me.

Oh god, what is this?

He offers his hand, and I look at it with dread and anticipation before slipping my fingers into his. He grips my fingers lightly as I slip into the seat, the touch lingering long after he lets go and closes the door.

Then he's in the car, shutting his door and enclosing us in the most confined space we've been in since we met. His scent envelops me along with the leather of his car, and my lungs start to ache with every breath I take.

As I dressed, I kept telling myself that I didn't need to look perfect because nothing would come of it. But I actually spent more time than ever thinking about what I was going to wear and wondering how he'd feel about it.

Dean sent a message instructing me to wear something comfortable because parts of the building were still under construction. I ended up wearing a favorite pair of worn jeans, a loose shapeless sweater I love writing in, and my warm boots, because I love having comfy feet. I'm a fan of chunky socks, my Uggs, and tucking my feet into anything soft and snug. But it doesn't matter whether he likes it, right? Because nothing can come of this. I'm working, and he's . . . well, he's being nicer to me than I ever imagined by giving me a tour in the first place.

"I hope I'm dressed okay," I whisper.

His green eyes run up and down my body, and suddenly

more than my feet are warm as a small smile appears. He reaches an arm behind my seat and faces me completely. "I like this almost as much as I love what you wore the day we met."

I cover my face and laugh. "You absolutely don't mean that."

When I force myself to drop my hands, he's staring at me. I really have never been looked at the way *he* looks at me, with that glint of mischief in his stare, sexy, dark, and deep, roiling with the most exquisite promises. When he teases me like this, my flesh goes warm and things happen to me that could only be explained by collisions and particles and energy and chemistry. I can't take it.

Without reassuring me any more about my looks or how much he likes or doesn't like them, he gets the engine roaring to life, checks his mirrors, and sends the tires squealing as he pulls into the street. The next second, I'm flat against the car seat and without breath.

"This car is meant to be driven like you stole it," he says.

He takes a curve a bit recklessly and starts to chuckle, the sound low and amused. "All right, Rachel?" He grins and squeezes my thigh, and I look up at him, the tingles of adrenaline and lust I'm feeling becoming bells chiming loudly inside me.

I smile and nod, but add, "You're a devil, though."

He slows down and starts driving like a normal person for the next couple of blocks, speaking low, with a sidelong, curious glance at me. "More devil than saint?"

"You couldn't be a saint if we got you a halo."

His lips tip upward, but there's something about the smile that doesn't reach his eyes as he turns back to the road. From the moment I met him, the air between us has felt different from the way it does when I'm not with him. Thicker, more electric, every glance or smile or word causing ripples in the atmosphere. But right now, inside his leather- and man-smelling car, I feel his presence with every breath. Every thought. Every move—those moves of his, as he turns the steering wheel, shifts gears. And those moves of mine: tucking my hair back, smoothing my hands over my sweater.

When we get to the Interface underground parking lot, he slides into the first empty slot, and I'm telling myself to *freaking forget about his delicious ghost kisses* as he removes his jacket and tosses it to his seat. But it's no use; the glimpse of muscles rippling under the fabric of his white cotton shirt doesn't help get my knees back into normal working order. He unknots his tie and pulls it loose, his biceps flexing under his shirt. My eyes—I can't pull them away from him. I feel his call viscerally, right in the core of my being. I watch him, noticing the hair that fell over his eye as he raked his fingers through it just now.

A ball of tangled lightning is in my stomach as I follow him into the elevator and we ride to the top floor.

His textured voice suddenly runs like a feather down my spine. "Do you want to talk about Interface now?"

I tear my attention free from that beautiful set of lips of his to find him watching me. His stare is too keen and knowing for me to hold it for long, but I can't look away, either. "I don't know."

"So you don't want to discuss Interface?"

His voice is gruff, deeper than usual, and the sudden smile on his lips is absolutely sensual.

I bite my lower lip, uncertain of what to say as he takes a step forward, looking at me questioningly and also . . . expectantly. My heart starts thumping. I feel like something is happening. A hurricane called Malcolm Saint is happening. I've been dreaming of him—of us. Limbs, flesh, touching, those grazing kisses of his right on the corner of my mouth . . .

A prickle of nervousness tightens every inch of my body as he moves his frame to stand before mine. He stretches his arm along the wall behind me, his eyes glowing. He's so close I can see the icy flecks in those irises, reminding me of other times, when those flecks seemed to have melted from warmth.

"Hey," he says, running his thumb along my jaw as he suddenly smiles down at me.

He smells of soap. His nearness is lighting up my nerves like a Christmas tree.

"Hey," I whisper, shooting for casual, failing miserably.

His closeness is unsettling.

He takes my fingers within one warm hand and tugs my arm up from my side, watching his fingers lace through mine as he holds my hand between us, at the level of our throats. "Ask me anything you want, Rachel," he says, his thumb rubbing along the back of mine, the touch electrifying my nerve endings.

He reaches out with his free hand and strokes the note cards I'm clutching in my other hand. He peers at the top card. "'Relentless,'" he reads out loud.

Startled, I jump into action and take the cards with both hands. His lips curve; he watches me shakily tuck the cards into my small bag.

You're really unfocused, Livingston! I don't know what to do, or what to say, only that this development is not good for *Edge,* for my career. For the exposé. Oh, fuck.

"You think me relentless?" He's amused.

As I search my brain, frantic for an answer, I find him peering down at me with a sober expression.

"I'm much worse than that," he murmurs.

The elevator halts.

Saint glances at the top. "We're here." We head outside.

Marble, windows, everything new and recently cleaned. To one side are paint cans, the scent of drying paint mingled with plaster and plastic. The ceilings have cables poking out. It's a masterpiece in progress, a visionary building for visionary people.

"Hey, come here, I want to show you something," Saint tells me, watching me walk over to where he's standing.

He leads me into a huge conference room.

I look at everything. "It's beautiful."

I realize he's looking only at me. He looks at me like he wants something from me, like he wants something very much, and like he's wanted it for a long time.

Aware that I'm blushing hard, I tear free of his stare and distract myself with the huge artwork on the wall to his left. The wall is so huge, I don't recognize the splotches of color as I take them all in, but when I focus on each and every one, I do.

Here, covering one of his walls from end to end, is the huge canvas mural Gina and I made at the park, along with nearly a hundred other people.

Dazed, I walk forward, scanning all the hands. There is Gina's. And, yes, there's mine.

"What do you think of it?"

I look at him, not believing what I'm seeing. On impulse, I turn back to the mural and lift my hand and match it to my red handprint, finger to finger.

How did he know? When I went to his office, I was streaked with red paint, and I told him where I'd been. Oh wow. I look at our hands, still disbelieving as I step back.

I remember riding in one of his cars once while he bid in an auction.

I remember all the things he handled in the space of mere minutes.

And I can't believe that one of those things, one of the times he was on the phone, one of these days, was regarding this one thing that means worlds to me.

"You see, I'm correcting an injustice," he says behind me. "Interface has contributed to the cause you believe in so much . . . and you can't give this one back."

I laugh and face him, my knees feeling weaker and weaker. "I really hurt your pride returning your shirt, didn't I?"

"I'm mortally wounded."

He's not grinning.

His pull is stronger than ever.

His stare greener than ever.

"The donations made by the institutions who acquire these go to the families of the victims. These donations really helped my mother when my dad died," I hear myself admit, with a ball of emotion in my gut. "It's such a great gesture. Thank you for helping."

His eyes go liquid, as if all he wanted was this meager thank-you I just gave him.

He smiles and nods his dark head, and suddenly, it's not enough. Not enough at all. I can't believe it—this gesture out of a hundred gestures. On impulse, I walk up to him, my Uggs silent on the marble. Then I push up on tiptoes and kiss his hard jaw. He moves his head, so I end up kissing the corner of his mouth.

Startled, I ease back, gaping.

His eyes are dark . . . but glimmering in delight. As if he wanted the thank-you but will take anything else that he can.

I realize several things. He's grabbed my waist to keep me from stepping back. His hands are on my hips. I shiver at his touch. I also notice the unmistakable, determined look of a hunter on his face, as if he doesn't plan to let go, and I'm dizzy with his scent. *Fast.* I didn't imagine the human body could want so fast and so much from one instant to the next.

"Put your arms around me," he says, his voice a gruff whisper in my ear.

My stomach grips tightly in surprise, small butterflies exploding from its pit to the tips of my fingers. His warm, long-fingered hand curves around my hip, holding me close.

"Put your arms around me," he repeats, slowly watching my reaction as he takes my wrists, lifts my arms, and links my hands together at his nape. He watches me as he ducks his head and, oh, the anticipation, the exquisite torture, of wanting this and not wanting to want this.

"I can't breathe," I whisper, somehow easing my head back as he edges forward.

His eyes start fluttering closed, the shadow of his eyelashes dark on his cheekbones as his lips come within a breath of mine. "I don't want you to breathe."

He kisses the corner of my mouth; my body tightens at the contact. He eases back—not a lot, as if he doesn't want to let go or leave me for more than an inch—and looks at me like I'm absolutely new and precious and he wants to play with me so much, he actually isn't certain if he wants to play with me completely or maybe save a little bit of me to play with later. And I . . . ?

I'm burning to my bones.

Beyond thought right this second.

I want him so deep I'll end up broken. I want to forget there are multiple reasons why this isn't a good idea—because it doesn't matter if it's good or even right, only that I give my body what it wants. And all I want right now is looking down at me as if he wants to give it to me too.

I'm scared, but that doesn't stop me from tipping my head up in offering, my lips parted in complete recklessness. "Do that again," I whisper. His eyes gleam as he watches me, his gaze somehow male and savoring as I lick my lips and squirm a little beneath him. "Saint . . . do it again . . ." I try again.

He ducks his head, and the second corner kiss is so close to the center of my mouth, I can taste him. Oh god, I want to taste him. He's teasing me now. Teasing me with kisses and desire, the kind I've never felt, and it's working; I'm aching, throbbing, wanting, dying.

"You like that?"

I nod fast, breathing heavily. "Again . . . *please.*" I tip my head farther back. He takes in my reaction with dark, hooded eyes, and I remain dazed, struggling to keep my lungs working. He tips my head back at the angle that he wants it.

The air between our bodies feels like fire, the places his thigh touches mine singe me, the tips of my breasts are crushed and hot against his flat chest.

He bends his head and takes my lips—front and center now. If I had just been burned at the stake, the impact would have been less than the hot feel of his tongue pushing my lips apart. I burst up in flames, and he pulls me closer with a rumbling noise as his tongue delves in and strokes mine, dominating, tasting, kissing.

"Do you like that too?" He dips his tongue, hot and wet, into my mouth; then he secures the back of my head in one curved hand and parts his lips and takes me deeper, harder. A rush of sensations knifes through me, and when he angles his head to get another, thorough taste of me, I part my lips wider so that he continues to do what he's doing, continues rubbing his tongue along mine and feeding me with his indescribably delicious taste.

"Yes," I moan softly, hungrily breathing his breath. "I can taste you in every inch of me."

The sound of his hands sliding down the length of my arms, over my clothing, is decadent and delicious. We slant our heads and kiss a little, then a little more. Then his lips soften . . . retreat . . .

A tremor racks through me as his lips brush across my soft wet ones, the ghost of a tantalizing touch.

When we finally part, my mouth tingles, and I can see him perfectly up close. I notice the shifting shades of green in his eyes, the copper flecks scattered inside—not cold, not an ounce of cold right now.

I feel his fingertips graze my temples as he brushes my hair off my forehead to look at me. His hands remain there for what feels like an instant and, at the same time, forever. I blink as I grudgingly remove my hands from his nape and bring them, trembling, to my sides, my eyes focusing on his stunning, virile face.

"I . . . this can't happen."

"It's happened. It's happening, Rachel."

His gaze is heavy, thick-lashed as he surveys his handiwork: my lips, wet. Swollen—at least that's how they feel. I find myself touching his shoulders, nervous. "Saint . . ."

God. I don't even know what it is I'm asking for.

He's the sort of guy who'd never be in any woman's friend zone or brother zone. He's the sort of guy you fantasize about having for a lover, and he wants me. When he ducks his head, I go up on my toes so our lips meet again. Then we're tasting, slowly exploring, and when I want to make it go fast because my toes are curling and my body's trembling, he slows me down with his mouth, his tongue. Perfectly in control, he's feasting on me and doesn't want to be rushed. My mouth has become his expedition, and I want to be explored, just like this.

He pulls away—I have to swallow back a protest then.

He stares at me. Eyes, lips, eyes, lips, prolonging the looks a little more every time. I'm in agony. Suddenly I tilt my head and kiss his neck. He groans softly, fisting my hair in his hand, tipping my head back. And there, his lips wait for mine. Our mouths fuse as if each was somehow waiting for the other for a long time. The touch, the heat, is so electric, I pull back with a shocked gasp.

Our eyes meet again. We're playing this game, kissing, stopping. . . . I can see by the curl of his lip that he's enjoying it. But I'm not. I'm pained with desire, panting as I fight the urge to rub up against him like a cat, tug his shirt off his chest. I want to eat him up alive, so hard and so fast, I have to fold my fingers into my palms to keep from doing just that.

His hand cups my jaw and holds me still now. He watches me until the very last moment as his lips descend to mine. He tastes me, savors me; then the heady taste of him hits me again, melting me. I catch the rasp of his jaw against my cheek, the moist heat of his tongue on mine. When I let out a moan that scares me, he eases back for another moment to look at me again.

Oh god. Trembling with how much we've kissed and how much I still want, I stare at his mouth. Every time he's stepped back, he's come back to kiss me harder. Harder. His mouth—was it really just on me? I feel in a strange way like it still is. My lips tingle from side to side, top bow to bottom curve. He's looking at them too. Then his hands tighten on my arms and his mouth crashes down on mine, hard this time. I stiffen against the onslaught, afraid of the cataclysm overtaking me. I try to move away and pull free, but his mouth shifts every time I do, and it is always there, ready to taste me again, the tip of his tongue brushing me open.

Excitement thrills through my veins as I dare open my mouth as wide as I can, and then he tastes me. A heart-stopping, whole-mouthed kiss that makes me dizzy and unsteady and amazed. My hands on his arms, my body leans on his so hard my breasts ache against his chest, and I taste him back. Not slow or in a savoring way; more in a way that means I will never be kissed like this again and I very much want him to eat me like I want to eat him.

This is Malcolm Saint—my dream story and the salvation of *Edge*—and I should've pushed him away. But I'm suddenly desperate. I've been paying attention to every visual sign, every word we exchange, trying to silence whatever it is he makes me feel. Some kind of need. Some blatant thirst. But his mouth is on mine, and I'm thirstier than ever.

We peel our lips apart, and his mouth immediately seeks a path down my throat. I turn my head and tug his earlobe between my teeth, running my hands over his hair. I've never touched a man like this, his hair thick and silky, dark as soot. He groans under my slow but impulsive caresses, and the sound runs through me in an erotic wave. His slow neck kisses drive me crazy, but I still crave his mouth; my mouth is sore, and it feels like the only way I won't be aware of its soreness is with his mouth on mine again, pleasing me like crazy.

I turn my head. He's there, as if needing my mouth too. Our lips open and fuse again. He groans; I moan. We taste each other feverishly. His tongue is hot and wet against mine, and this kiss alone has me more turned on than anything in my life ever has.

But . . . who do you think you are, Rachel? Come on! Elizabeth Bennett? Jane Eyre, perhaps?

Peeling away with effort, I shake in place, leaning my forehead on his while my breath stumbles back to me.

"We can't do that again." I ease back, running my hands down my hair. "Can someone . . . Can you call me a cab?"

He doesn't say no, only stares at me, then stares down at his hands, then up at me. He glances at my mouth with heavy eyelids.

"I'll drive you home. Just give me ten minutes to cool down."

"No, I'll take a cab. I need to cool down too. I can't see you except . . . for interviews." He looks so sexy, hot, and suddenly so attainable, I can't bear to stand here anymore. I pull my bag close to me and head to the door.

"See me outside in ten minutes," he says, his voice still thick with desire. "Just let me cool down," he repeats.

But if I see you outside, I'll be the whore who sold her soul for your story.

I shake my head, not turning around to see him following me to the elevators. "I need to go."

"Rachel. See me for drinks tomorrow," he says.

I press the "down" arrow several times and thank god the elevator door opens right away. "I can't . . . Saint," I say, and slip inside.

"Malcolm!" he calls back gruffly as I board the elevator.

I'm numb on the way home.

Malcolm.

I can't even think his name; it seems so intimate, after what we did.

What did we do? He touched my hand. He kissed the corner of my mouth. And then he kissed me, tongued me, put my arms around him, and he felt so strong, tall, solid, powerful, and I felt so weak, so liquid, so vulnerable that I wanted him to do more things to me, things that make me feel both more and less whole, that make me feel like air, like a pool of desire

We didn't have sex, but we hardly even needed to; I basically let him *eat me up alive.*

Exhaling noisily, I try to focus on the buildings ahead, on the people walking down the sidewalk. Get out of your head, Livingston. No, get out of your hormones. Use this for the exposé. Saint is challenged or intrigued by you, and soon it'll be over and you'll have everything you need, everything the world wants to know.

I pep-talk myself all the way home but nothing gives me peace.

The best work I've ever done in my life, I lost a little piece of myself. I can't bear to think what size chunk I'm gonna lose by the time I'm done with the exposé.

I'm horny, and my horniness is due to the fact that Saint wants to have sex with me. It's so obvious: his body was vibrating and his eyes were heavy-lidded, and against my body I felt the way he wanted me. Clearly he's a playboy. He uses sex for . . . something. I can't be used like that. I'm a professional. I need to keep barriers up—things like that can't happen. As long as I put up the walls between us again, it'll be good. It has to be.

During cocktails the next evening, Gina is outraged over Wynn's anecdote.

"I'm telling you, he stepped into the store and asked me to pose for him," Wynn assures us.

"Why, Rachel? Tell me why Wynn has a boyfriend and now has another guy hot for her. On her tail. And she did absolutely nothing but ask him if he was looking for any particular oil or candle from her shop!"

I sip on my cocktail, my brain all over the place. Maybe not all over the place; it's just not here. It's back in the top-floor conference room at Interface.

"Rachel? I mean, seriously, why does Wynn attract all the men? And let it be clear that I do not want one, but it would be nice if one wanted me, you know?"

God, he. Kissed. Me. HARD. I kissed him just as hard. We *made out*.

"So was he hot, at least?" Gina asks Wynn.

"Oh, he was definitely hot, but I'm with Emmett—I couldn't possibly!"

Okay, so the guy can kiss. He's a player, of course he can. But that doesn't mean it will happen again. In fact, it means that I really should *not* allow it to happen again.

"Really, Rachel, are you listening?"

Because my friends look so puzzled, I try to pull myself back to the topic at hand. Wynn, yes. And her ability to attract more and more men even while happily in a relationship with one. "Like attracts like, I guess. Rich people become richer, the poor poorer, isn't that how the saying goes? Give a poor guy a thousand dollars and he comes back with a pair of designer jeans; give a rich guy a thousand and he comes back with ten thousand."

"Give a thousand to Saint and he comes back with a million."

Saint, well, yes. "He does have the touch," I admit.

"And you know this touch?" Wynn prods with a little smile.

There's no way I'm divulging my darkest office-kiss secret, so I sip my cocktail.

"Oh, I know that look, the look of 'she's been dreaming of his touch,'" Wynn says.

I zip my mouth and throw away the invisible key, then I tease, "We all know you jinx your dreams if you talk about them." I shrug. "Plus, the dreams need to stay in bed because it's not happening. I mean, it's ludicrous to think of giving up a great career opportunity just for a fling with a known womanizer. Right?"

"Found anything extra juicy?"

"You mean other than him?" I arch a brow. They laugh, but inside, I'm aching. My body's aching in places it shouldn't even ache. I didn't know that your breasts could ache like this and it could have nothing to do with PMSing. Deep inside, between my legs, where I want him, I *ache*.

"I'm cutting tonight early," Wynn says with a quick glance at her watch, reaching for her coat from the back of her chair.

"No, come on, it's girls' night, we don't see you anymore," Gina complains.

"Well, because I have Emmett. Relationships need to be nurtured. Like little plants!" She grins.

"I'm in a serious relationship with Chris Hemsworth, he just doesn't know it yet." Gina sticks her tongue out and then sucks on her straw.

"You two, really. Sometimes I just can't take how you are." Hands planted on her waist, Wynn shoots us an I-don't-even-know-why-I-love-you stare.

"What? What's wrong with us?" Gina asks.

"Well don't you *want* it? Don't you really want to find it? Because out there, half the people have it, the others are looking for it, others just lost it, but it's there. You can't ignore what it is."

"It sounds like influenza," Gina grumbles.

Wynn shakes her head. "You two can say anything about me, but I'm going for it. And to you two cowards, I say you should go for it too. Find a guy who can love you like crazy and love him right back. What's the worst thing that can happen? That we'll need a couple extra cocktails when we meet next time?"

When neither of us says anything, Wynn adds, "I'll tell you what, they're on *me.*"

"The guys or the drinks?" asks Gina.

The moment Wynn angrily drops a bill down on the table and leaves, Gina turns to me. "I think she told Emmett she loves him and he didn't say it back yet."

I think of how humiliating it must be to tell a guy you went ahead and fell in love with him and not have him say it back as I swirl my cocktail.

The rest of the night Gina and I discuss everything except the one masculine, relentless thing in my brain.

My T-shirt feels extra thin as I go to bed that night, and somehow my skin feels extra sensitive beneath it. So when I wake up in the middle of the night again, sweating and whimpering, I'm not even surprised by who it is I'm dreaming of.

My blood is lava in my veins, desire rushing through my body to the point that every inch of me is trembling under the covers. I wish it were just channeled desire; desire to know more about the subject, deep things, silly things, things nobody else will know, even things I might not include in my piece just because I need to satiate this need to know. But it's also desire of another kind—uncontrollable, unreasoned, unplanned, and unwanted. Desire from the very pit of my being and not from my intellect but from something more primal and old inside me, something that hasn't ever really responded to anything or anyone before.

"Oh, Rachel," I groan when I find my hand wandering between my thighs. "Don't, Rachel," I say, stopping my hand on the inside of my thigh. For a moment I think I'm going to win, until I remember how he kissed me, remember how neither of us wanted to stop, and, because this is the only way I can let myself have him, I slip my hand deeper between my thighs and tell Saint how deeply and how *deep* I want him.

13

INTERFACE INAUGURAL

Come with me to the Interface inaugural tonight

M.S.

You mean as press?

Rachel

We can discuss when you arrive—Otis will pick you up at 8 p.m.

M.S.

I'd love to go as press. Thank you for the news opportunity.

Rachel

"Silver is the bomb on you," Gina says approvingly as I twirl around to get her verdict. She keeps nodding and nodding, obviously pleased. "Stunning, Rachel. He doesn't stand a chance."

"I'm not sure about this dress of Wynn's, it's so sexy." I take in the long, silky curves of my body in the full-length closet mirror. "If he doesn't stand a chance, neither do I." I laugh, then fall sober and feel my cheeks go hot.

I remember the way we both couldn't stop kissing the last time we were together, and wonder what he'll do when he sees me in this. The material is sleek, shiny, and cool. Fit for a mermaid, and the fabric clings to my every curve like a man's lips would, and his hands could.

"What do you mean?" counters Gina. "He's a playboy. Hello? You don't like that sort of guy. You and I are the smart girls, remember?"

Following the urge to inspect my feet, I then search for my clutch, tucking it under my arm. "I gotta go."

"Rachel!" Gina calls. "Just think of the story. You're flesh and bone, but try to leave the flesh and bone, the heart and the woman, home. Take your brain with you, that's all."

I bite my lip and nod, wishing I felt more confident. I need a Malcolm Saint vaccine, for immunity, and I need it now. "What are you doing tonight?" I ask Gina.

"I'm going with Wynn and Emmett to watch some movie premiere."

"Okay, have fun."

The night is cool and a little rainy as I slip into the Rolls-Royce, the driver shielding me with an umbrella, and my heart flutters when the scent of the car's leather interior, which I associate with Saint, reaches my nostrils again. I've got butterflies in my stomach, my chest, everywhere. I wish I could leave the flutters home.

As the Rolls pulls into traffic, I mentally caution myself against overthinking tonight. I'm obviously going to pretend we didn't kiss. Definitely that I didn't ask him to. Then I realize I've never really had the courage to speak to his driver, so this time I clear my throat and start with, "How's your day, sir?"

"Good, Miss Livingston."

"It occurs to me we haven't been formally introduced."

"Otis."

"Nice to meet you, Otis. How long have you been working with Mr. Saint?" I ask, trying to get back into investigative mode.

"I'm sorry, miss, but I'm not free to say."

"Oh, come on." I laugh a little, but he doesn't say more.

"Do you transport all his dates around town?"

A shake of his head.

"Give me one, at least," I insist.

"All right. No," he says.

"Only his businessmen?"

"That would be Claude."

I roll my eyes. "He has several drivers, of course."

He nods.

"Who do you drive around?"

"Usually? Saint."

"Why are you driving me?"

"Saint," he answers.

"And who drove Saint to the event if you didn't drive him?"

"Saint."

Amusement curls my lips. "Have you known him long?"

He hesitates.

"All right, so I know I said one. Just give me one more. Your boss is so elusive."

"I've known him since he was fourteen—and Mr. Noel hired me to keep him out of trouble."

I'm surprised into silence by this.

"Oh, I know it's coming. Fine job I did?" he asks.

"I didn't say that. Everyone knows your boss has a mind of his own. I don't think anyone could've controlled him."

"The more they tried, the less controllable he became." He shakes his head. "I've spoken too much." He looks up at me in the rearview mirror. "But he trusts you . . . and I trust his judgment."

"What makes you say he trusts me?"

"Hunch." He shrugs. "Comes from knowing him over a decade. First of his girls I get to drive around."

I blush. "Oh, I'm not one of his girls." And I'll never be.

He smiles knowingly and helps me out of the car, and one sumptuous lobby later, I step into the lap of absolute and complete luxury. Water fountain. Glowing crystal chandeliers.

Getting a little more nervous with each step I take, I walk down a long hall outside the ballroom and straight to the press entrance, where I wait my turn to give my name to one of the ladies in charge.

"Hi, Rachel Livingston from *Edge,* please."

"Good evening, Rachel, let me find you here on my clipboard list. . . . Hmmm. Well . . . let's see. . . . You don't seem to be under the *L.* Any middle name under which I can check too?"

When I shake my head, she goes over to one of her coworkers. They whisper for a bit, comparing clipboard pages, until finally, illumination seems to strike the woman I was talking to. Her expression changes from a worried frown to a beaming smile as she scrambles back to me. "Oh, well, mystery solved! You're with Saint himself—this is quite the development!" she whispers excitedly, pointing to the guest entrance. God, really? More flutters.

Pasting a false smile on my face as if I'm happy about this— well, am I?—I walk down a long hall and follow the sound of the music past soaring columns and below vaulted ceilings. I venture deep into the crowd, walking amid his eclectic group of friends and employees. I become aware of the women and how they instantly size me up as competition for Saint's attention.

The men stare too, their gazes appreciative. I've got great hair and long legs, and interesting eyes . . . maybe I'm not a buxom blonde, but I've got a great ass. Oh god, look at him. I almost stumble when I spot him at the far end, near a chocolate fountain.

His backside is to me—so impressive, my mouth dries. I can see the definition of his back and arms in the jacket he wears, his black slacks hugging the best male body I've ever seen.

Callan points Saint in my direction, and I spur myself forward again as he turns around. His eyes catch mine, and the whole time I approach with uneasy steps, they stay trained on me. His chest goes wide as if he's pulling in a sharp breath, and I can't breathe.

He's in black tie and a devilish suit, his hands at his side. He's unsmiling, his jaw tightening when he notices the other men looking at me.

I see the women flanking him, and I'm hit by a wave of jealousy so deep I tremble.

We kissed—that's all. I don't care what he does. I'm not interested in him in an intimate way, I keep reminding myself. Not in a woman's way, just a *reporter's*.

He's just a man—a playboy, womanizer, hell, a manwhore—and I just need to store all this information and then write an exposé so people can experience what I'm experiencing.

It doesn't matter that he stands with two women. They're not touching him, but oh, yes, I can tell from their glum expressions that they have before. He's used them. And they have used him. But it doesn't matter if people use him, or if people even understand or know the real him, because all I care about is getting this exposé right. Right?

This isn't about me, it's about a story about the man.

Still, my stomach aches with unfamiliar possessiveness as I

stop before him. He looks at me, straight into my eyes, and I look straight into his.

"Did you think you would get away with using the press entrance?" he asks me, lips quirking. Hmm. He's got me pegged, hasn't he?

"Did you enjoy not writing my name on the list and making everyone scramble to nearly kick me off the premises before they realized you wrote my name down next to *your* name?" I tease back, one eyebrow rising.

He laughs in true enjoyment. "Excuse us," he tells the group, earning me a couple of venomous stares from the women as he takes my arm and slips it into the crook of his and draws me away.

"That's quite a dress," he whispers with a twinkle in his eye, his dark head ducked so he can say it in my ear.

"What does that mean?"

He smiles as he leads me to the table where Callan and Tahoe sit, each with a drop-dead-gorgeous girl. Saint pulls my chair out, then sits next to me as the room continues filling up.

"Are all the new Interface employees invited?" I ask him, looking around.

He nods, looking at me intently. "There are several connecting rooms to fit everyone. This room is mostly for directors and members of the board." When I only smile, he spreads his arm out on the back of my chair and leans forward so that his voice is all I can hear, not the classical music in the background or the conversation. Just a voice in my ear. "Why do you insist on labeling yourself press?"

"I *am* press. I can't delay writing the Interface story anymore, my magazine needs me to turn it in."

"You don't need a press badge to catch my attention. Nor do you need a badge to interview me."

"Do you even lift anymore, Carmichael? Didn't think so," Tahoe baits Callan at the table. Because I'm so unnerved and unused to having a man's attention like Saint's attention is on me, I try to divert myself with their antics.

"I lift," he argues.

"Haven't seen that since I last fed my unicorn," Tahoe drawls.

"It's true, bro," he answers.

"Saint, do you mind a suggestion for later?" Tahoe asks as Saint shifts in his seat to face him, the move bringing him closer to me. I instantly sit up straighter.

Saint sips his drink lazily, lips curling. "I'm down for whatever."

"Good. Because you know what we should do . . ." Tahoe begins.

Saint: "That always precedes a terrible idea. So naturally, I'm game."

"Let's hit the pool on the top level."

He chuckles and then looks at me only, his attention drawing my own helplessly back to him. "I like your friends so much better than you," I say softly, so that only he hears.

In the warm lights, his gaze gleams like something liquid. His voice is quiet. "Do you really?"

"Yes. Really."

Silence. My heart beats fast. He lifts his hand and brushes my hair behind my ear, and my earlobe burns when we hear a woman say from nearby, "Saint, I left my shoes at your place the other day. Can I still tell you about the charity I was hoping you'd—?"

"Monday at M4," he says without inflection, his attention fixed on me.

The woman shoots me a look of pure hate, then is gone. I wonder if he's sleeping with these women. I wonder—

"At least I know what they want. My bed or my wallet. Or both," he says, as if reading my thoughts. His lips twisted adorably at the corners, he studies me. *What do you want from me?* those eyes ask.

"You should work out with Saint sometime. He'd kick your ass, probably. It'd be fun for you two," Tahoe tells Callan from a distance.

As Sin looks down at me, I feel his hand slip under the table in search of mine. There's the barest brush of his thumb when he finds my fingers, and then we hear the voice of an elderly man up on the podium.

"Ladies and gentlemen, thank you all for coming today—we're very excited about the inaugural dinner for the one and only Interface. I know you're all as excited as I am to be part of this innovative family. And here with us is the genius behind it all, a man known for his edge, wit, and incredible zest for life. I give you, Malcolm Kyle Preston Logan SAINT!"

"I'll be right back," he whispers, his breath hot in my ear.

I'm blushing bright red from the touch of his hand, imprinted on my back as he stands and caresses me under the fall of my hair. As he heads for the podium, I can't take the stares coming my way and the way I feel hot under my dress, moist between my legs, so completely affected I decide I can't be with him tonight. I can't sit here and pretend to be his date. It's too wrong and it's too much work for me.

I stand quietly as I hear him greet the crowd in that authoritative voice of his. "Good evening, and thanks for that, Roger."

As I slip out the entrance and head to where the tables for press badges are set, I spot his assistant Cathy.

"Cathy, hi, do you remember me? I met you at—"

"Miss Livingston, of course." She motions toward the ballroom. "Everything okay with your table?"

"Oh, it's the best table, which is why I really can't sit there. I'm here as press, you see. It's such a misunderstanding, and Mr. Saint is so busy . . ."

I'm surprised by the way her face basically blooms when I mention him. "I understand," she says quietly. "I did worry a good girl like you might be concerned about his reputation."

"No, I mean . . . well, yes, that's exactly why I need my badge. I don't want anyone to get the wrong impression."

"Especially him?" She looks at me, and I blush. "I can give you a thousand badges, Miss Livingston, but if he wants you, he's going to come after you. He does have the patience of a saint when it comes to getting what he wants."

And you're in love with him, I think, but say nothing because, thankfully, she's printing my badge. "You're happy working for him?" I ask.

"I wasn't working at all until I began working for him. He was the only one who would give me a chance." She smiles and hands me the badge.

Quietly, I head back into the room, and when I hear his voice in the microphone, rushes of electricity crackle down my spine. A wave of applause sweeps the room as everyone claps in excitement.

Standing in the back, I'm turning my badge over in search of the clip when I realize dozens of heads are swiveling in my direction. There's no more Saint up on the podium.

Because he's wending his way through the crowd, his wide torso carving a path as he comes straight for me.

"Are you done?" He doesn't sound angry or impatient but . . . almost.

"I . . . yes." Quickly, I lift the badge and try to attach it to my dress.

He takes my hand in his. "I do love those ears of yours,

but they don't seem to hear very well," he murmurs in amusement. "You won't be needing this." He plucks the badge from my fingers.

"What? Why?"

"Saint!" a voice nearby calls. It's a member of the media, asking for a shot, which Saint denies with a hand signal.

He then tucks my badge into his jacket pocket and takes my hand back into the crook of his arm. "Come," he whispers in my ear, already leading me to the side of the room, to the doors that lead out onto a terrace overlooking a golf course. He steps out onto the terrace with me, and only then do I manage to pull my hand from the warm crook of his arm.

"I don't think we should be here. Everybody saw that."

"So?" He lifts his eyebrows, and I stand there, at a loss. His eyes gleam in the moonlight, and he looks succulent. Edible. Not just his lips, every part of him.

Slowly, his gaze slides downward. He radiates a vitality that draws me like a magnet. It unnerves me, but something in his voice soothes me. "Do you blame me for wanting you to myself for a few minutes, Rachel?" he asks, his voice husky.

I have a thousand pictures of him, but none like this. The face I see right now isn't for any camera; it's for nobody to see. Not even me. There is pure, organic, unfiltered emotion etched across his features, roiling in his eyes.

He squeezes my hand to keep me from backing away from him, and then he reels me closer to him, his lips pulling into a smile because I resist a little.

"Come here," he coaxes, finally managing to make my body loosen up enough for me to go where he wants me. Close to him.

He's so magnetic, so beautiful as he looks down at me and brings me close enough to smell him. I imagine reaching out to touch his hard jaw, running my tongue up his tan chest to that laughing mouth.

I'd give anything to know what he's thinking. Why he's smiling like that. There are smiles that just make you want to smile back, but *this* smile makes you want to kiss it *so* hard.

He's the first to move instead, his hand lifting only a fraction to rest on my face. "You look gorgeous," he murmurs, and he brushes my lips with the pad of his thumb. I shiver involuntarily. "I could feast on your mouth . . . even longer than last time."

"No, no kissing," I breathe, but for a second, I let myself absorb the feeling of being close to someone who's so much bigger and harder.

He runs his hand through my hair, and the sensation is so sweet and so intoxicating, I stay there. We stay like that.

He obviously knows he affects me. But he looks affected too, his body stonelike and buzzing with tension. We're both affected. He brushes the tips of his fingers along the bare back of my dress, the warmth of his hand sending shivers through my body. We're in an alcove, and there's this intense you-and-me vibe.

Intense you-and-me vibe . . .

"I never do this." I try to unwind his arms from around me. "Give me back my badge, please."

"What for?" he murmurs, scowling softly.

"I need my badge. I'm . . . this isn't . . ."

"No," he says softly.

"I feel naked without my badge."

He grins. "It's still no."

I groan and turn away, and when I glance at him, he's looking at me with perfect amusement.

"Can I ask you some questions?" I say, reaching out a fast

hand, catching him off guard and pulling my badge out of his jacket.

He laughs when I quickly step back so he can't recover it; then he falls sober and recovers the distance he lost, his steps slow and measured. "Do you want to talk about Interface?"

I feel like *Do you want to talk about Interface?* has become code for something else.

"Yes," I say primly, clipping the badge to my dress.

He looks at me. "Ask." He seems pretty content to be interviewed, so I breathe a sigh of relief at last.

"What are your goals for Interface?"

He tucks a loose hair behind my ear. My ear burns when he eases back his hand. "To be number one in the market, leave the competition behind."

I see him, hear him, his ambition, his determination, and their effects only grow stronger in me.

"Do you . . ." I trail off when he lifts his hand, caressing my cheek with the knuckles of one hand.

"You never stop working, do you?" he interrupts, scowling a little. "In that sense, you're like me."

I scowl too. "You're answering with a question."

"You're not asking the right questions."

"God, Saint! Why do you like to tease me so much?"

Laughing, he leans closer, until his face is level with mine and I can smell the soap on his skin. He holds me by the chin with the pad of his thumb and forefinger. "Why do you blush every time I do?"

"My skin is white, it's almost translucent. I blush easily."

"I only see you blush with me."

His eyes are both comforting and disturbing, hot and cold, closed off at the same time they seem to be stripping me. "Do you think about me, Rachel?"

"At work, yes. I think about you in the office. Is that what you wanted to hear?"

"Partly, yes. I think about you in the office too, but I also think about you in bed."

"Saint, the commissioner would like to speak with you. Miss Livingston, I'm Dean."

I'm so hot right now, I'm mortified I get to meet Saint's PR person like this, but I shake his hand nonetheless and try to act calm and collected, not in the least Saint-affected. "Dean, oh yes, so nice to meet you."

Malcolm extracts the badge from my grip. "Press time is over," he informs me. All the cold has fled his eyes; they look beyond warm, blazing like fireballs as he looks at me. "Take care of her, Dean."

"I will."

He goes inside.

Dean and I soon follow.

I ask Dean how long he's worked at M4, how the hiring process was. We're talking about his job, and how impressed I am with Interface, when I spot a familiar face across the room. I stiffen when the hawklike, tiny pointy nose and the long dark hair register in my brain. Victoria?

Her eyes widen from across the room, and she points at me, to my complete and utter horror. She starts charging over.

"Rachel?" she calls.

God, seeing a colleague from *Edge,* one whom I don't trust and one who knows exactly what I am doing here, I did not expect to feel so small.

I brace myself for a second, then I stand to greet her.

Playing the perfect innocent, she seems absolutely delighted as I perform a quick, perfunctory introduction to Dean.

"Dean, wow, and you're Saint's PR person?"

"Victoria . . . meet me at the ladies'? Dean, will you excuse us?"

I try to appear calm and mermaid-like as I start in the direction of the restrooms, keeping my eyes ahead while Victoria walks smugly next to me.

Even the way she walks is like she's having sex with the floor or something.

"Saint is absolutely *eating* you with his eyes. Why aren't you clinging to him, chatting him up?" Victoria says when we're finally in the ladies'.

I make sure that all the stalls are vacant, then go to the sink and open the water.

"It isn't like that."

"What? It isn't like what? Like that dress isn't begging to be peeled off—"

"Shhh!" I glance around at the stalls, checking a second time that they're empty.

She follows and inspects every one of them herself. "Don't worry, I'm not telling. Helen will kill me if this blows up."

I rub my temples and sigh. "Can you explain to me what you're doing here?"

"I called a few of my contacts when I heard you weren't on the press list. I wanted to get the deets."

"The deets on what, Victoria? I'm *here.* This is my . . . I'm here. And it's all under control."

She eyes me dubiously. "Okay. Well then." She makes a ceremony out of washing her hands, taking forever to pat them dry. Then she checks her makeup. "I suggest you go out there and use your feminine wiles. You're a woman, a pretty one. And in case you haven't noticed, every other woman out there is giving Saint come-hither looks but *you.*"

She leaves.

I stand there, looking at myself in the mirror. I've lost all semblance of color from my face. I feel physically ill. I'm certain that if I walk out there, Saint will see right through me. He'll know what I want from him, that I want everything including his secrets, and he'll know why I shouldn't have kissed him the way I did at the Interface building. What we did there felt so intimate to me, so . . . so unprofessional on my part, considering what I have to do.

All my insecurities rising to the surface, I call for a cab with my cell. I wait a few minutes, then slip out of the bathroom and find one of the women from the press-badge table.

"Could you please tell Mr. Saint that the woman whose badge he has in his pocket had to leave, she wasn't feeling well?" I ask her, grateful when she agrees.

Outside, my cab is waiting across the street, and I leap over a few puddles and climb inside, the bottom of the dress completely ruined. I thank the driver when I get home, then I pull off my dress and my shoes, slip into my Northwestern T-shirt, and sit on the bed, motionless, thinking and feeling blank and numb.

I never thought I would ever do anything to hurt somebody. I always thought I was on the good guys' side, on the side of rightness. Seeing Victoria today while I was both working and not working made me see what I am. What I'm doing.

I'm a hypocrite. I'm . . . a liar.

That little game bullies try to make you play when you're a little kid—if you were forced to kill one to save the other, your mom or your dad, who would you choose? Sometimes in life you have to make a choice like that, a decision so hard you can't make it, you would rather sacrifice yourself. But that still means *Edge* goes down.

I peer into Gina's room, but she's not back yet. I go back to my fetal position on the bed and I turn on a local gossip show on television, trying to distract myself.

"Tonight at the Interface inaugural, Malcolm Saint speaking..."

A snippet from a while ago appears, and my stomach tumbles as if I've just taken a steep drop on a roller coaster. The video cuts back to the news anchor and an image of us, Saint and me, as he took my hand and led me to the terrace.

OHMIGOD!

"A young lady's early departure is causing confusion among the press; this is the image taken earlier of Saint with her, arousing much speculation as to whether Saint's got his eye on her. Early word is that she's a member of a small magazine in the area but wasn't on the scene as press. First time ever Saint's been linked to a reporter. It will be interesting to watch future developments."

"Agreed," the coanchor says.

"Ohmigod!" I turn off the TV, toss the remote aside, and cover my face in my hands. I'm breathing in and out, in and out, when my cell phone vibrates. It's Helen.

> You're on the news. Vicky texted. Said he looks absolutely hooked? I'm impressed

I groan, "I'm going to throw up now."

Sick with self-loathing over my disgusting duplicity, I grab a pillow and bury my head there. I don't answer Helen. I delete her text instead, then I reach for my lifeline, the only thing that has kept me going when it's gotten rough:

> Love you, Momma

14

AFTER THE PARTY

My mother's probably asleep. She hasn't answered. I still feel like shit. Hell, I *am* shit. Groaning, I pull my T-shirt over my knees and wrap my arms around my legs; then I bury my face there. I've been here for a while when I hear the downstairs buzzer. I'm not answering. I really am not.

The third time it buzzes, I give up and go answer from the kitchen. "Yes?"

"It's me."

Malcolm.

I glance frantically around the place I share with Gina. It's in a Chicago factory-turned-apartment building. The doors to our bedrooms are both in a short hall, one on the right side, one to the left. Painted wooden bookcases and framed metal columns stand between the kitchen and living room. We have a hole in the wall between the dining room and the pantry, and the cheapest alternative we could think of at the time was to hang a huge whiteboard over it on the dining room side, where we write things when we get drunk or just feel like it. It used to be my idea board, but the girls hijacked it.

It's . . . home. My home. What will he think of it?

This apartment is my pride, my little spot of peace, and now HE will be in it, and it will be intense. It's been a while since my friends and I have had this conversation, but no man has crossed the sacred barrier of my apartment threshold. Ever. He's the first. The very first.

I'm nervous about him seeing my place, my safe zone, my pride and joy, through eyes that have seen far too much of the world. Far more than me. What is pretty to me may be simple and uninteresting to him.

"C'mon up," I murmur and buzz him in, then hurry back to my bedroom, slipping on some leggings and exchanging my T-shirt for a long blouse, checking my reflection in the bathroom mirror.

Sighing in despair over my swollen eyelids, I scrub my face with soap and head to the door. He's waiting outside when I open it, leaning against the wall, one hand in his pocket, staring down at his shoes, his eyebrows furrowed.

He looks up at me. My legs feel paralyzed, as if they're not getting enough blood. He doesn't know how monumental it is for me to step back and wave him inside. God, he looks so good—as good as he did minutes or hours ago—that I almost trip on the rug.

"Do you want coffee?"

He glances around my place with a nod.

His tie is unfastened and hanging around his neck, the top buttons of his shirt undone. His hair curls at the collar of his shirt, and when he rumples it and keeps surveying my place, it sticks out all over his head, dark and lovely. I have to fight the urge to reach out and touch it. Instead, I bring us two cups to the coffee table. I take the couch and watch him lower himself into my favorite oversize reading chair, the one I do my best thinking in. I'm a little afraid now that I won't ever use it again without remembering he was parked right there.

"I'm sorry I bailed," I whisper, sliding a cup across the table and retrieving my hand before he can reach for it.

"I heard you weren't feeling well." He leans forward, ignoring the coffee. Ignoring my apartment and everything except me.

His dissecting look makes me lower my face and exhale. "Yeah, I guess," I agree.

"Somebody hurt you, Rachel?"

"Maybe . . ." I raise my head at the protectiveness in his tone and cross my arms over my chest. A male figure has never been concerned over me, protective. I like it so much I smile a little in happy amusement. "Will you punch her for me?"

"Her?"

"Me," I specify, shaking my head. "I'm referring to me, she's the one who hurt me." I tighten my arms because seeing him in my place makes my mind keep going elsewhere, to another time, at the top of the Interface building. I can't believe I've kissed those lips. I can't believe he kissed me for so long.

He laughs softly, runs a hand through his hair. "Then no, I won't punch her." A pause, a laden look.

Then kiss her again, I think recklessly.

Groaning inwardly at the thought, I put my face in my hand for a moment.

Saint seems to be beyond puzzled by me right now.

"Is this a girl thing?" His voice brings my head up, his tone a mix of confusion and amusement that, coming from such a hard and closed man, is unexpectedly sweet.

"It's a me thing," I admit. "I saw someone tonight—she

works where I work. She's always so spot-on. Everything she writes is absolute gold. Her topics, her metaphors, her similes!"

His chuckle fills the room—a rich, beautiful sound—and then he reclines farther back in the chair, the embodiment of a businessman relaxing.

"I'm personally a fan of your work, Rachel."

My . . . *what!?*

"You always lay out your topics with refreshing honesty."

"You've been reading me?" I'm sure my voice and round eyes betray my surprise.

That small smile again, combined with a scowl this time. "You think I give interviews to just anyone?"

"Honest?" I ask.

When he nods, I dip my head low. "I thought you saw my boobs pushing out of that top on my profile picture and told Dean you'd see me."

His eyes crinkle with humor, but then we stare for long, heavy minutes, and our smiles fade.

"I read your column before that interview was granted."

"I must've been such a disappointment in person. That first interview? It's the most embarrassing interview I've ever had," I admit.

We stare again.

I want him to say something, so I wait.

"I thought you were lovely."

I'm blushing red.

He's not known to be big on compliments, or a big flatterer. He's known to be blunt, his honesty close to making people uncomfortable.

I'm uncomfortable now because I feel him looking at me with new intensity, and when he speaks again, the girl inside me feels euphoric.

"It gave me great pleasure to watch you walk out with my shirt. It seems every single one of my employees who saw you knew that I wanted you. Everyone knew this except maybe me."

My breath catches.

"Oh," I say, when I manage to expel it.

"I didn't know *then*," he specifies, his stare unflinching.

The desire I feel is so absolute, so powerful, I cannot think of anything else but him and the fact that I cannot have him.

I'm acutely aware of the distance between us—of exactly how many feet lie between him and me in my living room. I turn on a lamp, and the room becomes more alive; all the light seems to make love to him, to the angles of his face.

"Why are you here, Saint? If it was because of what happened at Interface, I made a mistake."

"Then let's make another one. A bigger one."

I laugh nervously. "What is this? Am I a challenge to you now?"

His lips quirk. "A challenge is something you stop wanting once you acquire it. I can't know if you're a challenge yet until I make you mine."

I can't believe how sexy that short little word, *mine,* is when the man I want utters it. I want to hear him say it so many more times, in my ear, closer to me. Oh god. *Livingston, get under control.*

But how can I? The tension is so thick in the air. I inhale the scent of him with every breath; every breath reminds me my body is tight and throbbing, every breath hurts because of him.

He's watching me as if he wants to figure me out. "So, your friend . . ."

"Victoria. She's my age, but she's had short stories published already, she's writing a children's book for sex education, she makes success look so effortless. I can never do as much, think of the concepts she comes up with."

"Use it, use it to become better. You do your best when someone else is right there trying to beat you. I was . . ." he begins, then laughs softly as if amused at himself. "Okay, let's try this." He edges forward in his seat. "I was a disappointment to my father." He speaks casually, but he watches me as if he wants to be sure his words have an effect. "I'm not sure if it's been since I was born, or later . . . when I got sick. Dad never forgave me that weakness. He asked for DNA testing, sure my mother had had an affair, wanting to prove I wasn't his son. I got bigger, faster, stronger, just because the one man I wanted to prove myself to underestimated me."

"Was he a tough dad?"

"Tough as nails. Nothing anyone did was good enough to suit him."

"Is that why nothing you get is good enough, why you're always chasing after more?"

"Not because of him. It's because it never *feels* like enough. I never stop unless I want someone else to catch up."

"You're tough as nails too."

He laughs and shakes his head, his hand restlessly running over his head. "You okay now?"

I nod. "Thank you," I whisper.

"For what?"

"You being here right now is holding me back from a pretty nasty hell."

He stands, and my heart stops beating as he comes and drops next to me. I'm pudding when he tugs me into the nook in his strong arm. "Come here." He holds me for a while, his arm encircling me. He's not soft at all—his chest is hard, his shoulders square—but I feel his warmth and heartbeat, and suddenly I realize I'm pressing my mouth to his throat.

He circles my waist with his arm and traps me against his chest. He caresses my neck from my collarbone to the edge of my jaw.

I slide my hand up his chest.

He meets my eyes with blazing force, and I start chasing my breath in fast pants as he ducks his head.

He kisses the edge of my mouth. My lids sweep closed from the pleasure, and I don't dare move a muscle.

He frames my face with the palms of his hands and slowly brushes his lips against mine. He eases back an inch, looking at me again, making sure I'm okay before bending again and opening his lips against mine.

He holds me loosely as I kiss his mouth, as if giving me space, letting me get accustomed to him. Everything about him is hard. His jaw. His chest. His arms. His hands. But oh my god, his lips. His tongue. His lips are warm and soft, kissing me hungrily. His tongue lightly slipping through my lips, making me melt into him.

We sink into the couch and I let him kiss me because it's the most exquisite thing I have ever felt. I open my mouth wider, savoring every minute, every second, that his lips are on mine. He kisses me for a long time, over and over again, until I'm breathless. I never want to stop. I could do this for hours. It feels perfect. Amazing.

He draws back and rubs his thumb across my bottom lip.

My brain is thinking so many things at once it isn't thinking anything at all. I'm breathing hard, looking at him with his hair tousled, eyes hooded, and lips slightly swollen, and he looks back at me like a tiger does its prey. We shift, and I sit on his lap straddling him. He kisses my jaw. I hold on to his biceps, big and strong. He kisses the side of my mouth again, reassuring me that I'm okay, while parting my blouse with his hands. Then he leans down and places a kiss right below my throat.

I look down to his jet-black hair, feeling his warm mouth kiss across my collarbone. He places another kiss right between my breasts, then all the way up to my jaw. He kisses my throat again. Sucking a little here, licking a little there, kissing a little more. I'm looking up at the ceiling, trying to memorize the feel of his lips on me. I feel like I'm separate from my body. If someone were to talk to me, I probably wouldn't hear them. All I want in life right now is for him to never stop.

He makes his way back to my lips, giving me another soft kiss. I open my mouth immediately and wind my arms around his neck to hold him to me. His hands are big and warm on my thighs—without them I would probably float off somewhere near Cloud Nine. Or in this case, Cloud Ninety-nine.

I melt when I hear his hot voice against my skin. "I keep thinking of that day. And you couldn't have possibly tasted this sweet. . . ."

I open my mouth, and suddenly I'm kissing him with my whole heart. He is exquisite. Kissing me tenderly, and then kissing me hungrily. The smell of his cologne surrounds me, the heat from his body warms me, and his lips slowly drive me crazy. This little make-out session of ours is going to end up with me in a psych ward.

"Don't stop," I breathe, rocking my hips with the sudden ache to get closer to him, to feel his skin on mine.

My body's trembling. He raises his head and kisses the edge of my mouth, starts nibbling. He groans, and I can tell he's really getting into it. "Don't stop," I beg.

"I'm not stopping until morning." He draws back and cups

my face in both hands. I'm looking into his glowing green eyes, which stare at me with a light in them I can't describe. He's looking at me like I'm a goddess. Like he could never have imagined me. He's looking at me with so much need and tenderness I can feel my throat tighten again. I'm not ready for this. I'm scared. I'm nervous.

"What in the—"

The overhead lights snap on and I sit up in confusion, covering my hot face with my hands.

Gina blinks.

Saint closes his eyes tight, then opens them, and he looks so perfectly hot, so manly, so angry and so debauched by me, I reach out and quickly start to button his shirt, too jealous to let Gina see his chest, his abs, what I'd just been touching so madly.

"I hope what's happening here isn't really happening." Gina scowls with her hands planted on her hips.

"It isn't," I blurt; then I look at him as he looks down at me in complete puzzlement, eyebrows slanted low. His hair is standing up adorably, but his expression is beyond annoyed.

"Your roommate," he curses under his breath as if he should've remembered I had one.

Mortified, I pull him to his feet—with much effort—and then to the door. "That . . . was beyond a mistake. I don't know what got into me."

His stare is dark as night and his voice is gruff with desire. "I know what got into you—the same thing that got into me."

"No." I go into the hall, call up the elevator, and then push him in with all my effort. "'Bye, Saint."

"I'll call you, Rachel," he murmurs as he grabs my face and kisses my mouth, rubbing his tongue a little over mine and making me moan before I tear free and the elevator leaves.

Oh. My. God. *What have I unleashed?*

"What was that?"

"He was saying goodbye."

"I'm Gina, remember. Your best friend. I can tell when you're lying. Were you guys . . . sleeping together on the couch like some item?"

"I had a few drinks. So did he. We had that . . . thing. I'm beyond . . . not thinking well."

"Okay. 'Cause we know deep down he's Lucifer, right? The Arch Douche himself? We don't sleep with the bastard, we do not drop our walls!"

I nod and go to my room. I scrub my mouth with the back of my hand and brush my teeth and then look at my face in the mirror.

What am I doing? I poured my heart out to him. Why didn't I just tell him I was writing an exposé?

This wasn't part of my plan. I'm supposed to write an exposé about him, not let him expose *me*.

But I can't sleep. I remember the frustration on Saint's face when Gina came in. A little later, I turn on my lamp and get my cell phone.

I'm sorry about the way I said goodbye, I text, but before sending the text, I dial the number and wonder if he'll answer. I don't wonder for long: I hear the sound of him picking up, his voice saying hey.

"I'm sorry about the way I said goodbye."

There's a smile in his voice when he answers, relieving me. "If that's what it takes to get you to call."

I laugh, then go sober and cuddle up in bed with the phone

to my ear, shyly whispering, "You're different with me than anyone."

"Because of the 'fragile, handle with care' sign you wear."

"I'm not fragile."

"You're so fragile you've boxed yourself up so you don't break."

"I like my safe zone."

"Nothing happens in the safe zone."

"That's the point—you control everything and it's predictable and . . . safe."

There's a long silence.

Then Saint says, "When you come outside of your box, I'll be waiting."

15

A MAKEOVER

What did that even mean?

I don't want to be unsafe. It's the last goal of my existence. I've always liked that I have never been reckless.

On Friday, I pour myself mindlessly into a piece Helen wanted for the week. I can't think; I can't stop to think or I'll start to drown in my own fears and confusions. I tell myself to stay detached and keep my eyes on the prize, and that's all a sensible reporter would do. And I am sensible. At least, I was for the twenty-three years before I met Malcolm Saint.

I'm typing furiously when my phone buzzes and I peer absently at the screen, only to have a heart attack when I see the word I saved him under in my contacts. SIN.

Meet me tonight at the Tunnel?

What is my heart doing right now? It's doing cartwheels in my chest. I've become this girl, this ridiculous girl. The Tunnel is a hot spot known for its dark and winding rooms, its loud music. Hardly anyone comes out sober or unmussed from the Tunnel. *Rachel, you can't go with Saint to the Tunnel unless you're totally prepared to get your libido in check, and you've been doing a lousy job of that.*

"So are you ready?"

I lower my phone when Victoria tries to peer over the top of my cubicle. "Ready?" I repeat. "For what?"

"Don't you remember? Your beauty day! Getting you prepped this weekend to *work*."

"I . . . ah. Right. How could I forget? The clichéd makeover. Normal girl gets her hair cut, gets the guy, lalalalalala," I say as I grab my things.

"Yes." She laughs.

I get my phone and close the file I had open on my computer with a few too many links—but never enough—featuring what Malcolm did this week. In all the pictures there were girls too, but he looked detached. He didn't look like he was having fun, but then, he's hard to read.

Once I close up my computer, I follow Victoria to the elevators and we head to a spa. Pedicure, manicure, a trim.

"Highlights."

"I'm platinum blonde, Vicky, it doesn't get lighter."

"Slightly lighter streaks and slightly darker ones give light to your hair."

"I'll take the haircut, but I won't be enslaved by hair color until my hair turns gray. It's a tip I learned from my mother."

"What Saint likes is a good ol' easy woman. He's not used to working for it—it's always available to him, and that's how he probably likes it. Though he really did seem thoroughly hooked on you, Rachel."

My phone buzzes. I stare at the caller ID, my body once

again getting into the action. SIN. Flushing just at the thought of him, I tuck the phone aside and watch my toes get a nice pink coat of paint.

"After the toes, full-on bikini wax," Victoria announces from her seat next to mine.

I wonder whether she could speak a little louder so that not only the entire spa but the outside world as well could hear.

I lean forward and drop my voice. "No thanks."

"Um. Hello? Not a question."

I laugh. "Girl, I've got it perfectly maintained. Leave it!"

"All right." She slaps down the magazine she'd been reading and sets it aside. "But guys like Saint like Brazilians." She smiles secretively. "And of course, all those gorgeous *girls* from Brazil too." She chooses a new magazine and continues in her role of advisor, like she's an expert on him. "Womanizers like all girls; it's part of their charm. They're perfect specimens, and we can't help but be drawn to that." She smiles. "You know that earthiness about you, that gentle fierceness—he can be drawn to that. I *saw* that he was drawn to that. Under that drive, you're sweeter and more gentle, and he's more like fire, more forceful, more ambitious. Saint plays around but he's hard—as everybody who's done business with him knows."

My phone vibrates, and this time it's a call. SIN.

Force and fire.

Hard.

I want to answer. I want to hear his voice.

I also want to *not* want these things.

I swear, if the knot in my stomach gets any tighter, I'm going to implode.

I'm staring at my phone when another text pops up.

What does a man need to do to get you to say yes?

Chewing on my inner cheek, I stare at my phone for what feels like forever. *Yes! Yes! YES! But also NO. We cannot. NO. NO. NO.*

Finally I focus on the job, tell myself it's a *yes* with an emotional and physical *no* attached, and answer:

I'll meet you there

My hand is shaking as I tuck my phone away again and try to come back to the present. Spa. Makeover. Victoria. Oh yes, Victoria. Very interesting development here. I scrutinize her in confusion, then say, "From what you just told me, I'm starting to think you actually want me to succeed."

To be honest, I don't bother to hide my surprise because, well, I've been surprised by Victoria in a great way today.

"I *do* want you to succeed—why wouldn't I? I love working at *Edge*. Where am I supposed to go?" A look of puzzlement crosses her face. "We all know we're on our last breath. Nobody's taking over. Our print run gets tinier by the second. Every one of us will end up without a job." She shakes her head. "I don't want that." She sighs. "I want to be looked upon favorably by our bosses, but to be honest, I'm not sure what I'd do with Saint if I ever had him."

"Oh, that boy just can't be had." I laugh lightly, but inside, this makes me sad. That Saint is so apart from the crowd may make it harder for him to feel like he "belongs" anywhere. That he will never belong to anyone at all.

"What do you mean, 'he can't be had'?"

"He just can't be had, not in any way that matters to him. Nobody's gotten more than just a tiny piece of Saint. Not his dad, not even his mother. No woman. Not his friends or his businesses. He spreads himself around, even in his interests.

Nothing really claims him. He keeps that to himself, all that fire. He just gives you a glimpse of the spark."

"Well"—she fans her face with her hands—"you already have a better grasp of him than I do!"

A little before 8 p.m., I enter my apartment, remembering I'd promised Victoria I'd wear a dress. "Try not to reveal too much. People always take their tops off for Saint. He might like wondering what's underneath instead."

"He won't get to see it, so he can wonder to death," I flippantly said.

But I'm surprised my tongue didn't catch fire, because I don't feel flippant. I feel anticipation of the kind that makes you concentrate on nothing. Makes you try to do ten things at once and fail at them all.

I haven't seen him since he Frenched me outside my apartment right before the elevator doors closed.

By the time Gina gets home, I've got clothes strewn all over my room. I had texted her: Sin is at the Tunnel tonight and we're going!

Whereas I'd been deliberating what to wear since before I even opened the door, she instantly storms inside and takes charge.

"What are you still doing in bra and panties? Get dressed! Wear that top that's cool and modern in blue and white that says MY BOYFRIEND IS A SAILOR, just because you want to appear taken and like you didn't try too hard."

"Not try too hard? I spent four hours at a spa. I paid for my silly makeover."

"Wear that top anyway that says your boyfriend is a sailor. If he wants in your pants, he's going to loathe that."

I pull the top out of my closet and eye it, my nerves sky-rocketing as the seconds tick by. I decide maybe I will wear a skirt and the boyfriend top. Not as seductive as a dress but still, he can get an eyeful of long legs now that they're slick and oiled up nicely. And why are you wanting to show him your long legs, Rachel?

"Is this a good idea, G?" I leap into my skirt.

"It's a fucking great idea, it's exactly what you wanted!"

"Um, no, it isn't. I wanted research, but this is almost like a date."

"No, it's not. Saint doesn't date. He just hooks up."

God, I'm wishing he'll drool for me.

I'm wishing that at least one night, one night in his existence, he will have a wet dream about me.

But I'm still so uncertain. I turn and ask Gina, "Is this all right? I'm treading such a fine line. . . ."

"Rachel, just remember he's using you, you're using him; you're not in a relationship, nor will you ever be. Just do the job and don't get involved."

"Okay," I quickly agree, just to get her to stop saying the word *using*.

I gulp back a ball of nerves the size of a lemon and as bitter as the peel, then grab my bag and tell myself that I can do this, that I want to do this, that I want to do this more than I want to do him.

16

TUNNEL

"Okay, we're mingling. Help me find Emmett."

Wynn, Gina, and I roam the mazelike rooms inside the Tunnel with the smells of clay walls and sweat filling our nostrils along with perfume, cologne, and alcohol. Flashing lights and music hit us as we head toward the heart of the Tunnel, the "pit." Wynn leads the pack while I trail behind, head turning as I look for him.

"Bet he's there." Gina points at a room to the right, which is filled to capacity, so I can't even see past the wall of glittery dresses and skin at its fringes.

"Why there?"

"Hello? Where there's smoke there's fire? Where there's Saint, there are GIRLS."

Frowning at that, I wedge myself through to the busiest corner, and my heart stutters because there he is, the Guy Who Owns My Hormones. While Callan and Tahoe look good, Saint could be wearing a sign that says BRING EXTRA PANTIES.

Two women sit on each of his friends' laps, and a pretty blonde socialite is talking to Malcolm, looking at him in complete rapture.

Music pulses through the speakers. Bodies bump and jostle as I steal this moment to watch him while he's not watching me. Tan, his hair standing up a little bit, his shirt rolled to the elbows like it always is at the clubs, where it gets hot and crazy. *God, butterflies.*

He's laughing as he turns, rather casually scanning the room, and then his shoulders tense. My heart stops, flips, because he's noticed me. Then I'm subjected to the seriously uncomfortable pressure of his scrutiny.

He cocks a brow, and once again he gets that curl to his lip. *You going to stay there all night?* I can almost hear him say.

Saint sets his drink down on the side table and comes over. Every step makes my heart beat faster and faster. He looks at me, starting at my feet and working his way upward—his eyes miss no detail.

"Rachel." He draws me into his strong arms and presses a kiss to my cheek, the brush of his lips so incredibly light I can't believe such a minuscule gesture can do so many things to my body. I'm having a war inside myself as I try to steady my breathing as he takes my hand and tugs me to their table in the back. I was born a girl; I've got proof of that on my birth certificate. But I've never felt so much like a girl until this moment, when my hand feels tiny and fragile in his strong grip.

Callan and Tahoe greet me through the music. "Hey Rache!" "Hey Rache!"

I slide into the booth and Malcolm settles down beside me, his shirt stretching in so many places I can't help feeling constrained in my own skin just by the sight.

He orders a drink for me, then sits back, looking as relaxed as I am tense. Something happened when he visited my apartment. The fact that it mattered to him if I was feeling well or not touched a chord, but also, he opened up to me in a way that surprised me, and, even more surprisingly, I opened up to him. We both shared things—real things. Now, the intimacy between us is so palpable right now that every inch of me aches to get closer, as close as we felt that night.

His arm outstretched behind me, his friends continue to banter and do wicked things to their whores with their drinks. "How was your week, Rachel?" At Saint's question, a warm glow of excitement flows through my veins, because there's real interest in his gaze.

"Good. My work is good. My mother's good. I . . . well, I don't want to bore you." But I smile. I can't remember when anyone's looked so attentive listening to me describe what my week was like.

Then I ask him about his trip to London—because of course I read that he was there for forty-eight hours—and he says it was "good," then shifts the subject back to me.

"What are you writing about now?" he whispers.

He's always so focused on everything I say; people pass and slap his back or call his name, and never once does he lift his head to acknowledge anyone apart from me. Just as engrossed in him and having trouble steering away from dangerous topics, I hedge and say, "Researching for next week's column."

I notice one of his outstretched arms is farther down on the back of my seat, and think, My topic is you.

A painful yearning hits me dead center. Whoa. Where did that come from?

I glance down at my lap as I try to regroup. *Why, oh why do these feelings of instability have to happen to me with you?*

Is it because I want to draw you out when you get so serious and you're not teasing me?

Or is it that you really want to know, for some inexplicable reason, the things that move me?

Or maybe it's because you make me so nervous . . . or maybe, simply, because you asked?

I drag in a breath, aware of being watched through those thick lashes by those boundless, deep-set eyes, green like the forest, hiding all the secrets of somebody who's never really reveals his cards until the game is won. Cunning eyes. Male eyes. Interested eyes. I want to shut myself up and not keep putting myself out there with him while he's still giving me back hardly anything at all, but I can't help wanting to answer him when he asks me questions. I glance at the dance floor and slowly rise to my feet, tugging his hand.

"Dance with me," I tell him.

I'm sick and tired of wondering, stressing, wanting and fighting it. I'm tired of thinking, of trying not to feel. Suddenly all I want is to dance with him. An hour of fun, an hour of being just a girl with a guy.

He cocks a brow, says nothing . . . but he stands. He stands slowly, like a serpent uncoiling. I laugh and tug on his hand a little more to lead him to the connecting room, where the dance floor is. "Dance with me, Saint."

His hand is large and long-fingered in mine as I tug him forward, and he lets me lead him, like a lazy wild animal indulging his prey before pouncing, and he steps onto the dance floor with me, his hands lifting to my hips. A fire churns inside me when I glance up to see the wicked tilt at the corners of his lips.

He watches me as I move sinuously under his hands, up and down and sideways, using him as a pole. A pole I want to kiss, just like any other girl, because it turns out I'm pretty human after all. He starts letting his hands roam up and down my sides, his eyes glinting like a devil's. I take his hands and put them on my nape so he holds me close. My stupid head can't think—my thoughts are all blanked. I want him naked, sweaty, out of his element, not smirking, not amused, definitely not in control.

"Is that the best you can do?" I taunt, surprised when he yanks me closer.

Then, with my hips in his hands, he moves me. *Wow.* He's hard. All. Over. People jumping around us, bumping against us, Malcolm dances like his body is an extension of mine. He draws me against him with very little effort on his part, and the stubble of his jaw scrapes against my nape as he pulls my hair to the side and runs the silver rings on his hand up the column of my neck. I'm so shocked by the soft sensuality in his movements and touch, the stealth and ripple of his muscles against mine, how safe and excited I feel in his arms, I'm high on this feeling. On him. On this night. I'm stealing touches that might definitely be too close to the fire, but my hands have a mind of their own. Part of me is crazed. His lips were made to kiss, his hands to touch; that's the sole purpose of his thick hair: for women to cling to while he pounds them hard. His eyes seem to offer peeks into heaven and into some kind of party in hell, and I'm maddened by it all.

I run my fingers up his shirt, around his square shoulders, savoring the rock-hard feel of his muscles. I couldn't stop the way I want to touch him even if I *tied* myself up!

The song ends, and he takes my hand and leads the way back to the table. Beads of perspiration run down between my breasts. Dozens of stares come at us; nearly every woman in the room is surveying me, head to toe, most with expressions that tell me they want to claw my skin off.

I almost wince.

At the booth, Callan is relating Saint anecdotes to the socialite whores.

"Oh yeah, but Saint crushed those rumors."

"Crushed!" Tahoe proudly echoes, fist to palm.

Ignoring them, Malcolm pulls me into the booth with him and resumes his position with his arm on the backrest of my seat, his head lowered in my direction so I can feel his warm breath at the back of my ear. "Hey . . . look at me," he coaxes as he slides his hand to my thigh and my thoughts scatter.

The touch sparks all my nerve receptors, all my yearning. I don't know if it's been building for minutes, hours, days, weeks, or my whole life, but I know I'm never aware of it unless he's near. Ruled by impulse now, I turn around and lean a little against him. He shifts so that his arm is now loose around my shoulders, and shiver as his fingers wander under the fall of my hair. His friends are talking. Saint whispers in my ear, "You look very pretty."

Suddenly my cheeks are burning and my stomach turns into a live thing.

The music stops and "Kiss You Slow" by Andy Grammer starts. He cups my face, his eyelids at half-mast. He kisses the corner of my lips.

The air feels like a lick of fire on my skin.

He gathers me tighter and flatter against his side, then drags all four of his silver-ringed fingers down the side of my face, his eyes following their path. "I'm with the hottest girl in the Tunnel tonight," he murmurs as he rubs my lipstick off my mouth with the sexiest brush of his thumb I could imagine.

And there, in his beautiful eyes, is a wild desire mirroring the one inside me. Desire unlike anything I've ever known clogs my throat, drives me to gently nip his thumb. I shouldn't be doing this, but I can't stop. The song is talking about *kissing slow* . . .

My perspective zooms out for a little bit, and I become aware of his friends making out in their corner with their whores just like Saint is making out with me. Of my friends mingling out there, somewhere. Of people dancing, others glancing in our direction. And of my life, changing, right this moment, somehow, as he stares at my face, the colors in his eyes shifting like a kaleidoscope as he seems to battle with the same confusing emotions that I am.

He takes my hips and slowly guides me to his lap. I go all too willingly, loosening my body so he can sit me sideways while I clutch onto his neck for dear life.

"Do you want this?" he whispers as he reaches beneath my skirt and I feel the warmth of his hand caressing the inside of my thigh.

Heart violently fluttering in my chest, my fingertips slide up his neck as I try to press closer. His neck is hard and thick and I duck my head to smell him. Then I whisper recklessly in his ear, "I'm with the most handsome guy."

"You fucking sly dog. You're probably going to do some jousting later on with Rache, too!" Tahoe calls from his seat, lifting his wineglass at us while his floozy tries to readjust her dress.

Saint's hand pulls out from my skirt, but he squeezes my thigh as he looks into my eyes regretfully. "Busy, T," he growls. He levels Tahoe a look that could just about flay the skin off his bones.

I blow out a breath, remembering the images and the rumors already going around about me, only making my job so much more risky.

"Not here," I tell him when I recover at least a little bit of my brain.

Making out in a club? Really, Rachel? With Saint?

Malcolm seizes my hips and helps me down off his lap.

"Hey, he really likes you," Tahoe calls to me, wagging his eyebrows as Malcolm summons a waiter and asks for something that makes him rush away, only to come back and nod.

"Mr. Saint, follow me," the waiter says.

Malcolm grabs his jacket from the bench and then takes me by the elbow, murmuring in my ear, "Come with me, Rachel."

We're led into a private room. There's a table at the end with little electric candles. A wine bucket, two wineglasses, a vase with a single pink tulip, dimmed lights. The same song playing outside but far more intimate.

"Anything you need, Mr. Saint?" the waiter says, and when Malcolm pushes what looks like several bills into his hand, the waiter almost falls apart.

"Thank you," Saint says. He guides me by the hand to the couch, and the waiter shuts the door with a soft, heart-dropping little *click*.

My legs can barely hold me but thank god, Saint sits me down. He shifts his toned, beautiful body so he can look at me. God. His eyes. I can't even hold them with mine for more than a few seconds; my heart is pounding in my chest, my skull, between my aching legs.

"Malcolm . . ." I start.

He seems to have a one-track mind right now as we settle back on the couch, and he ducks his head and presses his lips to my neck. I moan and slip my fingers into his hair, feeling how thick and soft it is while a burning, boiling need circles around in my veins.

I shudder when his lips press to my pulse point. Then he's tasting me with his tongue, slowly exploring the tender skin of my neck, and my toes are curling and my body's trembling as he cups my breast in one hand and gently squeezes while he strokes his free fingers up my bare arm, up and down. "Are you okay with this?"

He leans back, lips curled as he looks at me, and when I nod, completely and totally breathless, he holds me by the back of the head and presses a slow kiss to the corner of my mouth. He's gentle. Too gentle. Within a minute I'm too drunk, lust drunk, Malcolm drunk, to do anything but exist. Kisses. Touches. Kisses he sets on my ear. The corners of my mouth.

He slides his hand under my skirt again. "What are you wearing under there?" he husks out.

"Something." My voice shakes with desire.

"Something you want to show me?" His lips curl again.

I'm helpless under his probing stare as he tugs my skirt up to reveal my panties. I don't want to breathe, I don't even want to live after this moment when he's looking at me the way he is.

"Malcolm," I plead, feeling all wanton and nervous.

"Shh," he says softly as he takes a good look at my tiny, see-through lace panties, "I won't hurt you. All I want is to look at you."

"Only look?" I don't know if I want him to say yes, no, I don't know . . . what.

"And touch," he coaxes. He draws my leg up to his hip and pulls me closer so that I half straddle him as his fingers skim the back of my knee. Suddenly a thousand nerve receptors awaken, so sensitive to the lightest pressure of his fingertips, I moan against his throat. When he pulls my hair up and ducks his head and uses his tongue on the side of my neck, I moan deeper . . .

Usually I'd expect him to head straight for my hottest, wettest spot, but this is one knowledgeable guy and he doesn't do anything I expect him to. His lips press to my temple as he teases with his fingers up the back of my leg and then he grazes my inner thighs with his thumbs. My breath hitches, my nipples poking into my silk top and into his chest.

I arch my neck, pulling in deeper, faster breaths that smell of his cologne and intoxicate me. I think I just moaned his name. Using one hand, he slides a few fingers along the crotch of my panties.

"Tell me you want my fingers here," he whispers. Against my temple, he's smiling in obvious male delight because I'm absolutely wet already. I close my eyes and wrap my arms around his neck, and I imagine us naked, moving together.

He keeps one hand caressing my inner thigh and the back of my leg while he slides his other hand under my top. A restrained squeeze on my thigh and I can tell he's getting serious. I can already feel an earth-shattering orgasm building, and I'm starting to get more than my little share of fear.

"Sain . . . um, Malcolm . . . don't stop touching me, I just . . . need to slow down. . . ."

He eases back, and we separate for a moment, our breathing audible. My pupils can't focus, he's a blur. A blur I'm supposed to write about, not to have.

"Give me your hand," he whispers. Lightly he reaches out and holds my hand in his strong grip, and I can feel his eyes, liquid and green, watching my reaction as he dips his finger to my palm. Suddenly I'm reminded of each of the forty thousand nerve endings in this very palm. He strokes between the base of my fingers and knuckles, the caress stimulating like electricity.

I watch, transfixed, as he interlocks our fingers and uses his thumb to massage my palm up to the base of my fingers in slow little circles. My blood vessels feel too close to my skin. A fire builds in my body as he holds my hand and slowly straightens out my arm. Gently, he kisses along the inside of my elbow, fluttering his tongue across my skin and bathing the warm spot with his breath. What he's doing feels like a drug, a drug I never want to him to stop shooting into me.

Slowly, he tugs my top upward and tucks it into my bra strap so it stays up.

I've read the solar plexus is a powerful nerve cluster, but I've never experienced it before. He starts below my breasts, caressing upward, spreading me out on the couch so that he's kissing me softly around my belly button. When I moan, he soothes and whispers, relaxing my body, my abs uncontracting so that all the blood heads to the part between my legs that's on absolute fire. It burns and tingles at the prospect of being touched. He's so close and at the same time so far away. He caresses up my ribs and down. Ducking his head, he uses his tongue around my navel, then dips it, hot and wet, into the tiny nook. A dozen erogenous zones awaken to him. Nerve endings never before stimulated like this tingle and scream, my hot zones alive. All of me. Alive. I'm excited mentally, physically, emotionally.

"You have no idea how much you excite me," I hear myself admit as I caress his hair and he lifts his head, tugs my bra down off one swollen globe, curls his fingers around my breast, and gently suctions the tip of my nipple with a hungry sucking sound.

"I want you beneath me tonight, Rachel." His lashes sweep upward and he looks up at me, the gold rim around the green of his eyes gleaming with intent. Every breath, every undulating move of my body under his as he suckles me, everything undoes me from the very core outward. "Writhing," he says. "Panting. Wet."

He takes the hardened, already sensitized nipple back into his mouth. I slide down the seat, part my legs, and try to pull him above me. Instead he lets his hand slip in between my legs.

My arms wind around his shoulders tight enough that I can feel the muscles flexed and taut under my fingertips as he slowly tugs my panties aside with his thumb and slides one finger inside me.

The touch triggers a cascade of pleasure through my body. I arch, a tiny sound of need and ecstasy slipping through my lips. I can see the mask of control he always wears slipping as he watches me, his lips curling with a soft smile. "For me . . . Rachel. *Let go for me.*"

One rub of his thumb on my clit. One deft finger inside me. Those male eyes, glittering, watching. That voice, coaxing me. And I come, twisting with a soft cry, unable to stop it, unable to tell him that I wanted him to let go for me, too.

I gasp and pant for a while longer. He shifts his big body and watches me with that soft smile as he tugs my skirt back down and lets my top drop to cover me, using a hand to smooth it back in place as he whispers in my ear, "I've wanted to do that since the day you crashed my Ice Box party."

He's teasing me. I've gotten to know that tone now. So I tease him back. "I was dared by friends. Guess now I can say I met you and you were the heartless bastard everyone says you are."

"Who's everyone?"

"Your ex-girlfriends."

"I don't have girlfriends."

"Ex-lovers, whatever."

"I have something to say about that, too."

"Oh really, what is it?"

"I'm innocent?" He smiles.

I laugh. I want to kiss him, kiss him real hard, and fuck him harder. Oh god, I want to give him what he just gave me, but then what? "Are you having fun with me?"

"That was me actually attempting to let the lady have fun with *me*."

I put my hand on his thigh playfully. "You make my world spin a little faster."

"I'd like to rock it even more," he rumbles, and I laugh.

He looks at me, his grin, his eyes, all of him mischief to the tenth power. Mischief and sin.

"What's your idea of rocking a girl's world?"

"You tell me." He trails his eyes down my body.

"Me?!" I cry. "What do I have to do with it?"

"I've never wanted to rock a woman's world the way I want to rock yours."

It seems my lungs just froze on an in breath.

He leans forward in his seat, and instead of doing the expected, which is teasing me because he shocked me, he looks absolutely sober. "You've got to know this about me," he says as he cups my face in his warm palm. "I indulge in anything that I want. I'm not in the business of denying myself what I want. I'm not in the business of denying those around me of anything they want. I'm yours if you want me, Rachel."

He gazes at me quietly.

"We don't fit," I say. "I just want to find a spot, warm not cold, with a nice view, everything I could want, and I want to stop moving and stay there—in that spot. And you will never stand still."

His eyes darken more; he doesn't answer.

He strokes the back of a finger slowly down the curve of my cheek, his eyes looking into me like he wants something from me. Like he wants more than something—everything. Or maybe anything, that's how hungry they look. "I think we fit just right," he murmurs at last.

The door swings open and my best friend appears. "Why am I not surprised right now?"

I groan and push to my feet, uselessly trying to hide all the evidence of a make-out: hair tangled by my own head as I rolled it on the couch, smeared lipstick, rumpled clothes. I'm blushing hard, and Malcolm is clearly amused by my embarrassment. God, I must look ridiculous with my blonde hair and red face. I turn to him and point in mock warning, "And don't think you're getting a free pass, I'm hearing that story," I tell him, for Gina's sake.

"Hey, you're staying with me tonight," he says, confused.

I stand there, looking at him as Gina tugs on my hand. "Sorry," I finally say, wincing a little. "Gotta go."

On his feet, Saint lifts his jacket, and he looks at Gina as he folds it over his arm. "How about I drive her home?"

"How about 'no'?" She smirks.

"I'm Malcolm, by the way."

"I saw you at our place, remember? I've also seen your face on only every magazine and despite the fact that you're hotter in person, I'm *completely* immune. Say goodbye to Rachel now."

She takes my arm, and Malcolm says, "Do you want to go with me tonight, Rachel?"

His face is inscrutable now, but he's putting out some major waves of annoyance.

"No, sorry. I have a campout in a few days, so I really should get some rest. 'Bye," I awkwardly say as I turn to leave with his eyes on me. Oh, shit, fuck, that went so bad just now!

I run my hands over my hot cheeks before Gina drags me down one of the long tunnel halls. "Nothing happened," I mumble, in answer to the big bold question mark pasted on her forehead.

"Okay, I'm saying it," begins Gina. "Saint is absolutely bad news. Workwise, heartwise, you could not pick a worse guy than Paul except for Saint . . . and his two friend creeps. Rachel, you don't have to tell me what happened, I can already see he's totally got you pinned against the wall. You're blushing like a carrot."

"What do you mean I'm blushing like a carrot? I'm *orange*?" My eyes wide, I'm freaking out.

"Rachel, you don't know it yet but you don't stand a chance! And that dude Tahoe totally eye-fucked me right now when I hunted you at Saint's table."

"I do not blush orange, Gina!"

"I swear Tahoe totally eye-fucked me and my heart still hasn't recovered."

"Orange? It has to have been the Tunnel lights! Please tell me you meant cherry. At least cherry is a prettier shade of blush than freaking orange?"

"You're red! Okay? Relax, Saint won't know your name in a few days when he wakes up with four naked floozies."

My mouth flaps open to reply, but all I can say, as I come down from my orgasmic high, is, "If Saint's bad news, so is Tahoe, okay? I don't want him playing with you."

"I don't like any of these manwhores playing with you. I'm starting not to like this project." She seizes my shoulders and whips me around. "Tell me you don't like Saint?"

"I . . ." I don't know what to say. I don't want to hurt her, I don't want to lie, I don't even know what I'm doing, so I say, "My ovaries kind of like him." I add, "A little," when her mouth purses grimly.

"Oh no." She shakes her head wildly. "No, Rachel."

It's no use. I came in his arms at the club. I move in bed tonight and I can smell him on my skin. I can still hear him inviting me to be with him while I find my safe spot. I want to know what it's like to lie next to him without anything between us. I have a thousand questions floating in my head, and one single ache between my legs. More than anything, I want to text him and say, *I had a good time tonight.* But do I really have the courage to open up this way? Maybe if he had a different history. Maybe if he were that normal guy. Maybe if I weren't so focused on a job rather than a partner. Maybe in another life.

Monday trails on at a tortoise's pace. Wake up. Coffee. Work. Emails. Editing yesterday's draft. Helen's interrogation about what's going on. Victoria coming over with wide eyes. "It worked, didn't it? I heard Saint was seen with a platinum blonde on his lap!"

"Shh," I laugh and pull her close, and then I don't want to talk about him to her. Sometimes when I write I don't want to talk about my subject: I protect it and nurture it in my heart before I pound the keys and then it's out.

It's different with this man. I can't bear to share him at all. Not even with my friends. I don't understand why I feel like putting a bubble around us where nobody can have an opinion and nobody can take him away. Not floozies or his lifestyle, and not my friends. "I did have luck but nothing happened. You know those guys—they just flirt."

"Oh, well, flirt back harder." She winks and walks past.

Fuck. I groan and slump in my desk when Valentine walks by with much the same tune.

"Platinum blonde? People are asking on his social media. I

know of only one platinum blonde . . . so speak now, platinum blonde. In fact, give me a few tips for tonight's date."

"Valentine, you have a date? Wow, love is in the air. Boy or girl?"

"Female. I'm taking her to greasy Chinese to make sure she knows how to pig out properly. I hate having dinner with a little stick. Which is why it's so hot to dine with a man. Nothing gets me going like a healthy appetite."

I keep surfing the internet, researching.

"Did you know penguins are monogamous?" I ask.

"Yes, I was among that tribe once but have rebelled. See, I'm no longer going to be restrained by traditional dating rules, and neither should you. Oh, wait, you don't date. Do you?"

I smirk. "Just because *you* didn't change my mind doesn't mean nobody else can."

"See! You ARE dating him."

"NO! NO! Just . . . silence, please. You need to go and . . . meditate. To your desk. Shoo!"

I field questions all day, pretending that last night didn't give my little world a little too big of a shake.

17

NIGHT

This Sunday, at another neighborhood campout, I'm still thinking about the club as I scan my phone for new links about him. Strange. He's been rather socially quiet lately. There's hardly been any big party he's been linked to since that after-party he refused to allow me to attend.

I notice in the back of my mind that there have been about five guys parading in and out of the park, setting up what I think is the biggest-ass tent I've ever seen in my life. Everyone is settling into their sleeping bags, snacking on nuts and berries or marshmallows. I turn to look at the big-ass tent again and wonder what the hell is going on.

"Hey, do you know whose tent that is?" I ask the girl settled next to me, a frequent campout attendee named Rio who's organizing her stuff next to her sleeping bag.

She turns to look at the big-ass tent situated at the edge of the camping site and shrugs lightly. "I have no idea, but whoever's in that tent really wants to make a statement."

I laugh a little and turn back to my sleeping bag. The men haven't come back in like ten minutes, so I think the tent is finished.

I place my sleeping bag next to Rio's. The sun is setting, and everyone seems to be winding down. Deciding I need to tune them out and try to relax and gear up to hunt you-know-who next weekend, I take out my earplugs and listen to some music, lying down on my back and looking at the sun drift in through the leaves of the trees. Occasionally a gust of wind comes, and I feel it cool my skin and move my hair.

I breathe in deeply, enjoying the feel of grass beneath my flimsy sleeping bag. I've had it for years now. I took it to my first sleepover in seventh grade, and I've been using it at these campouts, so over the years it's lost a lot of its cushion, but I refuse to get rid of it.

Rio taps my side and I sit up for a moment, reaching out to take a marshmallow from her hand, and in my peripherals, I see a dark figure. I turn around and see Malcolm Saint getting out of his car, swinging a duffel bag over his shoulder. I feel like my heart just tripped inside my chest. I turn to look at Rio and see that everyone is glancing at Malcolm and whispering in each other's ear. Great.

Rio stares. "This is not the kind of candy I expected us to have at the campout."

I gulp and focus on chewing the stupid marshmallow in my mouth.

Malcolm makes his way over to his tent, admiring his employees' handiwork and placing his duffel bag on the ground. He scans the crowd, looking for someone, and I feel my heart stumble again. Everyone's trying really hard to act normal, but I can sense their attention is fixed on the six-foot-plus man in black slacks and a white shirt standing next to a big-ass ten-person tent. Like Rio's, their faces display open amazement as they speculate and probably start catching on to who that man is.

A young strawberry blonde stumbles over. "Saint? What are you doing here?" she asks as her chest starts to heave a little too fast.

Saint looks at her. He seems to be trying to place her when the blonde speaks again.

"Tammy!" she tells him, almost giggling and ready to explode. "Tammy from the Ice Box, remember? You were there with your friends, I was there with my friends. . . ."

"Oh, that's right," he murmurs with no inflection, and then lifts his hand in a casual goodbye. "Good to see you, Tammy."

He leaves her gaping longingly at his retreating back and heads straight—straight—toward me. Oh god. Since when did he spot me?

I faintly hear myself saying, "I'll be right back" to Rio, or maybe to myself, as I sling my bag across my chest, stand, and dust myself off. I feel several pairs of eyes follow me toward Malcolm and his big-ass tent.

I can hear the grass and leaves crunch beneath my feet as we walk toward each other. He's smiling at me, and once again, I feel myself blush a little.

"Aren't you a little out of your element, Saint?" I laugh. He's wearing his black suit with ease, those black slacks covering his long legs, and a white shirt that molds perfectly to his toned chest.

He smirks and eyes me up and down. "I was looking for you."

"How'd you know I'd be here?" I ask.

Then I remember what I said at the Tunnel. My heart kind of warms a little bit that he came looking for me tonight. *Why?*

I gesture to his tent. "Nice little house you got there."

He laughs. "House?"

"Yeah, you can fit what, like, ten people in there?"

"I was only planning on two," he says in his deep voice.

I raise my eyebrow at him. "Two?"

"Yeah." He adds, "You and me."

My breath kind of gets stuck in my throat.

"Um, I'm sleeping with Rio over by the oak." I point back to our sleeping bags.

He scrunches his brows. "Where's your tent?"

"I don't have one, my sleeping bag is all I need."

He looks at me like I'm crazy.

I laugh. "Do you always have to be the center of attention? You know everyone else is sleeping in sleeping bags just like me, right?"

"I don't care about everyone else—I care about you." He looks down at me with those killer green eyes. "So you're sleeping in my tent."

Before I can protest, he takes my hand and leads me to the tent.

"Wait, I need to get my sleeping bag."

"You don't need it, I brought one," he says over his shoulder as he continues pulling me inside the tent.

Once I'm inside, I can see this tent isn't for ten people; it's probably for like twenty. The ceiling is about seven feet tall. Or maybe a little lower, since Malcolm has to bend down a little to fit inside the tent. There's a huge sleeping bag already inside that looks more like a mattress to me.

I can't help laughing.

"What?" He's grinning at me and he looks so delicious I laugh harder.

"Nothing."

I sit down on the mattress/sleeping bag and pat the seat next to me. He sits down, his huge body warming mine just with how close he is. We're not touching, but I can feel his hand is close to mine. I can see his profile from the corner of my eyes: his strong jaw, sexy-ass lips, and spiky black lashes. He is too beautiful. I have no idea how it's even biologically possible to look like he does.

I'm left thinking about his strawberry blonde. And her long legs.

Her lips.

Her breasts.

And whether or not he slept with her.

"I bet she made you a great girlfriend," I whisper.

He looks at me, his eyes sparkling. "I don't kiss and tell."

"You just kiss."

"Exactly." God, he's teasing me again.

And I'm one big throbbing nerve of want and obsession.

I wonder. About those kisses he gives. I've read quite a bit on it, actually. His activities. Day, morning, and night, four women a day sometimes. And why not? Sexual energy courses through his veins. His body hums with it.

"Is it true you only sleep four times, tops, with a woman because your favorite number is four . . . ? "

"I eat babies, too."

"Malcolm! Serious."

"Do you waste all this energy thinking about me?"

I blink.

"Do you?"

"No," I say. "In fact, I'm super tired after just two minutes of trying to figure you out."

"Don't try to figure me out," he helpfully suggests.

I tear open a package of marshmallows. I turn around and see him lying back on his elbow, watching me curiously.

I take out a marshmallow and place it in his hand. I pop one in my mouth. "It's for eating?" I tease him. He laughs because my voice is muffled by the huge marshmallow. I laugh too and he pops the marshmallow I gave him into his mouth.

His lips. His mouth . . .

Lust slams into me like a train at full speed, and I'm suddenly trying to think of anything but how close we are.

The voices are dying down outside, and it's already dark. The wind rustles the trees and I yawn.

"You're tired?" I lie on my side and face Malcolm, who's looking down at me with a look in his eyes I can't describe as he waits for me to answer.

"Yeah . . . I think it's lights out for me." I look behind me at the sleeping bag and then back at him.

The air seems to shift and I clear my throat, stuffing another marshmallow in my mouth.

Am I supposed to put on my PJs now? Should I just get into the sleeping bag and sleep? What if he doesn't want to sleep yet?

My questions halt when Malcolm unbuttons his shirt and throws it across the tent.

The next thing my eyes see are miles of tanned, muscular chest and a tight six-pack.

He takes off his shoes but leaves his pants on. His back muscles ripple as he turns his back to me and settles into his sleeping bag. The night is hot as it is, but Malcolm Saint shirtless makes me feel like I'm in some kind of sauna.

He gestures to his sleeping bag; he wants me to join him. This realization makes my heartbeat almost triple in speed, and

I can feel my stomach start to flip with excitement. Or maybe fear. Or maybe anxiety. But I mean, what did I expect when he said he wanted the tent for both of us? I don't know. All I do know is that I feel like the next in line to ride a big-ass roller coaster, and I want to get on, I've been waiting for it for a while, but I can't seem to move. I want to stay in line a little longer. Except this big-ass roller coaster has his hands hooked behind his head and is looking at me with such a penetrating stare, I actually get an adrenaline rush.

I breathe deep and walk to my bag, untie the strap of my halter dress, and slowly slide it down my body until I'm left in my bra and panties. I reach down in my bag and put on my big cotton sleeping shirt. Malcolm is still looking at me, inviting me to come into his sleeping bag. I pad over in my bare feet, feeling the grass softly crunch underneath the tent floor.

He opens the flap of the sleeping bag. I slip in, making sure there's some distance between us, because I don't want to seem eager. I settle into the surprisingly comfortable sleeping bag, looking up at the ceiling. I can hear soft chatter outside. The crickets chirping. The wind rustling the leaves. And I can feel Malcolm's body beside me. His heat. His cologne. I don't dare look at him because I know that if I do, anything can happen. We're surrounded by a couple dozen people, but inside our little tent, our little bubble, there is just me and him. No one else. And that scares the crap out of me.

Just then I feel Malcolm shift, and his hand makes its way across my stomach, to my waist, and he draws me up against him until my back is to his chest.

Holy shit, I'm spooning him. Or he's spooning me. Holy shit.

I focus on breathing. The back of my head is tucked beneath his chin, and I can feel his chest expand with every breath. His heat flows through my cotton T-shirt, warming my stomach and back. His face is so close to mine, if I turn around my lips will touch his.

I nervously move my arm to cover his, and he turns his hand to intertwine our fingers.

All I can hear is my heart banging in my chest and my pulse ringing in my ears. Just being around him makes me lose myself. He makes me feel a thousand different things, so I snuggle a little closer to him, the daredevil that I am, telling myself there's nothing wrong with wanting a little warmth. Even though it's not that cool in here. He nuzzles my head, tightens his hold on me, and places a little kiss on the top of my head. The feeling I get when he does that is indescribable. I feel butterflies in my stomach, and my throat tightens. I want to turn around and wrap my arms around him, and I want to kiss him, because feeling his huge chest against me makes me crazy. He is enveloping me completely, holding me in his arms, his big, strong, warm arms. Being drawn against his chest, having his arm hold me against him. It's the safest I've ever felt.

I crack my eyes open, hearing voices outside. I hear movement, some laughter, and the sunlight is shining through the tent's ceiling.

The *tent's* ceiling.

Malcolm Saint's tent's ceiling.

Malcolm Saint, who's currently lying beneath me.

HOOOOLY SHIT.

My arm is thrown across his chest, and my head is settled in the crook of his shoulder.

My leg is thrown across his body, resting between his legs.

What the hell is wrong with me? Holy crap.

Second thing I notice: he feels very muscular against me.

Okay.

My heart is beating so fast I can feel it threatening to burst out of my chest and run away.

I start to unwind myself from Malcolm, and I feel him stir, tightening his arm around me. He groans a little, and I can feel him move his arm a little lower.

I try to unwind myself more, and his hand ends up splayed across my butt cheek. His hand is huge; it covers my whole butt cheek. I try to contain my panic and some other emotions boiling up in me as I manage to lie on my back. Malcolm shifts again. He drags me up against him and I gasp. The bastard is awake, isn't he?

His face is nestled between my breasts.

"Malcolm!" I shout-whisper.

He stays silent.

"Malcolm, I swear to god, someone could come in here any minute; get your face off my boobs!"

At that he laughs and picks his head up, looking at me quietly.

My breath catches in my throat. He looks gorgeous. His lazy stare, his bed hair, his body deliciously warm and holding mine. I feel something stir in the pit of my stomach. He lowers his head back down.

"Don't be mad at me," he whispers to my neck. His voice sounds even deeper in the morning. I groan inwardly because my anger vanished the moment he opened his eyes and smiled at me.

I don't answer, because I know my voice will betray me.

He looks up at me again. I frown and attempt to scowl at him, but I don't think it works that well, because he just smirks and lowers himself back to my breasts, then moves lower still.

He plants a kiss on my stomach; then he raises himself up and places another kiss on my neck.

"Are you mad at me?" he says again.

I don't even know what he asked me.

"What?" I ask.

He places a kiss on my shoulder, then takes my hand and kisses the inside of my wrist. He keeps my hand in his, his fingers playing with mine. "Are you mad at me?" he teases, brushing my hair behind my ear in a move that suddenly just fills me with longing.

"Yeah, I'm mad. I'm mad because . . . What are you doing here? I can't sleep with you."

He chuckles.

"I can't sleep with you, Saint. I won't."

His gaze goes liquid as he rubs his thumb up my arm. "Yeah, you will, Rachel," he promises.

"I won't," I promise him.

All the laughter fades from his eyes and he says nothing. He surveys me, and I can almost hear the wheels turn in his head as he figures out how to break my walls.

"Is there a man in your life?"

"No!"

"Then I don't see a problem."

"The problem is"—I jab a finger in the direction of the tent's zipper—"Tammy . . . and all your other floozies. I don't want to be one of them!"

"Then don't be one of them," he whispers in my ear.

When he offers to give me a ride home so that I can change for the office this morning, we don't even tease each other at all.

"Come here so I can kiss you," he coaxes from the bench across from mine in the back of the Rolls. I feel vulnerable and raw, like someone just opened me up and peered inside. He knows I want him, and I can tell from the look in his eyes he won't let up until he gets me. I shiver. "Rachel," he says, when we get close to my place.

"We can't keep doing this."

"Rachel, there's nothing I won't do to get you in my bed," he says, his eyes hot and hungry.

My body responds, and it takes all my effort not to leap across the car, wrap myself around him, and let him kiss me stupid like he always does.

"Thanks, Saint," I murmur as the car stops before my building.

He murmurs, "Malcolm," as I get out.

I pause and look at him. I feel like I'm kissing him again when I concede and murmur, "Malcolm."

He looks at my lips like he's definitely thinking of kissing me again. Like hearing his name in my mouth just fondled him somewhere . . . maybe his beautiful, perfect dick. Ohmigod, what am I thinking?

I turn away and hurry upstairs.

On Thursday, he asks me out to dinner.

My heart leaps and vaults—*he wants you, Rachel, he's actively pursuing you*—but my brain puts an end to that ridiculousness. I can't risk being seen by more press—my true story being discovered. I am also afraid of seeing him in any sort of dating sense again. Look what happened last time?

I tell him that I'm busy and he just texts back: OK.

I wonder if he's calm about me denying him or if he's frustrated. My own sexual frustration is so acute I beg the girls to please let's have a night out at our favorite Japanese restaurant because I need the girl therapy. Distraction. I just really need to stop thinking of him.

But it seems they both found out, through word of mouth and everyone's best friend, the internet, that Saint was at an End the Violence campout, and they can't believe he actually went looking for me after my casual mention at the Tunnel.

"Okay, so let me get this straight. This guy, a playboy who doesn't truly know you, is willing to do what Wynn and I aren't?" Gina says.

"Don't look so stumped. You're with me when I'm painting murals, you're great supporters."

"He wants to get laid—that's a powerful motivator. Wynn and I, on the other hand, want nothing from you but your friendship."

"Does he want to get laid? He's a guy who gets it whenever. He's the kind whose body just begs for it." I blush. "He's getting it somewhere."

"Get out and get drunk, have fun, and get it somewhere too, then," Gina says.

I'm sleepless and tired, groaning. "Not really up for that."

"You'll get rolling once you're a few cocktails in."

"You're worried that you like him?" asks Wynn.

"No. This isn't a relationship, I'm just worried that he's much more than a manwhore. He's pretty cool."

Wynn: "It's so nerve-wracking but exciting not to know in those heart-pounding early stages what he's thinking."

Gina: "Oh, trust me, all he's thinking of is his cock in your mouth."

"When you say you worry," Wynn says, "you mean you worry the man wants you or that you may not be as strong as you thought, strong enough to resist him?"

"I am resisting him. Otherwise that night I could've just torn his clothes off and ravaged him."

"Rache!" Wynn scowls. "Physically denying him is only making you more obsessed. Just fuck the guy and get your head straight for the article, and he'll move on, giving you plenty of fodder."

"True," I agree.

Wynn: "And you'll think clearer."

The thought of doing Malcolm is wreaking havoc in me. "It feels like danger zone to me."

"It's a fucking suicide mission. I don't like it," Gina says.

"More danger zone to keep prolonging the inevitable time when he moves in—just get it over with and get your piece written," says Wynn.

Sex with Malcolm. I'm growing obsessed with it.

That's what Gina strives for now, just sexual hookups. It's strange how circumstances that burn the people around me, like Gina, could have such a profound effect on my love life. But they have. I have been reluctant to start anything with any man my entire life.

And now I choose to want to sleep with this one?

Really?

It's like waking from a nap to find yourself dropping down into the world's deepest chasm.

I have a job to do; I wanted to do it, and I didn't plan to sleep with him to find out what makes the man tick.

My life has been all about studies, work, my mother, a great job, Gina and Wynn. With the girls? We've been friends since middle school, all through high school—we even managed to survive those college years when Wynn went away. Every Christmas and Thanksgiving and summer we'd meet up, catch up.

We all "lived" the Paul issue. He was so nice and so in love with Gina. I used to fantasize about meeting my own Paul. Paul was what Wynn and I aspired to. Until he did the Paul move, and our best friend was broken, not only brokenhearted, and we struggled to help her pull through. Wynn got over it, she still believes there are good men out there, like Emmett. I, on the other hand, developed a fear of guy love that has made me determined to avoid heartache and heartbreak at any cost. And it also, in a sense, made me avoid sex and focus on work.

Gina and I like men—but we don't want them close enough to hurt us. And we feel lucky that we know. We're in the smart girls' closet, where all the girls who never want to be brokenhearted go. Right?

True, when Emmett proves us a little wrong and Wynn comes to brunch looking flushed and excited, it's a bit of a downer. But all we need as a reminder that we're right is another tale from a guy like Paul, and our goals are reinforced. Our careers, our moms, and our friends are what matters.

Now I'm not so sure.

Now I think about Saint's anatomy all day. Maybe I chose the wrong career. I should've been a chemist. A doctor. Because I keep wondering why he has this pull on me. I keep wanting to go crazy, have my way with him, and watch him dump me and then write about it.

"Rachel's clammed up, I think a plan is forming," Gina says worriedly.

I groan and shake my head.

"Don't sleep with him, Rachel, not him," Gina murmurs.

I look at her and nod.

The thing about having such close friends like Wynn and Gina is that we are determined to fix each other's lives. So now Gina and Wynn are determined to fix mine. And if they can't, it seems they're ready to fix me up with a guy.

"Okay, so not him. I know who. He's Emmett's cousin and he's the complete package," Wynn insists. "The reason you're attracted to Saint right now—"

"Is because he's Saint," Gina groans.

"Well, true," Wynn agrees. "But you've been focused on work too long. Every extreme is bad news, even in dieting, even in sex or abstinence."

"Guys, stop. I don't want to date, okay? I want to feel secure in my career first before I let some guy take me out for a spin. . . . Look, *don't worry*," I assure them. "It's all work for me from now until I get this piece done," I vow.

I imagine his flesh against mine, him sliding inside me, his mouth on me, his moan of ecstasy, and I wish things were different for me, that I could actually have him. But this, this story, is all I can really have. Isn't it?

He's not a man to give anyone more, and I'm not the kind of woman to change all of her life for the wild dream of love. But what if for one night, one night, I let myself spend it with him?

18

SPINNING

Later that night I'm feverish, gathering more data at 12 a.m. It suddenly seems imperative that I get the exposé done as soon as possible because, despite what I assured my friends, I'm afraid I've developed somewhat of a crush.

Mooning over his pictures on the internet.

What the hell is up with that?

I stumble across another YouTube video of his father. Saint isn't in the video, but his father is ranting about his own son on television. "He's had business luck, he has a shrewd mind and his mother's inheritance, but my son has no idea of the responsibility it takes to run a billion-dollar company."

"Well, he's proved you wrong, hasn't he?" I mumble to the man.

He's a handsome man, maybe fifty-five years old. He looks nothing like Malcolm, except that he's large and virile. Malcolm got that from his father, but he got his mother's beauty and her dazzling smile.

When I research her and her death, I find out several things. Catherine H. Ulysses, one of Malcolm's assistants, the one I'm sure is in love with him, seemed to be at the funeral, standing close to a young Malcolm, which confirms that she's known him for a while. And second, I find out something surprising about his mother. Saint's mother, Juliette, was apparently big on animals, and every year made huge donations to activist groups. The day Saint saved Rosie, it was the anniversary of his mother's death—I track back in time and find out that every year since she died Saint has saved, or adopted, one animal. Every year he visits her gravesite afterward (his cars have been spotted in the cemetery parking lot yearly).

My heart tugs. I saw him that day, and maybe he was hurting the same way I do when it's the anniversary of Dad's death. I remember we dropped Saint off at M4 and his car was waiting, and I never expected that he'd be heading to the cemetery, but it makes me wish I'd known before. It makes me wish I knew what makes this man tick. I could've been with him tonight. I could've let him take me out to some fancy event and then . . . *then what, Rachel? Then do the most reckless thing you've ever done by sleeping with him, even with your most precious story on the line?*

Utterly conflicted, I keep clicking links, especially the ones about him and his parents.

Gina's chowing on cereal in her effort to get rid of the cocktail buzz she's still harboring when we get a knock on the door, and all I hear, after she goes to answer it, are the words ". . . apartment 3C . . . dead . . ."

My blood freezes in my body as I watch Gina close the door, put her hands over her face, and burst into tears.

"Gina!" I gasp.

"Miss Sheppard," she chokes out.

An image of her smiling, just the other day, with her pets outside, hits me. One second my face is dry, the next it's wet with tears. This scene, this fear, of huge, unexpected loss, has haunted me my whole life. It's been there since my father's death, even before I had reason enough to know it was there. A feeling of complete vulnerability. Of having your world always spin and never be still for a minute for you to get your bearings.

It turns out that Lindsey Sheppard, our neighbor a few floors down, was shot and killed by a group of young men driving by in a vehicle only an hour ago.

Miss Sheppard didn't make it to the hospital alive.

Gina and I are so shocked that, after crying passionately for ten minutes and hugging each other, we turn on the TV and watch the news. I snivel, she snivels, we both snivel. I call my mom and ask if she's all right. She asks if I'm all right. I lie and say that I am.

"I swear I will die happy the day I don't see all this in the news," Gina sighs wearily, grabbing the remote and switching off the TV. She flips open my laptop and settles next to me so that we can search the news online.

When the information we find is a repeat of what we watched on the news, she gives up and pads over to the kitchen.

I've got a ton of new Google alerts, which I'd set with the keywords *Malcolm Saint.* Impulsively, I click on a few and am led to a popular news and gossip blog. I scan the heading and today's date and play the video. After a fifteen-second advertisement, I see Saint's face flash onto the screen, and a slow, dull ache begins to grow in my chest as several pictures of him pop up on the video screen. He's in a black suit, black tie, his hair slicked back, walking through a throng of people. He looks untouchable and mentally elsewhere.

The clips are apparently from earlier tonight, where he was present at a business function—*and the corporate shark was remarkably alone,* says a background voice. *Speculation regarding whether he's in his first serious known involvement with a young reporter has been storming the Net. . . .*

"Maybe he was alone at the function, but I bet he's not alone now," Gina offers as she pours herself some water and promptly takes one of her sleeping pills.

Since my little crush seems to be developing into a big one, her words don't make me feel good at all. In fact, after what happened to Miss Sheppard tonight, I can't feel anything but wretched now.

"Don't gooooo," I whine, grabbing her arm as she heads to bed. "Gina, stay, I won't be able to sleep."

"Ah, you poor wee baby." She pats the top of my head and says, "Good night."

I sniffle a little more and try to remember the last time I saw Miss Sheppard. I'd been heading out, ready for my tour of the Interface building. She'd been walking her dog . . . and she'd been kind to me, as always. I feel bad for her dog, her cat. I feel bad for the entire world for being without Miss Sheppard.

Then I keep watching the news and listen to them speak of M4 venturing into pharmaceuticals.

I realize he's this sexy daredevil and I'm this safe, scared workaholic who lives with her heart on her sleeve and therefore is always vulnerable. *When you come out of your box, I'll be waiting.*

Oh, Rachel, what are you doing?

I charge to the bathroom and slip into the shower, tying my hair up so it doesn't get wet. Guilt is such a volatile thing. I always feel guilt when somebody dies like this. Guilt for not doing more; guilt for being alive. We use so many defense mechanisms to cope. Anger, denial, tears, but my mechanism has always been action. Many of the actions I've taken in my life have been taken to combat my fears and numb the pain.

I never, ever expected they would lead me to a man. Much less *this* man. I pick out my lingerie with him in mind. White, because I know he's experienced, but I'm not . . . and I want him to be careful. My dress? With him in mind. My black pumps too. Hell, I breathe right now with him in mind. And I comb my hair fast and hard until it gleams and falls behind me, and as I grab my keys from my vanity and look at my reflection in the mirror, I wonder who the sex-starved, desperate crazy person looking back at me is.

I've heard Saint has several places in Chicago, but the only one I know for certain that he's been using lately is the huge penthouse crowning the top of a billion-dollar mirrored-glass skyscraper that overlooks both Lake Michigan and Michigan Avenue. I leave a note to Gina saying *out tonight,* just in case she wakes up and worries, then I head down to the lobby and outside to a taxi.

He may still be at the fund-raiser, Rachel, I chide myself. He may be heading somewhere else after that—and not alone.

But nothing I can say is really filtering through enough to change my course as I climb into the taxi. I feel like I've been at the end of a rubber band stretched to its breaking point and now I'm flying in the air, not knowing where I'll land.

I just want to see him.

I tell myself that is all I want.

I'm not drunk.

I'm in full possession of my senses, but at the same time, I've lost them all.

From the back of the cab, I peer out at the looming highrises, the shiny windows, the bustling streets, and then, with the big ol' knot I get with anything Saint-related, the luxury high-rise where Saint is supposed to live as he gets a "bigger" place renovated comes into view.

Unease accompanies every click of my heels on the pristine floors as I cross the lobby. "Hi." I approach the concierge, wondering what Sin will do when he sees me here. "Rachel Livingston to see Mr. Saint. He's not expecting me."

He assures me not to worry as he promptly dials a number.

Judging by how quickly he's handling this, I assume this happens often.

He announces me, then instructs, "Please. Straight to the top." A staff member by the elevators slides a key in, I suppose to secure top-level elevator access, and then he hops off and sends me on my way.

Oh wow, what am I doing?

Please god, don't let him be with a floozy. . . .

Or let him be with a floozy so I can just go back home and forget I ever wanted this. . . .

Or if this is a super-bad idea then just let the elevator get stuck until I get my brain back, and I will never come back from the scare I'll get and the claustrophobia. . . .

When the elevators open straight into his apartment, I hear music. *Oh no, fuck, I didn't mean it.*

I should probably back out, but I feel an unnatural jealousy take over me. I don't back out. Instead, I force my legs to work, the minimalist yet palace-like luxury of his apartment enveloping me so that I almost feel I'm in another world.

His jacket is on the back of a long modern L-shaped couch. I try to place the song playing in the background. Classical, I've heard it before. Chopin, I think. A single wineglass sits on the coffee table, its contents drained. I wonder if he's entertaining. *Maybe God answered your prayers and he's not alone, Rachel. Maybe he's having a threesome, and the concierge thinks you're going to be the fourth.* For some reason that stings, and I really want to cry now. I'm wearing a lovely black dress but an awful cry face, and that's not a good combo. Is it? Not a way to lure a womanizer. I'm seriously contemplating leaving when he steps out of the hall, buttoning a white shirt. Holy god. He is so beautiful. He appears distracted, his hair rumpled. He's barefoot . . . and so hot. I see the open laptop on the coffee table finally—next to the wine. He was working?

Yes.

"Something wrong, Rachel?" He scans me, head to toe.

I feel beyond vulnerable for being here, all of a sudden. I'm dressed to seduce a man, to seduce *this* man. This man who makes me achy and twisty and makes my heart work.

"Are you alone? Am I interrupting?" I'm dying from nerves. I'm dying to touch him. Kiss him.

His eyes narrow to slits. "What's wrong?"

"One of my apartment-building neighbors died tonight." I rub my hands over my arms, chilled to the bone. "She was divorced. She lived with a dog and a cat, and she was nice. You know? Lonely. Lonely and nice."

He runs a hand through his hair in a sign of restlessness and drops it. "I'm sorry. Come here."

God, I want those arms. One, two, three, four, five steps later, I slide into his arms and wrap mine around his waist as he pulls me close, pressing my cheek to his chest with a hand on the back of my head.

Oh god. Since when did I become this girl? This girl needing to be coddled by the guy she can't stop thinking about? All the times I saw Wynn being hugged by her father, by her boyfriends, I really yearned for something like this. But I never knew how much until he moves his hands up and down my back in soothing motions. He held me like this the other day, at my place. But I had been too scared; I hadn't really enjoyed it until now.

I press my nose into his chest, and it smells absolutely good.

"I *am* sorry," he whispers gruffly in my ear.

He takes my face in his hands and looks truly sorry, his eyes tender and fierce. And something happens when he kisses the corner of my mouth. Almost a brotherly kiss. A feel-good, *I'm sorry, I'm here* kiss. One second my body is in sleep mode and the next it's speeding in full-operation mode, recognizing these delicious ghost kisses only he gives me. My nerves tangle in my belly, and everything is gone save for this feeling of my heart pounding, my blood just gushing through my ears. This incredible, amazing feeling where one second everything is dull and the next it's bright and fiery. One second I'm scared, the next I feel like I can do anything. Scream. Leap. *Kiss him.*

"Do you still want to have sex with me?" I whisper, tangling my fingers in a handful of his shirt.

His eyebrows pull low. "Right now? You've got to be kidding me," he murmurs.

I grit my teeth, grab a fancy-looking suede pillow from the couch, and hit his arm as he steps back. "Do you?" I cry.

His jaw is absolute granite as he stalks to the corner of his apartment and presses some sort of alarm code at a receiver on the wall. Then he grabs a cordless phone, punches two numbers, and he whispers, "No visitors."

He hangs up, and with purposeful strides heads back to me.

"I'm a bastard, Rachel, but I'm not the bastard who's taking advantage of you tonight."

"You're *not* taking advantage. You are so not taking advantage."

"Yes, I am. Look at you. Look at your face, Rachel. If you only saw yourself the way I see you right now, the last thing you need is a fuck." He laughs at himself, curses under his breath, then gathers me in his arms and turns my face up to his. Our noses bump, and I gasp from the feel of his lips so close.

"Saint," I whisper, grabbing his jaw. "Please."

"Tell me why you came tonight."

"You know why."

"For sex?" he asks in a rough voice, rubbing his thumb along my cheek.

I swallow and press my face back to his chest. "Why don't you do something?" I moan.

His arms feel amazing.

"You're as close to a god as we have in this town," I whisper. "So many people wake up one day to find their lives will forever be changed, that they'll live trying to fill up this emptiness. . . . You have all this power—you can *do* something. Talk about it. Bring it to people's attention?"

He's quiet. Then he takes my hand.

"Come here." We head down a hall past many doors, and then walk into a huge modern bedroom done mostly in dark woods and light fabrics. "Get comfortable."

He hands me a men's shirt from his closet and disappears into a spa-size bathroom, rolling an oversize mahogany pocket door closed behind him. My heart aches as I grip the shirt and impulsively smell it. I hear the shower water, and I wish I had the balls to just strip naked, walk in there, and join him.

Instead, after smelling his shirt to my heart's content, I remove my dress and briefly wonder if I should remove my underwear. I keep it on, which I'm glad of seconds later, because nothing prepares me for the intimacy and panty-wetting sensation of slipping on his shirt.

I feel a strange tingling awareness when it envelops me. I hadn't realized how much I missed his damn shirt. A part of me still hoping I can change his mind, I try to run my hands down my hair, wipe my tears, and slide prettily into his bed. His mattress is huge, the kind that feels like heaven beneath you.

When Malcolm steps out of the shower, my stomach's gnarling with all kinds of warmth and need. He's in slacks and bare-chested. His hair is wet, and he's barefoot as he lowers himself and stretches out on the bed beside me. I press up to him, closer. The scent of his soap reaches me as he gathers me even more tightly to him. His skin has a scent and I'm addicted, pressing my nose to it. Suddenly I want to make him breathless and groan, feel his big body against me, feel him quiver for me.

He's in bed with me.

God, it's like a dream come true. All these nights dreaming. I tip my head back.

He regards me quietly, his lips quirked. "Livingston, if you could read my mind, you would start feeling really shy around me."

No. He can't possibly know what I want. How crazy I feel. How much I want him. How I can't stop thinking about him. But the intensity in his eyes mystifies me, and the air crackles with so much desire, it's hard to lie here and do nothing but look at him and want him and feel crazed with desire for him. He doesn't move closer, but he doesn't move away, he keeps me in the bestest embrace that's ever been around me. His lips are here, so very near, two inches from my mouth, as he studies me with an expression of utter determination.

"So tell me about these plans of yours," he says, and though his voice is low with desire, I can hear the sincerity in his tone as well.

"We don't have to talk, we can go for the other option," I whisper. But when he only smiles ruefully down at me, I sigh and snuggle back against his chest. "I've never in my life managed to feel safe somehow. But you're not afraid of movement, you always keep moving. . . ."

Silence.

"Why?" I ask pensively. "Why are you always after something?"

He chuckles. "I don't know. Because I want to. I want everything."

"Even women?"

He doesn't flinch, answers with a soft press of his lips against my temple that makes me melt. "Sometimes women."

Jealousy sneaks into my guts, but I try not to let it stay there. "You're always surrounded, Malcolm, by so many people. I'm surprised I found you alone tonight."

He hesitates. Again, his lips graze my temple. He shifts his body so that I'm almost spread out on top of him, my bare leg folded over one of his black-clad thighs, his hand splaying over my back—over his shirt I'm wearing. "The company I've been keeping doesn't seem to satisfy me anymore," he whispers in my ear.

If I keep turning into the consistency of honey like this, I don't even know if there'll be anything left by morning. Brushing my lips over his tiny brown nipple, I murmur, "Why do you surround yourself with so many people?"

"Because of the meningitis. Remember my father couldn't stand that I got sick? At five, I was a kid in the hospital with meningitis. My mother stopped by for an hour every day before her tennis classes. The days went by so damn slow. So damn slow that I would look at the clock and one minute would trickle by. Then another. I waited for the last of my IV to drain so someone would come in and change it."

He felt lonely. In a private room. Alone. Isolated.

I look at him, and he's big and powerful. But still, there is always the sense of him being surrounded but alone.

Squeezing my eyes shut, I lick his nipple, suck it, kiss it, and when I feel him tense and lift his hand to my hair—ready to pull me back to stop me—I ease back, then gaze up at him with a fierce ache in my gut.

"With Stop the Violence, I sometimes visit family members of the victims, and some of them are so alone. People don't realize that even if they don't have money to donate, so many of us just want company."

Another rueful smile, but there's nothing rueful about the raw desire on his face as he looks at me. "Come here, Rachel." He pulls me back to his chest, where he caresses a hand down my hair and whispers against my temple. "I'm very sorry about your neighbor."

My brain is muddled with his nearness, his unique aroma of male and soap and his shampoo and cologne and aftershave. It's such a powerful combo, an aphrodisiac to my senses. I close my eyes and stroke my fingers over his chest—just a little. I don't mean to be devious about it, but I can't stop touching his skin and his muscles; I can't stop my heart from beating fast, my chest from feeling knotted over what he just told me.

Want.

I want to run my fingers over the stubble on his jaw. I want to press my lips to the top bow and the bottom curve of his lips. I want, want, want.

Want is such a short word, and yet it can encompass so many infinite things.

Saint is momentum. Movement. He's a man who's always moving forward, pushing for more.

He will never stand still until he owns the world, and I just want to find my place in it.

It couldn't be more wrong.

He's a womanizer. No one woman will ever appease whatever thirst he has for more and more and more.

Love is for romantics; I'm a journalist.

Still, I lie in a man's bed for the first time in my life and can't help but want . . . for a night to be someone else.

19

MORNING

W_e wake up, his hair bed-mussed, his face fully rested, a scratchy beard on his jaw. He was watching me, and I feel myself blush because I slept so well. I feel loose and relaxed. "Hey."

He touches me. And I edge closer and move my head closer to his hand. It's a really tender gesture, and I worry I'm starting to crave them.

His shirt still hugs my body—the feel of the fabric brushing against my skin beneath, the same fabric that touches his bare torso too, warms me to my toes. It's a struggle to hold my reactions under control. I'm in bed with him, my hair falling past my shoulders, our bodies only partly dressed, our stares equally restless and ravenous. All the ice inside his eyes is gone, replaced by a thermal heat that causes a pooling of volcanic matter inside me.

"I'll get breakfast for us," I murmur.

I head to his kitchen in his shirt and, after a bit of fumbling, I get his fancy coffeemaker to work. Then I make some toast.

He comes out fully dressed in slacks and a white shirt and hangs his jacket on the back of a chair. His hair gleams from his shower, wet, dark, slicked back from his smooth forehead, his features sharp and tan.

There's intimacy between us as I curl up on the chair and have breakfast. Saint drops down and reads the news on his iPad. I don't want to take his shirt off. I miss having it in my closet. I never realized how much I want it. "Is it okay if I take your shirt? I'll dry-clean it and bring it back . . ."

"Don't bring it back." He sets his iPad aside. Leans forward, his business shirt all over his muscles the way I want to be. Saint spreads his large palm over my cheek as he pushes my hair aside and kisses me with painstaking gentleness. "Rachel."

That's all he says. That one last word sounds frustrated, aroused, annoyed, confused—almost pained. Before I can get him to get into the kiss, Malcolm takes my face between his large hands and looks at me with ice-green eyes that carve into my soul. "I'm not the guy anyone comes to for comfort, Rachel. But I like that you came to me."

I realize that he looks rawer this morning, on edge, his eyes not shuttered or icy like usual. He looks . . . like he's burning on the inside. I swallow the strawberry jam and lick the corner of my lip, finally realizing how much last night must've tested him.

"You didn't sleep, did you?" I whisper.

He brings me closer to him, his breath hot against the back of my ear as he lowers me to his lap. It feels so good, and at the same time I can't stop shaking.

"I haven't had anyone in bed with me for a while. It's harder for anyone to hit my engage buttons. It's because of you." I can't help but notice how heavy his lids seem to have become. I lick my lips, anxious.

His attention drops to where my breasts press into his chest, and my body homes in on how good this contact feels, how oversensitized the tips of my nipples are.

"Saint . . ." I trail off.

He cups the back of my head; then he silences me by pressing his mouth to mine and sweeps his tongue into my mouth.

"I'm obsessed with you," he says.

He tastes of toothpaste and coffee as he teases my lips apart, one of his hands planted on the back of my neck. My hands seem to get away from me, and before I know it, they're caressing his hair. "Saint," I moan, pushing my breasts upward.

He groans, pulls me over and around him, adjusting my body over his in a straddle position, his hands on my ass.

I'm aware of the heady friction of our clothes as I let him adjust my body so that we're both fitted so right; if our clothes weren't between us, he'd be inside me.

And that's the way he kisses me for a long while. A piercing need floods me, the kind of longing I've never known before. He opens my mouth with a firm parting of his lips; then he tastes me, his tongue relentless against mine, pushing hungrily over and around. The heat and seductive dampness of his kiss make me quake for more, every stroke thrusting me deeper and deeper into a whirlwind that revolves and focuses entirely on him, Malcolm Saint, the one who makes my heart race, my life spin faster and faster, my every waking thought now centered on what he does, who he's with, what he likes, who he is. . . .

He doesn't break the kiss as he keeps me on his lap, all while his greedy mouth keeping mine attached to his.

I straddle him better, shifting on top of him, seeking to bring the biggest, most delicious hardness I've ever felt as close to me as I can; he's so big and thick, I almost jump from shock but instead I rock against it, wanting it. Needing it. A pained groan rumbles up from his chest as he brings me down by the hips, rocking me harder against his hard lap, his breathing rough and uneven in my ear.

"Come back tonight. I'll send someone to pick you up after work. We can grab some dinner. . . ."

"No! No dinner."

"Why not dinner?"

Because I can't bear to be online like one of your floozies. I press my hands against the smoothly shaven flesh and hard bone of his jaw and whisper in his ear, horny as fuck. "Because you know what I want," I breathe. It presses between my legs. It looks at me. It's touching me. It smells good, tastes good. "Because," I say, "I want *you.*"

20

TONIGHT . . .

I'm at my desk, editing, when a flower arrangement almost larger than the guy carrying it stops by my chair. "For you," the guy says from behind the forest of orchids.

Shock freezes me for a second. I glance around, narrow-eyed. Did somebody in the office decide to play a prank on me? They're all typing, but some are glancing curiously my way.

Then I realize the poor guy is about to pass out from exhaustion. I scramble to clear a little space for the vase and let him set it down. Then I stare at the most wild arrangement of orchids you can imagine. I pluck the card nestled in between all those white and purple beauties, and my heart quivers so hard I need to sit down.

IT DIDN'T SEEM RIGHT FOR YOU TO SPEND ANOTHER
DAY WITHOUT THE LUXURY OF A GIFT FROM A MAN
WHO THINKS OF YOU.

M.S.

I shake my head and put the card down. Sandy, one of my work colleagues, stops by to see them. "Wow. A man after Rachel's heart!"

Valentine peers into my cubicle. "Trust me, he's aiming lower."

Victoria and Helen want to know how it's going. "I've got so many folders," I tell them, hedging but trying not to appear that I am.

I tell myself that the time I spend with him tonight will be just mine. Just mine and his.

I'm stealing it, and this makes me a complete sinner, but I'm aching to Sin. Throbbing.

Thank you, I text him.

Thank me in person tonight

He knows; we both know what's going to happen. I can't wait for it to happen. I'm anxious for the day to end, can't eat or think without him present in every thought in my head.

Everyone in the office seems to have Saint on their mind; they can't stop discussing how fresh and exotic the explosive combination of flowers is, how perfectly they're arranged, how much they must have cost.

Victoria comes to peer into my cubicle and tries to open the card. I snatch it away and quickly tuck it into my bag.

"Wow. Protective much?" Her eyebrows furrow, but then she laughs lightly and strokes the petals of a small fuchsia orchid with her fingertips and smiles. "Best quality."

"I'm busy, Vicky," I sigh.

"You didn't look busy." She crosses her arms and leans her hip on the edge of my desk. "You were staring off into space. Into the space of *these* flowers." She happily points at them.

"Did you need anything?" I ask.

"Yes. Tell me. Does Saint usually send flowers to the women he seduces?" She taps the corner of her mouth and pretends to think. "Hmm. I'd never heard that before. What's the secret?" She smiles in mischief. "You're playing him well and good, aren't you?"

I think of how seduced I feel. How much I ache. His kiss. His touch. How I can't sleep. How I can't breathe. How I can't go on without feeling him inside me at least once. And I can't help but feel like the one being played expertly could be me. . . .

I'm so in over my head, I'm drowning in air.

But I stand and lightly brush her away by pulling out the files under her bum, and say, "Trade secrets. Now scoot, you're breathing my fresh, flowery air. Go get your own flowers."

When she leaves, I look at mine. Majestic and unapologetic, they take up all of my oxygen in a way I love, and I swear to myself I'm going to look just as good and smell just as good for him tonight.

I doll up for him that night. Pink lace undies with a little bow at the top, the same bow in the middle of my front-clasped lace bra. I slip on an A-line skirt that twirls a little when I walk, and a slinky spaghetti-strap ivory-colored top that lets him see the pink strap of my bra peeking out from underneath. It screams *I want you* in the most blatant way I know how to say it.

He texts me that he's outside my building.

Gina isn't back from work, so I leave a note like the kind I leave when I'm camping out with Stop the Violence, saying: *Sleeping out tonight. XOXO R*

Both an eternity and a heartbeat later, I climb into the back of the Rolls and see him. Did he dress up for me too? He's so handsome in a black button-down shirt and black dress slacks that my breath can't seem to go past my throat. His hair looks wet from a recent shower, the top button of his shirt undone and the cuffs rolled to his elbows. The glimpse of his golden body under his clothes makes my heart beat more rapidly. The privacy glass is in place, and he whispers, as if for my benefit, "He can't hear or see us." I didn't know I was so desperate, but when he reaches out and pulls my body closer to his and slides his hand under my top, to the bare skin of my back, I wedge a little closer.

Another corner kiss.

I shiver.

He grazes the second corner now, his lips warm but firm.

I slide my hand up his hard thigh, wanting to know he's hard, not certain if I have the courage to let my hand wander higher. It feels so hot, his skin under his clothes. His eyes are so green and so dark.

"Where are we going?" I whisper.

"My place," he murmurs. He brushes my lips with his and looks at them, then edges back so he can look at me completely.

I start to put a little distance between us, trying to get myself under control.

"Come here, I want you close to me."

He slides his hand around my waist, and with a small press of his fingers on my ribs brings me closer. Heat bubbles in my veins as I press my lips to his thick throat. He lets me. I rub my fingers up his shirt and he slips his hand under my top.

We shift so that I'm straddling his thigh.

I lick between his lips.

He drags me over his lap so his erection is right between my legs. "I'm so hot for you," he rasps.

Pleasure ripples through me when I feel the hard erection beneath me. I wanted to know? Now I know. He's pulsing. Huge and perfect, hard as steel, his need a living thing biting between my thighs. In contrast, his lips are soft and brushing feather-like against the edges of mine, incredibly gentle. "I want to taste you here, right here. To take you all night. My god, you're ravishing," he whispers, drinking me in with his eyes and savoring me with his hands.

My responses are ungoverned. Unplanned. I nibble my lip, aching.

We share a stare—eyes, lips, eyes, lips, lips. Lips. He ducks his head, and the idea of not tasting him is suddenly intolerable. We kiss. Just lips first. A graze, a press, then easing back, breathing hard.

He trails his hand down my back. "How do you want it? Hard? Soft?" He looks down at me like I'm some goddess.

"Hard. No. Soft. Soft, then hard."

I'm so excited and nervous.

He eats me with his eyes as he pours wine for us, and we drink and look at each other, and when I set my cup aside, he does the same and pulls me close to him so he can tease my lips apart with his mouth and taste the delicious red wine I just sipped. He smiles when we arrive at his apartment building. We head into the lobby, and I feel the knowing glances come at us from every corner.

Saint curls his hand around my arm and tugs me into the elevators.

"How many women do you bring here?" I ask. He gathers so much attention. I can't imagine ever getting accustomed to that.

"I haven't brought one in a while," he admits as the doors close and we ride alone to the top. "Since I saw you."

I laugh. "You don't have to say that."

"Why would I be lying right now?" He tugs me closer to his hard lines, my breasts aching as they press against his chest. "You're here, aren't you?" He runs a hand down my hair, and suddenly I feel so precious under those twinkling, knowing eyes. "You've got every intention of letting me do anything I want with you," he whispers in my ear.

"You really haven't brought anyone?"

I can't seem to make my voice rise above a whisper. My body feels so tense with wanting, it's an effort to stand here and not let my fingers and tongue have their expedition on his body. God, my attraction to him has nothing to do with reason. *Nothing.*

He shakes his head, his gaze intimate on my face as he basically admits to being celibate for what has to be a record time. I'm so undone by the thought, I drop my lashes and gaze with sudden shyness at his throat.

"What about the after-party I couldn't go to? You got a show from . . . those girls?" I quietly ask him, stroking one of his shirt buttons with a fingertip. Why does he make me so shy? I'm afraid he'll see that I'm jealous, but I have to ask.

It feels like this elevator is our own cocoon and nothing can come between us right now, nothing in the world outside this perfect space.

His throat: it's so masculine. I watch the thick tendons and his Adam's apple move as he answers now, his voice warm, his breath moving the hairs along my temple. "The Ice Box that night was a way of me distracting myself—I had every intention of fooling around. But you appeared, the very thing I wanted to distract myself from, and I couldn't go through with having anyone else after the way you looked that night."

The elevator stops at the penthouse, and I blush as he takes my hand and leads me in, my brain almost flooded with pleasure from what he just said.

He called his friends when he was riding in the car with me on our second interview. He was attracted to me then, while I'd been fascinated with the water he'd drunk, almost wanting to drink from the bottle he'd left behind—not even understanding what was happening to me.

Saint would've seen me for another interview—I would've made sure of that—but I'd have never known whether, while I lay wanting at night, he went and buried his desire for me between another woman's legs.

I'm glad to know; he didn't need to tell me this, and yet he did.

"Do you do that often?" I whisper. "Take just any woman in exchange for the one you want?"

He lets his head fall back and shouts with laughter, squeezing my hand. "Rachel, I never settle . . . not in business, not in pleasure. You were going to be the exception because you were a reporter. I never mix business and pleasure."

"I ended up being that exception. To not mixing business with pleasure," I say, almost to myself, flushing again when I think of the way I've totally mixed things too. I step away for a moment and stare out his massive windows at Chicago, admiring the thousand tiny, flickering lights that awaken in the city after sunset. "Your views are incredible. You have a completely different view of the world . . . both from your office and from here."

"I like my view right now." He speaks from behind me, and I inhale sharply and savor the butterflies in my stomach, the melty sensation in my knees. His voice is like tree bark now, raspy, firm and steady underneath, firmly rooted. When his tongue plays with my earlobe, I feel weightless, leaning back against him.

I part my lips just to breathe, noticing the large erection swelling prominently against the small of my back. Oh, how I want that. I want that so much. He turns my face to him. He slides a hand to cup my breast.

"I'm so ready, we can skip the foreplay," I breathe.

I frown a little when he stills his hand. Um, not the reaction I was going for. I twist my neck a little.

His lips curl, a glint of mischief entering his gaze. "I'm taking my time, Rachel."

Oh no. More foreplay? How wet does he want me to get? I'm so swollen I'm afraid nothing could go in right now. "Saint, don't be a dick! I want you—"

"I want you too." He kisses the corner of my mouth; then he heads to a huge black granite bar and brings us each a glass of wine.

He sits down on the couch and looks at me. It's too easy for me to lose myself in the way he looks at me. Too easy to do anything else but want. Want, want, want.

"Come here." He offers me a glass. "I want to know if you liked my gift."

"I drank enough in the car. Didn't you?"

He sips calmly.

I frown.

Suddenly I want to just toss his cat-and-mouse game right back at him and go home, but something in his expression stops me. It's so male. So completely concentrated. Somehow it makes me wetter. Whatever it is I see there, the energy and power of a male establishing domination over a female, it pulls at me harder than my pride can. I've never had a relationship. I've never been attracted to a man as infuriating, impossible, and beyond hot as him.

I would physically fight a woman right now, naked and in mud, for the rights to him tonight.

So I tug my top down my arms and let it fall on the floor, barely suppressing the urge to cover myself when he has his first full look of me. Oh, fuck, did I just strip like a hooker? Before Saint? I did.

His voice is thick. "If you're going to do that, do a little dance at least."

"Fuck you," I murmur.

"I'd rather you do it."

I open my eyes, and he's sipping his wine, devouring me with a small smile. He's so virile, testosterone pulses around us. I want to rip his shirt off. God, I want to be reckless with him, wild with him. Somehow, within that recklessness, he gives me a measure of safety.

"In case you missed it, I'm willing to have sex with you," I tell him, flat-out pushing my shyness aside.

He laughs softly, slowly setting the wine aside.

I start for him in anger. "Saint! I hate you! I am throwing myself at you here! At least fucking catch—"

He yanks me down on him and presses his mouth to mine. "Shh. I think I like you mad." Then he sweeps his tongue into my mouth. He pulls me over him, adjusting me with his hands on my ass. He sucks on my tongue, and the low sound he makes along with his greedy sucks give me the most exhilarating, delicious sensations I've ever felt.

"You do want me," I breathe.

He lifts me up in his arms as if I weigh nothing, and I hang on with my limbs around him as he carries me to his room. He lowers me down on the bed and I sink into all that softness. Then he edges back, his breathing as ragged as mine. His eyes are green lava. All the pent-up desire of the past weeks is about to explode inside me.

"Malcolm," I beg as I pull open his shirt and pop his buttons free. He stands at the edge of the bed and lets me get on my knees and push it off his chest. Then he quickly shrugs it off his shoulders and lets it fall while I run my fingers up the grooves of his abs, his flat chest, pressing my lips wherever they fall. I manage to free his belt and throw it aside too. He pushes my hair behind my forehead, and I ease back on the bed, locking my hands on his nape so that he has no choice but to follow me down. He sweeps his head down and his lips are hot, tasting my mouth as he slides his hand up the side of my body. His mouth goes downward as his hands go upward.

He nips at my breasts and uses one hand to unhook my bra, his breath hot on my skin and his tongue wet and warm.

"God, you did that with one hand?" I gasp.

I feel his smile against my skin as he reaches between us and rubs one nipple with the pad of his thumb. And then his smile is gone and so is mine, our breathing starting to change as the air between us heats up.

My head rolls a little on the bed as he licks one nipple and then the other, waves and waves of pleasure rolling through me.

"Dibs," he says as he runs his tongue down my navel. Its soft, wet strokes tickle me as it goes into my belly button. I laugh a little, then moan when he goes higher to lick my nipple again. Then he's tugging my panties down my legs. His eyes go even darker when he pushes my thighs apart and visually drinks in my wet folds. I stay there, memorizing the raw need on his face as he takes me in, my breasts heaving, my pussy swollen, my hair spread behind me.

"Relax," he says when I try to close my legs as he slides his hand up my thigh. "Relax," he says again as he pushes his middle finger inside me. It feels so good I almost leap off the bed, but instead I arch and let a moan of ecstasy escape me.

"Don't be shy with me, I want to look at you. I want to hear you let go," he murmurs huskily in my ear as he rubs his finger inside me and then sucks one nipple into his mouth. Pleasure shivers through me.

He smiles, coos down at me, and caresses my pussy with his middle finger once more. Slick sounds mingle with my breaths as he eases his finger into me. "So beautiful, I can't wait to be in here."

He rubs little circles over my clitoris with the pad of his thumb, and my hips start rocking up to his touch.

Catching my lower lip with my top teeth, I look at the bulge under his slacks. I want it so bad, in my hands, inside me, he's so beautiful. I want to go up on my knees and pull him out, see and touch him, lean and kiss the tip, then open my mouth, taking everything I can, the whole shaft. I want him to groan, I want him to never forget me.

But the arousal Saint stokes in me is so powerful, I'm nearly paralyzed in sensations, shivering.

His eyes are a green no living plant can compete with. He kisses my breasts, suckles me, sucks me. He pets and rubs my clit, the pleasure out of this world. I come quickly on his fingers. He holds me in his hand. "God, look at you go off for me," he rasps. "You're beautiful—do you know how beautiful you are?"

"I feel beautiful right now."

When he reaches for his slacks, I whisper something

encouraging like "please"—god, I'm so unoriginal. But I can't think. I'm throbbing with need, desperate for him to fill me.

The frustration of all these nights and days, the knowledge that this is only a stolen moment, temporary, only makes me ache for it more.

He tugs the zipper of his slacks downward, and I'm in complete museum-quality silence. He looks like he works out every day of the week, his chest ripped, tanned, gloriously defined and perfectly shaped, muscles rippling with every yank. A sound of need leaves me as he pulls down his slacks and I get to see him. A storm of desire racks me as he comes closer. His cock is bigger than anything I imagined. I lick my lips, anxious, my eyes running up his length, up to the swollen head and the glistening drop of semen at the tip.

I can't . . . I can't wait. I want every inch of that inside me. Every inch of him.

He smiles when he notices my blush and leans over me, caressing my pussy. His fingers quicken, and then he replaces his finger with his thumb, the pad rolling my clit in little circles while he tastes my mouth. I'm galloping to the brink again.

"You're so responsive, Rachel, you get wet with a look, soaked before I get to touch." He slowly wedges himself between my thighs.

I claw at his arms. "Saint," I moan breathlessly, rocking my hips as he opens a condom packet and sheathes himself.

He curls his fingers around my waist and pins my hips down, pushing the first few inches of his cock inside me. I yell, and he holds me pinned, watching me as he plows inside a few more inches. Ecstasy sweeps through me. I rock my hips in my greed to get more of him inside me, pulsing. He flexes his hips, moving his cock in deeper. I lock my ankles together at the small of his back, clasping him to me. Tightness. Fullness. He pulses inside me. I clench my fingers in his hair, wanting more, afraid of more, and he makes a sound that rumbles in his chest and that I can actually feel against my breasts. In my ear: "Can you breathe now?" he husks.

A sound tears out of both of us as he immediately withdraws, prolonging the moment, watching me with those burning green eyes—then he thrusts all the way in, our stomachs slapping, our bodies arching. A sound rumbles up his chest, low and deep. There's this hunger. This need to feel him, connect to him. There's nothing else. Only us moving. The sounds of the sheets rustling beneath us. Our breaths. Our mouths as we suck, taste—lips, nipples, skin.

"A little. Oh god, Saint."

With every thrust I feel so full, my spine arches, my nails claw at the taut skin and muscle at his shoulders.

I'm between screams and pleas, laughter and tears. I don't know what to think or say or do. It feels like a dream, or a nightmare. Powerful . . . his pull to me is undeniable. I'm scared out of my mind and at the same time I'm helpless to resist. I want more. I bite his neck. I claw at his back. *Saint, Saint, Saint,* I cry, thinking incoherently that nothing is enough, nothing until I get his every secret, every name of his lovers, his fears, his dreams, his heart, until he comes for me, in me.

My breasts bob between us, his body powerful and more precise as he prolongs every thrust. "And now?" Making me nod as he takes me higher and higher. His muscles bulge. His head ducks and he tastes the tips of my breasts again, tugging with his teeth, smoothing with his tongue.

The brief teasing we've enjoyed, the little playful flirting and foreplay, those were tentative questions, born of curiosity on both our parts. This is an avalanche of ravaging desire. He thrusts again, his mouth on mine, his body relentless, neither of us letting the other breathe, or think, or stop. I won't last another minute. *How can I have gone years without this?*

"And now, Rachel?" he growls through his harsh breaths.

Arching upward, I sink my nails into the back of his neck. "Please, Saint," I moan out.

He rubs my clitoris a little bit with the pad of his thumb, and my eyes shut in bliss as my orgasm thunders through me. My skin melts; I fly away, ecstasy ripping through me. I clutch myself to him and feel him groan in my hair as he comes, his body tensing and flexing powerfully against me.

After a few minutes of lying together, I'm obsessed. I'm addicted. I'm bewildered. I want to know how many girls he's made out with. I want to rank as one of the best. I want to do it again. I want to touch his body. I want to let him do whatever he wants with mine. I want to stop breathing forever. "What do you like? Blow jobs? Making out . . . ? " I whisper into his neck. "Teach me, Saint."

"You know what I like?" he whispers huskily in my ear. "I'll show you what I'd like to do right now."

He's a beautiful man, with a beautiful, muscled ass that makes my mouth water as he disappears into his spa-like bathroom. I sit up on the bed, studying his bedroom. I hadn't really been paying attention before. It's pretty minimalist—bare. Almost emotionless. Almost icy, like his eyes.

There are no photographs, not even of his mom or of his buddies. But there are pictures of race cars all over the room, old vintage Ferraris. I suppose to a guy who grows up with more toys than people, the toys become important somehow.

"You should get some sort of fancy fur-like coverlet for this bed," I say, loud enough that he can hear me in the bathroom, I hope, shivering as I tug the sheet to my breasts. *Things that make love to you.*

Suddenly I look at him at the threshold and he just looks like a man who needs to be made love to often. Not because he's sexy, because now that he's made love to me, his energy is calmer, more subdued.

I like that lazy, half-lidded look he wears when he comes back out of the bathroom naked and grins when he sees me in bed with my hair falling down my shoulders and the rest of me pretty much naked under the covers.

"You felt good, Rachel," he says, his eyes—*god, my heart*—his eyes look more thirsty than anything I've ever, ever seen.

I blush completely.

"I'd bet anything that you taste just as good too," he says.

Oh, fuck, he doesn't really mean . . .

He's looking at my legs. I'm starting to melt under the sheets. His pupils are dark and liquid with a strange mix of tenderness and need, and his cock is . . . oh. "I . . . wouldn't know, I'm not into being given . . . you know."

He raises an eyebrow as he ventures forward, back to bed. Okay, I don't want him to kick me out or anything, so I ease out from under the sheets, crawl down to the floor to get my panties, and slip them on as I nervously explain, "Not sure what it is about it, but I just couldn't ever do it. I feel too exposed."

He stops before me when I stand up, only to graze his thumb over my panties, up, down, around. "It's not much different than me touching you like this. Except my tongue caresses you."

"Why do you want it? Why do men like it?"

He chuckles and guides me back down on the bed. "You won't need to ask me that when I'm through." He tugs my panties down my legs, and I'm already so nervous about what I can tell he wants to do my lungs have already started to overwork.

"Promise to stop if I ask you to."

"You won't," he assures, caressing a hand up the inside of my thigh.

"Promise."

"Don't make me promise."

"Why?"

"Because I've broken every promise I've ever made, and promising will only make me want to break yours."

"Why do you break your promises?"

"Because I can. Part your legs." He urges my knees apart. I'm squirming inside from nerves and anticipation. He leans between my legs and takes my thighs gently in his hands, parting them. He licks his lips when he looks at me, and I don't think he realizes he's savoring me like that.

"Oh no!" I laugh when he starts to lower his head. I clench my legs and stop him by grabbing a fistful of sooty black hair. "It's too intimate! I can't."

He trails a hand down my curves, his eyes glimmering, but not with a smile, with challenge. "Let me taste you," he says, husky and hot.

I go quiet and melt as his lips press to my stomach, my navel, lower.

"Malcolm." I protest at first, holding my body tense on the bed.

His first lick I tense up, my hands in his hair ready to stop him. "What if I don't taste good?" I breathe.

He runs the tip of his tongue over my clit and dips it inside, to the complete massacre of my senses. "Mmm. You do." His hand smooths over my navel. He licks me slowly, savoring. I peer between my legs and see his eyes are closed, his lashes two half-moons. I start relaxing and let my fingers wander up the bulging muscles of his back, then I moan softly when he tongues there, harder, as if it were my mouth.

"You're very good at this," I choke. Suddenly I can barely formulate an audible word, much less several.

He caresses his fingers up the inside of my thigh and rubs my clit under the pad of his thumb as he shushes me and tells me to stop talking. The ceiling blurs and I lick my lips, panting as the pleasure escalates. I grab the comforter and hang on as I come and twist.

Wow.

I am deliciously numb.

I'm still panting while he's still kissing me there. Instead of coming up fast, he then works his way up my sex, up to my belly button, between my breasts. By the time he puts on a condom and expertly thrusts inside me, his body made for this, to take me like this, make me quake like this, I'm a big ol' quivering mess. A big ol' quivering mess who's delighted that, as he holds me to his body, he says the dirtiest, hottest things to me.

I've got to go.

Saint looks so delectable in bed as I gather my clothes that I almost can't bear to look back when I'm finally dressed and at the door. Whatever just happened here, I don't think either of us wants to face it. Especially not him. He once told me he didn't do sleepovers . . . and though I slept with him before, this was so different, I couldn't take it if he had regrets because . . . I don't.

I sensed him put up a huge wall as soon as he was done coming. He roared out my name, hard and deep, like a war cry that made me explode on the spot. We were both mute afterward. When he came back to bed after getting rid of the condom, he didn't touch me as he doodled on his phone.

I quietly start dressing, eager to go to my bed, where I can process this better. *Or try to forget.* He just crosses his arms behind his head and stares back at me, and I hear him call his driver to pick me up at the door.

"'Bye, Saint."

I see him nod and hear him murmur, "Let me know when you get home, Rachel" as I head to the elevator.

"I will," I murmur.

And once in my bedroom, I text.

I'm home

I can still taste you

I smile and slide into my bed, groaning into my pillow, thinking of that big, hard, beautiful part of him. *"I want to taste you too."*

21

AFFAIR

Facebook wall:

Saint, saw those pics of you with a new chick on *The Toy*. Got bets going on if she's a weekend-deal?

Twitter:

@MalcolmSaint hey I'm not sure you lost my number? It's Deenah from the Ice Box—call me

Please follow me @MalcolmSaint!

Instagram:

Who's the chick on *The Toy*, Saint? She the flavor of the hour?

After scanning Sin's Twitter feed, I toss my phone aside, turning around in bed, wanting him again. Pale morning breaks overhead. It steals in through my blinds and falls on my second pillow. I imagine him lying on it, the sheets draped low on his hips. I'm here, close, so I can tuck my face into the crook of his neck like I did yesterday.

Yeah, like he'll ever let a woman see him like that.

It doesn't matter, it probably won't happen again. Remember that he ran instantly cold after all the heat? Still, last night feels like a dream. An amazing dream. I should probably feel remorse, because we probably shouldn't have done what we did.

But I can't. I melt when I remember. I can't even believe this feeling. If only I could bottle it up and get high on it when I'm away from him. He oozed confidence. The way he worked me into a fever. The way he made me cry out. The way he controlled himself. The way he gave me oral.

Urgh. I'm so comfortable right now. I could stay here all day remembering. But I must. Fight. Bed gravity!

I manage to get out of bed, brush my teeth, and head to the kitchen. I look around as Gina pads in. I know deep down what I'm doing is so wrong and inherently risky. Proof of that is that I haven't told my friends I slept with him.

We talk about the lamest things. I talk to Gina and Wynn every day, even if there's nothing to talk about. We usually don't even have anything significant to say except: "I just pigged out on a sundae."

And I will be: "Oh, those are good."

And: "I watched *Sleepless in Seattle* again; I can't believe how good that movie still is, so many years later."

"Oh, I love Meg Ryan and Tom Hanks. Where are those two, anyway? Where's Meg? I miss her. . . ."

Sleeping with a guy after a three-year dry spell—and only having slept with two other guys in my life, neither of them anything to scream about—definitely classifies as noteworthy material. Sleeping with Malcolm Saint is a ten on the Richter scale. It deserves waking the girls up, if need be. It deserves screaming and scolding and more screaming, it deserves a day of daydreaming—*What if he really likes me?* and *What if it happens again?*—but because it's him, and because this is me, and because everything is more complicated, I can't say it. I can't share it, and I can't bear to share him or hear anyone's advice or opinion when I'm so tangled up about it all.

"What's up with you?" Gina asks.

"Nothing. I'm going to write," I murmur lamely.

I head to my laptop and stare at it, not writing a single anything at all, my fingers just stroking the keys as I glance at my phone.

Oh god, I'm such a fucking slut. I force myself to exhale the breath I'd been holding and read the text I just sent him:

Tonight?

Tonight, he'd answered.

We're heading back from a night out with Callan and Tahoe. I can't even believe how turned on I got watching Saint have a sportgasm when the White Sox won. His friends had one too. They yelled in Tahoe's apartment. Tahoe started running around like a madman, banging his chest. Callan opened a bottle of champagne and gave us all a bath. Malcolm's muscles gave my saliva glands quite a workout when he took off his shirt, balled it up, and threw it at the TV. "FUCK THAT, YES!"

He kept staring at me as I went to and fro.

"Hey, we're having a good time. Why don't you call the girls?" Tahoe says.

"No, thanks. You can leave your paws off my girls," I say.

"We're actually bailing," Malcolm says. I look up at him, and he's looking at me meaningfully.

"Aw, Saint. Hey, can we hop by your place later?"

"Later," he says.

I don't know why, but I'm already shivering like crazy.

Fifteen minutes later we're in his bedroom, and I roll over to straddle him, aching for his mouth, and we kiss again. We're naked, my breasts bare so he can toy with my nipples and drag his hands over my arms and then my spine. Our bodies shift as he sits up and pulls my legs around his hips. I'm so excited to feel that he's thick underneath me, I can't stop kissing his jaw, his lips. He's so thick he groans when I rock my hips a little bit.

God, he really wants me. . . .

"This doesn't mean anything, right?" I ask, panting and ready, so sopping wet I'm a little embarrassed about it, because his fingers are already trailing there.

"Right." He drags his tongue over my ear, his hand sliding over my pussy lips.

I watch the harsh look on his face as I move slowly over his lap, teasing his hardness with my wetness, until he rasps in my ear, "A guy would kill to live here."

He seizes my hips and urges me down on him; in this position he fills me to the hilt. Our eyes meet and cling. I lick my lips, and he runs his keen male attention over every part of me he can. He slides his hands down my butt, the backs of my legs, to curl over my ankles, his thumbs rubbing my ankle bones as I do the rest of the work.

My breasts bounce. He lies back on the bed, watching, as he drags one hand down the flat of my abdomen and fondles my clit. "Look at you," he croons huskily, ducking his head to suck on my breasts in a way that makes my eyes roll into the back of my head. I just lose control.

"Malcolm," I moan, wrapping my arms around his shoulders, savoring how they flex.

We hear the door.

I stop riding him for a second, but he's so big and full inside me, I don't want to stop.

"Shh." He sits up, hands on my hips, locking me on top of him. "It's just the guys, they won't come in here."

He sucks the tip of my breast into his mouth. My head falls back in pure red-hot pleasure as I move again.

More noise.

"Mmm," I moan, savoring him. Every pulse in his body, I feel too.

"Saint!" they're yelling.

He lifts his head. "BUSY!!!!"

Oh god, I can't. I lift up on my thighs and pull him out of me, too nervous about being heard to continue.

"No, come here." His arm locks around me, gently tugging me back to him.

"They're going to see I'm in here with you!" I hiss as I squirm free and start gathering my clothes.

"So?" As I get my pretty little thong and my bra back on, his attitude becomes more serious.

"So I really don't want to be your new whore to everyone. Just to me and you."

I slip into my top and skirt, and he jumps into his jeans, still hard, his face completely remote now. He comes and wraps his arms around my midriff. "Stay here, and I'll get rid of them."

I close my eyes, his touch, firm, persuasive, inviting me to stay and have my way with his hair, his lips, him.

"It's okay," I whisper.

"You sure?" The mere touch of his hand on my chin sends a warming shiver through me, and I nod.

We go outside in silence. He gets me a cup of coffee and then brings a bottle of wine out from the wine room.

"Hey, bro!" The guys high-five him, and he gives them a si-lent look that clearly speaks volumes. As in: *Why are you here?*

"Well, hello there, Rachel." Tahoe waggles his brows as he and Callan settle down on the huge leather living room couches. "You know, Rache, people have been asking me about you. Especially old Saint acquaintances," Tahoe tells me.

"I can imagine. I've lately experienced a friend surge on Instagram, FB, and Twitter since the Interface inaugural," I reply.

"Callan's gotten more inquiries than me, even," Tahoe adds.

" 'Cause you're a man beast, chicks are partly scared of you." Callan nods at him and looks at me. "He didn't hit puberty, he beat the shit out of it."

I laugh.

They both look at me as if waiting for me to explain the situation, but I won't. I think those two are too scared to drill Saint. So the guys start talking.

I'm trying to take mental notes, but mainly they're talking about the White Sox.

I curl up on the couch and set my cup to the side, grabbing a little pillow. Sin sits across from me, maybe because I told him that I didn't want them to think I was his whore. I smile at him in quiet gratitude.

He smiles at me and sips his wine.

I'm trying to convince myself that it's better if I go home—though my body protests at the mere thought of not seeing him until I don't know when—when I hear Tahoe casually tell Malcolm, "Her girls are coming over."

My cup of coffee comes down with a clatter. "What?"

"Yeah. I invited them."

"You? How do you even know my friends, Tahoe?"

"Succulent Gina?" He smirks. "Saint's got dibs on you. And he's got your landline."

I stare at Malcolm, flushing when he returns that look with a straight, unflinching stare.

And true to Tahoe's claim, in fifteen minutes Wynn and Gina appear at Saint's place, dressed to impress. They gape a little at their surroundings, and I'm almost embarrassed for them at how long it takes them to recover. The guys usher them to the living room with the huge cinema-size screen. "What are you girls up to?" Tahoe prods—gazing directly at Gina. "What were you so heatedly discussing coming off the elevator?"

"Um . . ." Wynn says, hesitating. "We were talking about Rachel's love life," she blurts out. "How she's lived perfectly well without a man her whole life. Not even a boyfriend, ever, really."

"Really?" Tahoe asks. "So is she like, a virgin, or what?"

The silence from Malcolm's vicinity feels leaden, and then he growls, "Dude, Rachel and I . . ."

He falls silent upon my glare, and then the silence grows endless.

"You're what?" Tahoe asks.

He raises his eyebrows and looks at me in question.

"You're what?!" Gina echoes.

Malcolm keeps looking at me, as if just now realizing I hadn't wanted my friends to know, either. I'm frantic wondering what the hell he's going to tell them we're doing. Well. What *are* we doing?

"You two are sleeping together, holy shit, I could stick a sock in my mouth right now!" Wynn says.

"I could do that for you if you're into that," Tahoe offers.

"It's nothing, really," I quickly say, to appease my shocked friends. "We hooked up, twice. So."

I'm aware of the way my friends stare at me in confusion, Malcolm in quiet assessment.

"Just twice, dude? And looks like there might not even be a third!" Tahoe laughs.

"Shut up, asshole. I've got this pocket on lockdown." Malcolm crosses to my couch and drops beside me, reaches out and kisses my temple, his whisper low and husky so that only I can hear, "This Hershey's Kiss, all mine."

"Malcolm." I swear I just blushed from the roots of my hair to the tips of my toes.

"Look at that pink on your skin." He laughs softly, clearly amused, a smile on his face, his eyes dark and gleaming.

"Twice?" Gina explodes in delayed response to her shock. "And you did not think to tell your best friends?"

Saint heads to the wine room, a cold space encased in glass near the back of the bar, bringing out a bottle of wine and a handful of glasses, all the while looking at me with curiosity. "It just didn't seem important," I hedge uncomfortably.

"Considering . . ." Gina scowls. "Considering." She gestures at him. "It *was* important."

Gina looks at him.

Then me.

"It's not important," I repeat.

"Oooooooh, that's bad, man," Callan ribs Saint.

"You fucking sly dog," Tahoe says. God, that man is obsessed with dog references, I swear. "You've been jousting all this time. I bet you were jousting right fucking now when we came in."

Malcolm's eyes flick up to me in quiet evaluation and then he whispers, his voice low, "Rachel's a lady."

I'm tomato red.

Malcolm's eyes are totally talking to me. *What's this about?*

"Hell, I bet you joust with the lady when we leave!"

"Drop it, T," Saint murmurs, draining his wine, looking at me still with that quiet concern. He's trying to know what to do; I can tell he wants to get a cue from me, but I can't even think of what cue to give him now. Oh boy.

"Let's bet on it," Tahoe suddenly tells Callan and then turns to Malcolm. "If you get the lady under your charms, I give you my wheels. If you don't, you give me one of your insects."

Saint sets his glass down, and I stare at him, waiting.

My friends stare at him too.

It seems like the one question they're all asking—are Saint and I are sleeping together?—will be answered right now.

And Saint looks at me, a look that's part challenge, part quiet command, and says, "Done. I'll get both your wheels when I do."

The guys woot.

My blood rushes through my body, hot with arousal, and also hot with humiliation.

"Saint! You said she was too good for you!" Tahoe jabs a thick finger in his direction. "You wore her down in true Saint form."

I stare at Malcolm, and he's still staring at me, a small smile of victory on his lips as he pours himself a fresh glass of wine and sips it. As if now all is right in the world because he's on top of it once more.

I explode.

"You did not seriously just bet your cars that you're going to . . ." I trail off, and when he nods, I go get my bag. "Okay, enough. We're leaving. Thanks for the great time, Sin," I mumble, charging for the elevators.

He comes over. "Get back here, Livingston. Everyone's leaving but you. . . ."

I walk by, and he moves his big body so I can't leave. "Didn't you hear what I just told the guys?" he asks me softly.

His eyes are curious and look completely puzzled by me, as if I should be ecstatic he claimed me like this.

"I did, and that's exactly why I'm leaving."

I stomp away, and at the elevator I swing around and glance at him one last time, and his eyes are as shuttered and unreadable as his expression is.

The girls follow me into the elevator. "Rachel, you're in deep. You've already promised the story to Helen."

"I know, Wynn." I shake my head because both my friends look so concerned about my situation. I just realized how reckless I've become.

I pace around. Suffering for the way I left.

I can't believe how these powerful businessmen are, deep down, also such boys. But I *still* like one of those boys very much: the ruthless one who is too ambitious for his own sake. Who doesn't like to lose. I *like* that boy; I still wanted to be with him today, and before his bozo friends arrived to chill out, I know he only wanted to be with me.

"He's really dicking you out, isn't he?" Gina says as if she can read my mind, turning around to see if Wynn is with her. "It's a bad idea, Wynn. Do you agree?"

I don't even let Wynn reply. "You two have always been pressuring me to hook up with someone. Well, I hooked up with Saint."

"Who's also your research material," adds my roommate.

"Thanks, Gina, for reminding me. Fine, so I had a moment of weakness. Or . . . several. He's so easy to be with. He's different than what I expected, and he's got me in a tangle." I scowl. "Look, he's fair game. He's single, isn't he?"

They're both silent.

Gina whispers then, "You slept with him and you didn't tell me? I'm so hurt right now, Rachel."

"What can I say? The power of Sin compelled me to?"

"You two spent all night playing jack-in-the-box, Jill, and we knew nothing!"

I groan as we hit the lobby, then realize I don't want to go. I stop and say, "I'm going back."

My friends gather close around me by the elevators. "Rachel, I totally approve of the hookup, but there's a reason he always keeps it to three times. . . ." Wynn says.

"Four, actually. He's big on the number four."

"And I'm not doing this to be a dick," Gina tells me. "I'm doing this because you're my best friend and I love you. You don't date a lot, you never wanted to, but I'm telling you right now, I never, ever want you to feel the way I did when Paul left me. I wouldn't want my worst enemy to feel as used, as worthless, as small, unbeautiful, and completely foolish as I did for having loved him."

We both stare.

"You know if you go for this thing with Saint, I'll be there to pass the Kleenex, like you were. But I hope you know that I care about you enough that when you go out there and get your heart broken, you're going to break mine too."

My eyes sting a little. There's the kind of support you ask for, and the kind that just is there. We hug a little and I promise I've got it and ride the elevator to the penthouse again.

I walk in. My body pricks everywhere when a particularly sexy green stare lifts from what seems to be the start of a poker game and targets me. He drops his cards and stands up, a flash of pure primal need in his eyes. I feel it in my *core*.

My voice is husky as I whisper, "Gentlemen." I address the

two stunned men, "If you don't mind leaving your keys with the concierge."

Saint's devil grin: I will never forget it.

My girl parts scream for mercy as Malcolm tells his guys they have to leave. "Now."

My girl parts scream for mercy, for him. They scream as he points me to the bedroom as he watches the elevators take them down and then pulses an alarm code so that nobody can interrupt us while we're here. My senses still scream as he follows me to the bedroom, and as I back in the direction of the bed, he walks straight to me.

He says nothing, just looks at me, then slides a hand around my waist and I'm yanked flush against him. I feel the feather-light brush of his lips first, warm, light, then the pressure as he locks them over mine, fitting perfectly, so perfectly he swallows my "god" . . . It's a kiss that goes from dry to wet, from slow to fast, from light to deep. . . .

I'm starting to pant, sliding my fingers up the placket of his shirt.

And still he kisses me, longer and wetter. A soul-searing kiss. A kiss I can tell he means. He cups my breast, caresses it, his thumb on my nipple, rubbing lightly, his expert touch promising me no one will ever sate, take, or please me the way he does.

"How many women have you kissed?" I ask against his mouth, his glorious mouth. I'm jealous of all the women out there, asking his friends about him. When he only looks at my wet, reddened, Saint-kissed lips, I edge free and start backing for the bed.

How many women are asking about Saint . . . ?

I bite my lower lip and feel the ache between my legs run upward. I wonder if some of these women have done what I shocked myself wanting to secretly do when I met him, which was to just totally rip his shirt off. He exudes all kinds of sexual pheromones, and I have this big little ache and I want to smell, touch, taste that wide, flat chest and those big square arms and that full male mouth. I bet those women tasted more than I've ever *dared*. I bet—

"Come here."

He takes my hand in his and stops me from backing away any more. And I'm breathless. He's staring down at me with glowing green eyes and lids that fall halfway over them. . . . They look at my hair, those eyes, and at my lips, and at our joined hands.

"Kiss who?" he finally asks. His thumb strokes across the top of my hand slowly as he reels me back toward him and brushes his lips across my forehead.

"Kiss who, where? Here?" he lightly teases me in a gruff, textured voice.

"No." I moan and laugh lightly and bury my face in his chest. He smells clean, minty, and . . . just manly. His hand is still holding mine, his fingers intertwined with mine. He reaches his other hand out and cups my cheek in it, kissing the tip of my nose. "How about here?" He dips his head and starts kissing my neck, lightly tasting me with kisses from my collarbone to the edge of my jaw.

"No," I breathe. My chest is rising and falling quickly, I'm trembling all over. I just want him to keep touching me, holding me, kissing me.

"How many men have kissed this?" His smile fades, his eyes burning with smoldering intensity as he rubs a silver thumb ring over my lips.

I tip my head farther back and offer him my mouth. "Two . . . and you."

"But no one's been here?" In one sinuous move, he dips his thumb inside. "No one's come inside this mouth."

"No . . ." I urge his shirt out of the waistband of his slacks. "I want *you* to."

I push the fabric up his chest and he jerks it over his head with a tug. His hair ends up tousled and glorious as he discards it, giving him a bed-mussed look that makes him even more gorgeous in my eyes because he looks approachable. Powerful but human. So human I can feel his body heat. Chasing my breath as I reach out and caress the hard planes of his pectorals and chest, suck his nipple. I smooth my fingers up his biceps.

The palms of his hands are holding my face upward, to his kiss. I give up my mouth with no protest, letting him move it at will.

His kiss makes me feel like my blood is gasoline, running through my veins. And Saint's lips are the fire, lighting me up.

I let him caress me, his tongue lightly stroking my own, and then he's heatedly kissing my throat, the peaks of my breasts. My breasts are heaving, and I can't believe how much I hurt between my legs.

He places a kiss right between my breasts, then teases the tip of one nipple over my top. I feel the lick arouse me. Shivering, I don't move a muscle, so he doesn't stop.

He makes his way back to my lips. I open my mouth immediately and wind my arms around his neck. I'm kissing him back with abandon, holding nothing back while his hands steal under my top.

Holding me close, he backs toward the bed and drops down, pulling me over. Quickly he shifts us around so that he's on top. He props himself up on his elbows at my side and looks down at me. Beautiful. I look up at him, his lids low and his eyes dark with desire. I lift my head and twine my tongue with his, my tongue circling, pressing, tasting. He hunches over me and tries not to crush me but gets close, so deliciously close. He feels so good, and tastes like heaven. I reach out and slide my fingers along his abs, needing to touch him.

His cock was made for sucking and for fucking, his cock, and I feel its hard length with my fingers. Then his hand is easing between my legs and teasing me with his fingers, and he's asking me, "Do you want it?"

Hips rolling to his touch, I gasp, "Yes."

He nibbles my lips slowly, taking his time. "You smell good," he whispers in my ear. He wants me, lust humming between us. I smell like a woman who's ready to be taken, my perfume and shampoo and soap mingled with the scent of Saint driving me crazy.

I'm gasping for air: every breath smells of him, every part of me remembering how he feels when he's in me. In the moment now, I slip my hands into his hair and open my legs so I can feel him right where I need him most. He lifts me against him by the ass and takes my mouth in no hurry, and I realize he's going to take his time—he's going to take all night, till he's done with me. When I realize I will be sexually tortured some more, I moan in aching misery.

He tilts my head back so that we make eye contact. He cradles the back of my skull while his free hand curls around my neck and he caresses my pulse point with his thumb. "What do you want, Rachel?" he whispers quietly. "Tell me how you want it. Do you want it now?"

Watching me, he slides his hand along my throat, my collarbone, flicks open my bra, and easily discards it. "You're so responsive when I touch you, it pushes me over the edge to watch you fall apart." He reaches to my waistband and flicks open my skirt; then he eases it down my legs. He is in no apparent hurry, but I am. I'm in such a hurry to see him naked that I kick off my skirt and reach out like a frantic nymphomaniac, my fingers trembling as I unzip his slacks.

"Get naked, get naked, Saint," I beg on a cotton-like breath.

When his super-warm, smooth skin connects with mine, I'm in heaven and in purgatory, running my hands down his back, gripping his hard ass to pull him above me. He trails his tongue, hot and wet, across my nipple. I moan. His smell enthralls me, and the hint of his taste lingers on my lips. If that isn't the most delicious form of torture, I don't know what is.

He ducks his head and slides his tongue over my other nipple, and I shudder and part my legs when he teases two fingers across my folds, and I'm saying, "Please." He teases the strong tip of his middle finger inside but pulls it out immediately. Fierce desire pools between my thighs as I lift my hips and, aching, try to follow his thumb's retreat. He keeps me there, where he wants me. Beneath him, helpless and quivering. He nips my lower lip, pulling it away from the top. Achingly gently.

I mew softly and he shifts above me so that his hard body is aligned with mine. God help me, he owns me. "Sin . . . *Sin* . . ." My thoughts scatter as he dips his tongue sinuously into my ear. This man will turn the entire world into a sinner.

He looks at my reddened nipples. I groan when he sweeps down to lave and taste them as he caresses my sex with smooth, knowing fingers. First brushing on the outside. His middle finger across the length. The pad of his thumb, in little circles; then his thumb rubs me and his middle finger eases inside me and I'm undone.

I pull his face down to me, trembling with desire as I kiss him, angling my head and sucking his tongue hard. He groans when I let him slide up and down between my legs. I'm so hungry that if he enters me, I'm going to get there before he does. But he's savoring what he's doing to me, and he seems to want to make it last. The head of his cock massages the outside of my sex.

He's beautiful and untamed and powerful and I want him to come inside me. But I know it would be reckless, and so I pant and watch him roll on a condom and look at me, his chest jerking with his deep breaths.

We hold gazes as I part my legs and he rubs against me again. He spreads out over me again. In one swift move, he curls one of my legs around his hip, opening me, and he presses in. I groan and sink my nails into his muscles. He watches my face as he starts to penetrate me. His body shudders, and my breath leaves me when he draws out his cock and then puts it inside me, all wet from me, and so hard. I can't think or speak, I just take him, take his mouth, take the thrill of the way his eyes watch me. My every undulation, my every gasp, every whimper of helpless abandon.

He reaches between us and rubs the pad of his thumb just a bit over my clit, and he watches, breathing hard, with the merest tiny circular rub of his thumb while he presses his cock in as deep as he wants, ready to enjoy the tightening and loosening ripples in my body.

An orgasm. Fierce and wild. It sweeps through me like a wildfire, no corner of my body untouched. Saint pins my hips down and rides me through it, keeping my orgasm going with the most delicious thrusts of my life as I twist around, my mouth seeking his. He gives me a crushing kiss, and I can feel when he reaches that point, that magical point, because the energy seems to coil in his body, which grows tauter and tauter with each thrust.

I'm still enjoying the aftershocks when his body tightens and I feel the jerks of his cock as he jets off inside me. He grabs me by the cheeks, holding my face as he slows his rhythm. We share a slow but deeply passionate kiss as our bodies loosen.

"Wow," I say, panting.

"Yeah," he says. A soft laugh follows, and it comes with a gleam of satisfaction in his eye. He looks pleased with my sincerity. Or maybe just . . . with sex with me.

He shifts so he's facing the ceiling and I'm draped to his side, his arm holding me to him, the other folded under his head, his chest heaving. He looks down and brushes a tendril of wet hair from my forehead. "I'm nearly about ready to go at it again. You?"

I can't breathe, but who needs air? "Me too."

What am I doing? What am I doing? WHAT ARE YOU DOING, RACHEL?

"One more time before I leave," I say, rolling over on top of him. And, oh god, he's so good, I'd keep him if I could.

One sex marathon with multiple orgasms later . . .

"Why didn't you tell your friends about me?" Malcolm asks.

I hesitate as I dress.

His expression is not annoyed, but I can't say that he looks happy either. He looks a bit closed off, his lids heavy from his last orgasm, his gaze shuttered.

"Same reason I didn't want your friends to know."

"What reason?" he asks.

"We were just fooling around. It means nothing." I zip my skirt and then stand there, looking at him. "You're mad?"

"I'm curious."

I stare. "So you're used to parading your lovers, and they love flaunting the fact that they slept with you; I don't do that."

"Aren't we a little old to play the hiding game, Rachel?"

"Aren't we too old to be betting on whether you can have me?"

His lips twitch, but the smile doesn't reach his eyes.

"You can't stand them thinking you wanted me and didn't get me."

"That's right, I can't."

"Why?"

" 'Cause I called dibs."

"I don't understand you, Malcolm. See, this is why I don't want a relationship. It would kill me to try to figure out my man."

"It's killing *him* trying to figure *you* out."

I blink.

He goes on, as if what he said wasn't something monumental. As if my heart isn't just something frozen with a strange hope and fear in my chest.

"See," he continues, "usually girls *like* people knowing they landed in my bed. Some girls claim to have landed there and I've never even met them. You're the first who's been there but doesn't want to be."

I duck my head as an awful feeling of betrayal and dishonesty sweeps over me. "If I didn't want to be here, I wouldn't be here," I murmur. "I'm here despite . . . despite the fact that I shouldn't be here at all," I explain, raising my eyes to his. I should not be here, Saint, I think miserably.

But he just stares at me with that same puzzled look he gets when he's trying to figure me out. I grab my top and feel him watching me as I dress. This is the kind of conversation you don't expect to have with a one-night stand. But he's not a one-night stand. *What is he?* "I don't want to be a number on that list. Just thinking of all the women you've slept with makes me want to go sign up for a pole-dancing course."

He laughs. "Why?"

"Because I'm vanilla. I'm just some normal . . . girl. And you're you."

And I'm addicted.

It's past 3 a.m. We're both rumpled and supposed to be relaxed after the way we fucked like crazy. But there's tension in his jaw, and my muscles are tight with it. I want to jump him again and work out this tension the way we've been doing, but I'm beginning to grow scared of this addiction. Scared of him. I stand at the door and turn to say goodbye, but he's already slipping into his sexy black boxers and then his slacks.

"It's not safe out there this time of night," he murmurs.

"It's never safe out there," I mumble.

Bare-chested and barefoot and still giving me butterflies even after he had his hands all over my naked body, he accompanies me to the elevator and waits next to me as it arrives. When it tings, he turns me to face him. I let him kiss me on the lips and I kiss him back, wrapping my arms around him just for a second. Two. And then I peel myself away and hop onto the elevator. "'Bye."

There's something intimate in his gaze as he watches me, holding eye contact right until the doors shut between us.

God, I never thought a man could look at me like that.

I'm walking out of the building when I see his driver emerge from the Rolls.

"Miss Rachel," he greets, and opens the door.

"Oh, Sin, *really?*" I look up to the top of the tower but I can't even see it. I'm about to argue with Otis, but it's 3 a.m.

As I slide into the back of the car, I hear someone say, "Mr. Saint, good eve—good *morning*," behind me. I'm barely seated when I see his face and *that* happens; that way my heart keeps leaping when I see him.

"Rachel," he says as he takes my arm and pulls me out of the car.

"What . . . what are you doing?"

"Something I should've done before."

I refuse to take a step as he takes my hand and tugs me toward him. My eyes are huge. "You've lost your mind."

"I have," he agrees, then he lifts an eyebrow. "Are you coming up, or do you want me to carry you?"

"Please don't carry me," I beg, aware of Otis's absolutely *stunned* stare.

"Then come with me."

I take one step forward, his fingers lacing, strong, through mine, and then we're back on the elevator. When the doors open, when nobody else can see us, he swings me up on his arms and folds me over his shoulder.

"Saint! Malcolm SAINT! Put me down, what are you doing?"

"I'll put you down soon." I fall still and melt a little inside, my heart done for. "You're not doing this," I say in swoony disbelief as he drops me down on the bed.

"Yes, I am. You're sleeping over. You're staying the night here."

Looking pretty serious about it, he tugs my top over my head to get me comfortable, and I know I should probably not stay over, I know I shouldn't like being together so much, and I know I'm not thinking straight right now—no, I'm not thinking *at all*—but that doesn't stop me from unbuttoning his shirt with reckless speed, until I quickly pull it off his chest, sighing when he spreads his body above me.

⌣৯

@MalcolmSaint is it true you have a girlfriend? #imsad
#pleasesayno

I lower my phone and turn in bed two hours later to stare at the sleeping man beside me.

I reach out and touch his jaw. I stare at his sexy mouth, completely still as he sleeps. I just slept over after wild, hot sex sessions. *Me.* My entire life, my fear of rejection and of being hurt by a man has made me focus solely on things I can control. My studies, my career. My body and its needs have been overpowered by my brain for years, it's true. But not now, not tonight, not with this male.

The way he wants me . . . it takes my breath away.

Before I realize what I'm doing, I stroke my fingers over his face, tracing the contours of his jaw first, marveling over the abrading feel of his night stubble.

His lips are plush, firm, and so pink, my pulse accelerates as my own lips tingle in complete envy of my fingertips.

Without even thinking, I hold my breath and try to be as quiet as possible as I bend my head. *You're making my world spin so hard and so fast.* The words shudder in my heart as I cup his jaw in both hands and press my lips as softly as I can to his without waking him up.

Something gooey and warm washes over me. *Oh god, Malcolm . . .*

I press my body closer to his, feeling him, looking at him. I never thought I'd see him like this, asleep with me, after sex. I've been admiring his smiles, the twinkle he gets when he teases me or amuses himself at my expense, and how protective he gets when his friends want to horse around with me. I never thought I'd connect with a man like this.

I love that he is centered and logical, but that with his friends, he is sometimes just a teenager—a very big, very handsome teenage boy with very expensive, very powerful toys. I love to work on him and interview him because I feel hungry for every bone he throws me. I love to be just a little bit part of his life, and right now, seeing him in a way I never thought I would, naked, in bed, sleeping, I'm so much more into him than I ever thought possible.

So when his arms come around me, and his mouth opens under my lips, and he slides his warm, damp tongue inside me, and a thousand flutters of pleasure race to my nerve endings, the only thing I can do—the only thing I want to do—is let both it, and him, take me.

22

EXCITEMENT, ECSTASY, AND EXPOS

We spend Sunday with the guys watching another White Sox game.

I fully intended to write notes on my phone to keep adding to my file, but I'm so relaxed, I'm letting myself chill out for a while.

I'm starting to feel comfortable with them—they're like the noisy big brothers I never had. They both seem to have gone to some sort of function because they're in suits, their ties discarded on the side, one's jacket slung over the chair, the other's over a sofa.

The announcer's voice is saying something about a goal, or maybe it was a touchdown or whatever, and the boys are glued to the television screen. I'm sitting next to Malcolm, who is wearing a light blue cotton T-shirt that clings to his shoulders and light-wash jeans. He looks comfortable and commanding, sprawled on his couch. Callan and Tahoe are saying something about some player and Malcolm still has his eyes on the TV, occasionally taking a sip of his wine. That's right, no beer for these boys. They watch their games with Pinot Noir.

A day in the life of Malcolm Saint. I laugh inwardly and try to focus on the game, but all I can think about is Malcolm's arm behind my back. He looks so inviting in that T-shirt, all I want to do is cuddle up closer to him and bury my face in his chest and have him hold me to him with his strong arms. Instead, there's about three inches of couch between us, which I deliberately put there for the same reason that I want to crawl into his lap. I need to calm down.

Just then, Malcolm drops his arm around my hips, and he draws me to him in one swift motion. I end up with my thigh touching his, and his arm around me.

"That's better," he says, satisfied with himself as he leans back again and keeps watching the game. Another sip of Pinot Noir.

Tahoe seems to have seen Malcolm's little move, because he starts laughing. Malcolm shoots him a glare and draws me closer to him.

Men. I roll my eyes and bite the inside of my cheek to keep from laughing. I turn to see Malcolm staring at my lips, which are pursed and lightly twisted in a barely controlled smile.

"This mouth," he says, reaching down and using the pad of his thumb to pull my lips apart. He's still looking at my lips as he withdraws his hand. He leans down to kiss me, and I freak and turn my head away. He just chuckles and places a big kiss on my cheek.

"Damn, I've never seen that before," says Callan.

"What?" I ask.

He motions to Malcolm. "The king being rejected by a woman."

"I didn't reject him!" I say quickly. I'm pretty sure I'm blushing. I turn to look at Malcolm, and he has a slight scowl on his face. I'm sure he's making a mental note to kick Callan's ass later.

"You did," insists Callan. "You're gonna have to nurse that wound later." He winks at me, and I feel Malcolm grow tense next to me.

"What? What did I miss?" says Tahoe, with his eyes still glued to the TV.

"Oh, nothing, it's just that our boy here just got—"

"OOH!! FUCK YEAH! THAT'S RIGHT!!!" Tahoe shoots up from his chair and claps his hands together. "Let's go, let's go, let's go!!!"

I think something good just happened. Callan and Malcolm look back to the screen and join Tahoe's little celebration. I feel Malcolm's chest vibrate with his deep voice, and I feel my head instinctively sink a little closer to him.

He leans his head down to my ear and explains what happened. I nod, but all I can think about is how his voice sounds. Deep and manly. And I just want to crawl into his lap again.

He plants a kiss on my temple and looks back up at the screen.

This is too much. I try to move away from him, but he just tightens his arm around me. *Fuck.*

I hadn't really been into baseball so much until now, and even though I'm so relaxed that I could tune out, Malcolm keeps reminding me that he knows I'm here with his stupid little touches. Sometimes it's a kiss on the top of my head, or his hand on my thigh, or his thumb rubbing across the inside of my wrist. Each and every touch makes me dissolve and dissolve and dissolve. They're little, insignificant touches, but they make my head swirl and my stomach flip.

I promised myself I wouldn't, but by the end of the game my head is on his chest and his arm is holding me against him. Callan and Tahoe keep staring at us A) like we're some kind of dinosaur/extinct animal they can't believe is actually there before their eyes, and B) like we're some kind of magical sight that might disappear in a blink of an eye. I can tell they're not used to seeing Malcolm like this. And I feel like I'm playing with fire. I feel like the closer I cuddle into him, the more I relax into him, the more I let my head settle into the crook of his shoulder, the harder I'll burn later.

At one point in the game, I stand up to get some air because I feel like I'm doing something I really shouldn't be doing. It takes every single ounce of self-control I have to edge away from Malcolm's huge chest and go to the kitchen. It's like leaving bed on a Sunday morning, Malcolm being my own personal king-size mattress. The moment I leave I miss his warmth, his arms, the sound of his voice next to my ear when he talks. I remember I could even feel his abs move under my head. His stomach is rock hard. I shudder and focus on getting my cool back.

When I come back, I sit down with ten inches of couch between us again, hoping that I'm sending him a message. He doesn't even think about it this time, just looks at me like I'm doing something funny, and snakes his arm around my hips again to drag me back to my place. Which, in his opinion, is under his arm and against his chest. And so we stay like that for the remainder of the game. Tahoe actually stands up at one point and gives my leg a little nudge because apparently I'm falling asleep.

They joke that it's time for my afternoon nap, and Malcolm just tells them to shut the fuck up and watch the game. The fact is, I *was* actually falling asleep. He has a very comfortable chest—the asshole. I hate that he's making me feel these things. I hate how I feel naked if I'm not next to him. I hate how I feel like a part of me has been ripped off if I'm not lying on his chest or his arms aren't around me. And I hate how the guilt creeps up and starts to corrode me.

"Do your parents know you're here? Bartender, you might want to check this girl's ID again," Tahoe says.

I glare. "Why do you insist on joking about my age?"

"T."

Tahoe grins. "Yeah, Saint?"

"Leave her alone."

I twist my hair up in a bun, suddenly feeling very female under Saint's protectiveness. The sexual chemistry leaping between us is undeniable. The more I try to suppress it, the more I'm aware it's there.

Tahoe laughs and reaches out to tap my shoulder, presumably wanting to tell me something.

"Don't touch her, Roth," Saint says.

Tahoe leans back. "Dude, do you have to have them all?"

"You can have your pick of anyone."

"Well then—"

"Except her," he says, not even looking at me to see if I agree. "I won't say it again."

He stands to go get more wine and Tahoe grins, while Callan leans across the coffee table. "He's in a piss mood."

"Why?"

"Old man is having a commemorative event for his mother. If Saint has a button, that's it."

"His mother? Or the dad?"

"The combination," Callan says.

I can't ask him anything else because Saint comes back and glances at me with all the concentration of a torpedo. He takes his seat and puts his arm around me and runs his thumb over the side of my neck, and I blush beet red, my body hot. "I like your hair up," he tells me.

"Thank you."

He smiles and runs his finger down my jaw like he does.

I exhale through my lips; I can't believe how easily he arouses me. All of me. All my senses; hearing, sight, smell, taste, touch.

"Stop sweet-talking her, Saint, her ear is going to fall off," Tahoe ribs him.

I study Malcolm's somber, brooding expression as he sits quietly beside me. "Right? His talk is cheap but very, very sexy," I tell Tahoe, trying to make Saint come out of his man cave. "He doesn't have to worry. I'm so emotionally unavailable right now, he has no clue," I say dramatically.

"Trust the man! He knows all the locks and bolts to go through to get a girl like you to open up."

"I'm not a regular vault."

Malcolm says nothing. I look at him, then lean in and whisper, as I trail my fingers up his chest, "I want to cheer you up, Malcolm."

All that does is get him to shoot a frown my way. "Who said I needed cheering up?"

"Don't sound mad. I can tell the difference between you being simply quiet and relaxed and quiet and mad."

He takes my chin in his hand. "I'm not mad at you."

Yeah, I guess. Still, I want to see that smile reach his eyes, I want to kiss his wounds better, but I know there are those that no Band-Aid can touch. What kind of wounds made such a hard, unemotional man?

I'm quietly pondering that when he drives me home that

night. "I have something tomorrow. I'll see you another day?" he tells me as he walks me quietly to my apartment door.

I really ache a little. I want him to share, but he's a man, and we're having a . . . what? A prolonged one-night stand?

"Sure, good night," I whisper.

But before I go in, I lean back against the door, wanting him to kiss me.

So when he curls his hand around the back of my neck, I instantly go on tiptoe, wrap my arms around his shoulders, and meet him halfway. His kisses are my number-one addiction. One minute becomes two, then three, until he pulls away and looks at me. "I've got to go." He runs his hand restlessly through the sexy disorder of his hair and heads off.

I want to call him back. He seems on edge and as if he doesn't trust himself to be with me and in control like he's used to. "Saint," I call to him as he gets into the car. I consider asking him to spend the night, but he doesn't hear me.

I scowl and go inside, then rub my hand over my chest. Did you want him to spend the night, Livingston? No man has spent the night here, and Gina would *flip*. It was better that he leave, right?

So what are the pouty feelings for? Did you actually expect him to invite you tomorrow, Rachel? Really? To his *mother's* commemorative event?

Well, maybe I did. And I hate that the next day, I feel like a voyeur looking in on his pain as pictures flash on the internet. Saint, his father, their faces, the tension. The event is held in memory of his mother, who died of leukemia; his father hosts the yearly gala to raise money for a foundation in her name.

"Noel and Malcolm Saint, as we can see, are still not talking to each other. . . ."

I slam my laptop shut and go do something productive instead. I start scanning all of Gina's fashion magazines. "Don't unfold the folded corners," she warns from where she's on her laptop, listening to music on the living room couch. I untuck a folded corner and wonder why she marked the page. Maybe the cute boho bag? Or the yellow shoes the model is wearing? I'm mindlessly flipping, then I see his text message.

You busy?

My heart leaps so hard in my chest I forget the cardinal rules of not texting back too fast. I instantly text him back, No

I wait, my pulse fast in my body as the image of him standing tensely by his asshole father comes to mind.

Pick you up?
Where are we going?
Anywhere
Give me 5 mins

I leap to my feet and hurry to change. "Oh no," Gina groans from the living room.

I slip into a pair of sexier underwear—white lace. White lace for Malcolm. Then I select a cute little skirt and top. I know Saint is closed off. There's no real hint of his inner psyche, aside from his rebellious nature, in anything online that I've read. The fact that he texted me when I know he's had a difficult evening makes me feel somehow protective of him in a way I've never been protective of anyone except my mother, Gina, and Wynn. I can barely stay inside my skin when I spot the Rolls out the window.

"I'll see you tomorrow!" I tell Gina.

"Rachel!" she calls worriedly after me, but I'm trying not to hear that right now. I can't. There's no place in all of Chicago I'd rather be than at his side, and that's all there is to it.

I climb in the car, my eyes hurting from my glimpse of him across from the bench I sit on. He's cloaked in shadows, but some of the lights outside the window fall on his neck, his square jaw. His lips. As I grow accustomed to the dark, I slowly study the clear-cut lines of his features. He's so handsome, with those emerald-green eyes and a secret expression, and suddenly the cool ice in his eyes warms when they fall on me. "You look edible."

His voice ripples down my body. Quiet, but not cool as usual—warm. Quite unexpectedly warm, as if I've just heated up his whole existence.

"Yeah? I've got news for you," I say with a sultry little smile. I value words, but Saint is a man who values action and I want to take some action tonight. I lift my fingers up, tug my sleeve a little to the side to reveal a creamy expanse of shoulder. "I *am* edible."

"And I want a bite."

Seized by my own desperate, growing, clawing hunger, I pull it downward, Saint's face absolutely livid with lust.

"Where? Here?" I ask in a sensual whisper as I brush my fingers over my shoulder. I can't even find words to describe how much I like when his voice goes rough like tree bark.

"Right there. I'm running my mouth up your neck, down your shoulders, your arm."

My breath's gone.

Like a living, breathing thing ready to devour the both of us, desire leaps between us, arcing from him to me, from me to him. "What else will you do?" There's need in my voice: arousal. I can't hide it, not from him.

"I'm going to make love to you hard, and then I'll take you softly. Show me your other shoulder, Rachel."

I do.

The car is rolling down the street now, but if you ask me, the entire universe is in this car, looking at me.

My veins sing happily over his stare as I drop my top sleeve as far as it will go, baring the most of my shoulder possible. Every day my desire for him deepens and intensifies, magnifying my attraction to him to a level I could have never imagined. I know him by heart now, the different angles his mouth twists to create each of his smiles . . .

"I'm going to run my tongue over its curve, dip it right where your pulse beats fast," the Universe says. "Show me more," he coaxes.

"Mmmm. You're so greedy. Will anything in your life ever be enough, Malcolm Saint?"

He shakes his head very slowly, as if in warning, a tinge of amusement in his voice. "Nothing's ever enough and it's especially true when it comes to you. Show me more, little one."

I tug my top down an inch, enough that he can see the top swell of my breast beneath my lace bra. He growls in his throat, and I blush and go warm as I straighten myself. "I was happy to hear from you, big one."

He chuckles. Then, more tree bark, rasping over my skin. "I was happy you could see me tonight. . . ."

I angle my head a little and study him, the roiling energy circling around him. His thirst, his desire, his frustration evident in the fists at his sides.

My heart tumbles over itself to get to him.

"Rough evening?" I ask softly.

"It's looking up."

The ice that's usually in his irises is completely subdued as he reaches out for my hand, pulls me across the car, sits me as close as possible to his side, and starts kissing my mouth, running a path to the shoulder I bared, running his fingers over the curve. Heat, moisture, the softness of his lips with the strong movements of his mouth. "Definitely looking up," he rasps. "And you?" He nibbles a path up to my mouth. "What were you doing before I came calling?"

"Hmm. Let me think," I say, pretending to think hard about it. "The real answer? Or the one you'll like most?"

Shifting so I can watch my fingers slide up his throat, I run them to his square jaw, a jaw that is so stubborn—as stubborn as him—and I like that he lets me touch him like this very much.

"Both." While he caresses my shoulders with his hands, his thumbs dip into my top, slowly tracing my collarbone.

"I was working." My own thumbs run over the stubble of his jaw now. "But while I was doing that, I was *anxiously* waiting for you to text me and invite me somewhere."

"Anywhere," he corrects, husky.

"Exactly." I press my mouth to the corner of his mouth, not even thinking of what I'm doing, acting by pure instinct now. "Are we there yet so I can gorge on you too?"

His arms tighten around me, and one of his hands slips under my shirt to explore the hollow of my back. "Rachel . . . I didn't want you to see me when I'm not at my best."

"On the contrary, I want to see you like this. I desire you, I crave you, and I want to comfort you and give you whatever you want."

Hot lips nibble on my shoulder. "Then I want you."

"Anywhere" turns out to be *The Toy*. Away from prying eyes and from the public—to my complete relief and delight—it feels like we're in another world. The yacht is docked and the crew is not aboard, so it's just Malcolm and I sitting in silence up on the top deck, both of us still a little sweaty from the hard, and then the slow, fuck he just gave me.

He's wearing his black slacks but nothing covering his chest, while I'm wearing the shirt he was wearing not long ago. He's brooding and silent, and I've never felt so protective toward something so large and strong before.

"M4," I whisper, my cheek resting on his chest while the rest of my body conforms to his hard lines. "You do things by four so many times, I've noticed. Why four?"

We're almost to our fourth time together. Are we over then too?

He exhales and sips the last of his wine, sets the empty cup aside, and we stare at the Chicago skyline. "I have a temper." He stares into the distance, his profile thoughtful.

I reach for his hand on his knee and link my fingers through his.

He looks out, his voice coming lower, husky, almost regretful. "It was worse when I was young. Control is something that's always taken me some effort. The staff kept quitting because nobody could keep me under control; the more they tried, the angrier I became. But my mother was the embodiment of patience. I guess this is why she could tolerate my father. She was patient, far more understanding than anyone should probably be. When I lost it, my mother said to count to three, and I'd argue that I had. That I'd counted to three—it didn't work. So one day she pulled me aside, worried because my father has a temper too—she could predict the worst for me and the ways I seemed to push his buttons. And she told me I'd need to count to four. And that's what I'd do. More than anything else, that's what came with being a Saint. If you were asked for three minutes, you gave four. If you had to count to three, you counted to four. I do things in fours."

"You even like foursomes."

He lifts his brows. "Not with you. I enjoy taking my time with you." He runs his hand up my spine, under his shirt. I shiver.

Shiver and want and melt.

And most of all, I'm crumbling to pieces inside and eaten alive with guilt over knowing such an intimate detail about him.

Heavy with feelings I can't even process, I roll to my back to put a little distance between us. He props himself up on one elbow and flicks open the button of my top, and oh, god help me but there's definitely more melting, melting, *melting*. I don't protest, don't move, only helplessly watch him pop a second button. Then three. Four. While the body beneath the shirt he's parting open starts trembling in every centimeter.

I want to tease him, to lighten the intensity of the wild ache building in me. I whisper, barely managing to get it out, on a breath, "Take your time with me. It doesn't bore me one bit."

Four buttons. Five. And six. Until he spreads my top open and leans forward to kiss the center of my throat. The centers of my breasts. The center of my abdomen. And the center of my sex. Four kisses, then he nuzzles me between my legs. "I'm not one bit bored with you either, Rachel."

I remember being so shy before. This time, when he flicks his tongue across my clit, I moan and spread my thighs wide open, rocking my hips up wantonly as I whisper, *"Malcolm, Malcolm, Malcolm . . ."*

"Hmm," I whisper an hour later as he nibbles my ear, waking me from a little doze I was taking in the cabin.

"Your ear," he rasps against the object of his delicious attentions. "I'm partial to it, and it matches your other one."

I stretch with a smile, and he eases back to look down and watch me.

"I love it here on your yacht, it's so peaceful," I say, walking my fingers up his tanned chest.

"I'm never here alone. Too peaceful. I can hear my thoughts too well." He frowns as he gets up from the bed and heads for his clothes. Dreamily, I roll to my side and stare at his absolutely mesmerizing physique as he jumps into his slacks. "Are you happy at *Edge*?"

I shake off the sleep fog, then sit up, one sheet clutched to my chest as I feel around in the bed for my underwear. "Why do you ask?"

"Rumors are it's coming down." He rams his arms into his shirtsleeves, measuring my reaction as he slowly starts to button up.

"I hope not. I like *Edge* very much." Somehow I manage to find my panties and bra, and have to drop the sheet to get them on. "Why? Are you venturing into publishing . . . ?" I ask, afraid.

He's quiet as he tucks his shirt in, adds his belt—becomes Malcolm Saint right before my eyes.

"No, I'm not buying the magazine—that's not where I see the money going. Businesses require time and vision. Reviving businesses is not where my passion is." He looks at me for a moment. "Is owning your own business a dream of yours?"

"No, I want to write. I want to earn a good living so I can write more. More than more."

He smiles. "You're so little. I get a kick imagining those little hands typing up your big ideas."

The fact that he thinks about me at all makes me butter.

He watches me dress. "So you see your future at that magazine even if you had a broader range of options?" he asks.

I'm taken aback. A grain of concern suddenly drops, like a tiny, uncomfortable little pin, in my belly. I think over my answer carefully.

"I guess . . . in a *general* sense, my ideal future is to feel safe in my career and, I guess, in my life. I want my mom to be and feel safe, and if I could help make the city physically safer for others as well, it'd be a dream. That's the kind of thing I want to write about. But that kind of journalism takes time, and *Edge* has given me better opportunities than anywhere else. I feel linked to it, somehow. If it grew and I could grow right with it, that'd be a dream, it really would," I admit.

He comes to sit on the bed and he edges forward, his expression intense. "Like, what would you like to do for the city? What's your idea?" He tucks my hair back from my forehead with one large hand, searching my face.

"I don't know. Change doesn't happen unless there's a huge collective effort, unless you're very powerful."

His lips quirk and his eyes glimmer with a predatory light that never fails to thrill me. "You're sleeping with a very powerful man."

I bite my lip. "Yes, yes I am." I laugh and feel myself blush. He cups my cheek, and once again, I tuck my face into his palm, seeking his touch. "You're not how I imagined you'd be, and I have a good solid imagination," I whisper.

"That's because you're *all* good. Terrible things made me."

"Oh no." I laugh, but he doesn't laugh. He's quiet. "We're all made of good and terrible things."

"Are we?" He studies me again. "What do you see in me?"

I frown. "What do you mean?"

"I'm a difficult man, I'm not easy to handle—some might argue I refuse to be handled. I'll never commit to anyone—I never have, and I don't think I ever could. You don't want my money, you don't want to party with me—not the way others want. You almost wouldn't sleep with me. But then you come to me as if you want my protection, and it makes me want to be that man."

I stare at him, quiet.

He's always said I confuse him, and he looks so confused right now, I'm confused by his puzzlement too.

"Malcolm," I begin, but what can I say? So many truths, and in the end, he'll think all of them a lie. It breaks me to think about it all of a sudden.

"When my mother was diagnosed . . ." He pauses. "I promised I'd be there for her. By her side. She was given two years. She still had a year and a half left . . ." He pauses again but never takes his eyes off me. "She didn't want me to know the leukemia came back. And when it was only a matter of hours, my father refused to let anyone tell me. He thought I should be punished for leaving the country for Tahoe's birthday." I can feel the blood drain from my face. "So you see? I'm no good with promises. But I'll take your cause as if it were mine."

"I'm so sorry. I . . . when my father died, I was too young. But I have nightmares sometimes about the way he died, alone."

We share a stare.

"She died asking for me." He looks away, then heads for his phones and other items, his jaw completely flexed.

"She knew you loved her," I whisper.

"Did she?"

"Women know these things. My mother said . . . she knew even before my father did that he loved her. Women know these things. Your gender wasn't made for subtleties, you need to be hit in the head with it, and sometimes love just creeps in even when all your doors and windows are shut to it." He stares, and I add, "Everyone is born with a natural love for their parents."

"You outgrow that love. There's no point to love. Truth, loyalty—there's something that lasts."

Speechless, I'm not sure if I'm more surprised by the words or the casual tone he used, which only brings home that the sentiment is so completely natural to him.

The fact that he has no trust in love, *any* kind of love, astounds me.

I drop my face a little to hide the tender emotion I'm sure he'll be able to see reflected in my eyes. My chest feels suddenly swollen with it.

But we have so many things in common—Saint and I. We love to work. We work hard, squeezing in a little fun but not much else. We're both proud, maybe closed off. I also thought I didn't believe in love, not romantic love like Wynn does. So why do I suddenly feel like changing my mind?

I finish dressing, unable to look at him again.

After the "truth and loyalty" comment I've gone quiet, very thoughtful because, naturally, I'm questioning what the hell I'm doing with him right now. What do I think will come out of this affair?

I didn't think, I guess. I only wanted. I wanted, obsessed, and had to have, like a young, reckless girl. Like a girl he brings out, someone I'd never been until now. I'm acutely aware of his effects on this girl as he drives me home.

I should feel satiated, content, and happy by now. Instead I don't want to say goodbye, and when he tells Otis to wait for him as he walks me up, I feel frantic that he won't stay. That I'm not truthful and loyal, and he will soon go away.

"I have work tomorrow," I say, just to give him an easy out.

"I have work too," he says, but he keeps following me to the door, waiting behind me as I open.

I shiver when he nibbles the back of my ear, his hand running up my bare arm to caress the shoulder I teased him with hours ago when he picked me up.

"Do you want to come in?"

"Yeah." He kisses my ear.

I can't even explain the way my heart unravels in my chest, spreading warmth all over me.

Not wanting to bump into Gina like this, I press my finger to my mouth, hook my little finger in his, and pull him into my bedroom. We shut the door. He looks big and beautiful.

"Sit down," I gesture toward the bed, my hormones already joining the party.

He starts unbuttoning his shirt as I go and slip into my Wildcat T-shirt. I walk back to my bed. He looks at me with that naughty curve to his lips, and from his expression you'd think I was the sexiest thing to come out of my university. I look down-to-earth, while he looks exquisite, his shirt stretched in all the right places.

Quietly I straddle him and unbutton the rest of his shirt while he eases his hands under my T-shirt, squeezing the flesh of my ass.

"Malcolm, I don't have condoms. . . ."

He kisses me slowly, deeply, savoring me. "Don't worry, I got us covered."

In less than a minute we're all set, all naked, and I'm pushing him down to my bed, delighted that he lets me straddle him. Run my hands up his massive chest. Watch him watch me move over him. I take him in my body, and my breasts feel heavy with need, tender from his fingers as he caresses them, raises his head and licks and laves the sensitive tips. He sits up with me, then, eye to eye, we move together. He pounds me with his hips, pulling me down harder to meet him. He comes fiercely, my orgasm tearing through me at the same time.

Our breaths come fast. He looks confused, awed, grateful. He wanted to break me, but I could almost see a crack in his huge, huge walls as we made love. Because that's what it felt like. Strangers who should be fucking somehow ended up giving more and opening up more than planned. Content, I rest against the hard, warm lines of his body for a long time, his hands lazily trailing a path up the line of my spine.

I go out on a limb and whisper, "I like being just like this with you."

"Do you?" he asks, his look soft and teasing, tender.

I nod.

He pats his chest. "Then come back here."

I put my hands around his neck and curl into his chest. He smells like safe. Like strength. Like his shirt I now have tucked in my closet. He smells like control and power, and he also smells like sex and connection and happiness to me. I turn the feelings around in my being and then in my head, but I won't be writing these words on my note cards. These are just mine, and though they'll leave my mind, the feelings behind them, I know, will stay.

He says, "Hang on," grabs his phone, then sends off a text. "You okay if I spend the night?"

I smile, nod. "Did you tell Otis that you are?"

"I did. You sure it's okay?" His eyes twinkle. "We won't get much sleep if I stay."

"Who needs sleep with you in bed?" I grin; then he makes the bed squeak as he rolls to his side to watch his hand caress my abdomen on the way up. I watch my own fingers crawl up his throat, his jaw, and I whisper in his ear, "Help me keep quiet. I don't want us to make noise."

He rolls me to my back and sinks his hips between my thighs, his palm spreading over my cheek. He presses his thumb between my lips and strokes it against my tongue so that I can suck it instead of make noise. There's such raw need in his eyes. Suddenly I'm jealous thinking of him giving this to anyone else. I'm so jealous I can't claw my way close enough. A moan flows out of my mouth as I press my body upward. "Come closer. Come closer and tell me what you want, say it dirty," I beg in his ear.

"Tell you?" he says in his quiet voice. "I'm going to show you."

Watching me, his fist slides over the length of his erection until he's grabbed the base; slowly, he introduces the head into my body. "How dirty?" he coaxes, eyes gleaming in the lamplight. "Rachel?" The desire in his voice excites me even more. "How dirty do you want it? How hard?"

He slides, inch by inch, between my legs, and stops midway. Warm hands take the backs of my knees, and then he spreads my legs over his square shoulders. The move opens me up like a flower, my pussy exposed. His hips settle between my thighs, deeper this time, and he enters me the rest of the way, and I take him with a long, erotic moan, the pressure of his cock entering me robbing me of my breath.

Alight with exquisite pleasure, my body's throbbing for him. We both begin rocking in unison, seeking the ultimate closeness.

My nails sink into the back of his neck as my legs loosen so he can fold me over and get as deep as possible. His powerful body moves above mine in a ripple of muscles and a flex of hips and arms. God, the friction. The friction brings him balls deep. Every in-stroke brings his body to stimulate my clit. Slowly, but with expert control and powerful thrusts, he moves above me. Inside me.

The pleasure is exquisite torment: my senses attuned to his breath, warmth, weight, I don't want it to end.

He fucks me hard, every controlled thrust bursting with power, his growls a low vibration in his chest until he has no choice but to duck his head and bury the gruff sounds against my hair, and me, in his throat. We undulate together, straining to get closer, and it feels so good, so right, that instead of slowing down, I let my virgin little bed scream for mercy.

There's something so intensely good, a fierce connection—invisible but intimate—in waking up to find a man watching you sleep. It's not the first time I catch Malcolm watching me, but it's the first time I don't start. The first time I open my eyes, meet his quiet stare, and feel a pool of heat in my stomach build and build as I slowly start to smile.

"Hey," I say.

"Hey." He cups my cheek, and the brush of his thumb over my lips makes me turn my head into the touch and savor it a little. "Hmm," I say, admiring how adorable he looks recently awake.

We have officially hit the "four" mark in the sex department, and a part of me wonders if this is it.

He looks at me with respect this morning, as if he liked all the sides of myself I showed him yesterday, and I can't miss that glint in his eye that somehow silently tells me, *I know how you like it.* Lazily, he asks me about work, specifically he asks me what I'm working on. It's the second time he's asked me—the first was at the Tunnel. My heart leaps a little bit, but he's too relaxed after all the night's sex to notice.

I turn the topic around with a frown mixed with a smile. "Don't you have work too? What are you doing in bed with me?"

"Getting hard."

I laugh.

With a wry smile, he tilts my chin. "I had a good time last night." He kisses me softly, no tongue, and it feels as intense as if he'd tongued me.

I count down to ten. Then I groan in protest as I wiggle out of his arm. "Be a good boy and wait," I say. "I don't want Gina to have a heart attack."

I kick the sheets off, slip into my terry robe, and pad out into the kitchen to put coffee on. I come back into the room to brush my teeth and wash my face, then I ponder whether I should put on some makeup. I stare at my reflection. I look bare . . . my skin pale, my sad-panda eyes all dark and tired after last night. But my irises are glowing bright and I can't really keep my lips from curling upward at the corners. I grab a lipstick and a brush, but then stop myself. It's not like this is going anywhere, is it? It's not like I want him to fall in love with me—it was just a hookup. So I force myself to drop the brush and to leave the lipstick where it is. Shaking my head at myself, I don't bother primping when I go back out to check on coffee and then come back to my room with a cup for each of us in my hands.

In true man-form, Sin's spread on the bed, completely useless and clearly spent from fucking this lady right here. The duvet is at his ankles, every inch of him bare, one muscled arm behind his head, the other stretched out under the pillow I was on. Fucking god, he's glorious. I want to catalogue every detail of him—I know Gina will want to hear all about it . . . so will Wynn . . . but he's in my bed, and I don't even want to share the details about how he looks in it with my internal journalist.

"What's that?"

Checking out the goods I carry, he sits up, the muscles of his arms rippling with the move, and smiles at me. When I automatically smile in return, I feel vulnerable, real . . . and human. Why I chose to open up to a guy like him is beyond me. But I feel like my walls are still not erect. I don't want to put them back up yet.

"Coffee, or me?" I lift the coffee cup and my eyebrow at the same time.

His laugh is soft and raspy as he drags a hand through his rumpled hair, looking even more handsome as he tsks and shakes his head. "You don't know by now?"

"How greedy you are? You're right, I do know. I bet you want both."

He flashes an all-mischief smile as he pats the side of the bed, calling me back to him.

I head over with the coffee, and when he takes his cup, I slide into bed with him. We sip coffee in silence.

Before I'm finished with mine, he takes my cup and sets it on the nightstand closest to him. In one smooth, strong move, he presses me down on the bed and I fall back, breathless as he braces himself above me, his arms long and taut. He takes my fuzzy socks off. His fingers brush my arches, and I can't hold back a choked little laugh. "Your feet are ticklish, Rachel?" He's amused. I love how he says *Ray-chel*.

I nod, growing more and more breathless.

He presses his lips to mine, hard, not forcing me to open up, just soft, warm, demanding lips pressing down. I feel myself yield; and I love how he softens the kiss the moment he feels my resistance vanish. And I love what he's doing now, giving me some earlobe love, licking me, tugging and kissing my lobe, his breath warm on my ear. "You're such a man-eater, Rachel. I'm disappointed we didn't break your bed, though."

He stands, and he is beautiful and virile and edible as he dresses. "How's Saturday?" he asks.

"Excuse me?"

"How's Saturday for you?"

"I, um. For breaking my bed? I might be free Saturday."

He laughs lazily, completely relaxed this morning, all the tension from last night's event with his father completely gone. He totally fucked it out of himself. "Pick you up at noon? Wear something comfortable."

"Wait. What? Where are we going?"

"You'll see."

Butterflies in my stomach. Followed by tangled ropes, re-minding me I can't be feeling like this. I'm not a girl anymore, I'm not free to fall for a boy like this. Not this boy. I could not have chosen a worse time, an even worse circumstance, or a more elusive man to fall for. "Sin, no, I just remembered I can't. I just can't."

He studies me; then he nods quietly. "I'll call you, then."

"I'll be busy all week," I lie.

I need space between us, I need to get back to the groove of work. He stops by the door and I already miss him—the distance between my body and his suddenly too much. God, what's wrong with me?

A minute later he drives off to his office, I suppose, and when I can't seem to work, I unhook my phone from the charging outlet, power it on, and, like an addict, already worrying about when her next hit will come . . .

On the other hand, I just moved some things. Saturday is great.

I step into the shower, then check his message when I step out and wrap a towel around myself.

Good

Oh typical. He's so limited with words! I quickly wrap a towel over my wet hair and text back:

You know, I like words. You can totally use a few more
Good girl
Hahah OK.
I had a good time
Me too. I already miss you

Oh boy. Did I say that? I stress about it. Then before he can answer or feels obligated to say something like that, I quickly text:

Ok, gotta get back to work. XO

I set my phone aside and then take out my notepad, trying to write something, but I find myself doodling his name.

Malcolm Saint

23

STATUS

He changed his status.

He actually *changed* his Interface, Facebook, and general social media status.

I feel like there should've been an alert, something like an earthquake. If my stalking has told me one thing, it's that he's never done it before. *In a relationship*, it says. And considering mine still says I'm single, I wonder if Malcolm is even talking about me.

It's the weekend after he slept over, Saturday, to be exact, when I text Gina. DID YOU SEE?

She doesn't answer. I call her cell phone.

"Did you see?"

"Hmm."

"Where are you?" I demand.

"Rachel, I'm sleeping. I'm next door."

"Are you alone?"

"Of course I'm alone," said Gina.

"I'm coming over."

I flip my laptop open and cross the apartment to her room, make her scoot over, hop on her bed, and show her. She reads, frowning as if she can't figure out the emergency, then her mouth flaps open.

"Wow."

"Come on, it's more than wow."

"Double wow."

She looks at me, scowling bleakly. "Wow!" she explodes. "This is a whole new level of playerness that's just . . . so Paul-like." She scowls and is agitated and mad. Normally I'd agree with her. This is a douchebag move. But she doesn't know the details—that he is also a human being. That he has, incredibly, not really been accepted by his parents.

She doesn't see things through my eyes, the way he has this really, really genuine smile, and a wholly different smile when I'm amusing him.

"Aren't you outraged?" Gina explodes.

"I . . . well, I—"

"Rachel. Rache. Do not go Wynn on me."

"Wynn is adorable. She always gets the guy. You know why? 'Cause she thinks she deserves him, and that it's possible." I pull my phone out, my heart doing things. Excited, weird things. "I'm going to text him."

"Text what? He might be in bed with the girl he's in a relationship with."

"Then I'm going to call."

I hit dial and wait for him to answer with his usual curt *hey*.

"So I want to take you out tonight. But as I see you're in a relationship, I wanted to check if you were still available."

He laughs.

God, his laugh.

Butterflies.

"Where are you?"

"Golfing with the guys."

"When did you change your status?"

"What?"

"On Facebook."

"I didn't change it. One of my assistants must have."

"Oh."

He laughs and I feel like a dick.

"You're disappointed, Rachel?"

"No, I wouldn't even expect monogamy from you." I guess I'm testing him with that comment. I'm doing a girl thing, needy for reassurance, needy to hear him define what it is we have going on between us.

He doesn't give me much, but he says, "I do. From you."

"What? You think I can tackle any other guy at the same time I tackle you?" I ask.

Oh, my heart.

"Tahoe's dicking with the golf cart—I'll call you back."

"Fucking Tahoe," I mumble to myself as I hang up.

"Tahoe. I swear he needs something to *do*," Gina says.

"Like you. Just say it."

"Never."

"He's the product of your every fantasy."

"He's an animal."

"He thinks you're succulent."

"What?"

"Yes, he asked me your name. 'That succulent friend of yours.' "

"He did not. Motherfucker!"

I sit there staring morosely at my "single" status.

Gina sits there, stumped because Tahoe thinks her succulent.

She recovers first. "I feel awful for you, but you walked into it with your eyes and, apparently, your legs open, Rachel."

I roll to my shoulders so I can face her. "Gina, just having feelings for him makes me feel like I'm betraying me and you. We said we wouldn't do this."

"And now you'll have to make a choice, Rachel: the job or the man."

"There is no choice! If I choose him he'll fly away like some wild falcon before I can even hold him for long."

Gina grimaces. "Then pray he ends things soon."

"It hurts praying for something you don't want."

"Then end it yourself. Get it over and done with."

I sigh.

"Rache, did he really say that?"

"Tahoe?"

"No, his dick. Of course, Tahoe. Well, Tahoe *and* his dick."

"Yes, but I don't want him near you."

She scowls. "I hope he stays away from me next month—it's the anniversary of Paul's dumping me, and I always feel particularly vulnerable."

I groan and fall back on the bed, rubbing my face. "Gina! What's happening to us?"

"Man. Mankind. Manwhores."

Sigh.

"You and Saint." She studies me dubiously. "You ever wonder if you and he could have an epic relationship?"

"You mean epic disaster."

"No, I mean"—she shrugs—"he's excitement, and you

could ground him. It could be an epic relationship if he doesn't fuck it up . . . or you."

"This from you? I'm blown away right now, Gina."

"I'm just asking. You have to have wondered. You know. Like a sex fantasy but without sex."

"I do," I admit. "I wonder what it would be like to be a part of his life, not just his bed. I know it was me who set up the relationship that way . . . not wanting to be part of public scrutiny. But I also know deep down it would never work. He can't be had, G." I shake my head. "Saint will never be had." And even if he could be, a scenario of what it could be like pops into my head. "Plus I'll live in fear of every other single woman out there and of Malcolm's nature to fuck around just because he can."

"Then just enjoy it, Rachel." She sighs and pats the top of my head, saying exaggeratedly, "You have my blessing, child."

"Do you mean that, Gina?"

She smiles. "I wish you wouldn't, but you're too far in. Plus, if I say no, you're going to keep doing it behind my back. Please don't. I'm your friend, that's what I'm here for."

"Thank you." God, it's like an enormous weight has been lifted from my shoulders. It's torture to be on a roller coaster, unable to scream, and that's exactly how having to bottle up the experience has felt.

I stare blankly at the ceiling, and then just smile because . . .

Well. His assistant changed his Facebook status. Cathy, maybe? Oh, how I wish I could have coffee with Cathy one day and know everything.

Everything.

I grab my phone and text him:

My hands would be very busy if you were next to me right now

My mother answers.

Hey darling. What do you mean?

I text him:

OMG I just sent a dirty text to my mother

Then to my mother:

Yes, Momma, I'd love to massage your neck. New technique I
learned

Sin's text:

Resend to me

Me:

SIN! This was an absolute mood killer. You'll just have to
wonder what it said ;)

The next day, I'm worn out from going hiking with him. I'm also
sleeping at his place. Pushing up on my arm, I take inventory.
 Every chiseled feature on his tanned face. LIKE.
 His wicked mouth. LIKE.
 His gorgeous, tiny brown man-nipples. LIKE.
 Oh god. I LIKE him so much.
 Sighing, I slip back into his arms. I LIKE this too much, too.

He picks me up in the Rolls two days later. Otis opens the door for me and Saint's just landed, back from some hot-shot conference in New York. He is the epitome of a sexy and golden black-haired god in a suit.

SIN, IN A SUIT.

I shift on the seat and slowly slide to the car floor, inching between his hard thighs, grinning up at him when he stops talking on the phone. Because yes, he's talking on the phone. Doing business. How strange? Ha ha.

I rub my jaw on his thigh and slide my hands up the hard muscle. "Yes, Charles," he continues. The mystery in his gaze as he watches me beckons me. Smiling in mischief, I rub my cheek on his other thigh, then my lips, then I nuzzle my way upward until my mouth and jaw rub against his erection. He's hard as rock under my lips as I lightly scrape them over the fabric, the thickening texture of his voice thrilling me. ". . . the short sell . . ." I hear him say, and as I look up to see if he likes what I'm doing, his eyes are gleaming down at me like glassy volcanic rocks.

The sound of my breathing echoes in the silence as Saint allows this Charles guy to speak—then *zip.* I lower Saint's zipper, then pull open his belt, never once taking my eyes off his face. His beautiful face. His lids look weighted as he watches my every move, and his gaze flares hot and tender as I take him out. He is all smooth velvet flesh, all of him, hard and thick. So strong. So vital. So *ready.*

I lick him, base to tip. I encircle his cock with my mouth, my tongue roaming, pressing, tasting as I feather my lips across the head. He tastes exquisite. His cock was made for sucking and for fucking, and right now nothing will convince me it wasn't made for me.

His fingers slide into my hair as his cock swells even thicker and longer between my lips.

I suck harder, the head of his cock massaging my throat.

"That sounds right," he says quietly into the phone. As he speaks, he brushes my hair behind my shoulders. *He wants to see my face,* I realize.

He wants to see mine, and I really want to see his.

Prolonging our eye contact, I continue savoring him, getting lost in the moment, and he tightens his hand on my hair. I pour myself into it. I want this to be a most memorable blow job, just like I love to mentally replay the times he's gone down on me.

He is enormous, pink flesh straining to be inside me—to be pleased. And right now I have one goal only: to make Saint come inside me. He's beautiful and in control and powerful, and I want him to come in my mouth.

My sex throbbing, I hear his voice as he tells Charles to keep him posted; then he hangs up and tosses the phone aside.

"Rachel," he says in thick approval, cupping my face with both hands, smiling down at me with pure heat. He rubs his thumbs over my cheekbones as he pulls my face up and back as he leans forward to kiss my lips. "Do you like it?" he asks.

I nod. Stroking his thighs, up his abs, I whisper, "I want to taste you. . . ." I'm beyond happy when he sets his hands at his sides and lets me get back to him.

I stroke my fingers up the length of his shaft and kiss the wetness at the tip, my body one single throbbing nerve as I savor his breath changing, one hand reaching out and his fingers clenching in my hair, the words he whispers to me as he starts pushing me and losing control. *That's right, Rachel . . . God, that's right. . . . Do you like it . . . ?*

I don't even realize my own hands are acting wild, rubbing up his chest, clawing at him, up his neck, the back of his head, as I try to get closer to intensify my blow job, to give him the kind of pleasure he gives me.

As I suck with more vigor, he whispers, his voice raw and low, "I come with *you*, Rachel," and he pulls me up with his hands on my face, then urges me down on the car bench as I start yanking down my jeans with record speed. He strips them off my legs, and then his hungry lips nibble a path up my stomach to my breasts as he pushes my top upward and my bra downward, freeing my nipples. A soft, helpless moan leaves me as I arch my body, offering him everything I have and more.

"Oh, yes," I moan, raking my nails over his back, wanting to feel his skin on mine.

He claims my lips. I'm not sure we can deal with this, with how we feel. No. Maybe only *I* feel like this, but he feels something for me too, I can feel it in his hands, his looks. So this is what we do. He nibbles my lips, urges my legs open with his palms. I've stopped breathing when he lowers his head. He tastes me. Firm strokes of his tongue.

He turns me into a bubbling mess, torturing me, pushing me to the brink of orgasm and then . . . making me wait as he tears into a condom packet and sheathes his glorious cock.

He covers me with his body, and the next second we're locked, groaning in relief. His torture doesn't end there. He drives deep and slow, forcing me to savor every pulsing, delicious inch of every thorough and perfect plunge. I can't keep still. I can't hold back the fierce sensation of something building inside me, straining for release. My mouth sucks his beautiful full mouth, his ear, his neck, his jaw raspy under my lips.

I'm so scared to consider what it is. I'm so scared he'll hurt me. I'm so scared I'll hurt him. I suck back a quiet sob as I start coming, shaking and trembling in both excruciating pleasure and quiet internal pain.

My eyes blur. I hear his loud bark as he comes, feel the long, deep pulses of his body coming over mine, and I take advantage to wipe my eyes and then kiss any part of him I can.

Saint invites me to dinner at some posh, top-rated, hard-to-get-into place, but I tell him I don't want a crowd. So he does something I don't expect; he gets us into Navy Pier after hours. We walk the long, quiet path that usually bustles with people; tonight it is quiet and empty, except for us. On one side are the stores, games, little shops, and on the other, the pier.

"How did you pull this off?"

"Otis knows one of the night guards." He chuckles.

"Let's go into one of those." I point at the Ferris wheel, and we get into one of the empty seats, shielded from the wind as he asks me if I ever came here when I was younger.

"Sometimes, with my mother," I say. "You?"

"My mother wouldn't have been caught dead here."

"But here you are. You look just as handsome in those jeans as in your suit." I touch the collar of his crisp white button-down shirt. "I love these shirts of yours. Sometimes I want to see my lipstick on one, just because."

He laughs, the sound full and rich. Mischievous, I lean over and press my mouth to the collar. His smile fades. "You have a rebel streak in you, Rachel." His eyes are admiring, filling me with heat.

"You bring it out . . ." I accuse, laughing as I step back, and I swear he looks even more powerful, more unattainable, and more handsome with my lipstick on his shirt. Just a little bit mine.

He asks me to visit him at his office, teasing me on the phone that he's got an opening. Do I want to talk about Interface? he asks.

Why, yes, I say.

I drop in at the time he indicates, and then he stands there, taking me in, his shirt up to his elbows as if he'd been knee deep in work, his hair rumpled. His voice sounds tired as he tells Cathy to leave us, and then he asks me, "How are you, Rachel?"

"Good now," I whisper, and we start kissing, the papers on his desk shoved aside with one of his arms as he props me there like his most pressing business, and he goes right to taking care of it.

I text him in the afternoon, wondering what he's doing tonight. Just then, he appears inside *Edge,* to everyone's shock. My eyes widen, sure that my stomach just flew to my throat, and I glance over to see if Helen has seen him. She's both pale and flushing. I hurry to ask her, "Helen, can I—?"

"Go!"

I grab my bag and come out of my cubicle. "Hey," I say.

He smiles at me, especially at my bag. "I hope this means you're coming with me," he says, eyes twinkling, the entire office melting right with me. Even Valentine.

"'Bye, Rachel!" he calls excitedly.

"'Bye, Valentine," I say, slipping my arm into the crook of Malcolm's.

"Friend?" Malcolm asks me about Valentine. Sizing him up. The girl inside me shivers as I wonder if he's jealous.

I nod. "Fan of yours," I whisper.

He cocks a brow. "Not heterosexual?"

"Not fully. More like bi."

He bursts out laughing, a sound that is rich and makes my knees weak, and I grab his face and flat-out kiss him in the elevator, pulling that laughter inside me. "I like to hear you laugh," I whisper.

He doesn't say anything, but I feel thoroughly liked when he looks down at me, his lips smiling, but his eyes hot and admiring.

I'm staring at my computer screen.

Every link I click about Saint is talking about him having a possible relationship with ME.

Speculation is fierce.

Somehow, people are more interested in wondering whether or not he's in a relationship than they ever were about him womanizing.

His Twitter feed is full of questions about his girlfriend.

I'm stressing about it, wondering what I've gotten myself into, until I spot a new tweet from Tahoe appear in my feed.

So the guy actually tagged me.

Hanging tonight w/ my boys unless @MalcolmSaint girlfriend @RachelLiv objects

Fuuuuuck.

A dozen replies have followed up in the next few seconds:

I give it a week

Saint could not be monogamous if he wanted to, he needs the variety

She's not pretty enough!

Is this for real? I thought this was some sort of publicity stunt.

Saint really has a girlfriend?

Hours later, I see Tahoe deleted the tweet, and I'd bet my life Malcolm made him.

Later that week, Saint asks me out.

"I can't, your social media is already ablaze about us."

He ends up taking me to *The Toy*, and we go out onto the lake in the afternoon.

He spends all of the first hour doing business. "How many hours can you be on the phone, who are you talking to?" From my lounger, I attempt to pry his phone away, and he holds it above his head, out of my reach.

"Do you see the blonde on that other yacht?" I point, distracting him.

He's wearing shades, so I can't see what he's looking at, but he keeps his phone in his hand and leans back casually on a folded arm. The sun really loves this man. He's gold, his hair gleaming, my own reflection in a blue bikini staring back at me in his mirrored lenses. He doesn't bother to turn around to scan the girls on the other yacht nearby. "I see the one in front of me," he murmurs huskily.

"Blondes are your type, no?" I point at her again—she's on the top deck of the other yacht, in a striped navy-and-white bikini, definitely looking this way. "Look at her. Pretty. Just your type."

He tucks his phone under his lounger. "I don't have a type, not really."

"Am I your type?"

"You're the first of a type."

I laugh. "You're the first of your type. Unfortunately, I don't think there's another one quite like you." I look at the girls again. "The other one is beautiful too. Malcolm! Look at them!"

He sits up now, lowering his elbows to his knees as he edges closer to me, the line of his mouth curving a little. "The things I used to like in a woman have lost some of their charm."

"Why?"

I pry his sunglasses off. His eyes shine under the sun and sparkle with secrets, and my stomach dips and my breath goes when they meet mine. "I look at them and see one glaring fault in them all," he tells me soberly, and he tsks and shakes his head, his gold skin gleaming under the sun. "A pity, really."

"What?"

"They're not the blonde I want."

I stare.

My knot as tight as ever.

"They're not you, Rachel," he specifies.

He leans forward to seize my chin, forcing me to look at him.

"Now, why do you want me to look at them? Do *you* like girls?"

I burst out laughing and push at his hand. "Malcolm," I chide.

"Do you?" he laughs, taking my chin again, teasing me.

"No! I would never share my man!"

With a low laugh, he leans back on the lounger, taking his sunglasses from my hand and trying them on my face. I giggle and pose; he chuckles and gives me goose bumps as he does then he plucks them off and encloses them in his big hands.

"That must sound terribly boring to a man like you," I say. "That I won't share my man."

"I'm not contesting it."

"The boring part?"

"The second part."

"You'd be monogamous for a girl?"

"I would be, for *my* girl." He leans forward again. "See, I've never had a girl I saw as mine. They've all been public property." Smirking, he sets his sunglasses next to his phone under his lounger, then looks at me with the same brilliant, thick-lashed, deep-set eyes that have been appearing nonstop in my dreams. "But there's this one girl. My private property."

"I don't know who you're talking about, but if she had any sense in her, she'd run away as fast as possible. It's not sexy to be considered anyone's property, Malcolm."

"Come here. You know I'm talking about you." His arm sweeps out and he seizes me by the waist.

"No, I don't, because we said we were just sleeping together, just—"

I squirm a little as he draws me to his lap. "Why do you fight me on this?" He smiles and scowls, both at the same time, then settles me down on his lap and stares right into me—dead serious. "I'm good at the one-night-stand thing," he tells me. "I'm excellent at fooling around. I was made to fuck around. If anyone can tell the difference between fucking around and the real thing, it's me."

Oh god. I'm melting.

I spread my hands on the sides of his jaw. "You were made for great things. Everyone can see that."

"You want to be with me," he murmurs. "I see the way you blush, hear you stop breathing, and I like being the cause of both." He stares at me soberly, and I'm scared. I'm so scared, I'm trembling in his arms, on his lap.

"I'm not your girl, Saint. I'm probably the only girl you know who doesn't want to be your girlfriend. I think you're suffering from the wanting-what-you-can't-have syndrome."

He looks down at me, tender-eyed, as if he understands the battle in me. As if he's been there or knows instinctively that I'm going to lose—but he will still have no pity on me. "I don't think so, Rachel. I've got you right where I want you."

"On your big yacht." I roll my eyes.

"Nah. Next to me." The comment makes my stomach dip and the backs of my ears flush hot.

"You're teasing me."

"You're blushing."

"It's a suntan. I'm tanning right now. You know. On your big yacht. You've lost the ability to make me shy. I no longer blush."

He tugs my bikini top open, and I yell, "Malcolm!"

"Not a suntan," he says, his stare hot on my breasts as I scramble to tie the top up again. "You're blushing all over, every inch of you," he says approvingly.

Before I know it, we're kissing, hot and lazily, for what feels like a minute and an hour. We're so hot by the time we peel our lips apart, I'm sure he'll pursue this in the bedroom, but he's got a dinner, and we have to head to the docks before we can get into it.

"You sure you don't want to come?" He rumples my hair on his way past me.

"And be the feast for all those reporters? No, thank you," I mumble, stealing glimpses of him as he covers that god's body in his sexy business clothes.

He zips up his slacks, then starts to work his buttons with fast, nimble fingers. "It bothers you that they're after you?"

I shrug as I force myself into my slim-fit jeans. "How do you live with it?"

"I don't have a choice." He looks at me, watching me and my jeans battle it out. "It's new to them because you're new to me. Are you uncomfortable, Rachel?"

"A little. Not in my jeans, with those assholes who are after you and, now, me."

He chuckles deliciously, then shakes his head and rakes his fingers through his hair. "Then I'll take care of it."

"Don't, it'll fade away along with your interest," I call after him.

"Not happening anytime soon," he says flatly, out of the room already.

By that night I have several texts from Helen.

Rachel I need something this week.

Call me when you can

I hope everything is going smoothly

And I've got the worst case of writer's block. I have a brick in my head instead of a brain, and it's absolutely silent. I stare at my screen, unable to write even one sentence. Nothing. I open my box of note cards and notes, then turn back to my online list of links.

Still nothing.

I'm so restless, I can't write, and my deadline looms like a DEAD END sign ahead. I thought things would have cooled down with Saint by now, but instead . . . where is this going?

Distracting myself, I start looking for new links when I see an article online.

Tiger Can't Change His Stripes—Saint Reverts to Old Ways
After Rumored Split with Possible Girlfriend

And I see an image of him, sharp in a suit, with the event banner in the distance. Today's event banner, to be exact. And a beautiful blonde who looks like *me* standing with him, looking dotingly up into his face.

My face just pales, and my stomach aches. I lift my finger to his face. He looks so detached and remote. I can't believe this is the same man who was teasing me only hours ago.

I sit there and see her with her arm linked in his, and he looks beautiful. It's the most coveted spot in Chicago, that arm of his. Who wouldn't be happy and proud to stand by Saint's side?

You, because that's not your place; your place is at *Edge,* in your own safe life, not in the crazy whirlwind of his. Slamming my laptop shut, I head out to the living room, having no room for jealousy tonight or anything other than writer's block. No, thanks. Getting possessive over a man who's proven to be unattainable for years is not what I need right now.

What I need is to let my brain rest so that my muse can come back.

What I *also* need right now is to start focusing on my project, not on sex and Sin.

"What are you watching?" I go sit next to Gina.

"Moulin Rouge," she says, sniffling.

"Oh, I can't watch *Moulin Rouge* right now!" I pound my fist on the seat beneath me; all the anger I feel bubbles up with that sentence, and I end up heading to my room as the song "Come What May" follows me.

I curl up on my bed with my phone in my hand, staring at his name. *Don't text him, Rachel.* He's with another girl, the perfect out for you so you can stop seeing him and get straight back to work.

I lie in bed a little after midnight and then I see:

SIN
Can I come over?

I scowl. I don't answer, but I keep the phone in my hand, unable to set it aside.

It vibrates.

SIN the screen blinks.

My heart leaps as I sit up, inhale, then answer as casually as I can. "Hey, I thought you had something tonight."

"For you, I do," he growls softly, voice husky with lust. "Can I come over?"

WAAAAANT.

I want him, want him. WAAANT HIM. Just his voice on the phone runs in my veins like a shot of arousal. "I'm sleeping."

"Lucky you."

"Did you have a good time tonight?" I ask.

Is she going to be your favorite now?

"It was okay."

"Oh."

"I put an end to the rumors about us. Press should be off your back for a while."

"Oh." Delighted surprise flits through me. Is that why he was with her? "Thank you, I guess."

"Maybe now you'll go with me sometime to one of these events, Rachel."

"I can't," I say, bed squeaking as I shift to my side and get more comfortable. "But what did you do tonight? Tell me what I missed out on." I pull my covers over me, waiting for his voice to soothe me like it does.

"Same ole. Most interesting thing of the night was meeting one of my employees. A man who was in a coma, woke up able to speak several languages."

I laugh. "That's unbelievable! I love hearing about such inexplicably fascinating things."

"I thought you'd find it interesting," he says with pleasure. I hear the sound of a car door. Did he get home just now?

"Which ones? Languages, I mean."

"German, French, and Russian." Silence. Then . . . the elevator ting? "See, Rachel"—a teasing tone comes into his voice—"you would've enjoyed yourself. I'd have taken care of you tonight."

"Oh, I'm sure you would have. Plus I have a thing for other languages. A man speaking German, oof."

"I can speak German in your ear tonight."

I laugh, then fall sober. I hear footsteps, then the door. I picture him in his room, want to be there with every inch of me. "No, we really can't," I breathe.

I hear a creak.

Did he just jump into bed?

"We can, you're just afraid to," he murmurs.

"Aren't *you*? Afraid? Concerned?"

"I'm not concerned, I'm fascinated by this. By us."

I feel all my shyness returning. Saint is so perceptive.

Does he feel this pull as strongly as I do?

When I hear him again, his voice surprises me with that deep, almost reassuring quality, its timbre as thick as syrup. "Considering I never expected to have an addiction like you, much less for it to last the week, I'm not letting this go, Rachel," he whispers.

Hot from the tip of my head to my toes, I stare at the ceiling, warm and afraid, uncertain what to say and where we'd go if I admitted just how far into him I really am. I feel him in my body, still. I feel him still inside me. In places you can't tattoo. In places nobody's ever ventured to.

"A challenge, then," I say. "I'm a challenge."

"Maybe," he says, still husky. "The challenge of my life."

I laugh. "You're teasing me now."

He doesn't laugh.

We stay silent for a while, so silent I can almost hear his heart beating through the phone. His slow breathing. "Good night, Saint."

"Malcolm," he quietly corrects.

"Malcolm."

He chuckles then, at last. "Good night, Rachel. Think of me."

Oh fuck. I groan.

What does he want from me? What do I want from HIM?

I need to talk to someone who won't remind me what a mess I've made of things.

24

MOTHERS KNOW BEST

I need to see my mother. First, because I need to see that she's looking a nice healthy color, not gaining or not losing weight because of unstable blood sugar. Second, because I know that she will have something wise to tell me, something that will help me see that maybe there's a positive to take out of this freaking mess I've gotten myself into. I ask the girls to come over with me. I need girl time, which usually makes me feel wonderful. Tea, carbs, talking about Wynn's aromatherapy shop and Emmett, Gina's anecdotes about the department store, my mom telling me she's stolen some time to paint in the room that used to be mine, and topics for my column.

My mother looks perfectly stable. She swears to me that her insulin's working like clockwork and she's had no recent blood sugar spikes, no episodes of hypoglycemia.

She's enjoying the girls' updates with a big, wide smile and eyes that are, by the second, getting bigger and wider than that.

"So she's now going to take him down," Wynn finishes filling my mom in.

My mother looks at me in surprise, then laughs. "Oh, but those young boys, they're just being boys. They're just being themselves—they're certainly not evil. Malcolm Saint has been some sort of bachelor hero since he was born to that devil of a dad!"

"I didn't say he was evil," I quickly say, prickling in defense. "This story . . . it's a job, it's like pulling the curtain away from something, or revealing something new about a topic people are crazy about. I am certainly not going to write that he's evil!" I'm getting defensive, so I scowl. "I'm not a mean person, Mother, I'm just trying to do my job."

"So what will you say? That he's a womanizer? These girls maybe *want* to be taken advantage of. I know I did. Your father—"

"Stop!"

Her eyes widen at my outburst.

"I need to write this exposé, and do you know why? Because if I don't, I'll get fired, and I don't know how I'll get by. And even if I don't get fired, *Edge* is at the edge of *collapse*—and dozens of people are going to end up without jobs. And this, Mother, this is my opportunity to get you a house—a house of your own so you can paint for the rest of your days and maybe have me support you. So I will *write* this exposé because I'm a professional, and then *Edge* will get a new edge and my job will stabilize or even catapult me to another level, and then I'm going to buy you a big-ass car and a big-shit house with the money that rolls in, and Saint will be on his yacht with a dozen lovers and he won't even give a shit." My voice breaks and my eyes start watering, and Gina and Wynn, who'd been busy flipping through my mother's magazines, suddenly look up and lower them.

My mother's face softens. "I don't want a house, Rachel," she says, slowly setting down the tea box she'd been pulling out of a cabinet.

A stray tear comes to the corner of my eye, and I dab at it. "Well, you're getting one. You deserve one, Momma."

"Rachel, did you miss having a father so much? Did it hurt you so much?" She comes over and sits by my side, and reaches out to take my hand in her warm, soft one.

"It didn't make a dent. I had you," I assure her, blinking because I've never, ever had an episode like this.

"So why do you need to do something that is clearly not sitting too well with you?" she continues in that understanding way of hers.

Another tear, in my other eye, escapes. I free my hand from my mother's and wipe it, aware of Wynn and Gina being so quiet, everyone being so quiet except me, breathing fast as I try not to cry harder than these measly little sniffles. "Well, isn't that what life is about?" I ask her. "Making hard choices? Isn't that what you choosing to stop painting so you could get a job was about? It was a choice that broke your heart but you had to do it because there was no other choice. Not really. Was there?"

"This young man, how does he feel about you?"

"He's not in love with me, Mother. He's not my dad. It wasn't love at first sight, it wasn't two soul mates connecting. He doesn't want to be with me like Father did with you. He didn't see me and think, 'That's my soul mate, that's the woman I want to spend the rest of my life with, no matter how short'!"

I can't go on. My throat clams up and my chest hurts. "I'm a challenge to him," I add in a little voice. "I'm just this challenge to him. He's not a man to feel love for a woman, he's not made like that. He and I . . ." Something in my chest keeps tightening, like a noose, and my eyes are on fire. "We wouldn't last even a season. And just like my dad, one second, poof, he'll be gone, and it'll be just me and you. Me and you, Mom. Like always."

I don't think I can bear to hear a reply, any reply, whether it's to soothe, to reassure, even to agree, which might hurt even worse, and because I'm being stared at by the three of them as if I just grew a thousand worms out of my head—because I'm *evil* and that's what happens to *evil* bitches like me—I push to my feet and head down the hall to my old room and close the door, breathing as I sit there on a stool before my mother's unfinished canvas, my eyes leaking tears. I don't even know why I'm crying. It shouldn't have been this hard. I never expected it to be this hard. But my friends and my mother are starting to think I'm making a mistake.

I groan and lie down on the floor where my bed used to be, staring up above. I stared at this ceiling when I was just a little girl who wanted a dad, who had dreams, who wanted to make a difference, who wanted to write because writing made something . . . it made something out of nothing.

I used to lie here as a girl, and before I met Gina and she met Paul, I would wonder if I'd ever fall in love with a man the way my mother fell in love with my dad. My mother loved my dad before he even had the chance to disappoint her or break her heart. My mother has the purest view of men in the world, that they are inherently good—the yang in the world, the perfect complement to our yin. And I used to be a girl who would wonder who my yang would be. What he'd do. How he'd look. How hard he'd love me.

Never did I imagine twinkling green eyes and dozens of smiles, and a man who challenges me, teases me, is about as flawed as he is perfect, and makes me want to know him down to his every last thought.

My girl . . .

God. I've made such a huge mistake.

By fighting him, I've only intrigued him more.

Yielding to him, I've only doomed myself to pain.

My mistake wasn't accepting the assignment to write the exposé, it was that I dropped my walls and got close to him to the point where he feels like part of my soul. My mistake was taking his shirt in my hand, and going to his club, and to his yacht, and moving my lips beneath his, and going to his place and begging him to make love to me even after I promised myself it would never happen.

I need to put an end to this, but I can't rationalize right now. The thought that I need to end it makes me crave to see him all the more.

I impulsively pull out my cell phone and dial. His voice mail answers. He's probably fucking some other chick, I tell myself negatively. I leave a message: "Hey, it's me. I guess . . . nothing, really. Call me. Or not. 'Bye."

I hang up. Then I wipe my tears and get a grip. I had a goal, a chance to write an exposé, to get my name out there, advance my career, reveal the real Saint and not the legend. Maybe I can open a girl's eyes and avoid one broken heart. Maybe they can realize that Saint won't love them. Nobody is going to love them except themselves, if they work hard at it. And their friends, if they choose wisely. And their families, if they're lucky. This is my side of the story—the side of the little girl who grew up wondering what it would be like to live with a man's love, then grew determined to prove to herself she didn't need it. I know there are a lot of girls out there like me. Those who didn't get the guy at seven, at thirteen, at fifteen—they didn't even get the guy when they were born. Why will we get the guy now, when we've grown up already? *We don't need him now.*

He calls me back. "Hey. You all right?" he asks.

"I . . ." Something unknots in my stomach at the sound of his voice. I've never felt so connected with a guy. Where you can hear the concern in his voice, and you're sure he can hear the sadness and frustration in yours. How can this be? I wipe the corners of my eyes. Hate, hate, hate crying. "Yes, I'm okay. I just wanted to talk to you."

I clear my voice, hating that it wavered a little at the end. There's a tense silence. Way to go, Rachel. Say goodbye to Saint now. Do you think he wants to deal with a crybaby right now?

"Where are you?" he asks.

"I'm at my mom's. Heading back to my apartment."

"Otis will be there. Spend the afternoon with me."

My voice gets shy and I admit, "I'd love that, Malcolm."

He's quiet, as if taken aback by how vulnerable I sound. And then he surprises me too, his voice just as low and fiercely husky and tender. "Me too. I'll see you soon."

I hang up and stare at my phone, my heart literally in pain inside my chest. Am I in love with him? Why am I so consumed and so confused? It seems like my brain points me in the direction of my logic and my lifetime career dream, but the rest of me doesn't want to go there if it means having to leave him.

I glance at my mother's painting and am struck by its raw beauty. It's like nothing she's ever painted before, as if all these years what she couldn't paint just simmered inside her, creating a powerful force that, once set free, fired up and took over the canvas. Even the room itself.

Just like an affair with Saint is taking over me.

25

NEEDING A SAINT

Two hours later I reach the docks, and when I see him waiting for me on the deck of *The Toy*, I inhale, long and slow. I'm wearing a yellow dress that's quite informal, because I hadn't planned to see him today, and I need to flatten my palms to my thighs to keep the dress from going up when the point is for it to fall down.

The wind flaps my hair as I board, also pushes the fabric of his white polo against the planes of his chest. He wears baggy white cargo shorts with that shirt, his legs thick and muscled.

He picks me up and swings me around and onto the deck, then takes my hand and leads me to the top deck. We don't even say hello. There's no need. I hadn't realized we were at that telepathic point I've only ever been at with my mother and friends, where you know what the other needs and you say nothing, you just stand there and be there. And that's exactly what he does for me as he keeps my fingers within his strong ones and brings me to the sitting area. I feel fragile, like if he touches me more,

I'll break. So I pull free, take a seat on the chair across from the couch, and just sit there quietly as the boat engines hum and we head into open water.

"Want to talk about it?" Malcolm asks from where he sits across from me, reaching out to brush my hair back. Eyes like blades slice through my walls.

Malcolm is such a sex god. He's a playboy and a player, but nobody sees past that. That he's funny. Also, in a way, very reserved. He's kind . . . I've seen it firsthand. He's kind with me, with his friends, never denying any request for charity. For anything. If he doesn't want to sleep with me ever again, he's a man I'd be honored to call my friend. I've come to respect him that much.

I'm also feeling so jealous over him, to know I have to step back so others can have him kills me.

"I'm having one of those days when my family . . . well, my mother and my friends and I aren't seeing eye to eye," I murmur.

The concern in his eyes is almost too much for me right now; right now when I hate myself for my job. For what I've been doing.

"Malcolm." His name escapes my lips in a soft moan.

He reaches out and draws me between his widely spread knees. "Never saw eye to eye with my family," he offers, sitting me on his thigh, and I'm surprised that he's willing to go there again. On his own. A tiny voice in my mind tells me, *He's doing it for you, Rachel. To connect with you.* "It made me feel all sorts of fucked up. Like there was something wrong with me. It doesn't matter what they believe. What do you believe?"

That I suck! I want to cry. I look down to his hand on my hip, and I slip my hand over his just because I don't want him to remove it—and I know that when I turn in the exposé, I will never feel this big, strong hand holding me by the hips again. Can I really do this?

"We didn't see eye to eye on anything," he continues. He brushes my hair behind my ears as the wind flaps it around, then grabs it in his fist and holds it to the nape of my neck so we can look at each other. "Nothing I did was good enough. I could never live up to the Saint name."

"So since you couldn't live up to the Saint name, you gave it a whole new reputation?"

His eyes glint greener. "Nah. I just did my own thing, tried to be happy regardless."

He watches me as if wondering why I'm not happy.

No. He watches me with intensity as if he's wondering what *he* can do to make me happy.

"Most times, I am happy," I admit. "Others it's like I keep waiting for something. I feel like I've lived with this little hole all my life."

"I know that hole."

When he nods, I tease him a little, reaching out to jab him. "I thought all your toys filled it up quite nicely. And your blondes."

"Not the toys." He laughs, then he catches my arm before I stand and ends up pulling me down on his lap with a forceful tug. The moment I land on his lap, well, let's just say it's not a soft landing. "Only one blonde."

He wants me.

His cock is so hard it's throbbing prominently against my bum. A heat rises in me as he slips his fingers into my hair. He whispers in my ear, "You look wound up and ready to be loved."

"And you don't waste a boner," I tease.

He laughs, and our smiles start to fade as we look at each other.

"I saw . . . how you got rid of the rumor about us," I finally tell him.

He looks at me, as if waiting for the question.

I want to ask, but I can't. It would be so hypocritical of me to ask if he'd slept with her when at the same time I want to keep our relationship casual.

"No, I didn't," he answers, watching me, and I'm sure he can see the tumult of feelings I have for him in my eyes.

I'm aware that I'm falling, I'm falling so hard my tummy aches. I'm playing with fire, putting my heart right on the train track for it to be squished soon. But neither the threat of being burned nor the oncoming train can stop me.

"You totally could," I say, as nonchalantly as I can.

"Yeah, I know." His lips twitch, his eyes sparkling tenderly, as if I amuse him.

Heart pounding, I wind my arms around his neck and whisper, "I'm glad you didn't," and rain slow, deep, anxious kisses up his thick neck while I tug his shirt out of his waistband.

"I won't," he rasps, and for a man who makes no promises, this feels like one, like a warm promise on my ear as my fingers slide up the bumps of his abs. It unravels me, all the knots inside me, so hard and so fast that a tremor racks my body and he notices, smiles at it.

"Malcolm," I breathe, all of a sudden as wet as I've ever been, feeling like he's mine right now, all mine. He lets me do the kissing for a moment while he drops his nose into my hair as his hands tangle in the length of it.

I slide my fingers under his shirt and push it up to kiss his abs, every single square inch revealed for me, up to his brown nipples. Then I lick my way up to his nipple while he pulls my dress up to my waist and grabs my panties in one hand, tugging them downward. I stand until I kick them off, and he takes advantage of that to unzip his shorts and pull himself out.

Desire trembles through me as he puts on the condom. He reaches for me, and I lift my legs and fold them at his sides, lowering myself, the skirt of my dress falling over us so that no passing yacht or boat can see, exactly, what we're doing.

He's so big, I moan every time he's fully seated inside me, but he likes it, he likes making me moan.

He likes making love to me.

Slowly, our bodies connecting, our mouths searching, the pleasure escalating. Our clothes lie between us but his flesh is inside me and I'm gripping him hotly, tightly, every rock of my hips meant to drive him deeper.

He murmurs something hot and dirty against the top of my head, and I nod without even being certain what it is I'm agreeing to, only saying yes.

We head to the cabin after a delicious meal. He sleeps without a stitch on, and it makes sleeping with him my first ever addiction. I slide under the sheets and press my cheek to his chest and listen to his heart as I fold my leg and hook it around his long, hard thigh.

I can't even say how safe I feel right now.

"Do you feel better?" he asks in my ear.

"Much," I admit.

I start to relax and think about what Gina asked. Whether he and I could have any future at all. Whether we could have something even remotely resembling a romance. I don't want to hope that, even if I worked out my job issue, we have anything. But it's hard to convince myself as he trails his hand up and down my back and we're quiet, comfortable, as if we've done this a thousand times and could do it a thousand more.

I'm exhausted, but at the same time, I can't sleep tonight. No matter how much I braced myself. How many emotional bulletproof vests I tried to wear. How much I fought myself. How many "stories" about Malcolm Saint I used as ammunition against the reality of him. I'm not immune. He affects me like nobody ever has. Knowing all of Malcolm's faults did nothing to stop me from getting attached. Instead, knowing his faults endeared him to me.

I connect to him. I connect *with* him.

My exposé . . . what will I expose now? I came in intending to discover and unmask a legend, but what I found is now lying sweaty and sated in my arms, flesh and blood, imperfect and irresistible. And this—with him, here—is the first real spot I've ever been in in my life where I want to stand still.

We had an extensive sex marathon at night, so we've been dozing off this morning as *The Toy* smoothly glides through the water. My skin prickles under the warmth of the sun, the wind playing with my hair, the soft rocking motions of the yacht. The engines hum softly, lulling me to a near sleep.

Saint just hung up his phone from another business call. Now he's lounging right beside me.

The sunlight strikes the lake, causing the yacht's shadow to shimmer across the water. I stretch out and flip onto my stomach, untying my top so I don't get a tan line.

Malcolm instantly caresses that spot, his hand spreading all over my bare back. "I'm going to tan with your big hand on me!" I laugh.

He chuckles and moves it to curl around my neck, then up to my scalp. His phone rings again, and he stands and paces while he talks. I watch a smile flash across his face.

He runs his fingers through the sexy disorder of his hair. "Yeah? Good."

I grin like a dope, addicted to watching him work, wondering what he's doing. When I'm with this man, I can never think of anything but all that makes him who he is.

He glances at me with his cell phone to his ear, crooking a finger to call me over. God, he's so bossy. I frown, but I sit up and try to tie my bikini top, curious as to what's going on.

I pad over and he hangs up. He whispers, "Got to show you something. Come here." He hooks a finger into the side string of my bikini bottom and uses it to have me follow. We go to the sitting area on deck where suntan lotion and fruit are set out, along with his laptop and tech gadgets. He pulls open his laptop and types in some passwords.

I sit on his thigh sideways to allow him to type. He logs on to some administrative page, then clicks a button and a window pops open with an image of a street.

"What is that?" I frown and stare closer at the screen.

"Something," he says in his low voice, "I believe the lady will like. Look at the screen."

The screen displays several images—a grocery store entrance, a street corner. "End the Violence has been pushing for citizen surveillance," he explains.

Shock flits through me.

"I know."

"I funded their movement. The government's got several satellites up already, with a few more to follow."

I'm so stunned, one of my hands is covering my open mouth, my obvious disbelief making Malcolm's eyes fill with amusement.

"Nothing to say?" he prods.

Forcing my mouth shut, I stare at him wide-eyed: *him,* an ever-changing mystery. Always surprising me. Teasing me. Annoying me. Seducing me. Enchanting me.

"This just brings me one step closer to that coveted moon you say I want," he teases me softly when I can't speak, when I'm still *blown away.*

He's peering at me, a smile twisting his lips as he runs his knuckles down my jawline. "You bring out a side in me I thought I didn't have." His voice is low and reverent somehow, as are his eyes, knowing and grateful. "I've been told that I'm reckless, that I could not be relied upon, that I couldn't make a difference for others—just for myself. My father looked at me as if I was to blame for everything, and Mother as if I would get myself killed. People look at me like I can get them the moon, but you look at me like I already did. Like all I need to do is exist, and you would be happy," he murmurs, tracing his thumb down my earlobe as he smiles at me, his eyes happily twinkling. "I *like* it, Rachel."

"I'm so alive with you," I whisper, without being able to even think of my words before I whisper them. "I'm so alive with you, you make everything pop for me, everything stand out."

"Ahh." He throws his head back and laughs deliciously then scrapes his hand over the stubble of his jaw, his smile both sexy and humorous. "See, that makes me feel good in a whole other way."

"Because you're arrogant and nothing's enough for you, no amount of admiration or respect. I love . . . this. I love this so much, Malcolm."

I duck my head, blushing because I thought the word *you* before the one I actually said, which was *this.* It popped into my head, so real and unfiltered, I'm blushing as I try to push it down. "I do love this," I add, focusing on the screen again.

He turns my head around and looks at my lips, rubbing them a little. "Good. My girlfriend wants to change the world, and I want to own it."

"Why do you insist on me being your girlfriend?" I complain, but when his eyes slide up from my mouth to lock on mine, that typical shyness he brings out in me comes out with a vengeance.

"Why do we want anything?" he asks me, one eyebrow up.

"Because it gives us pleasure, satisfaction, it makes us happy."

"So when can I call you my girlfriend?" he insists.

He's so stubborn! I giggle because his question is "when."

In Saint's mind, it's not impossible. He knows it's happening, he's actively carving his way to making it happen, and he's just curious to see how long he has to wait.

I feel a yearning to say, *Now!* But I can't. "Let's talk about it again later," I propose instead.

He takes my face in one open hand. "Next week."

Knots, knots, knots in my tummy, my chest, my throat.

"I might need more than a week to come out of the box," I begin when the flexing in his jaw and the tumult in his eyes tug at my heartstrings. Coupled with my own aching heart, resisting him is killing me. "But . . . will you be waiting?"

"I'm waiting, Rachel," he assures me, his tone steady, as if there's no doubt that he will wait as long as he needs to. He leans forward and gives me the sweetest, hottest kiss on the corner of my mouth.

I sigh inwardly, a sigh he doesn't hear, doesn't even notice.

His attention goes back to the computer as he starts to check out the software, and he works the keyboard with those long, blunt fingers that type, I realize, as fast as mine do—and I type like the wind. I'm sitting in his arms, watching him show me, so safe right now. His scent steals into my nose and I drag it inside, getting wet between my legs, happy in my heart. "I want you again," I whisper, in his ear.

He lifts a hand to cup my pussy and shift me, starting to caress me. "That was the aim of all this," he whispers, nuzzling my ear.

I turn around and his nose presses to mine, my breath on his lips as I speak. "I'm really wet," I admit. "Let me get pretty. I want to look so pretty I give 'your type of girl' a whole new meaning."

When I stand, he tugs me back down as if I'm being silly, chuckling, "Come here."

"No, seriously!" I laugh, then I say, "I'll be right back," and head quickly to the bathroom to get a little pretty. I see my phone messages.

Wynn: Hey we're worried, call!

Gina: Rachel where are you? You ok? We're worried

I answer them both.

I am physically okay but so absolutely in trouble

I toss the phone aside, and when I come out, Saint is lying back in bed, arms crossed behind his head, the sheets up to his waist, and he's naked already, his clothes tossed to the side. My stomach knots from the hunger, the fierce desire clawing inside me, begging for release. Begging me for him.

My hands shake from the heat already rushing through my veins as I slowly tug the strap of my bikini and start stripping for him. I prolong the moment, against every demanding throb of my body, every second that I'm not in that bed with him is torture, every pore in me trembling under the dark, tumultuous look in his eyes, eyes that make me feel owned, wanted, and absolutely wanton and sexy.

26

FRIENDS AND FANTASIES

Gina and Wynn are worried that I blew up at my mother's house yesterday morning.

After Malcolm drives me home, I ask Gina to give me half an hour to shower and change. I hop into the shower, day-dreaming a little bit as I rub my body and feel how tender I am between my legs. Gina is scowling and clearly concerned when I come out.

"What's going on? Talk to me," she goads as we head to meet Wynn that afternoon. "You were with Saint all this time?"

"Yes," I admit.

"And? Did you break it off? Or did you call Helen? What's going on? I've been deliberating and I don't think dumping your career for a man is a good move. Especially a man with a reputation. When he breaks your heart, you can't even say you didn't see it coming, Rachel!"

I tune out a little bit as she keeps going because, at this

point, my empty stomach is filling with bile over my own decision—the one I have to make soon.

When I don't agree with or reject her suggestions, Gina switches gears and suddenly can't stop talking about how great it is to be single. Does she want to make me feel better because obviously Saint and I are going nowhere? Or is she concerned and thinking I would actually dare go out with Saint publicly and expose myself to the same scrutiny he's subjected to?

No. She's in full protective mode, and she wants me to end it, and end it now.

"I plan to live my life eating cake without being judged, painting my nails in whimsical colors, spending my own money my way, and leaving with debt. That's the way I want to go. It means I took risks," Gina says.

"Huge risks, Gina," Wynn says sarcastically. She seems to be arguing the opposite side today as we sit in our usual booth. "Painting your nails and eating cake and spending money—the real risk is getting out there even after asshole Paul broke up with you.

"For a while now the only touch you've gotten is from your manicurist. That's how you and Rachel were both getting touched, just to get someone to touch you in *any* capacity."

"For your information, Rachel and I have been boinking our brains out. See, Rachel hardly has any left. She's in love with a guy who I bet slept with some waitress around here or something. And maybe even a few more. Maybe even one of us!"

"Gina!" I cry.

"Who are *you* boinking?" Wynn dares.

"My dildo!"

"Woo-hoo."

She narrows her eyes. "He broke my heart, Wynn! You're the one who always drops *your* boys. You both lose steam and you're gone. I love with my whole heart! He took my heart, all his warm shirts I loved sleeping in, all my trust. Even my coffee-maker walked out that door with him."

"Gina, Wynn, it's okay," I try to placate.

Gina stands. "I thought we didn't judge each other. I'm going to get a massage—and continue living my ideal life whether you like it or not!"

"Wynn, way harsh," I chide when Gina walks away.

"I don't judge, Rachel! I was arguing my point that at least I put myself out there and you two don't."

"We *all* do. What's wrong if sometimes it's so scary we want to do it in private in case we fuck up? Sometimes we're drawn out of our shells whether we want to be or not."

"I've never known anything to draw you out of yours. You've got your ideas and your safe zone and that's it."

"I'm in love, Wynn."

I sit here, and once the words are out, the feeling—inside me so long—suddenly has a name, and it's real. And it hurts. All this talk about the guy's shirts and coffeemakers and I realize I do sleep in his shirt, but I'd do anything to sleep in his arms more than a few times. To have more than one shirt to sleep in. I don't share a coffeemaker but I'd do anything to wake up another morning with him and have coffee with him while his hair is rumpled.

"I'm in love with Saint," I say softly.

Wynn is staring at me in complete worry and confusion, her blue eyes wide in shock. A lock of red hair had fallen over her eye a few minutes ago, but suddenly she has to reach out and push it back so she can stare straight at me.

"I've fallen completely in love. Spectacularly so. If you want a front seat for the debacle, I'm sure there'll be blood."

Wynn sighs, then grabs my hand. "There's never a right

time for you to fall. It's why they call it falling. It's an accident. In one second. Just pray that wherever you land, you're not there alone."

"Wynn, I didn't even know I wanted it. That I wanted to be worshipped this way. Even with no makeup and completely bare. I'd never wanted someone to touch me every chance he got. I'd never wanted to make excuses to touch someone else just so I can feel his warmth and how solid he is and know I didn't imagine him. My life has been inside this box and then he's solid and there and makes me feel something that is endless . . . I thought I knew what I wanted. Then I met him, and I don't know anything anymore."

"You want something else and that's fine," Wynn says, like it's as easy as changing nail color.

"It's *not* fine. Do you realize who he is? I'm setting myself up! I want the impossible. Men like him don't change."

"I beg to differ! People are always changing, it's the law of evolution; we change. For the better. To survive."

"Who thinks it's for the better?"

"*He* will. Because being with you means something, it means he gets to be a good guy. You can give him purpose. He can give you safety. A girl who challenges you and brings out the best in you, that's what a smart man values . . . even if he doesn't know it until he meets her. And Saint's a smart one, Rachel. Do you think he doesn't know what ninety-nine percent of the people surrounding him want from him? You're a *good* girl, Rachel. You can't cook to save a recipe, but any guy would be lucky to have you." She pauses. "Does he know?"

I shake my head and softly say, "Not yet." I've got a farmful of critters in my stomach just thinking of telling him, and the biggest of them is called fear. "Like you just said . . . I'm afraid to go out on a limb and then find myself just standing out there alone."

"Is he seeing other people?" Wynn asks, her expression concerned.

I wait for the waitress to leave a basket of Italian focaccia with a little plate of olive oil on the side before I continue. "I never went in having any expectations of him being exclusive, but . . . I don't think he is seeing anyone else. He still hangs out with floozies but . . . he and I are having a lot of sex. A *lot* of sex, Wynn."

Her eyes brighten. "For a nonmonogamous animal like he is, this is huge! Sex with only you?"

I feel myself blush hotly; all the talk about sex only reminds me of the powerful *high* of having Saint inside me.

"Don't be restrained by rules," she then chides. "Just go with your emotions. All those great romances, they're not planned, they just happen."

"That's the thing—no matter how crazy it sounds, I want to be swept away. I do. I want to believe it could happen to me for once."

"So?" she dares. "You're already headed that way. Wouldn't you rather go with it than fight some war you might not even want to win?"

"It's not that simple, Wynn." I fall back in my chair with a weary sigh. "I don't know how Helen will take it when I let her know I'm not doing this. *Edge* is on its last breath. Even if Saint could change and want something real with me, I'd be putting my own happiness before how many people's jobs? It's killing me."

"*Edge* will die anyway."

"No." I instinctively deny it with a shake of my head. "This would have injected new life. . . ."

"And you, Rachel?" She looks at me as if to her, my well-being is worth so much more than the well-being of the dozens of people working at *Edge*. She looks at me as if one small card—me—trumps all the rest. "And my friend Rachel, what about her?"

27

ON THE EDGE

The answer to Wynn's question eludes me . . . but I know by the next morning that there are some things we are capable of, and some we aren't. There are speeds at which we cannot run. And situations we cannot ever solve. We have limits within ourselves, and I have finally recognized mine. I grew up loving stories, sometimes loving stories more than people. Loving people in the stories, or because of the stories.

But today I love a man more than I love the story—*his* story.

So I walk into Helen's office certain that she's going to fire me. Fire me for real this time. Not only that, but I can't bear to look anyone in the eye today. Valentine at his desk, looking for the perfect stock images. Victoria isn't at her desk today, and I'm almost relieved I don't have her looking at me when I need to come to terms with the fact that I've failed. I *want* to fail.

Helen looks up from her desk, and her eyes are tired behind

her glasses. Her hair is a bit messier than normal. I can see the stress all over her and I can feel it around us as I take a seat.

She doesn't even greet me. I think she *knows*.

"This article on Malcolm," I begin.

"Malcolm?" she repeats, her expression one of complete and utter bafflement. She pulls off her reading glasses and pinches the bridge of her nose, then exhales. "Rachel, I've been very patient with you. You asked me for a chance. . . ."

"He's different than what we thought he'd be."

"Is he? I don't think so." She levels me with a hard glare. "See, I think he's exactly how we thought he was. And I think just like hundreds of women before you, you've fallen. You think that underneath all that rich bad boy there's a good man and that he'll change when given the chance to."

"He doesn't need to change. The media has used his image to their advantage but he's not who we think he is, who anyone thinks he is."

"Oh, and you know this because you've . . . what? Slept with him? Had a few cocktails with him? You've known him, what? A few weeks, Rachel? How is that enough to know a man?"

"You can know a man with one deed. Just one. It isn't about time."

"Ah, you're so deep," she says sarcastically, then sighs. "The answer is no. You owe me an exposé. Your work has suffered for weeks, I need the material, and I need it on my desk by tomorrow."

"I can't write it," I admit. "I can't even start. I physically get sick sitting at my computer now."

"Just write it, Rachel. He's not a one-woman man. He's got too many opportunities to cheat and be bad, and he can get away with it. He can have a blonde bimbo on the side who doesn't care if he cheats. Who encourages him to have other women."

"He's too smart. He may play with the bimbo but he won't be happy with one. He needs someone real," I whisper.

"What he needs is none of our concern—what *you* need is to do your job. That's the end of it."

I'm sitting here trembling. Quit. Quit. *Just quit.*

"Helen, I thought this exposé would give me a voice to talk about a subject people wanted to hear about, so that later I'd be heard when I talked about other things. This was also about my dad and telling myself we all have the same troubles and ups and downs in our lives, that no one has it better in all respects. I've felt underestimated and I wanted to prove I could do something more. I can, I'm sure of it but no, I won't.

"I met a powerful man and I've learned that just because you *can* do something doesn't mean it's right. Saint could do a million things with his power. He doesn't. He uses it to prod others to action, I've watched him do it. He's not the villain here. He gives as good as he gets. He's used in the same way he uses. That's what I call a trade. He's not all saint, but he's not all sinner."

"Good, very good, write all of that. I need it on my desk."

"I quit," I breathe.

Helen looks at me, sighing. "You can't quit, Rachel."

"I just did. Helen, I'm sorry."

"I'm telling you, you can't quit."

"Why?"

"Because Victoria just did."

"Helen, I'm sorry that—"

"You'll be sorrier if you don't go through with it now. Victoria quit. She's gone to our competition. They're printing a story about Saint's girlfriend secretly working to expose him. They're jumping in before us."

"WHAT?" I'm frozen.

"So you see, if you quit now, every one of your colleagues will soon be out of a job. *Edge* will get the last blow needed to finish it once and for all. Do you want to live with this, Rachel? At twenty-three, do you want to live with this on your shoulders? I've asked one special thing of you. One. To do your job."

"Helen," I plead.

"If you ever thought you could back out and it would all be forgotten . . . it won't. Your boyfriend will know what you've been up to by next week. If you thought you could salvage your own image in his eyes by sacrificing *Edge* . . ." She sighs and turns away. "You thought wrong. Victoria will run with whatever it is she accessed through our systems—surveillance caught her photocopying things from your desk, Rachel. You wanted a voice? You have one. I need it in my inbox by Monday to try to match their print schedule. If we want to try to salvage the magazine, we need this piece—and we need it *now*."

All I hear, as I leave *Edge,* as I gather my notes that Victoria may have photocopied and my bag, shut down my computer, and as I take the elevator downstairs, all I hear is my own voice, telling Malcolm that it wasn't Interface that I was researching.

It was him.

I find myself in the streets. Walking without direction. How long have I been staring at the word *Sin* in my contacts? I don't know. The wind bites into my cheeks. My fingertips are cold around my phone. I'm walking . . . but I'm heading nowhere.

I stare at Sin's name and realize it's the last contact I dialed.

It's barely afternoon—he has a thousand things to do at M4 and even has to fly to New York City, but I press "dial" and lift the receiver to my ear. I don't even know what I'm going to say. Only that I need to hear his voice right now.

He picks up with his lips sounding close to the receiver, as if he's with people. "Hey."

God help me, his voice will never stop doing things to me.

My eyes drift shut as a series of sensations flow through me to the tips of my feet. He is such an experience. Funny that he's known to be straightforward, a man of few words.

This seems to fascinate the world, and in contrast, the world speaks about him almost *too* much.

And now, Victoria is going to speak about *us*.

"Hey," I hastily whisper, "I know you're busy. I just wanted to hear your voice." I stop walking, lean on a lamppost as I feel myself blush beet red, and stare at my feet and the cracks on the sidewalk. "What time do you fly out?"

"Soon as I finish here, two hours at most."

He waits for a heartbeat, as though waiting for me to explain why I'm calling.

"Something up at work?" he asks.

"Only me, wanting to call you. I'm making it a habit, aren't I?"

"I'm not complaining," he husks out in a murmur. "But I've got some people waiting."

"Of course. Go get the world. Better yet, go get the moon!" *No time to have this talk now, Rachel. Just say goodbye, say goodbye and ask to see him soon.* "Let me know when you get back? I was hoping we could talk."

"Sure."

"'Bye, Sin," I whisper.

"'Bye."

After a full minute of regrouping, I look around, and though I know perfectly where I am, I'm lost.

I'm lost, and I can't find my way home.

I'm lying in bed, sleepless, when my cell phone buzzes on my nightstand and an unidentified number appears. I see it's almost midnight, and I almost don't answer, but I do—and that's when I hear it.

Saint's voice, kind of smoky, thick and low, through the background of jet engines. "What . . ." I grumble and shake myself awake. "I thought you were flying?"

There's pleasure in the low whisper. "I am."

"Of course," I groan. "Your plane has a phone. What else? Naked flight attendants?"

"I assure you they're perfectly dressed."

"Oh, but I bet *you're* not," I tease.

Surrounded by only dark in my bedroom, his voice is . . . everything.

His voice, his soft laugh.

It gives me such pleasure I can't stop smiling. "I'm glad I amuse you," I say softly.

"I'm glad too."

My turn to laugh.

But this time, Saint doesn't join in.

"We said a week, right?" Saint asks me.

"A week for . . ." I'm confused for a moment, but then I remember our conversation onboard *The Toy*, about him . . . and me. And I know exactly what he means. "Oh, *that.*" A hot flush creeps along my body, spreading down, down, down, all the way to my toes. "Yes, that's what we said," I admit.

"How about now?" he surprises me by saying.

Tingles and lightning bolts race through my bloodstream. The sensation covers my body from corner to corner. I try to suppress it; it's *wrong* to feel it. But I can't stop it, I can't stop what he does to me. "What happened to your legendary patience?"

"How about now, Rachel?" he insists.

All my guilt, my insecurities, and my fear are suddenly weighing down on me. It's really hard to speak as I shake my head in the dark. "I'm a mess, Saint," I choke out.

"Be my mess, then."

A truly sad laugh leaves me, and for a moment, I'm afraid it'll turn into a sob. "Oh god." I drag in a deep breath and blink the moisture from my eyes. "When can we talk about this in person?"

"When I land in Chicago. Saturday. Come stay over."

I nod. "God, I need to see you." I wipe the corners of my eyes. "I need to see you," I say, then laugh to hide the way my voice is trembling and boy, how I really, desperately want to cry and spill my guts to him. "I really need to see you, Malcolm."

"I'll send you a picture."

He's teasing me?

He's teasing me and I love it and I always have.

"Saint!" Thank god my voice didn't break just now, because the rest of me really wants to.

I hear his chuckle, low and savoring.

Worst of all, I can tell he's enjoying talking to me. And teasing me. I pinch my eyes painfully shut, savoring it too, "Don't hang up yet, just say something long and important. . . . Say your name! Your ridiculously long name . . ."

"Malcolm." He indulges me. Then, slowly, "Kyle," then "Preston," then "Logan," then "Saint." Then, more intensely: "I miss you, Rachel."

I wipe away a stray tear and strain my throat to say something in reply. "Okay."

"That's all I get?" He laughs, incredulous.

"I love you," I say. The emotion gets the best of me, and I repeat, "I love you, Saint," and before he can answer, I hang up and cover my face.

Oh god. Oh god oh god, I just said it. And I have no idea what effect it had! OH GOD.

Shaking from the adrenaline, I put my phone on my nightstand and watch it for a few minutes.

What. Did. I. Just. Do?

I fall back in bed feeling a mix of excitement and dread and . . . disbelief. Well, I did say "I love you" to a man for the first time in my life. Just like that—wham!—over the phone. To Malcolm Saint.

How silly it must seem to him.

I must seem so . . . *gah!* Stupid!

Why could you not wait until you talked to him in person, Rachel? Why?!

I wish I hadn't missed his face, his expression. I mean, he must have been completely dumbstruck. Dazed. Was he surprised to hear it? Pleasantly so? Or not-so-pleasantly so? Well, did he *laugh*? Or frown? Puzzle? Fuck my laptop, what did I *do*?

I lie awake for a while in full-blown stress mode, in his shirt, my body aching for his, haunted by his eyes and by the last time we were together and every moment in between.

Haunted by the dread of LOSING HIM before I can really be his girlfriend.

"*Dibs . . .*" I remember.

"*I'm an only son. . . .*"

"*Are you coming up, or do you want me to carry you?*"

I'm flooded with him.

Remembering the way I could almost swear he caught his breath when he saw me at the Ice Box.

The way he kissed the corner of my mouth first, always, leading into his bigger kiss.

The way he saved an elephant.

The way he saved me.

The way he fed me grapes.

The way he opened up to me.

Please come back to Chicago and let me explain, let me tell you why I don't deserve you . . . and give me your advice. Give me your wise advice on what to do. Because I should've come to you before anyone else. I should've trusted that you would help me because that's all I've seen from you—I've just never trusted a man before.

I hear my text beep and read:

Sin: I'm going to take that as a yes

28

TRUTH AND LOYALTY

"Wake up, Livingston."

I tuck my face into my pillow while someone who sounds a lot like Gina keeps knocking on my door. I groan, "I'm going to kick your ass when I get out of this bed."

"You're going to be too busy."

"Busy with what?"

"Rachel, the door's freaking locked."

"So?"

"So open up."

Hmm. Don't think so. My life's a mess. My life's a mess and I need to fix it and I need to think of how to fix it. And the only pleasure I can derive anymore is in thinking and remembering, remembering talking on the phone only a few nights ago; I dreamed he said some things, and that I said some *other* things, then I remember that, yes, I think it's true—I said I loved him.

Holy crap.

"Raaaa-chel," Gina whines. Hard banging at the door. "Open up, Livingston. You need to see this!"

"I don't want to see anything today. I'm seeing Saint when he gets back from New York and I want some beauty sleep, okay? It's Saturday," I grumble, but when she keeps banging, I leap off the bed and whip the door open, then rush back under my warm covers. "What is it?"

Wynn and Gina drop onto my bed.

Wynn is here too?

I'm aware of a strained silence while Wynn goes to open the curtains and comes back. Their stares . . . they look ominous.

A shadow of fear looms before me. "What?"

Their expressions alone set alarm bells ringing throughout my head. Leaping off the bed, I open my laptop and start scouring the Net, and all I can think is no, no no *noooooooooo*.

Within seconds, dozens of results with the words *exposed* and *undercover* and *lies* and *betrayal* pop up, tying Sin, my glorious Sin, to me.

"Rachel, you're all over the gossip sites," Wynn says.

The results come at me with talons. One after the other.

"Go here." Gina points at a website.

My hands have never shaken so hard on the track pad. I force the cursor to move and go to the site, and my stomach drops. I see Victoria's byline and realize they went ahead and released her story in blog form before going to press.

I can't see through my tears.

"That BITCH!" Gina yells.

As though someone else is speaking for me, numbly, in my own voice and with my own lips, I hear: "She's doing what she has to. She wants to succeed, like me," and as I speak, my tears keep gathering in my eyelids.

"She can suck my dick!" Gina yells.

I duck to read.

DECEIVED: Malcolm Saint's New Girlfriend Really Undercover Press!

If you've been waiting for the dish on one of the most unexpected "relationships" to arise with one of our bachelors, prepare to have your mind blown even further when I let it all out of the bag. At least, Malcolm Saint's girlfriend's bag. . . .

I can't continue. Each word is out there for Malcolm to read. Snarky, like the words of a real-life Gossip Girl amusing herself while my world is torn asunder.

My eyes well. "He's read this by now, ohgod."

"Rachel, calm down. . . ."

"You don't understand! Truth and loyalty are important to him! They're so important to him . . . I can't." I cover my head in my hands as I start to hyperventilate. "I'm going to throw up."

"Rachel." They try comforting me, both of them slinging their arms around my shoulders, but I'm beyond comfort.

My cell phone is buzzing madly. I suck in deep breaths, and when my phone falls still, the landline starts to ring. Gina lifts the kitchen phone in the air. "It's Helen, Rachel."

When nothing happens, she waves the phone at me.

"Helen's calling."

"Don't talk to her," Wynn whispers.

Gina covers the speaker. "Hello? Wynn? She's her BOSS."

I know what she wants, what she will say. I grab the phone while my hand trembles and the rest of me starts to grow numb inside. I have disappointed everyone in my life. "You saw?" she asks.

I can't answer.

Helen growls, "We'll ride this if it kills us. Get to work."

I've barely hung up the phone when Gina raises my cell phone before me, eyes wide and apologetic. "It's your mother."

With a moan of distress, I shoot Gina a "help me" look. What will I say to her? Well, let's see. That I lost my heart and my senses with it. That I lost the man I loved before I had the courage to let myself truly have him. That I lost a story to my colleague. That I might, if I can't find my balls soon, lose my job.

That I've lost all sense of direction. Of what's right and what's wrong. Of who I am and what I want—

"Heyyyy, adoptive mom!" Gina finally picks up on my behalf. "Yes! GINA! Oh . . . Rachel? She's super busy writing the article that will leave this other one *in the dust.* Oh, pfft! It's just a blog article! Rachel's will be IN PRINT, and it's much more important in that format. . . ." She starts to wax poetic to my mom while I go back to the computer and go to Saint's social media.

I scan a few pictures.

There he is.

I see a picture of him getting out of his Rolls and into M4. A picture of him *flipping off a reporter.*

A set of slick aviators shield his eyes.

He looks sharp and on top of the world as he gets out of the car and, just like that, flips off the reporter. And a caption beneath the image reads: "When asked by a reporter, outside his offices, what he thought about his girlfriend being undercover press, this is what Malcolm Saint had to say."

Saint is back in Chicago. He's back from his business trip. To find this.

He's being tagged. He's being BOMBARDED.

@malcolmsaint U deserve much mre and better than a cunt lke her!!

"I'm going to go talk to him."

I run into my room and change as fast as possible into a pair of black slacks and a professional-looking white button-down blouse; then I quickly gather my hair into a ponytail and, despite Wynn and Gina's reservations, take a cab to M4.

I cross the pristine lobby. If I'd thought it was difficult to walk up to the receptionists behind the oval desk the first time, it's even more excruciatingly painful now.

I know that they know what's going on; I can tell by their pointy stares.

My pulse is dangerously high. I can't imagine what it will feel like when I see him.

"Rachel Livingston for Mr. Saint, please."

It strikes me, after several heartbeats, that none of them wants to answer me.

"We apologize," the middle one with the tidy bun finally says. "But Mr. Saint just got into town."

"Yes, I know." I can't believe how calm I sound, considering how twisted up my insides are. "I'll wait."

"Miss!" she calls as I walk toward the elevators. "No one is to be allowed to the top without authorization today."

I stop mid-stride, puzzled. "Oh." I hesitate, and notice that the elevator bank is, in fact, quite empty today. "I'll wait here, then." I try to stay calm as I walk back in their direction. Did Saint cancel all the meetings in his "packed" day? I feel increasingly anxious about it. "Just please tell him Rachel Livingston would love to see him. It's terribly important."

"Like I said, he's terribly busy."

"I'll wait," I say, soft but firm.

I head to one of one of the lounges by the window. Huddled in my seat, I wait, feeling cold, remembering the absolute gossip storm taking place online. I shift uneasily from side to side, watching the elevators and the cars outside.

There are two or three people outside the building trying to keep their cameras hidden but occasionally taking snapshots of the building. So they want a piece of him too? Annoyance flares inside me. Annoyance, impotence, and loathing at myself for having caused this. The receptionist approaches moments later, and there's an intimidating bodyguard with her.

Slowly, I rise to my feet.

"I'm sorry but we can't have you here," the receptionist says. "He's busy, just arrived from out of town." I see anger in her eyes. My attention flicks to the large man and . . . I just can't believe there's a bodyguard. I can't believe he's having them escort me out.

"Tell him I stopped by," I murmur. Then I do them all a favor and take myself outside, using my hair as a curtain to avoid being recognized—glad that my hair can also hide the absolutely crestfallen look on my face. I head straight home, where Gina and Wynn appear to have been waiting by the door.

"How did it go?" Gina takes me by the shoulders and forces me down on the couch.

I'm still numb with disbelief. It takes me a moment to answer. "He's walling himself up. I couldn't see him. They . . . I was escorted out."

"What?" Wynn cries, outraged.

And Gina: "Didn't you tell me his staff is loyal to a fault? Of course they'd be overprotective of their Saint."

"But did he know Rachel was there?" Wynn wants to know.

They start arguing about whether or not Saint instructed them to kick me out, but I can't join the speculation. I'm feeling more and more hopeless as I look at my phone. My silent phone.

Locking myself in my bedroom, I call his cell phone and pace around as I leave a message:

"Heyyyyy. Hey . . . will you please call me back? I need to talk to you." I flounder with what to say next, my thoughts stumbling one after the other.

"Malcolm . . ." I trail off, but my voice breaks so fiercely, I hang up. I wipe my tears away and dial again. "Sorry," I whisper. I have never wanted to hear his voice so much. "I want to say that . . . I don't know. . . . I just wanted to hear your voice." I think of what else to say when I reach his voice mail.

I dial again. "You value truth and loyalty, and I . . . I need to talk to you, Malcolm, you need to let me explain. If that's all you do, please let me explain."

It's killing me. I can't sleep. Can't eat. I have a constriction in my chest and I literally can't breathe. This time it's not in a good way. I keep waiting to hear from him, keep expecting him to message me back.

I storm into Gina's bedroom. "Do you think it's over?"

She jolts up in bed. "You scared the shit out of me. I thought we had an intruder!"

"Do you think it's over? Not talking and this shit happening, it means it's over. Right? Who am I kidding? I wasn't even his real girlfriend. Not even for a day. There's nothing to be over." I laugh sadly and struggle with my tears, and with my conscience, and my desperate need for him.

"I feel bad for you, but Saint's a powerful man. When Paul betrayed me, I couldn't look at him, not even a single possession of his. He broke me. And this is . . . this is public, Rachel. How would *you* feel? If he came with something like this, throwing you for a loop? Give him time to assimilate what's being said. Maybe he just wants to rationalize."

Maybe he just needs to count to four, I think to myself.

"I have a temper. . . ."

One instant I'm trying to feel positive by telling myself that I will have a moment to explain, eventually, and the next I'm heavy with grief. The next, I'm one big, gigantic knot of regrets. Remembering those few, rare moments when he completely opened up to me makes me even more anxious to be with him right now, to explain. To make it okay. To hold him. To BEG him to hold ME. "Rachel, what are you going to do with your article?" Gina asks worriedly.

In my hand, on my phone screen, for the thousandth time, I look at that picture of him arriving at M4 after a business trip. Looking like a true, first-class billionaire . . . but flipping off whoever was snapping that picture. All of that glass and technology in the background, and him, in that killer suit, his dark head bent, his eyes shielded behind his aviators. *No comment,* the caption says. But the finger said plenty.

29

RESEARCH

A short while later I slip into my bedroom and stand, in my socks and his shirt, and stare at my laptop.

Inhaling, I bring it, along with my shoebox filled with note cards, to the little rug beside my bed. I sit Indian style on the floor and read my notes, one by one. Notes on him.

Truth and loyalty, I had written.

Traits he probably admires in his best friends. Traits he may never have found in the women who are after him. Truth and loyalty . . .

That's all I can write about. The rest of what I've learned is too raw for me to share.

But *truth and loyalty.*

Things Saint values above love.

Things he wouldn't find in me. I read the back of the card, my scribbled note, this one talking about me.

I SUCK SOOOO HARD.

He'd stood there talking about truth and loyalty while I sat there moved by everything we talked about, absolutely knowing that I was falling in love, helpless to stop it.

And still, I was taking notes. Studying him like a lab rat. As if he wasn't human. As if he weren't driven by the same things everyone else is: a heart, a mind, a body, hormones; as if he didn't need air and water and maybe even love; as if he were this robot to be scrutinized and picked apart for the amusement of the world.

Really? What does it matter that he's been with a thousand and one women? What does it matter that he's the city's obsession and now also mine? He's human. He's entitled to the little privacy he has. He's *so* damn closed off, he rarely opens up to anyone, and I know it's because he's always so judged and scrutinized.

My eyes water, and suddenly I grab the cards and start tearing them up, one by one. Then I lie with all the notes scattered around me and cry a little. Then I look at the scattered mess. What did I just do? *Oh god.*

If I want to save the magazine, I need to deliver something.

I breathe in and out.

"Rachel?" I hear Gina call.

She peers inside and scans the mess of torn note cards, and then me. As broken as the paper around me.

"Oh, Rachel."

I start crying.

"I need to write it."

"Rachel, tell him the truth. Tell him the truth. If he knows you well at all, he'll understand."

"What? That I'm a liar?"

"Tell him you love him," she says.

"He doesn't want my love. He values . . . truth and honesty, qualities I don't possess."

"You possess them in spades. You're loyal and honest with everyone."

"But not with *him*."

"From the moment you talk to him and come clean, you will be. Make him see it from your eyes. Maybe you can have it all."

"Whoever gets it all, Gina? Nobody. *Nobody,* that's who."

"But yet we all believe that we can. Isn't that the point of everything we do? We want it all. So write this piece. And if you still want him, then you should go get him."

I pause. "I *do* want him," I whisper, wiping my wet face with the back of my hand. "It's a million tiny things that, added up, tell me there is no one in this world, ever, who will have this spectacular effect on me but him. Sometimes I just can't see myself when we're together, I'm so lost in him." I wipe my eyes. "He's the only man I dream about at night, and the only man I want to wake up next to in the morning. Everyone is after his fame or his money, but I love him not because of anything he has but because he *has* me. . . ."

"Oh, Rache. Don't cry. Maybe there's hope for you two."

"How can there be? He doesn't want anything to do with me anymore."

"He's fucking hurting, Rachel! Even I can tell, because there's not *one* picture of him without fucking shades to cover his eyes. There must be hell in those eyes, Rachel. I can't believe I actually feel bad for him now."

"Because I was the Paul in our relationship. I was the liar."

"Paul played me. You never played him. Your feelings were real."

I groan and bury my face in my hands. I remember how

Helen warned me from the beginning. That I was too young, playing with adults. I hadn't seen all of this coming. She was right. I was not ready for this at all.

But I take the Kleenex Gina passes, wipe my tears, connect my laptop, boot it up, and write my heart out.

The day I turn it in, Helen tells me that the *Edge* email servers are bursting with hate mail for me, and she advises me to take the week to work from home.

The day it's published, I don't get out of bed. I don't answer my phone. My mother stops by, but she ends up chatting with Gina because I don't want her to see me like this; I'm too sad to fake it today, and she knows me so well. She tells me before she leaves, "I'm going to go paint."

She's telling me I should do the same. She's telling me I'm free to go out there and do something I love.

But what I love hates me.

Twitter:
Did you read your girlfriend's article? @malcolmsaint

On his Instagram:
No way @malcolmsaint would give that bitch a second chance!!

And the feminist groups online:
Rachel Livingston, our hero! Revenge on the playboys! Want to play with our hearts? Beware the time you will find your own weakness. Revenge is sweet!

Later that week I find enough energy to get out of bed and go to work, and I'm immediately called into Helen's office.

There's tension between us. Helen was not happy when I sent over the article. She said, "It's not what I asked for."

"No," I concurred.

Helen took it and printed it anyway.

Today, I'm surprised that she seems pleased to see me, genuinely pleased. "It's a circus out there," Helen tells me, waving me forward from behind her cluttered desk.

"I'm not online. Can you blame me?"

"No. But let me fill you in." She signs to a chair across from her desk, but I remain standing. "Your boyfriend," she begins with obvious glee, "pulled Vicky's piece. It can't be reposted without legal repercussions now." She eyes me with a new gleam of respect and admiration, and adds, "In case you lost me when I said 'your boyfriend'"—she laughs happily—"Malcolm Saint canned any print editions of Victoria's post—and it was removed from the blog." She nods ever so slowly and somberly.

My eyes widen. "What?" I finally speak.

"Victoria's article. Your boyfriend owns the rights. It can't be published anymore—not without his say-so."

"What? *How?*"

She shrugs, then leans back in her chair with a little creak of the wheels. "Seems like Saint doesn't want it out there."

Ohmigod, he made Victoria's story *go away?* "If he canned Victoria's, why not ours? Why didn't he can mine?" *Why didn't he read mine?!*

My heart is in a fist in my chest and so are my lungs.

"Guess he doesn't hate you that much." She shrugs casually,

but stops herself when she seems to notice—finally notice—
that I'm crushed. That my hair is a mess, my face is a mess,
I'm a mess. "Maybe he *does* like you, Rachel," she says softly.
"I'm impressed, did you know? I'm not the only one who's impressed. The world is impressed too. He hasn't been seen . . .
consorting with you-know-what types." She taps a pencil absently on her desk, her eyes narrowed on me. "But he's been
skydiving daily. You'd think he has a death wish or has some serious mojo to get out of his system."

I hardly hear her. I need to get away. From *Edge,* from
her, from this office. "Is it all right if I work from home today,
Helen?"

Though I sense her reluctance, she agrees. I go get my
things from my desk, aching to my bones.

Saint skydiving.

Saint buying Victoria's article.

Saint thinking I betrayed him.

Outside that afternoon, I stop when *Edge* stares back at me from
a newsstand, one copy remaining on this side, a few on the other.

"You read that yet?" The man behind the newsstand whis-
tles and laughs. "That reporter's got her panties in a twist over
the guy."

I lift my head, prepared to scream at the man. Instead, I
scan the picture of Saint that Helen used on the cover—those
icy green eyes staring back at me. And yes, this man is right. I
do have my panties in a twist over Saint. Not just my panties—
my entire body. My entire life.

I miss him like nobody's business.

I want to kiss him.

I want to squeeze him. With my arms. And my thighs. With my whole body until I BREAK or he breaks me, and that's just fine, as long as he comes after me.

"Smart woman," I finally whisper, emotion thickening my voice. "I think I'll take him home with me."

I buy the copy just because of Malcolm's picture. Sharp tie, perfect collar, and that thick-lashed gaze, screaming to be warmed, that gets me. It's a marvel how those eyes of green ice can so easily melt me.

I sit down on a bench with the magazine on my lap, brushing my fingertips over his eyes, wondering for the thousandth time if he will ever read what I wrote to him.

30

AFTER THE STORM

It's over.

There wasn't rain or thunder when we ended. We just ended like we began. There were no flashes of illumination that told me I would fall in love, that I would meet the one man who would challenge me, drive me crazy. Now it's ended, my project done. Completed.

My mornings have returned to normal. I still have brunch with my friends on the weekends. I still visit Mom on Sundays. My world is back to ordinary, almost the same as it was before I wrote the exposé. I hadn't realized how bleak it was. I'm afraid I will pick up the paper and there he will be . . . with someone. Or with three.

The crying spells are bad. You go out and accidentally smell wine and oops, snivel. And don't talk to me about elephants, that takes me to a whole new level of despair. But the fear is gone. You were afraid of going out and suddenly you're right there, daring the universe to take that from you or pleading with it to give you an excuse to feel like shit today. Gina passes me the Kleenex.

Some of my coworkers . . . some of them envy me.

"I wish I'd been asked to go after Malcolm Saint," Sandy, my coworker, tells me because of the positions I'm being offered, but most importantly because "being paraded around in a yacht and being pursued like that . . ." she says dreamily.

"Fess up, was the sex phenomenal?" Valentine asks.

I think they're trying to cheer me up . . . but I'm uncheerable.

I still stalk his Twitter feed. I can't help stalking him, wanting to know how he is. Though the social media around him has been more active than ever, Saint himself has been . . . quiet.

He's been asked about me—by reporters on live TV, and online. He says "no comment" or ignores the online jabs. Just like he's ignoring me.

"It wasn't going to last," Gina assures me when she notices I'm mopey. "It was a hookup. He's a womanizer to the next level."

But it kills me that I'll never know. I'll never know if all the times he said I was his girl, he meant to keep me.

I have all these unsent emails addressed to Saint, and very little courage to do anything with them when I know that I don't deserve for him to give me the time of day.

To: Malcolm Saint (Drafts)
Status: unsent

I have a thousand and one emails just like this that I won't send either. I just needed to write to you.

Please forgive me

Do you think about me at all?

Dibs on your mouth and dibs on your eyes and dibs on your
hands and dibs on your heart. Even your stubbornness cause I
deserve it. Even your anger. I want it all. Dibs on my man. See
#Iamsogreedytoo !!!!

Gina tells me that if she could survive heartbreak, *I* can survive breaking my own heart.

"Baby, I know it hurts. When I found out about Paul, I
wanted a meteor to fall on my head so I could go numb inside
a coffin."

"God, Gina, I know. I just want a chance."

I stare out the window this morning at the street. No more
shiny Rolls-Royce waiting outside on Saturday mornings to
take me "anywhere."

Is it funny, though? That I keep waiting to see it? That I
wake up with hope every day? For a text, a message, a call, the
car, a glimmer of a chance?

Stop being so hopeful, Rachel . . . he would have read it by
now.

*Maybe he did and he just doesn't care to let you know what he
thought of it.*

I found out so many things about him during all the time
we spent together, but I didn't really find out if he could come
to love me. If he'll be too proud to ever forgive me. If he'll seek
to ease the pain of my betrayal with other women, or if he'll
shut himself off, like I'm doing. I found out dozens of things
about him, but not the dozen ones that could give me any kind
of comfort right now.

We saved an elephant together, he took up my fight for a
safer city, but all I physically have to remind me of my time
with him is his shirt.

His shirt, which sits like a priceless trophy folded away in plastic, inside a box, in the deepest part of my closet, because I can hardly bear to see it now. I can't bear to wear it now. But sometimes when the melancholy hits, I go into my closet and pull it out, stark white and large, completely male against my frilly items, and still with his scent clinging to its collar. Self-pity washes over me on those days, and it takes one second, two, three, and then I think of him, and so I take four. Four seconds before I let myself breathe again.

EXPOSING MALCOLM SAINT
By R. Livingston

I'm going to tell you a story. A story that managed to pull me apart completely. A story that brought me back to life. A story that has made me cry, laugh, scream, smile, and then cry again. A story I keep telling to myself over and over and over until I have memorized every smile, every word, every thought. A story that I hope to keep with me forever.

The story begins with this very article. It was a regular morning at *Edge*. A morning that would bring me a big opportunity: to write an exposé on Malcolm Kyle Preston Logan Saint. He's a man who needs no introduction. Billionaire playboy, beloved womanizer, a source of many speculations. This article would open doors for me, gain a young hungry reporter a voice.

I dove in, managing to get an interview with Malcolm Saint to discuss Interface (his incredible new Facebook-killer) and its immediate rise to popularity. As obsessed as the city has been with his persona for years, I considered myself lucky to be in this position.

I was so focused on revealing Malcolm Saint that I let my guard down, unaware that every time he opened up, he was actually revealing *me* to me. Things I had never wanted were suddenly all I wanted. I was determined to find out more about this man. This mystery. Why was he so closed off? Why was nothing ever enough for him? I soon discovered he was not a man of many words, but rather a man of the right words. A man of action. I told myself that every inch of information I hunted was for this article, but the knowledge I craved was actually about myself.

I wanted to know everything. I wanted to breathe him. Live him.

But most unexpectedly of all, Saint began to pursue me. Genuinely. Wholeheartedly. And relentlessly. I could not believe that he would be truly interested in me. I had never been pursued like this, intrigued like this. I had never felt so connected to something—someone.

I never expected my story to change, but it did. Stories tend to do that; you go out searching for something and come back with something different. I wasn't looking to fall in love, I wasn't looking to lose my mind and common sense over the most beautiful green eyes I have ever seen, I wasn't looking to drive myself crazy with lust. But I ended up finding a little piece of my soul, a little piece that isn't really that small at all: it's over six feet tall, with shoulders about a yard wide, hands more than twice the size of mine, green eyes, dark hair, and it is smart, ambitious, kind, generous, powerful, sexy, and has consumed me completely.

I regret lying, both to myself and to him; I regret not having the experience to recognize what I was feeling the moment I felt it. I regret not savoring each second I had with him more, because I value those seconds more than anything.

However, I don't regret this story. His story. My story. Our story.

I'd do it all again for another moment with him. I'd do it all again with him. I'd leap blindly into the air if only there were even a 0.01 percent chance that he'd still be there, waiting to catch me.

31

FOUR

Saturday.

The fourth one since.

There are still dozens of messages in my drafts folder that I won't ever send to him.

I've still, more than ever, been living in the land of "what could've been" and trust me, this is a very sad place to live in. In the zip code of the lost, you breathe in regret with every breath, sadness permeating every space in which your body stands.

Of all the things that drive people to change, it is despair and sorrow that cause it most of all.

Sadness is so disempowering. Anger, on the other hand, demands action and empowerment. But I can't get angry when it was *me* who put myself right where I'm standing.

I've spent weekends at the window of my apartment, trying to make myself want to go outside and not really feeling like it.

Never let anyone tell you that your life will return to normal after a hurricane.

I've got folders and folders with pics I can't open.

A number I can't dial.

A shirt I can't wear.

A name I can't say out loud.

The memory of a pair of eyes that will haunt me forever.

I live in fear of never seeing those eyes again. And in even more fear of what I'll see in them if I do . . .

Helen had complained it was not what she had wanted.

She'd said it was "a love letter to Saint."

But we all know stories are like that. Stories change. Just like people change. We change when we suffer, when we take, when we give, when we love. When you lose the object of your love, your normal will be perennially changed; there's no returning to the old anymore. You have to rebuild stronger walls, change your expectations, and wait for the sunlight.

There's nothing like a sunrise in Chicago, the orange-gold light shimmering over the buildings' mirrored windows. I've watched the sunrises and the sunsets and I've watched it rain from this very window. I've watched Gina go out, and I've watched the cars drive by, not really focused on what colors they are, only that none of those cars belong to him.

My laptop hums nearby. Gina went out to lunch with Wynn, but I still can't seem to work up the enthusiasm.

I'm trying to work on a new story. A story with good stuff. Stuff about people. Loss. And hope. And . . . forgiveness. I'm pouring tea for myself when my phone vibrates. The number is unlisted.

I stop and set my cup aside, then answer.

"Miss Livingston, this is Catherine Ulysses."

I pause.

Saint's assistant.

"Are you there?"

My heart. My heart is going to literally leap out of my chest.

"Yes, I'm here."

"He'd like to see you in his office."

I close my eyes.

"Should I tell him you declined?"

"NO! I . . . at what time? I'll be there." My fingers tremble as I write down the time and start nervously scribbling when I hang up.

The world tilts a little when I force myself to lower the pen. I stare at the hour. The date. The question mark. The heart. And the name *Malcolm,* I wrote, with all of that.

I'm finally going to see him. I have no idea what I'm going to say, where I will begin, what can even make this okay.

I picture myself kissing him, having the courage to say I love him.

I picture myself getting teary maybe, too, because this has been the worst month of my entire existence.

I picture him in all his glory, and my chest can't take it without gnarling up like a live rope.

His office.

M4.

Saint.

I brush my teeth, take a shower, then hurry to my closet and swing open the doors, staring at my clothes, hoping something—the right outfit—stands out and yells, *WEAR ME, HE CANNOT SAY NO TO THIS.* Instead I see a lot of sleeves and nothing, *nothing,* fit for this moment. Hidden in this closet is *his* shirt. How I loved sleeping in this shirt. It engulfed me like his arms did, and I had the best dreams, sometimes even erotic ones, even after I was back from his arms, recently sated. I pull it out and look at it, missing it with an ache, then impulsively hide it in the long-dress section again.

I go for something white, a white turtleneck sweater, a pair of light-colored jeans, my lambskin boots.

I feel exposed, all my walls tumbled down. But I go brush my hair, add a light peach lipstick, and look at myself, my gray eyes staring back at me, as vulnerable as I've ever seen them.

Because I'll tell him the truth—the entire truth.

And I'll deserve whatever he comes back with; I'll deserve it, every bit.

At M4, I take the elevator, trembling.

Our every complex human emotion, bottled up inside our bodies, our minds and souls and hearts.

Every member of every ethnicity, every human in the past and the present and every one in the future wants to feel like this. The way I feel right now, just a girl hoping and craving, dying to see him, praying the guy she loves loves her back.

My throat is so tight I can't talk when I step out. His four assistants lift their heads from their computer screens. "I'm . . . here to see—"

"One moment," Catherine tells me.

I'm standing here wondering if he'll smell like I remember, look at me like I remember. If he'll smile or frown, if he'll hate me forever, if he thinks of me at all. If he misses me at all.

It doesn't matter so long as he sees me right now. That's all I want, to look into his face again. Hear his voice.

Finally Catherine hangs up and nods at me as she walks to the door and pushes it open for me, and I walk inside.

To be continued in the next Manwhore book . . .

ACKNOWLEDGMENTS

This book wouldn't have been possible without the support of my fans, whose continued love, support, and enthusiasm for my work and characters continues to fuel me, day in and day out. My utmost love and gratitude goes to you!

Thank you so much to my early draft readers. Amy, you light my way. Dana, who brought me Chicago. CeCe, you get it every time. My lovely daughter, you inspire me, my love. Kati D, as always so smart and illuminating, it's never "done" until you read it, Kati. Monica Murphy, who not only reads early drafts but knows both the best and worst of me. Jen Frederick, from the moment *REAL* and *Undeclared* released we met online and became friends, thank you for that friendship. Thank you to the mega-talented ladies, Lisa Desrochers and Angie McKeon, some of my closest author friends. And my friend since our teens, Paula, who has lunch with me to talk about books every time I'm in town. Sylvia Day, I've admired you for a long time, thank you for the read and the amazing blurb; super honored to have my cover wear it.

To the amazing Kelli for lending me her eagle eye, and to Anita S. for helping me proofread and polish up my babies—but only to the point where my voice remains as natural as possible. :)

I also want to thank all the bloggers who have supported me from the moment my debut book, *REAL,* was released into the world. Your excitement over every work that has followed, your reviews, and your help in connecting me with readers have given my books a platform they couldn't have without you. With all my heart, thank you!

To my assistants, Lori and Gel, who help me keep my head straight when I'm in the writing cave.

Thank you to the most wonderful agent I could've asked for, Amy Tannenbaum: you get me, you inspire me, and you keep amazing me with your superhero talents! And thank you to everyone at Jane Rotrosen: you are among the most enthusiastic and talented people I know.

And speaking of amazing, talented teams, to my thorough, witty, and dedicated editor, Adam Wilson; to his wonderful assistant, Trey; and to the unforgettable Lauren McKenna. To Jen Bergstrom, for her belief in me; to Kristin, who is a genius at publicity, and to Gallery Books' art department, copy editors, and every gem of a person who does their best to bring this book to you as early as possible in the best possible shape we humanly can. Also, to Gregg Sullivan, from Sullivan and Partners, thank you for being part of the team.

To my Real Series Facebook group, readers who are so devoted and such cheerleaders, they touch my heart every day. To all my readers who've emailed, tweeted, and sat down to read one of my stories. Like you, I feel knots and butterflies when I watch two people fall in love. Like you, I cry and smile and ache for more and want to yell. It's the greatest joy ever to know that you enjoy my works the way I did when I discovered them. . . .

To my beautiful family, who is patient and loving, even when you laugh at me humming with my Beats on, typing away. I love you with all my heart.

To my muse . . . delicate as a butterfly. I thought, once, that I might lose you. That I would never be able to write again. You came back, book after book, again and again. And though you've proved me wrong, that fear of losing you is never gone, and so I wake every day hopeful that we will have a date, you and I, and that you will show up because our characters are waiting. I cannot thank you enough for what you give me. You bring me joy like only the best things in life could.

And last, but never least, thank you to you, right at this moment, for taking the time to read my story. XOXO

ABOUT THE AUTHOR

Katy Evans is married and lives with her husband and their two children plus three lazy dogs in South Texas. Some of her favorite pastimes are hiking, reading, baking, and spending time with her friends and family. For more information on Katy Evans and her upcoming releases, check her out on the sites below. She loves to hear from her readers.

Website: www.katyevans.net
Facebook: https://www.facebook.com/AuthorKatyEvans
Twitter: https://twitter.com/authorkatyevans
Email: katyevansauthor@gmail.com